DEAD WAVE

OTHER BOOKS BY ANTHONY GIANGREGORIO

THE DEAD WATER SERIES

DEADWATER
DEADWATER: Expanded Edition
DEADRAIN
DEADCITY
DEADWAVE
DEAD HARVEST
DEAD UNION

ALSO BY THE AUTHOR

DEAD RECKONING: DAWNING OF THE DEAD
THE MONSTER UNDER THE BED
DEADEND: A ZOMBIE NOVEL
DEAD TALES: SHORT STORIES TO DIE FOR
DEAD MOURNING: A ZOMBIE HORROR STORY
ROAD KILL: A ZOMBIE TALE
DEADFREEZE
DEADFALL
DEADRAGE
SOUL-EATER
THE DARK
RISE OF THE DEAD
DARK PLACES

DEAD WAVE

ANTHONY GIANGREGORIO

ACKNOWLEDGMENTS

A big thanks to my wife, Jody, who's continuing support allows me to keep writing. My son, Joseph, who is becoming a very good editor in his own right. Thanks to Roger for helping me with the first draft of this novel and for always listening when I get idea an idea for yet another story. Thanks to Eric, Chris, Marc and Jim for their continuing support and their positive thoughts.

Thanks to my father-in law, John, who has read almost everything I've written. His support and that of a few others is all I need to know that spending hours in front of my computer is worth it.

Of course to my Mom and Dad who have done what good parents are supposed to do, by telling me everything I write is good, even if it's not.

And to my son Domenic, who will hopefully follow in my footsteps and be the next big thing someday.

AUTHOR'S NOTE

This book was self-edited, and though I tried my absolute best to correct all grammar mistakes; there may be a few here and there.
Please accept my sincerest apology for any errors you may find.
This is the second edition of this book.
Visit my web site at undeadpress.com

DEAD WAVE

Copyright © 2009 by Anthony Giangregorio

ISBN   Softcover ISBN 13: 978-1-935458-04-3
                       ISBN 10: 1-935458-04-3

This is a work of fiction. Names, characters, places and incidents either are the product of the author's imagination or are used fictitiously, and any resemblance to any actual persons, living or dead, events, or locales is entirely coincidental.
This book was printed in the United States of America.
For more info on obtaining additional copies of this book, contact
www.livingdeadpress.com

Chapter 1

Henry Watson's head rocked sideways, the punch from his adversary powerful enough to fell an ox if the animal was hit head on. Despite the fact the blow only grazed his jaw, it still felt like he had been struck by a truck.

Backing away and rubbing his face, he gritted his teeth and prepared for the next assault.

Looking over his attacker's shoulder, he could see his three friends still tied to the poles they had been secured to only hours ago. On the far left pole, Jimmy Cooper's face was red with anger, the young man only wanting to burst free of his bonds and come to his leader's aide.

The large biker swung at Henry yet again, and he weaved away from the massive arm to come up under the larger man's defenses. He shot a right hook into the biker's kidneys, but the powerful brute barely grunted.

Rolling back out of reach of the massive arms, Henry grunted. "Okay, so much for Plan B."

"Get him, Henry, kick his ass!" Screamed a blonde woman tied next to Jimmy. She had a trim figure and sharp features. Despite the anger in her eyes, and the scowl on her face, she was beautiful. Cindy Jansen and Jimmy had been an item for almost six months now, the two people seeming to be almost perfect for one another.

Where the young man was wild and sometimes didn't think things through, Cindy was levelheaded and always knew what to say in any situation.

The rest of the motorcycle gang stood around the rough circle, cheering their leader as the bear of a man continued trying to reach Henry. So far, Henry had managed to stay out of those large, ham-size fists, but with each roll away or dodge, he was slowly growing tired.

"Come on, Steele, finish him!" Yelled a dirty biker from the sidelines. His name was Morton, if Henry remembered right, and he was Steele's second in command. The other bikers were a blur of beards and dirty faces. A few hardened women were scattered amongst the men, each a warrior in their own right.

A woman's voice pierced through the yells of the bikers, trying to cheer over the howling gang of cutthroats, giving Henry her support. "Don't listen to them, Henry; you can take the big idiot! Don't give up!"

Henry shifted his head slightly, seeing the brown hair and fiery eyes of Mary Roberts. Like the rest of his friends, she too, was strapped to a pole, each of them waiting on their own fate if Henry lost his bout with the leader of the biker gang.

He wanted to tell her thanks for the support, but instead had to lean back, Matrix style, to avoid a mighty swing from Steele. It didn't work quite the way he had planned it and he ended up falling flat on his ass, only to scurry away to the edge of the circle like a crab.

The bikers closest to him laughed and forced him back to the center, Henry cursing as he went with the push.

The sun was behind him, causing Steele to blink, trying to see Henry in the glare. Henry used this to his advantage, always trying to keep the same position, but he knew sooner or later he would either have to engage the six-foot three brute or risk the deal he had brokered for him and his friends.

With a roar, Steele charged at Henry, legs pumping like a bull. Arms were outstretched, prepared to wrap around Henry and it took all of Henry's skill and reflexes to wiggle away from the large man.

Henry's arms were covered with a sheen of sweat, the skin tanned a deep brown from the sun. Henry was a far cry from the man he had once been. Where once there had been the forming of a beer belly, now his stomach was hard and flat.

Living on the run, dodging zombies for over nine months would do that to a man.

His hair had turned a light grey, almost white, with a few streaks of brown on the sides, and the lower half of his face was covered with a light dusting of a beard.

With no time to shave, he'd been forced to let his facial hair grow. Now, with the worst of the itching over, the mostly ash-grey beard gave him an air of dignity, as if he was the captain of a naval vessel or a statesman.

But from the neck down he was all mercenary. With his shirt off, numerous white scars covered his torso, souvenirs from the many battles and scuffles he'd managed to escape from over the months since the world fell apart under a wave of death.

Now he traveled across what was left of America, with his three companions by his side. Before the zombie apocalypse, he had been content to stay in his small town in the Midwest for the rest of his life, but once the world fell apart and the dead started to walk, he had become a wanderer, moving from place to place like the nomadic tribes of the past, always moving, looking for something better over the next horizon. Plus, to remain in one place for too long would allow the dead to find him easily. Stationary places, such as towns and villages, tended to be overwhelmed and slaughtered, the numbers of the undead growing larger every day.

His companions had agreed with him and the four of them had traveled across the states until eventually ending up in New England. They'd had some difficulty in a shopping mall a few months ago, but once the problem had been sorted out with a few bullets, they had settled down for the long New England winter.

With the coming of spring, Henry and the others had grown restless and had decided to strike out on their own once again.

Saying goodbye to the few friends they had made, they'd been driven to the city limits and had moved on.

A little more than one week later they had met up with Steele and his gang of roving killers. The large gang had survived on the road since the first tainted rain had fallen from the sky. They had taken whatever they wanted and killed anyone stupid enough to get in their way.

Though bastards, every one of them still rode with an antiquated kind of moral code, so when the companions had found themselves surrounded on the outskirts of Rhode Island, they were captured and taken back to their present camp; nothing more than a wide open clearing in the woods.

Motorcycles had been set up in a rough perimeter and guards had been posted. Though the camp was not too close to any cities or towns, the undead could be anywhere, wandering the landscape looking for prey.

Henry was brought back to reality with a blow to his jaw that had him seeing bright flashes of light. Blinking his eyes quickly and shaking his head, he tried to clear his vision.

When his vision finally cleared, he was looking down at the face of Steele, who had run up to him and had wrapped Henry in a massive bear hug that threatened to snap his spine like a dry twig.

Steele grinned as he looked up into Henry's face, the smaller man's feet dangling off the ground like a child.

"I've got you now, little man!" Steele barked.

Henry said nothing, but instead reared his head back and brought it forward, his forehead striking Steele on the nose.

The large man roared in pain, dropping Henry and reaching up to his shattered nose. Henry didn't let up, taking advantage of the situation, swinging his arms into the biker's ribs, his fists beating like a drum on the man's body.

While Steele was larger than Henry, the small warrior was no slouch, either. Henry had become hard, surviving on the road, his muscles honed from endless battles with the dead.

When he had given all he could for the moment, Henry backpedaled away from the brute, breathing heavily from exertion.

Steele was holding his ribs with one hand, his nose with the other. Henry looked into the man's eyes and saw a grudging respect for him appearing, and something else as well.

Fear perhaps?

Henry didn't have much time to examine the nuances of the man's facial gestures before Steele came to his full height, and with a loud roar that overrode all the other voices in the clearing, charged at Henry, spittle mixed with blood from his shattered nose dripping down his chin.

Henry realized this was it. He was backed against the edge of the circle, the other bikers prepared to force him back if he tried to escape.

Steele plowed across the clearing, arms wide to embrace Henry, this time for keeps.

When Steele was no more than two feet away, Henry spun around in a circle, his right leg out at waist level, his left leg crouching low to the ground.

Steele was moving too fast to stop his forward motion and could only watch as Henry brought up his outstretched foot, even with the man's groin.

Steele plowed directly into Henry's boot, his testicles becoming crushed as they were forced up inside his body.

The large brute let out a loud wheeze, air whistling out of his lungs like a foghorn and he tried to take in a new breath of air, but failed miserably. Like a mighty oak, the man fell over onto his side, a puff of dust circling him when he landed.

Silence descended over the crowd of bikers, all too shocked to speak.

Coming to his feet, Henry strode over to his opponent and looked down at the leader of the biker gang.

Steele's eyes were filled with tears, his face scrunched up with the unimaginable pain he felt below his waist. He tried to raise himself off the ground, but failed miserably and collapsed again, his chest rising and falling steadily.

"Finish him," one of the bikers screamed, "it's the rules!"

Henry turned to look at the surrounding bikers and then said: "No, I won't kill him, there's no need, screw your rules." Then he turned away, dismissing them.

"I don't think you'll be fathering any children anytime soon, Steele. What do you think?" Henry joked as he looked at the wounded man and then back to the surrounding bikers.

He was greeted by mirthful calls and chuckles, the other bikers clearly seeing the fight was over. As one large group they swarmed into the arena and slapped Henry on the back, cheering his fight and dexterity.

Henry took it all in stride, not caring for any of it, but knowing it was a necessary evil if he wanted to free himself and his friends.

After more than five minutes of cheering and slapping, Henry thought his legs were going to collapse and he raised his voice over the din.

"All right already, enough guys!" He hollered. "I've done what you wanted and I won; now release my friends and give us our weapons back!"

Morton worked his way through the throng of people and when he was next to Henry, he nodded. "Sure enough, Henry, you beat our leader, though I can't believe it." Turning to look at a few bikers behind him, he pointed to Jimmy and the two women. "Release them, we honor our promises!"

The bikers nodded and did as ordered, cutting the bonds of Jimmy, Mary and Cindy.

Stepping away from the pole, Jimmy rubbed his wrists, grinning. "Shit, that was close. I can't believe you beat him."

"Thanks for the support," Henry said, checking on Mary and Cindy.

Mary ran into his arms and hugged him hard. "Great job, Henry, but you can't blame Jimmy. Even I had my doubts. I mean, that guy is huge."

Henry shrugged. "Whether it's here or on the schoolyard, never underestimate a good kick to the balls, after all, there's a reason sports players wear cups," he joked.

"Still, I had my doubts," Mary said, hugging him yet again. Jimmy was hugging Cindy, both kissing quickly, before they separated again. Though they were off the poles they were far from free.

Henry turned around to see Steele was on his feet, though still bent over at an unnatural angle. Mary saw him and gestured with her chin.

"Why didn't you finish him off? He did say to the death, right?"

Henry nodded. "Uh-huh, but I figured we might get more cooperation from these people if we didn't kill their leader. Besides,

Steele knows the fights over and though the man may be an ass-hole, he has honor. He'll honor the deal I made with him."

Almost on cue, Steele called to Henry. Turning, Henry strode the few feet over to the man, grinning slightly.

"Looks like you'll live," Henry stated with a slight grin.

Steele nodded, wiping blood from his chin. "Yeah, I'll live, but now I'm going to have to kick every one of my men's asses to keep them in line. You beating me put a serious crimp in my leadership abilities."

Henry shrugged slightly. "I could have killed you; if I did, then you wouldn't be having these concerns."

Steele started to laugh, a high roar that filled the circle. "Fair enough, fair enough. Look, Henry, I'm a man of my word. You and your friends are free; in fact, you can join us if you want. We can always use a few more people that can handle themselves."

Henry grinned up at the large man. "No thanks, Steele, if it's all the same to you, we'll be going our own way in the morning."

Steele nodded. "Fair enough, but we still have the rest of the day and tonight. So let's party!" He yelled to his men.

Cheers went up in the crowd as men and women picked up looted beer and food. A small hibachi grill was fired up and the smell of roasted squirrel soon drifted across the clearing.

Mary jumped into Henry's arms, handing him back his shotgun and 9mm Glock. He had found the Glock on the corpse of a po-liceman in what seemed like a lifetime ago and the weapon had served him well ever since.

Sliding the Glock back into its leather holster, he immediately felt better. He had felt naked without his weapons. His eyes lit up when Jimmy strode up to him, his own shotgun and .38 on his hip, and handed Henry back his panga.

The large sixteen-inch knife was honed to razor sharpness and was one of Henry's most cherished weapons. Though technically a short blade, the long sixteen inches gave him the reach he needed to take out an enemy before they came too close.

Strapping the leather scabbard back on his hip, he grinned from ear to ear.

"Damn, it feels good to have my stuff back."

"I'll second that, I didn't think I'd ever see old Betsy here, again," Jimmy said, patting his sidearm.

Cindy ran up to him and almost tackled him, a beer in each hand. Handing one to Jimmy, she reached up and kissed him. Jimmy reciprocated and in a moment the two were making out in the middle of the revelers.

Henry chuckled to himself. "Ah, youth," then he moved away to give them some semblance of privacy.

Mary was off to the side, watching all the bikers. Though she seemed calm, Henry had known her long enough to see she was uneasy. Walking over to her, he immediately saw she wore her .38 on her hip once again. She had once used a .22, but had recently upgraded to the larger caliber weapon. Greater stopping power meant less likelihood of your opponent getting back up to attack you yet again, whether they were dead or alive.

"What's wrong? You look antsy," Henry told her.

She moved her shoulders, slightly, her shrug barely perceivable. "Don't know, but with all this yelling and screaming, if there's anything out there, it'll know exactly where we are. And look, all the guards have left their posts, there's no one watching the perimeter."

Henry looked out to the edges of the campsite, following Mary's gaze. Sure enough, all the guards had left their posts to party with the rest of their gang.

If there were undead out there, they would be on them before anyone could sound the alarm.

"Shit, you're right. Well, let's keep an eye out for all of us. I'll fill Jimmy and Cindy in on the situation, just in case," Henry said.

Mary nodded, hugging herself while she watched the woods. She was probably worrying about nothing, but still, a careless woman was a dead woman.

One of the bikers handed her a beer and she nodded a thank you, cracking the top and taking a small sip. She had never been much of a drinker, and now, out in the middle of nowhere in a world full of dead people, to get drunk and let your guard down was tantamount to suicide.

She looked all around her at the bikers, all chanting and yelling as they drank case after case of beer. Mary wondered where they had found the large amount of alcohol. As far as she knew, Budweiser had stopped making beer for at least the past nine months.

That was when the contaminated rain started falling.

The atmosphere had been seeded with a bacteria that when coming in contact with human skin, would kill the person in seconds. But the bacteria didn't stop there. Once the host was dead, the body would then revive as one of the walking dead.

For more than three months the rain had ravaged North America and some parts of Europe. Other countries closed their borders, hoping to prevent the contamination from spreading, but how do you stop rain clouds?

Months passed and the bacteria faded from the atmosphere in some parts of the world, in other parts the lower temperatures brought upon by the change of seasons killed it off entirely; but not before the bacteria in the undead mutated so that every zombie became a carrier.

To be bitten by a zombie would initiate the bacteria into the new host's bloodstream and after only a half hour, sometimes less, the new host would expire and return as one more soldier for the army of the dead.

Mary was shoved by a few revelers and brought back to the present. She searched the crowd for her friends and spotted Henry talking with Steele. Evidently the man held Henry no ill will, losing the fight fair and square. Searching the crowd some more, she spotted Jimmy and Cindy sitting on an old log, kissing and talking softly to each other.

She smiled, watching them. Before they had been captured by the bikers they had spent the winter in an old shopping mall. By the time the first signs of spring appeared and she had checked off the first days of March on her calendar in her room, Henry had already started talking about moving on.

Henry had a firm belief that to stay too long in one place was to invite disaster and the man hadn't steered neither Jimmy nor Mary wrong since they had first found each other back when it had all started.

He was their unofficial leader and his decisions were almost always right on the money. She loved him, but not in any kind of sexual way. She knew he loved her too, like a father to a daughter.

She would do anything for him and him for her, if the opportunity ever arrived, and in fact, had arrived already to many times to count.

Now, as she looked off into the surrounding trees, a little more than a mile from the closest highway, she had a strong feeling that she'd need to keep her friends in sight.

Taking another sip from her beer, she moved closer to Henry, though not so close that he would notice her. She leaned against the pole that had recently held her prisoner and took another small sip of her beer, planning to nurse it until the party was over.

As she watched the revelers jumping and wrestling with each other, her back was to the south side of the camp. At the moment, no one was on watch, all the bikers enjoying the chance to party once more, so no one saw the thirty or so zombies slowly shambling out of the tree line.

Just as Mary had suspected, a large group had been wandering through the woods, with no particular destination in mind. Until, that is, one of the leaders heard the faint signs of the party and quickly adjusted its heading.

The others followed, not knowing why, but doing so anyway, until the entire group was on a beeline for the campsite. Flies jumped from walking corpse to walking corpse, laying eggs and feeding on the dead skin.

Maggots fell off the bodies by the dozens, leaving behind a macabre trail of breadcrumbs for someone to follow if they so chose.

The smell of death preceded them, almost every one of them nothing but dried skin and bones. Internal organs were long dry and mouths hung slack, the lack of live prey becoming ever harder to find as the bacteria claimed more and more souls.

They were hungry and needed to feed badly and the sounds of the revelers were like hanging a carrot in front of a starving donkey.

One step at a time, they pushed through the foliage and brush, growing ever closer to the camp...and food.

Chapter 2

Henry and Steele were in a deep conversation at about the same time the first walking corpse stepped out into the clearing.

While he was talking to Steele, he marveled at how the man seemed to hold no form of a grudge against Henry for almost killing him, in fact, Henry now saw a new respect for himself in the big man's eyes.

Once Henry had passed the test, he had immediately become one of them, with all its perks. Steele was already negotiating giving Henry a couple of extra motorcycles the gang had, the vehicles becoming obsolete when a couple of the gang was attacked by a pair of roamers out on the highway.

There were two kinds of zombies in Henry's opinion. There were *roamers,* which had a wandering spirit and would travel across wide expanses of land looking for prey, and *deaders*, which Henry had nicknamed for zombies' that were in groups of two or three.

He had quickly tired of using the name, *zombie,* and so had used the new names to take something back from their out of control lives. Jimmy, Mary and Cindy had followed suit and now all four of them used the slang nicknames, sometimes to other's dismay.

"I'll give you the two Suzuki's, but I still wish you'd change your mind and stay with us," Steele said over a mouthful of beer.

Henry leaned back, taking a sip of beer from his own can. He had never been much of a fan for beer, but now with the supply almost non-existent, he couldn't imagine tasting anything so sweet.

"That's really great of you, Steele, but we're moving in a different direction than you."

"So change your destination. Maine should be beautiful nowa-days, especially with spring here. I figure there's dozens of homes just waiting for us to take them over. And there's not a lot of people, so it should be easy to kill the *'posers*."

'Posers were the name the biker gang had named the walking undead. It was short, for decomposing. Henry didn't much care for it, but he had heard numerous titles for the creatures. It seemed that no matter where they went, the people still trying to survive just couldn't get used to calling the undead zombies.

Henry didn't blame them, it just sounded too much like a bad drive-in movie.

Henry took another sip from his beer and shook his head. "Sorry, Steele, but we just left Massachusetts after spending the winter there and now I want to head back towards home."

"Oh, yeah? And where's home exactly?"

"The Midwest," was all Henry said. Steele waited for more, but soon realized that was all he was going to get. The big man finished his beer and crushed the can with his hand, tossing the can over his shoulder. Letting out a huge burp, he caught another beer from one of his men and then quickly cracked the seal, downing half the can in less than a second.

"Fine, man, suit yourself. Your loss."

Henry grinned. "Yeah, guess it is."

A scream sounded near the edge of the camp, but at first no one seemed to notice. The biker gang was partying hard, whooping it up something fierce. Henry readjusted the shotgun over his shoulder, the Glock still snug on his hip. He had once had a .38 of his own, but had traded it to an old codger he'd met on the road. The old man had plenty of ammunition for the shotguns both he and Jimmy carried, so Henry had parted with the extra weapon in trade for the shells.

Now the shotgun had a full load, plus he had two pockets full of shells; Jimmy the same, if not a few more.

Thinking back to the old man made him grin. The old codger had had a crush on Mary from the second he'd saw her, despite the fact the man had been nearly double her age, plus a few extra years.

But Mary had played it well, using his amorous advances to get the four companions the ammo they desperately needed, plus a few other supplies that had dwindled after they had left the shopping mall behind.

Another scream pierced through the din of the revelers and he looked up. At first he saw nothing amiss and was about to continue talking with Steele when yet another cry sounded from the edge of the clearing. This time the unmistakable cry was of pain, not pleasure.

Henry jumped to his feet, trying to look in all directions at the same time. He saw Jimmy and Cindy from across a group of bikers and from the look on the younger man's face, Henry knew Jimmy had heard the shout, as well.

Swinging the shotgun from around his shoulder, he pumped the chamber, preparing for battle.

Steele was right behind him, an Uzi sub-gun in the man's ham like fist. "Shit, there's something going down," he snapped, pushing bikers from his path.

Henry nodded in agreement. "Think so, you need to get your people in order. Whatever's happening is going down now." Henry caught a quick glimpse of Mary and then she was lost in a group of bikers. Most were so drunk they could barely stand, and Henry couldn't help but wonder, if this was how they acted when in dangerous territory, than how the hell had they managed to survive this long without being slaughtered?

Steele was slapping some of his men in the face, telling them to get their act together and to draw their firearms.

There had been a battery operated boom-box playing, cassettes spewing loud music, but someone finally had the good sense to turn it off.

The moment the radio was switched off, the sounds of screaming flooded the clearing.

Almost like a dance group, nearly the entire complement of men and women swung towards the screams.

Just at the edge of campsite, where the trees surrounded the clearing in a close-knit circle, were two of the bikers, a man and a woman. Both were in a state of undress, evidently going off to grab some privacy for a little recreational screwing.

They were both still on the ground, but now with the radio off, their screams of pain filled the area. One look at the edge of the clearing and the reason for their screams was obvious.

More than a score of undead were slipping between the trees, mouths open wide, hands out in front of them, squeezing the air, as they moved closer to the biker gang.

The man and woman were even now in their death throes, three zombies having fallen on top of them with teeth and claw-like hands ripping at the exposed flesh.

The woman screamed while she watched her intestines being pulled from her body, inch by inch, the zombies gorging themselves on her innards. The man's jugular had been torn out, his shrieks of pain already subsiding with the last pint of his blood pumping out of him to become soaked up in the dry dirt below him.

"Jesus Christ, the bastards just killed Christopher and Susan! Kill those deadfucks!" Steele screamed to his men.

Henry spotted Mary and he ran to her, pulling her to him and the both of them ducking for cover behind a log. With the biker's drunk they pulled weapons and started shooting, some of them accidentally shooting their comrades. Bullets whined overhead as Henry pushed Mary's head into the dirt.

"What the hell is happening?" She screamed through a mouthful of dirt.

"Just stay down or we're likely to get shot. They're shooting blindly!" He screamed over the roar of the gun blasts. Almost every conceivable kind of weapon was represented by the bikers, all the firearms scavenged from all across New England.

One man, a small guy with a scruffy beard and glasses, held what looked like a combination rifle and grenade launcher, though if the man had any grenades left, he wasn't using them.

As if on cue, someone did pull a grenade from inside their vest, chucking the small orb over the heads of the closest bikers. The grenade rolled across the clearing and came up against a walking corpse. The dead man looked down at the black orb, his head cocking to the side curiously like a cat when it had spotted something interesting. Then the timer ran down to zero and the corpse disappeared in a blinding flash, taking more than a half dozen with it.

A few of the closest bikers were peppered with bits of shrapnel and pieces of bone and blood from the exploding corpses, others falling to the ground to find cover.

Henry pulled Mary's arm to get her attention and the two of them crawled across the ground between pairs of legs, staying well below the line of fire. In less than a minute, he bumped up against Jimmy. Though the man had his shotgun in his hand, he had yet to fire a shot, realizing their ammo was limited, letting the bikers waste what they had.

"Some party, huh?" Jimmy quipped over the rattle of gunfire above his head.

Henry frowned. That was Jimmy, always had a comment, even when they were moments from death. A smartass to the end.

"We need to get the hell out of here before we're overwhelmed. These idiots couldn't fight off a deader tied to a tree!" Henry yelled, looking for a way out. Through a tangle of arms and legs he saw a biker go down, forced to the dirt by three rotting ghouls. Henry shook his head, sadly. The morons didn't seem to care that you needed to shoot for the head if you wanted to put one down. In their drunken stupor they were just shooting blindly and hoping for the best.

Henry poked his head up to sneak a peek at the edge of the clearing and he let out a few choice curses when he saw the first man and woman, intestines trailing behind her, up and about, now part of the army of the undead.

"Shit, the dead bikers are already coming back, that means even more of them to fight. We need to get out of here before it's too late!"

Jimmy nodded and waved to get Henry's attention, the gunfire deafening. "Follow me!" He yelled, starting to crawl away to the opposite edge of the clearing, Cindy by his side. She had her rifle cradled in her arms vertically, using her elbows to help pull her along the ground. The rifle had been with her since the mall and though only a .22 caliber, Cindy was deadly accurate with it.

Henry and Mary followed, weaving their way in and out of the forest of legs. Henry heard Steele's voice and he turned and looked over his shoulder. The large man was in the middle of at least a half dozen roamers, fists swinging like battering rams, knocking heads from skeletal bodies, his large Colt-Magnum handgun blowing fist sized holes in the enemy.

But he wasn't aiming for their heads and though the impact of the massive rounds knocked the ghouls to the ground, they were climbing to their feet only seconds later, prepared to take the attack back to the motorcycle gang's leader.

One slipped through his guard, teeth sinking into his massive forearm. He roared more with frustration than pain, picking the corpse up in his hands and bringing it down over his knee, the spine cracking in two, the zombie falling to the denuded ground, its legs useless. Steele swung around to attack the closest ghoul, forgetting the one he had cracked in two. But the zombie wasn't out just yet and dragged its legs and lower torso behind itself until its face was close to Steele's leg, hoping to take a bite out of his shin.

Steele roared yet again, this time in pain, kicking the ghoul away and bringing his foot down to crush the skull into the ground, bits of dust and blackened brain matter spreading over his boot.

Then the man was lost from sight, moving legs concealing him from view. Henry turned back to his front view and concentrated on not getting stepped on. Behind him, Mary let out a curse as yet another foot stomped on her hand. Knowing it would be suicide to stand up; she shook off the pain and carried on, following Henry and the others.

Jimmy crawled all the way to the opposite edge of the clearing, only standing when he was confident it was safe. Henry and the two women all mimicked him and soon all four were standing near the parked motorcycles.

A zombie had skirted the crowd and was about to approach the companions when Henry caught it in his peripheral vision. Knowing Jimmy was closer, he called to the younger man. "Heads up, deader at three o' clock!"

Jimmy looked where he was told and shot the zombie from six-feet away. The head disappeared in a spray of red mist, the body crumpling to the dirt.

Pumping the shotgun again, Jimmy grinned at Henry, proud of himself.

Henry frowned at his show of bravado. "Don't get cocky, Jimmy, we're not out of here yet."

"Yeah, but almost. Come on, these poor bastards are screwed, let's take some of the bikes and head for clearer pastures."

Another zombie spotted the companions and charged at them. Henry decided to save his ammo and pulled his panga from its sheath. Taking three steps toward the wailing corpse, he sliced horizontally across its neck, severing the head from its body. Only a slim amount of skin stayed attached and the head fell back to touch its back, the spinal column severed. The zombie fell to the earth in a puff of dust, arms and legs still twitching. Henry wiped his blade on the tattered clothes of the corpse and then slid it back into its sheath, ready for the next time he'd need it.

"Well, if we're going, then let's go!" He stated, climbing onto a KZ1000. Their backpacks had been thrown in a pile near the bikes and Mary ran over to retrieve them, tossing each one to its owner.

Another zombie ran through the bikers and Mary pulled her .38 in one smooth draw, shooting the ghoul in the head. A small black hole appeared on its forehead, the exit wound at the rear of its skull much larger.

After firing the shot, the zombie was forgotten, her confidence in her marksmanship complete.

Climbing on the back of Henry's bike, she kept her weapon in her hand, just in case anymore stragglers broke through.

Cindy was waiting for Jimmy to climb on board one of the motorcycles until she finally asked him what was wrong.

"I don't know how to ride one, I never learned," he said quietly, a little embarrassed.

"What! Well, I sure as hell don't have time to teach you now!" Henry said, surprised.

Then Cindy surprised everyone by hopping onto a 750cc Suzuki, turning it on, squeezing the clutch and starting the engine. The bike surged to life and she looked over her shoulder to Jimmy. "Come on then, let's go, you know, women can ride too."

"Hot damn, you can ride, oh thank God," Jimmy said and climbed onto the rear seat, wrapping his hands around her waist, one of his hands brushing her left breast by accident.

She grinned at that. "Just keep them on my waist, buddy boy, there's no time for you now," she joked.

More ghouls had broken through the bikers and as Henry scanned the crowd of undead, he saw that a lot of the animated corpses were now the bikers, once killed and now playing for the other team.

Revving his own engine, feeling the power under him, he let out the clutch and shot out of the clearing. He looked in his left, rear handlebar mirror and caught a last glimpse of Steele, still in the thick of a crowd of undead. He was almost a foot taller than most of his adversaries and he fought valiantly, pummeling one after another.

It was only when one of his own men, now returned from the dead, attempted to attack him that he hesitated for the briefest of moments.

That one instant of weakness was enough to turn the tide and the undead horde swarmed over him, sheer numbers forcing him to the bloody ground.

Henry looked away then, and concentrated on the road in front of him.

Next to him, Cindy handled the machine well, but as he glanced at Jimmy, he saw the man appeared to have a sour expression on his face.

"What's wrong, buddy! You don't look happy, I mean, we just made it out of there by the skin of our teeth."

Jimmy nodded agreeing, the wind blowing his hair away from his forehead.

"Yeah, I know, it's just I didn't realize I'd end up being the bitch on the back of the motorcycle."

Henry started laughing and Mary joined in.

Cindy heard the conversation and she leaned back, nudging her man slightly.

"Maybe so, Jimmy, but you're my bitch and I love you," she smiled, her blonde hair flowing around her head like a golden halo.

He leaned forward, chuckling at that and kissed her on the cheek.

"I sure am, baby, I sure am," then he reached up and cupped each of her breasts in his hands, giving them a playful squeeze.

She leaned back further and turned her head so only he could hear her. "Later, as soon as we stop, I promise."

He grinned back at her. "I'll keep you to that promise."

*   *   *

A few old wrecks were scattered across the road and Henry and Cindy weaved around them, the bikes easily fitting between the gaps.

Soon the exit for route 95 appeared and Henry drove onto the onramp, the bike revving as he gave it a little gas. The gas gauge read full and he leaned back and enjoyed the wind in his hair.

They had made it out of yet another tight scrape, only their intelligence and their respect for the undead the deciding factor.

As he shot off down the highway, Henry couldn't help but wonder about Steele. Had the man been torn to pieces or had he died and then returned again.

Deciding it didn't really matter, he revved the engine, a spot of open road in front of him. The feeling of being free flooded through him and he weaved the bike a little, enjoying the feel of the machine.

Mary leaned forward and kissed him and he turned his head to the side and asked: "What was that for?"

She shrugged. "Nothing really, just happy to be moving again...and alive."

He nodded, wiping a tear from his eye from a bit of dust. "I hear that..." he said, the engine drowning out the rest of his sentence. He let it go, not needing to say it again.

With a glance askance to check on Cindy, he shifted into fifth gear and shot down the highway, the woman right behind him. The sun shone down from high overhead, the blue sky clear of clouds as the two lone motorcycles disappeared over the horizon and were soon lost from sight.

Chapter 3

A lone ghoul stumbled down the middle of Interstate 95. It had been separated from its brethren for more than a month, the lack of prey reducing the walking corpse to nothing but a pile of skin and bones.

Its left eye was missing due to the fact that a hungry raven had decided it didn't want to wait for the corpse to fall over and so had dove in to retrieve the soft morsel of meat.

The dead man was missing his left shoe, the wingtip having fallen off months ago. The other stayed on by some form of miracle, the foot too shriveled to fit inside the footwear very well.

A rumbling noise caused the ghoul to look up from the asphalt, his lonely eye catching the sun's reflection on the metal as the two motorcycles drew closer.

He let out a soft groan that sounded more like a sigh, the lungs nothing but shriveled sacks inside the hollow chest.

With the motorcycles drawing closer, it raised its hands in anticipation of approaching prey. If it still had lips, it would have smiled, patiently watching the prey move directly towards it.

Then a gunshot rolled across the highway and a fraction of an instant later the dead man's head disappeared in a spray of dry brain matter and red dust, the body falling over; dead for good this time.

The two motorcycles roared by the prone corpse lying in the middle of the highway, Jimmy sliding his .38 back into its holster.

"Hah, told you I could hit it, you owe me twenty bucks!" Jimmy called to Henry from the back of his motorcycle.

"I didn't say you couldn't hit it. I said you shouldn't hit it. Shit, Jimmy, what a waste of ammo. It could be the round you just wasted that might save your life some day!" Henry yelled back.

"Aww, lighten up, old man. If we can't have a little fun, then what's the point?"

Henry frowned, spitting dust from his mouth. "The point is, we never know what's gonna be around the next corner and we need to be prepared. Christ, Jimmy, after all we've been through and I still have to tell you that?"

Mary rubbed his shoulder. "Lighten up, Henry, he's just blowing off a little steam, besides, that deader could have attacked someone down the road. Now that's one less to worry about."

Henry turned slightly to look at her. She was beautiful; her hair blowing behind her like it had a life of its own. Sighing, he gave in, as he so often did with Mary. She had become the daughter he had never had and he loved her dearly. And just like Daddy's little girl, he would sometimes give in if the moment allowed him too.

This was one of those times.

"Fine, all right, I give in, but next time just keep it holstered, all right?"

Jimmy nodded, grinning widely, then his face went into a look of disgust and Henry became alarmed.

"What's wrong, you okay?"

Jimmy nodded, squeezing his eyes shut. "Think so. But I just swallowed a bug."

Cindy laughed at that. "So what? It's protein after all, isn't it?"

Jimmy shook his head, clearing his throat. "Maybe, but if it was a bee it could kill me and I'm not quite ready to take the last train to oblivion just yet."

"You're allergic to bee stings?" Mary called from her seat, Jimmy almost next to her, so close she could almost reach out and touch him.

Jimmy nodded, slightly. "Yup, ever since I was a kid. One time when I was at a family picnic, I got stung on my pinky," he added to this story by waving his pinky in the air. "My finger swelled up the size of a small baseball bat and if my aunt hadn't had an epi-pen with her, then I would have probably died right there. After that, my mom always made me carry one with me, just in case."

"Gees, Jimmy I had no idea. At the next available town or camp we should see if we can find one for you, better safe than sorry," Mary said; the worry clearly visible on her face.

Jimmy waved her away. "Aww forget about it. Shit, nowadays the last thing I should have to worry about is bees. I would think the dead people walking around are a little more hazardous to my health."

"Well, still, if we can get one at a reasonable price, then better safe than sorry." Mary said, while spitting some stray hair that blew into her mouth.

Jimmy shrugged. "Fair enough, it's fine with me."

Just then, Mary noticed the bike under her was slowing down, the engine starting to sputter. Tapping Henry on the shoulder, she leaned in close to his ear. "What's up, we're slowing down," she called.

"No shit," Henry snapped back, "don't you think I know that!" At first Cindy pulled away from him, but when she realized something was wrong, she slowed her own motorcycle, becoming even once more

Henry called to her, his face filled with anger and frustration. "Shit, there's something wrong with my bike. We need to pull over so I can check it out."

She nodded and after only a moment of surveying the landscape around them, spotted a few trees just off the highway. Pointing, she turned towards them, Henry following.

In less than a minute the two bikes were sitting under the trees, the engines ticking softly as they cooled. The four companions stretched their legs, checking around themselves to make sure the area was secure. After only a few minutes, everyone was satisfied they were alone, the highway only a few hundred feet away, standing silent under the sun, waiting for their return.

Opening his backpack, Henry pulled out a water bottle, taking a long drink before handing it to Mary. She smiled at him, a silent thank you, and took a long pull from the water bottle, twisting the cap back on when she was finished.

Both Cindy and Jimmy were doing the same, Cindy repacking the bottle when they were finished.

Cindy walked over to Henry's bike, kneeling down on her haunches to inspect it visually. "So what do you thinks wrong with it?" She asked, while her eyes checked for broken wires or leaking fluids.

Henry walked over to her and leaned over the seat. "Don't know, I'm not much good with bikes, know how to ride them and change the battery when it's time for a new one, that's about it."

"Well, don't look at me. My boyfriend taught me how to ride; he had a big ol' Harley fat boy. We used to drive it on weekends when I was off from college." Her eyes seemed to look out across the barren highway as if she was seeing something none of the rest could see. "Seems like a lifetime ago," she whispered and then came back to reality. "Anyway, what do you say we try to see what's up?"

"Okay, first let's see if the bike has a tool kit," Henry said, popping the seat to see if said kit was there.

Sure enough, it was, propped up under the rear fender, along with the registration and inspection sticker. He held the papers up to Jimmy. "Look what I found, that's good I guess. Just in case we get pulled over. I wouldn't want to get a ticket or anything."

"Very funny, Henry, you're a regular laugh riot, just fix the bike already so we can go, I don't like being out here like this. You know, exposed."

"He has a good point, Henry, the sooner we're moving again, the better," Mary added.

"Don't you think I know that? Gees, Jimmy can crack jokes all day long and no one says a thing. I make one comment and every-one's all over me," Henry said, sarcastically while he dumped the tools out of the small black bag they were in all over the dirt and grass. He had to take a moment to assemble the tools, the screw-drivers and pliers in two pieces, the handles and the ends. Once finished, he popped off the side covers to the bike and started poking around. Not having a clue what he was looking for, but hoping for the best.

Jimmy walked around the side of the bike and leaned over so his face was close to Henry's. Henry tried to ignore him, instead concentrating on wiggling spark plug wires and checking for any loose wiring.

"Did you check the battery yet? That's what I would check first. The battery and then the carburetor," Jimmy said from his side.

"No, Jimmy, I didn't check the battery yet, give me a chance will ya, sheesh, everyone's a backseat quarterback," he muttered to himself.

For all the poking Henry was doing, he couldn't find anything amiss. Starting the engine again, it sputtered to life for an instant and then coughed once and died. Trying the starter again, the bike refused to start. Henry kept trying, but soon the starter started to whine slower, the battery dying. Jimmy stepped in and placed his hand over the button. "Whoa there, sport, stop already, you'll just end up killing the battery."

Henry's face curled up in frustration and he turned to stare at his friend. "Don't you think I know that, Jimmy? If I could think of something else to do, don't you think I would?"

Mary stepped in between the two men. "Take it easy there, Henry, it's not Jimmy's fault the bike's broken."

Henry sighed, his anger deflating. "Yeah, I know, sorry, Jimmy, it's just that we finally get some transportation that could get us around for a while and the piece of shit breaks down!" He finished his sentence by kicking the bike on its side, the handlebars gouging a trench in the dirt, dust puffing up around it.

"Now calm down, Henry, it's not the end of the world even if it doesn't start again. We've walked enough to know sometimes it's the best thing, anyway. Now let's rest a while and try again later." Mary turned to Jimmy. "Jimmy, would you pick up the bike so the gas doesn't flood the carbs?" She asked politely.

Jimmy nodded and though he had to strain himself lifting the machine, he managed to get the bike on its wheels again, slipping the kickstand down with his foot. When he was done, Cindy moved next to him and smiled.

"Oh mercy, you're a strong one, aren't you, mister. Why, I bet you could sweep me off my feet with one arm behind your back," she joked.

Jimmy gave her a mischievous grin. "Oh baby, you have no idea," he said, chasing her around the trees until they were lost in the bushes. Jimmy stopped for a moment and looked back at Henry and Mary, the smile still on his face. "We'll be back in ten minutes, so consider a do not disturb sign on that tree over there," he said.

"If it's like the last few times, we'll probably be back in five," Cindy joked from behind the nearest tree, the surrounding shrubs hiding her from view.

Jimmy looked at the two and shrugged. "She's joking. If I wanted to, I could last twenty, but you know; I don't want to be caught with my pants down...literally."

Mary crossed her arms over her chest and gave him a slight grin. "Sure, tough guy, just get going, the sooner you're finished the better."

Jimmy flashed her a sly smile and then disappeared behind the trees, already removing his shirt as he went.

The sound of giggling and shaking bushes carried back to Mary and Henry, the two friends only smiling shyly.

Then sighing, Henry got back to work, hoping by the off chance he might actually figure out what was wrong with his motorcycle.

Mary leaned against a tree and with her hand on her .38, kept an eye out for trouble.

"So how did you know to pick a bike up so the carbs don't flood? Do you know something about bikes you're not telling me?" Henry asked.

Mary shook her head from side to side, her hair covering her face. She pulled the stray strands away with a finger and shrugged. "No, not really, I had a friend when I was younger and still lived at home. He had a bike. One time it fell over in the summer. It was so hot the kickstand sank into the driveway and the bike fell over. He had told me how the gas would flood the carbs so he had to wait a little while for them to empty again before he could try to start it. Just remembered when I saw the bike in the grass, that's all. Just another useless memory from my past."

"No, Mary, it's not useless. All the things that happened to us before all this shit started is important. We need to remember how things were...and the people we've lost."

Mary nodded, agreeing with him, and stayed silent, looking out on the grassy plain.

With the wind blowing a cool breeze across the trees, the sun high overhead and the sound of Jimmy and Cindy's sexual antics filling the area, Henry tried to concentrate on working on the bike, while Mary relaxed and enjoyed the day, one eye always on the surrounding countryside.

Chapter 4

An hour later the four companions were gathered around the motorcycles once more. Henry was on his knees, still trying to figure out what was wrong with his bike, while Jimmy leaned over his shoulder, always suggesting he try something new.

"What about that wire? Could that be what's wrong?" He asked for the hundredth time.

Henry set down his screwdriver and turned to look at his friend. "You've already asked me about that and I told you, I just don't know; now if you don't get away from me so help me I'm going to kill you."

Jimmy stood up, frowning. "All right, fine, I'll go, but you're passing up on a well of knowledge."

"I guess I'll just have to take that chance," Henry smirked, picking up the screwdriver again and poking inside the chassis of the machine.

Mary strolled over and leaned down close to his ear. "So, seriously, Henry, how's it going? Maybe we should just leave it and start walking. We could always share the other bike until it runs out of gas," she suggested.

Henry shook his head back and forth with conviction. "No way, these bikes are a find and I won't just throw them away until there's absolutely no hope of salvaging it."

Mary sighed. "Fine, keep going, but another hour and you need to just accept that it's broke and beyond your knowledge to fix."

He nodded. "That sounds fair. Damn, I'm not looking forward to hoofing it if I can't figure out what's wrong, though."

"You and me both, brother, so get to work and fix it, will ya?" Jimmy said from the edge of the trees. Cindy was a hundred feet away, but still in sight. She was picking some wild flowers that were growing along side the tall grass and boulders. Jimmy thought it was such an odd contrast to see a beautiful woman picking flowers, but yet, the same woman had a rifle slung over her back.

But such was the world he now lived in, and planned on living in for the foreseeable future.

Cindy waved to him, and Jimmy waved back, smiling at his one and only love. Though he hadn't known her that long, about six months if he was right, he had already fallen head over heels for the blonde stunner. Her smile always gave him a tingle, even more so when said smile was aimed at him.

He was lucky he had found her, especially with all the death around every corner, or so it would seem. With the fall of civilization came the lawlessness that would inevitably follow. Now the way of the gun ruled the land and Jimmy, along with his friends, had learned to adapt well to the new world order.

Jimmy watched Cindy moving about in the waist-high grass as she gathered quite a bouquet in her hands. Looking past her, he saw the grass bending, like a soft wave. At first he gave it no notice, assuming it was just the wind waving the dry stalks, but then he realized there really was not much of a breeze, at least not enough to bend the grass the way it was moving.

"Hey, Mary, come here, will ya? I want you to see something," he said in a curious tone.

Walking closer to him, she leaned against him, the two as close as a brother to a sister. They had only become closer in the past few months, though there had been a time when they had almost become an item, but romance had turned to something more, and though they loved each other deeply, it was more familial then romantic.

"What's up, worried your girl is gonna come to her senses and realize what an idiot you are?" She jibed him.

"Ha, ha, very funny, no, have a look over there, just behind where Cindy is. Look at the grass, the way it's moving. Is that natural?"

Mary squinted, trying to discern what he was talking about. At first she saw nothing unusual, but soon the undulation of the grass showed itself and she frowned. "That ain't right. What do you think it could be?

He shrugged his shoulders. "Don't know, should we tell Cindy?"

"Definitely, but hurry up. Whatever it is, it's heading right for her."

Henry had walked up to the two of them, looking over their shoulders. "What's up, what are you guys talking about?"

Jimmy pointed to the grass. "Over there, the way the grass is moving; it just looks funny, is all. I was about to tell her, though for the life of me I can't imagine what it is."

Henry squinted into the noon day sun, his eyes spotting the grass as it flowed back and forth. Something was in there, moving like a wave across the prairie. Before either Jimmy or Mary knew what was happening, Henry had dropped his screwdriver and was running toward Cindy. "You two, get into those trees, now, I'll get Cindy!" He said, moving at full speed into the grass.

"Cindy, get over here, now, hurry up, they're coming!" He called, sprinting into the grass after the woman. Cindy looked up, not understanding what the problem was. She could see her three friends clearly and there was no apparent threat around them, for the life of her she had no idea what Henry was yelling about.

Henry moved through the grass, mindful of hidden rocks or holes left by rodents. In a little more than a minute he had reached the perplexed woman and he quickly pulled her to him. She dropped the flowers in her hands and she became angry.

"Hey, what's the big idea? I've been picking those for almost ten minutes, what's wrong with you?" She snapped at Henry.

Henry looked behind them at the moving grass and knew there was no way to make it back to the clearing in time. He spun her around to look at him and her eyes were wide with confusion.

"Listen to me, Cindy, and listen well if you want to live. Do exactly what I say and you'll live through what's coming."

"What's coming? I don't..."

He cut her off. "Just shut up and listen to me. Keep your eyes and mouth closed and don't move a muscle, no matter how much you want to."

"Yeah, but, why are they climbing into the trees?" She asked, watching Mary and Jimmy doing just that.

"Doesn't matter, just remember what I told you," he said, pulling her to him so the two were in a tight embrace. Then it happened, the grass exploded around them and more than a thousand rats were running past them. Cindy tried to scream, but Henry placed his hand over her mouth, prepared for just such an act.

The rats swarmed over them, climbing on their heads and sniffing at their faces. Henry could feel the tiny pinpricks of sharp claws through his clothes and he resisted the urge to open his eyes. If he did such a foolish thing, the rats would probably have his eyeballs out of his sockets in less than a second.

He could feel wet noses against his neck and one crawled under his shirt, moving around until it retreated back the way it had come.

Cindy's face was buried in his chest, the woman visibly shaking.

At first the sun beat down on his closed eyelids, the light still trying to penetrate, but then all was dark as the hundreds of rodents swarmed over his body and face, investigating him and then moving on.

In all, the wave passed them in less than three minutes, the seconds agonizing as he stood perfectly still with his hand over Cindy's mouth. She squirmed in his arms, but stayed still, doing what she was told, until the last rat had passed them and had disappeared over the highway and then became lost in the tall grass on the other side. Since the fall of humanity, the grass bordering the shoulders of the nation's highways had become a low priority, especially considering all the city workers were probably dead.

Cracking an eyelid, Henry looked down at his feet and with relief, took his hand away from Cindy's mouth. She stood perfectly still; small rips in her clothes from where tiny claws had left their imprint. Henry's shirt was in a similar state, though his jeans had faired better; the heavy denim tougher against the sharp claws.

Henry looked over to see both Mary and Jimmy climbing down from the trees; Jimmy running towards them as fast as he could.

Henry separated from her just as Jimmy ran into her arms, the woman crying slightly from her shock. Henry couldn't blame her; the chill up his spine from all those tiny feet and noses was enough to give him the willies for the next year or so.

Mary had come over as well and she looked him up and down, her mouth hanging open.

"What the hell just happened? It was like a black wave just washed over the two of you. Then as they got closer Jimmy and me could see they were rats, hundreds of them."

"Shit, more like thousands, but how the hell did you know, Henry?" Jimmy asked, hugging Cindy closely to him.

"Well, if you'll believe it, I saw a special on the nature channel one day about how animals can migrate in packs. Nothing like that, of course, but I guess it's as close as you can get. I didn't know they were rats, but I knew something was in there. I'd say we were lucky," he said, rubbing Cindy's shoulder.

She smiled at him, wiping a tear away and placed her hand on his. "Wow, that was one of the worst feelings in my life, all those tiny claws." She shivered again, Jimmy consoling her with an arm around her waist. "Thanks Henry, I don't know what I would have done if you hadn't been there."

"No problem, honey, glad to help."

The four companions walked back to the trees and their bikes. The first thing they noticed was that their backpacks had been ripped to pieces, nothing but bits of cloth and thread lying on the ground, and the small supply of food they'd had was now gone, eaten by the rats.

The rest of their gear was spread out across the glade, tools and spare ammo everywhere. It took a few minutes, but soon everything worth saving was back together in the ripped packs. Two of the four packs were beyond salvaging and the supplies were repacked into the two good ones. Henry looked at his motorcycle. The pieces he had taken off the bike, including spark plugs and wires were gone. He walked around the area and then over to the other side of the highway, but nothing was found but a few threads to the damaged backpacks and one sparkplug.

Walking back to the others, he was frowning deeply, his forehead creased in concern. "Christ, I can't believe some stupid rodent ate my plugs and wires, but their gone. How's the other bike?"

Jimmy answered by pressing the starter button, the engine surging to life. "It's fine, good to go."

"But what do we do with four people and only one bike?" Cindy asked, rubbing her arm where she had picked up a few scratches from the curious rodents. Luckily they had a few antiseptic bandages and would be able to clean the cuts easily.

"We take turns; two will ride while the other two walk. We'll keep changing until we either find some new transportation or the bike runs out of gas." Henry said.

The others nodded and prepared to get moving again.

Henry took one of their empty water bottles and drained the gas from the unrepairable motorcycle, topping off the other bike's gas tank, as well as filling the empty water bottle with the extra fuel. It wasn't much, but gas stations with accessible fuel were few and far between, and Henry had to wonder where the bikers had managed to find the fuel for their motorcycles every time they ran low.

One of many questions he would never receive an answer to, as the bikers were either all dead or scattered to the wind.

When everyone was ready, Cindy and Mary climbed on the motorcycle and prepared to leave. Both backpacks were strapped to the sides of the bike, giving both Jimmy and Henry a much needed break from having to carry them.

Then the companions started off again, walking back onto the highway and away from the clearing. The highway was covered in small black pebbles, waste from a thousand rodents when the small creatures had crossed the highway.

Henry wondered where they would end up and was glad he was going the other way.

Looking up at the sun, he held his hand to his forehead, shading his eyes. It was many hours till dark and hopefully before dusk came they would either find a town that welcomed visitors or a suitable campsite for the night. If the latter came to pass it wouldn't be an unpleasant night with no food and only a small amount of water, but if they were lucky they might bag an animal, a deer or something similar.

With his stomach already grumbling, he was fairly certain he might even settle for dog.

Chapter 5

Captain Daniel Snyder walked to the end of the pier with two of his men behind him, their weapons held ready in case of trouble.

At the end of the pier waited the man who now ran the naval station in Groton, Connecticut. Behind this man stood more than ten guards all armed with assorted weaponry.

Snyder recognized every firearm, a warrior in his own right. He had been in more wars than he could count, though nowadays, or before the contaminated rains came, they were called skirmishes or other such nonsensical names.

He had been in the naval service for almost twenty years and would have been looking forward to a nice pension at his twenty year mark. He had been planning on moving to Aruba or some such tropical paradise and would have spent the rest of his days sipping cocktails and playing footsie with pretty native girls.

But all that was just a dream now.

Though he could still do exactly what he'd planned, he couldn't leave his men behind, or his boat.

Glancing over his shoulder, the U.S.S. Valiant floated against the pier, his men even now securing the mooring lines. The Valiant was a fast-attack nuclear submarine and she was his.

So despite the fact that he could sail off to an island somewhere and live the rest of his days in peace, he wouldn't leave his boat in anyone else's hands but his own.

So he was stuck with her, and she with him.

As for his crew, they were welcome to leave whenever they wanted. The United States Navy had officially become nonexistent a little less than four months ago, when the President of the United

States as well as the Senate and Congress were all infected and
became zombies.

So really they hadn't changed that much, he thought glibly.

But with all the major heads dead or walking around as animated corpses there was no one left to delegate authority. As base
after base became overrun with the undead, anyone who could
take the reins of authority disappeared until there was no one.
True, some Captains of larger vessels, such as aircraft carriers had
tried to rally other naval vessels, but soon they too became infected
as the rains fell onto the decks of the ships, killing soldiers who
then went into the bowels of the ships to kill and feed on their
fellow crewmates.

As far as Snyder knew, only a few ships were still active, though
most had headed for clearer pastures. Most had ceased all contact
with other survivors, deciding to make it out on their own. Snyder
didn't blame them, but unfortunately he wasn't in a position to
make that choice.

His submarine was small, and though he could pack it full of
food and supplies, he was still only able to stay down in the murky
depths for a little over a month before needing to resupply. In the
first few months of civilization's collapse, he hadn't had much
trouble finding food and clean water, but over the past two months
it had slowly grown increasingly harder to restock his dwindling
supplies.

Which had brought him to the Groton Naval Submarine Base.

Groton was a major submarine base off the New England coast.
Portsmouth, New Hampshire had been completely overrun, leaving his choices of either Groton, or perhaps, Virginia, which was a
ways down the coastline.

But Groton wasn't run by a military presence any longer, instead a ruthless local criminal out of Hartford had managed to take
control of the base in the ensuing chaos of the viral outbreak when
most of the MP's had either abandoned their posts to go to their
families or been infected themselves by the rainfall.

So he had secured the base as his own small village using his
own men for security.

The man had reinforced the tall chain-link fencing with barbed
wire. The fencing surrounding the entire base, and had brought in

all the supplies he could manage before the surrounding town of Groton, Connecticut had fallen to the undead.

There was a full commissary on base, as well as a giant galley that had the capacity to feed more than three thousand soldiers at a time. All in all, the man had set himself up pretty well.

Which was why Snyder was walking down the pier to see the man. He needed supplies and this was the closest place to get them.

The Boss of the base was a fat man in his late fifties, with a balding hairline and chubby cheeks. From first glance it looked like the man had two chins, though the layers of fat tended to confuse one. Despite the world going to hell in a hand basket, the Boss of Groton wasn't suffering in the eating department. On both hips hung two silver plated .357 Magnums, the large side arms seeming like overkill on the man's five-foot-six frame.

"Ah, Captain Snyder, so you finally decided to grant me with your presence, after all. For what do I owe thanks for this visit?" Jordan Raddack sneered.

"Spare me your pleasantries, Raddack. We both know what I'm here for."

The fat man nodded, jowls shaking. "Yes we do. And I find it rather amusing that you're here. In fact, the last time we talked, oh I don't know, a few months ago, you said you would never give in to my demands and that you would find your supplies elsewhere. Have I recalled our last conversation correctly?"

Snyder looked over Raddack's shoulder at the men behind him. All were hard men with sneers on their faces. He knew if Raddack gave the command to fire, the men wouldn't think twice of shooting him and his crewmen down in a hail of lead.

Snyder shifted uneasily, admiring the shine on his boots. "Well, the situation's changed and I'm here. So are we going to do business or not?"

Raddack nodded. "Perhaps, but it depends on what you might have that I need. He gestured with his arms, spreading them wide at his sides. "As you can see, I have everything I could possibly need. We've even started growing our own food, did you know that? After our last conversation you left me with a bad taste in my mouth. You need to have something very impressive to grab my attention."

Snyder nodded, "I do, you won't be sorry."

"Fine then, let's go back to my place and discuss this more. You can leave your men here with your ship," Raddack told him.

Snyder frowned. "First off, it's called a boat, not a ship, and do you really think I'd go anywhere with you by myself?"

Raddack chuckled at that. "My dear Captain Snyder, if I'd meant you any harm, then you'd already be bleeding out on the wooden planks below your feet. Now, shall we go?"

Snyder looked at the men behind Raddack, each one bringing their weapons to bear on him and his two crewmen. Truth be told, the fat bastard was right. If he wanted him dead he doubted he would have ever been allowed to get this close to the man.

Turning back to look at his boat, he waved his hand in the air, first left, twice, then right, once. The signal told the men topside he was fine and not to worry.

"You two go back to the boat, I'll be fine," he commanded the two crewmen behind him.

"But, sir...!" one of them said, protesting.

Snyder held up his hand, stopping any further protests. "That's an order sailor and as long as you're under my command, I'm still in charge, now dismissed!"

The man immediately relaxed, saluted and then spun around, the other crewmen next to the man following him back to the boat.

Snyder was actually pleased with the man, though he wouldn't want to tell him. Discipline was everything. But the man showed loyalty and concern for his safety and what Captain wouldn't want that from his men?

Swinging back around to Raddack, Snyder set his jaw. "All right then, let's get this tea party going? I have places to be."

Raddack chuckled as he waved his transportation closer. "I'm sure you do, Captain. It must be hard trying to save the world with only a hundred men."

The Black, polished, Hummer pulled up and Raddack climbed inside, his body actually becoming wedged in the opening before he slipped through. Snyder had the urge to place his boot against the man's backside and push, but knew it would be tantamount to a death sentence.

Climbing inside next to the man, he felt the cool air from the air conditioning. This Hummer was a civilian model, dark black with chrome wheels. Raddack had probably procured it from a nearby dealership, as well as the dozen others he had for his men. Snyder ignored this bit of information as irrelevant.

The only thing that mattered was negotiation with this bastard and leaving with what he came for, then perhaps once he was floating free in the harbor, he just might send a few Mach-8 torpedoes back to thank the man for his generosity.

Though he wouldn't do such a heinous thing, not wanting to hurt the innocent civilians under Raddack's thumb, the thought of blowing the base to hell and taking the fat bastard with him gave him a warm glow in his stomach that even the air conditioning on high couldn't cool off.

The Hummer drove out of the lower base of the station, once used exclusively for submarines. As the vehicle drove through the open gate from the lower level, Snyder glanced to the guard shack, now empty with its door hanging on one hinge, swaying in the light breeze.

A pang of how things once were crept into his mind and he forced the useless thoughts away. To focus on the past was irrelevant; it was the present and ultimately the future that mattered.

The Hummer slowly drove up the meandering street, Snyder watching the people of the station going about their daily tasks. Still, he was surprised not to see more people about. He asked Raddack and wasn't pleased with the fat man's answer.

"Almost everyone is gathered over by the galley. You see, you came at quite an auspicious time. We were about to execute a few thieves when your boat was spotted," he said leaning back in his seat, his body far too large to accomplish the task. Sweat ran down his forehead, despite the fact the air conditioning was on high. "I decided to put things on hold for a little while, hoping you might want to join me."

"Do I have a choice?" Snyder spit, disgusted. He could only imagine what form of barbarity the man would use to punish someone that had crossed him.

"Not really, my good Captain, not really," Raddack sneered.

Within minutes, the Hummer was pushing its way through the thongs of people. Most were dressed in worn clothing, though some seemed to have better appearances than others.

The story of the poor and the rich. Even without governments and capitalism, the same song continued, only instead of money it was food or a better house to live in, perhaps even a few workers to do your chores.

The Hummer slowed to a stop in front of a large podium, Raddack had commissioned it built for times when he wanted to gather his people to him and make an example of some poor bastard.

Though the man wasn't exactly loved by most of his followers, he was respected and even the biggest malcontent had to give credence that Raddack had saved their lives from the infected even now clamoring at the fences surrounding the base.

Exiting the Hummer and stepping out into the light, Raddack strolled onto the podium and stopped behind a small dais in the center. Snyder was directed to take a seat behind the Boss, the other seats filled with people Snyder assumed played some part in ruling the station.

Watching the faces of the people below, seeing the rage and bloodlust in their faces for what was to come next, Snyder found himself appalled. Had man fallen so fast as to become nothing more than barbarians in less than a year? How could the simple loss of technology and electrical power toss man back to the dark ages so quickly? He had always known civilization was a fragile thing, but he had never known just how fragile...until now.

Raddack spread his hands wide and two guards on either side of him shot two rounds into the sky, the gunshots silencing the crowd.

"My friends; welcome and thank you for waiting for me to return. Behind me is one of the last commanders of a United States Naval vessel! Captain Snyder hasn't been here for quite a long time and I thought it prudent for him to see how we deal with thieves and murderers!" He yelled over the heads of the crowd.

The crowd started talking again, some shouts and cheers cutting through the din. Another rifle shot silenced them once more.

"Now I know why you're all here and I won't keep you waiting any longer! But remember, though these two wretches are paying for their crimes today, it could be any one of you tomorrow, so fly straight and tow the line and do what is expected of you, only then will we survive this hellish new world we've found ourselves in!"

Clapping sounded across the crowd, and Snyder tried to count the shifting heads. If he had to guess, he would have counted almost two hundred, give or take, plus however many hadn't made it to the festivities. He decided to ask Raddack later exactly how many people he had inside the base.

He looked up as two men were dragged onto the podium. Both were in chains and their clothes were nothing but bloody rags. The first man, no older than twenty had a giant black eye, the pus and fluids forcing the eye to look like a brown and black balloon on the man's face. The second man was missing numerous teeth, the blood still dripping from the side of his mouth. Both of his eyes were wide with terror as he looked to Raddack and then the shifting crowd.

"Please, Boss, don't do this to me, it was a mistake, I swear! Send me away, out into the city, I'll take my chances there, please, I'm begging you, for the love of God, please!" The man shrieked again and again, begging for his life until one of the security guards clubbed the man in the side of the head. He fell to the podium, spitting teeth and his countenance was of one with a lazy gaze, as he tried to focus his eyes, despite the concussion he had just received.

The two guards dragged the men over to the opposite side of the podium where, for the first time, Snyder realized there was some kind of fenced in corral, though from his position on the podium, he couldn't see what was inside it, and hearing anything was next to impossible with all the yelling from the crowd.

Raddack raised his hands for quiet and this time the crowd did as ordered, almost all voices growing silent at the same time.

Pointing to the two wretches, Raddack raised his voice. "You Simon, are accused of stealing food from your neighbor and you, Andrew, are accused of killing your friend and co-worker, Mark, in a fight at the bar last week." He lowered his hand and grinned at the two men. "Do you have anything to say to us?"

The man with the black eye tried to take a step toward Raddack, but his chains and the guards wouldn't let him. "Yeah, I got something to say, you fat fuck. This is bullshit and you know it. I killed Mark by accident and it was a fair fight. This shit is just an excuse to keep the rest of us inline." He turned to look at the crowd. "Don't listen to him, this is all bullshit! Rise up and stop this fucker before he gets you all killed!"

He was silenced by a rifle butt to the stomach, the man doubling over, bile drooling from his mouth.

Raddack turned to look at the other man. "How 'bout you, got anything to say?" The man merely nodded a no. "No reason, no one gives a shit anyway, just get this over with and stop bullshitting around."

Raddack turned back to the crowd, a wide smile on his face. "All right then, now that the preliminaries are out of the way, lets get this shit going!" He screamed; raising his arms out to his sides like a ringmaster in a circus would.

The crowd roared with enthusiasm, agreeing heartily.

"You two men are found guilty of your crimes and are sentenced to death, may God have mercy on your souls!" He yelled, more for the crowd than any actual sentiment he might actually be feeling.

Raddack gave the signal; to one of the guards and the man walked over to the small corral. On top of the corral were two posts and each had large mirrors attached to them. When the mirrors were bent back using long poles, they reflected what was inside the corral, much like a mirror used in department stores to see what was going on in the aisles by the management.

Captain Snyder uttered a gasp of surprise at the contents of the corral.

Inside it, moving about hungrily, were seven zombies, all in similar states of decomposition. All had dried skin and flaking scalps, along with mouths that hung slack, swollen tongues peeking out of their orifices like a snake smelling the night air before going out on a hunt. At the moment their torpidity was obvious, as they couldn't see any food nearby.

Both of the haggard men uttered a cry of despair and the one with missing teeth tried to make a run for it only to be knocked to the floor of the podium in a heap of arms and legs, unconscious.

"You can't do this, it's inhuman," uttered the man with the black eye.

"Perhaps, but we have laws here on this base and you broke them, now you must pay the price." Gesturing to the two guards he pointed to the rope hanging from a telephone pole over the corral. "Go ahead boys; lynch 'em up." Raddack said brusquely.

The man with the black eye struggled for a moment while he was hung by his arms and hauled up to hang over the corral. A crude pulley system had been erected, another guard winching the man higher and higher until he hung precariously over the putrid semblance of human beings, now nothing more than evil incarnate.

Below his swinging feet, the undead moaned and scrabbled against the wooden planks of their prison, desperately trying to reach the prey hanging only a few feet above their heads. The excitement was apparent as they fought to reach the hanging man.

Next came the unconscious man, and soon, he too, was swinging back and forth, his head hanging low, his eyes closed.

Snyder stood up and walked over to Raddack.

"Raddack, this is insane, don't do this, they're human beings for Christ sakes!"

Spinning on his heels in a movement that belied his size, he turned to stare at Snyder. "Human beings? Perhaps, but one is a thief and the other a killer. This is how I maintain order around here; now sit back down or you'll be joining them." He told Snyder, his eyes flaring wide in anger.

Snyder stood his ground for a moment, but then backed down, realizing there was nothing he could do for the two men but end up suffering the same fate.

Backing down, he lowered his eyes to the wooden floor of the podium and stepped away from him. "Fine Raddack, but I still want to formally declare this is wrong."

"Duly noted, Captain, now sit the fuck down, now!" He hissed the last words. Snyder did as he was told, his stomach rolling inside of him.

Turning to the guard holding the winch, Raddack held out his hand in a fist and pointed his thumb down. The guard did as he was told and slowly started to lower the two men.

Black Eye screamed for Raddack to have mercy as he struggled uselessly. Even if he somehow was able to slip free of his bonds, he would only end up falling straight down into the corral.

The man was doomed and after a moment when the first claw-like hands wrapped around his shoes, he knew it, too.

The crowd cheered, watching the visceral scene in the mirrors. Black Eye let out a shriek of pain as the first mouth found his leg and ripped a chunk of flesh from his calf, pants and all. A moment later the unconscious man came awake, a high-pitched scream, gelded with terror, escaping his lips as blackened teeth bit into his own leg. He kicked and screamed, managing to push the creatures away, but an instant later they were back, biting and clawing at his lower body.

Slowly they were lowered until more than half of their bodies were in the corral. The sounds of pain and feeding were almost enough to make Snyder want to vomit, but he held it down, not wanting to show weakness in front of Raddack or his men.

Raddack took one last look at the two screaming men and pointed to the guard holding the winch.

"Finish it," he said briskly, and the guard let go of the winch, the two men freefalling into the corral in a heap. Two of the zombies were crushed by their weight; their legs snapping like twigs, but the five others fell on top of the two men, the two with broken legs crawling into the pack, as well, and with the sounds of death filling the podium, the two men finally became quiet.

Time passed as the ghouls continued feeding, ripping organs from bodies and flesh from bone. Then as if a switch had been pulled, the zombies backed away from the two prisoners.

Snyder watched the mirrors and his mouth went slack as he saw the two dead men slowly raise themselves to their feet, now dead, but yet still alive.

They had become the undead, the other ghouls no longer interested in feeding on them.

Raddack smiled, his fat face seeming to split apart like a melon sliced in two.

"You see?" He called to Snyder. "That's how I maintain their population. When criminals go down, dead people come up," he chuckled and then ordered one of his men to turn the mirrors back down to the ground.

Turning back to the crowd, he held his hands out for order. In a few moments the crowd quieted down, waiting for their leader to speak.

"The punishment is done, but remember, cross the line and you'll be next. But do what you're supposed to do and we'll all keep living while the rest of the world goes to shit."

Clapping filled the area and Raddack waved one last time, moving across the podium to Snyder.

"Come on, then. I'm thirsty, let's go back to my quarters and we'll talk about exactly what you might have that I need." Then he moved down the steps, towards his Hummer, guards flanking him as he went.

Snyder stood up, taking one last look at the two men, who only moments before had been living, breathing people and shook his head with disgust.

Then he followed Raddack down the stairs and climbed back into the Hummer.

Raddack noticed the look on Snyder's face and grinned. "It had to be done, Snyder, and you know it. It's the only way to keep the people in line. I don't have enough man power to stop an outright mutiny, so I need to control with fear. You know, when you think about it, I'm really not doing anything our own President didn't do with terrorists and Iraq before the world went to hell," he said in an unctuous tone.

Laughing to himself and enjoying the analogy that he was in the same league as the President of the United States, Raddack tapped his driver on the shoulder and the man pulled out of the crowd. While Snyder sat in his seat, wishing he had a weapon to place against Raddack's head and end the man's tyranny once and for all.

Chapter 6

"Okay, Henry, how 'bout we switch, my feet are killing me," Jimmy said as he walked alongside the motorcycle Henry was riding, with Mary on the back.

Mary grinned at her friend. "Gees, Jimmy, I'd say you've gone soft after spending the winter in that shopping mall. We used to walk everywhere," she joked.

"True, but for the last few months the most I'd walk was from one end of the mall to the other, even when we went out foraging for food, me and the others usually didn't wander far from the drop off. You know, I realize it was time to move on, but I'll still miss that place. It was nice not having to look over my shoulder every second of the day."

"Guess you'll just have to get back in shape all over again," Henry said, stopping the bike and climbing off. Cindy hopped onto the front seat and Jimmy the back, happy to be resting his tired feet.

Once off the bike he continued his train of thought. "I agree with you about the mall, but we'd spent the entire winter there and you could tell things were changing. There's going to be a power struggle there, no thanks to us for taking out Barry, and I don't want to be stuck in the middle of it. Better we had just left before it all came down."

Cindy revved the engine once and started moving, so slow she was barely keeping the bike from falling over. So far the companions had managed to keep a good four MPH as they walked along the side of the highway. For a while no one spoke, each keeping his or her thoughts private.

Cindy checked the gas gauge, tapping it with her finger. "Hey, Henry, did you see the gas gauge?" She asked.

"Yeah, afraid I did, despite the fact we're not moving that fast, we're probably burning gas faster than if we were driving regular, plus, who knows when the last time the engine had a tune-up. Damn bike could be sucking gas twice as fast, thanks to a bad valve or something."

"So what do we do?" Jimmy asked from behind Cindy.

He shrugged. "Nothing we can do. Just keep using it until we run out of gas." He looked up at the sky, the sun just starting its downward spiral. "We need to find a place for the night. I don't want to be stuck out here in the middle of nowhere when night falls."

Everyone agreed, but kept moving. More time passed, the sun almost hidden from view. The sky was a burnt orange, all of them admiring the beautiful sunset, despite the foreboding of trouble if they didn't find someplace to hold up.

They had only come across a few scattered roamers on they're trek along the long ribbon of asphalt. Most had been in ones or twos and had been easily dispatched with a bullet to the head. Only one time had they had to deal with any kind of sizable threat. More than eight ghouls had come out of the woods bordering the highway and Henry had decided to leave them, instead retreating.

For the next mile the four companions had jogged, each taking turns on the motorcycle so that they stayed fresh.

Jimmy had argued that they should have blown all the roamers to hell, but Henry had stated that if they could outrun them, they should, thereby saving their ammo for future use when a time might come when retreating was not an option.

"We can't kill every single deader we come across, Jimmy, there's just too damn many," he'd told his friend.

Jimmy had reluctantly agreed and they had soon left the slow walkers in their rear-view mirror.

Another hour later, Henry was back on the motorcycle, Mary sitting behind him. He slowed the bike and stopped it near an exit sign leading off the highway, the off-ramp silent and empty.

The top green sign read, Connecticut, 42 miles, but it was the sign below it that first caught Henry's eyes. The second sign read,

WOODHAVEN, POP. 5,321, but the **5,321** was crossed out, a white line of paint through it, and someone had written below it with white spray paint, **595 *give or take***. Below that on a new piece of plywood in red paint were the words: *WE'RE STILL HERE! TRADERS WELCOME, THIEVES NOT. HOTEL WITH FOOD AND WATER.*

"What do you think? Might be safe," Henry said, looking at his friends.

"Yeah, or it might be a trap. The second we step into their clutches they kill us all and take our weapons," Jimmy said.

"Oh, Jimmy, you're so morbid. Not everyone in the world is evil, you know," Mary said as she climbed off the back of the bike, stretching her limbs. Her butt hurt and it was sweaty from the last hour of sitting on the bike, plus her right leg had fallen asleep. She had already decided she would walk the rest of the way. Jimmy could have her place on the bike if he wanted to.

"Maybe not everyone's evil, but lately it sure seems to be most of them. Christ, it seems everywhere we go someone's trying to kill us or control us." Jimmy stated.

Henry nodded, agreeing with him. "He's got a point, Mary. Since there's no longer any real law enforcement around, it's like everyone is out for themselves. And you have to admit, man as an individual is selfish.

"I'm not saying that you're wrong, but you can't deny we've met some good, honest people on our journey, too."

Everyone nodded, agreeing with her. Henry looked up to the darkening sky and frowned.

"Well, enough chatter. It's almost dark, so we need to decide. Are we going into Woodhaven or are we spending the night out on the plain somewhere off the highway, with a watch posted all night and no fire?"

The four companions looked at one another, each gauging one another's answer, and as one, all said the same thing.

"Woodhaven," they all said, smiling to each other.

"All right then, if that's settled, let's get going. Hopefully the town's not too far from the exit. And stay sharp, just in case."

With Cindy and Jimmy in a slight lead on the motorcycle, the four companions moved down the off-ramp, weapons primed for any surprises.

Within a half mile of the off-ramp, the first signs of the town came into view. Almost the entire street had been cleared of cars and wreckage, the vehicles used to construct a crude barricade. Henry looked to his left and right sides. The barrier continuing on until it was lost from sight.

This wasn't the first time they'd seen similar construction.

When the rains first came and the population became infected, crude barricades were formed out of whatever could be found in a short amount of time. Anything from old automobiles to parts of houses were stacked on top of one another, thereby keeping the walking dead from penetrating into the town proper.

The towns across America had become small forts in their own rights, where outsiders were frowned upon and everyone was distrustful. As for the major cities, well, they had become death-traps, filled with millions of an undead population. To venture into a major city was a death sentence, only the ridiculously brave or the unbelievably stupid were foolish enough to attempt it in the hopes of scavenging something useful. They had been nicknamed *deadlands* by anyone living near the dead metropolises and were shunned by nearly everyone.

But sometimes on the companions travels there would be towns that would welcome strangers for a chance to hear what was happening outside their debris-filled walls.

Henry hoped this was one of the latter as he had no patience for dealing with some asshole who thought he was king for a day.

Walking up to the center of the barricade, he noticed the guards standing watch. The sun was just about to set and a few torches had been lit along the balustrade to help the guards see better.

Henry chuckled to himself. Didn't the fools know with the torches next to them their night vision would be all but lost? Not to mention with the men silhouetted against the flames, they were easy targets for bandits.

Jimmy noticed where Henry was looking and he grunted in agreement. "Evidently these folks haven't had much trouble since the shit hit the fan."

"Then they're the fist lucky ones we've found," Mary added, looking up at the men on the wall.

The guards hadn't noticed them yet, but as Cindy revved the engine on the motorcycle a flutter of activity appeared as men quickly tried to aim weapons and see what was approaching them in the falling dusk.

"Who's there, identify yourself or we'll shoot!" A nervous voice called from above the four companions.

Henry turned and looked at the others, a slight grin on his face. They mimicked his expression, hearing the slight tremor in the man's voice from above. Whoever was calling to them was either very green or a complete coward.

"Don't shoot, we're friends," Henry called up to the guard. "We saw your sign on the highway and thought we'd take advantage of your hotel."

"You're not zombies?" The guard asked, hesitantly.

"Now how many zombies do you know that say hello and ask to come in? Come on man, you can't be that stupid, now are you gonna let us in or should we move on," Jimmy said, his patience wearing thin.

The guard's head disappeared for a few moments and Henry and the others could hear hushed talking. Then the head reappeared.

"What do you have to trade? We don't give food or border away, you know."

"Fair enough. We've got ammunition, rounds for 38's or shotguns, how's that?" Henry called up.

"How many you got?" the guard asked back.

"Well friend, that's really none of your fucking business if I'm not trading with you personally, now are you gonna let us in or are you just blowing smoke up our asses!" Henry called back, losing patience with the idiot.

"All right, I guess you're okay, but if you got weapons, keep them holstered, we don't want trouble. If you're friendly, we'd be happy to have you stay with us, be good to hear what's happening out there."

"Sounds good to us, and we'd be happy to tell you what we know," Henry finished.

As they waited to be let into the town, Jimmy moved close to Henry so his voice wouldn't carry. "They're letting us keep our weapons? Are these the most stupid people you've ever met, or what?"

"They're just trusting and I'm not complaining, now stop talking and keep your eyes open, we're not safe yet," Henry hissed softly.

Mary heard their raised voices but didn't catch the gist of their conversation. "Everything okay, Henry?" She asked.

Henry nodded. "Yeah, it's fine; just stay sharp."

She nodded, waiting for whatever came next

There was a rumbling and a Greyhound bus started moving to the side, opening a three foot gap in the barricade. Henry nodded approvingly. He hadn't noticed the bus as it was covered with sheet metal and had blended in almost perfectly with the rest of the barricade. But now seeing it moving, he wondered how he had missed it, even in the shadows of the quickly falling night.

He resolved to become more focused. Sometimes it was the minutest nugget of information that could get you killed, nowadays; or save your life.

With their entrance in front of them, they started inside, Cindy driving the bike solo, Jimmy walking next to her. Just in case things weren't how they appeared, he wanted to be ready and not sitting on the back of the bike like a sitting duck.

Once inside, Cindy turned off the motor and with the kickstand down, dismounted. Henry and the others were by her side and they all waited as the guard climbed down from his perch, the rickety aluminum ladder looking like it was about to bend, sending the man plummeting to the ground.

But the ladder held and within a minute the man was standing in front of them, the other guards now aiming their weapons at the four companions.

The man held out his hand to Henry, assuming he was the leader by the way the others stood a little behind him.

"The name's Collins, Brad Collins," he said pumping Henry's hand twice. Henry returned the greeting, pleased to see the man had a firm grip. He had always thought it said a lot about a man by the way he shook hands.

"I'm Henry Watson, this is Jimmy Cooper. That's Mary Roberts and the blonde on the motorcycle is Cindy Jansen," Henry said, introducing each of them.

"The hot blonde, I might add," Jimmy said to Cindy, flashing her a smile.

"Jimmy, stop, be serious," she chastised him, though she didn't mind the compliment.

"Nice to meet you all and I really mean it. You're the first people we've seen in almost a month." Collins said.

"Really, no one else has come by?" Mary asked, surprised.

Collins nodded quickly, his head looking like it was on a spring. "Yup, don't know where everyone is, but they're not coming around here. So you want to go to the inn? I'll bring you there myself. My watch is just about over anyway."

The man headed away from the barricade, walking down the middle of the two lane street.

"Cindy, leave the bike there and take the keys, don't see why it won't be safe, sides, there's not much gas left anyway." He told her as he turned to follow Collins.

Sliding off the bike, she caught up to Jimmy, who gave her a quick hug before they walked away from the barricade. Mary was next to Henry, her hand never far from her weapon.

So what do you think?" She asked softly, so Collins couldn't hear her.

"I think we just found the only friendly town in New England." He said; looking behind him to make sure they weren't being followed by a large group of men.

No one was there. It was almost unsettling not to see some coldhearts trying to sneak up on them and try to get the drop on them for their weapons or ammo, but it was true.

"So, Collins, how have you and your people managed to stay so trusting after all this time?" Henry asked, moving up next to the man. Less than a half mile in front of them, the lights of the city sparkled in the growing darkness, the small orbs of light seeming to flutter with a life of their own.

"Don't know really, guess we just all banded together and dealt with the situation. When the rains first came more than half the town became infected. It was hard, but the rest of us rallied and killed them off. It was tough, I tell you. I had to put my own Grandma down when she got sick and came back. Was the strangest thing I ever had to do in my life. Well, we got control of the situation and built the wall around more than half the city. That was a feat in itself. Almost everyone in town helped with that, thank God all our construction workers hadn't been infected, they knew how to use the cranes and other machinery to stack the cars, the rest was done by hand. We lost some good people defending the town while we built that wall. Others just left, thinking they could do better elsewhere. We never saw them again."

"But how do you feed yourself? What happened when the stores went dry?" Mary asked.

"Most of us have gardens in our yards and once we knew we'd run out of food we turned the gym in the high school into a giant greenhouse. We're able to grow food there year round. Plus, we still have a fair supply of canned goods from before, we use them sparingly though. Thank God winter's over and we can plant outside again. We've got more seeds than we know what to do with, so we should have a good crop come next fall."

"That's great, so um, when can we get some of this food, I'm starving," Jimmy asked, rubbing his stomach.

Collins turned around to glance at Jimmy. "Oh, don't worry about that, Mrs. Sanders will fix you right up. She runs the inn with her daughter, Missy. They've got a bed and breakfast thing goin'. Some of us guards stay there sometimes when we're two tired to go all the way home. She makes some of the best stew you'll ever eat, I tell ya," Collins eyes lit up as he talked about the stew and Henry felt his own hunger growing.

Ten minutes later they arrived at the outskirts of the town. On closer inspection the lights they'd seen from the distance were torches lit along the street and in front of some of the houses.

With electrical power a thing of the past, lighting and cooking became somewhat more primitive. Though some folks still had generators, they were usually used sparingly and only in dire emergency, the fuel to run the machines in short supply.

Collins stopped in front of a three-story brick building with an ornate canvas awning over the door with the words: **THE HILLCREST INN** stenciled in white

"This is it," he said simply, opening the door and gesturing for the companions to enter.

Henry did as he asked and stepped into a small, yet grand foyer with a high vaulted ceiling. Marble statues were spread out along the sides and oil paintings covered the walls. The carpeting was plush, with a strip of marble tile leading up the middle to a wide oak staircase.

A huge crystal chandelier floated over their heads, twinkling with the candle flames set where light bulbs once were.

"Beautiful, absolutely, beautiful," Mary said in a whisper.

Music could be heard coming from somewhere and though it was classical, Henry couldn't put his finger on which composer it was.

He looked across the room as a woman walked in. She was wearing a dirty apron, her hair slick with sweat. She was a little on the frump side, though Henry was fairly certain she had been beautiful once. Her clothing was covered in food stains and the woman was a stark contrast to the decadent surroundings.

"Do you like the music?" She asked, wiping her hands on the apron, actually making the sausage-like digits dirtier. "It's Beethoven, his Moonlight Sonata. I love the classical stuff, so full of romance and loss, don't you agree?"

She was looking directly at Henry and the man felt like a specimen under a microscope.

"Ah, sure, I guess, can't say I ever got into the classical stuff, myself."

Collins spoke up then, breaking the unsettling silence.

"Mrs. Sanders, these are some visitors, they say they got ammo for payment if you can put them up for a spell."

"Ammo, huh, can I see it? Wouldn't want to feed you and give you a place to sleep to find out you're all full of shit."

"Sounds fair," Henry chuckled and reached into his pocket and retrieved a handful of rounds for the .38 both Jimmy and Mary carried. His rounds for his Glock were safely in his jacket pocket and he would be keeping them at all cost.

The woman took a bullet from his hand and placed it between her teeth, biting down on its surface slightly.

Pulling it away, she eyed it again and then smiled. "All right then, these seem genuine. We'll work out how much later. You folks hungry? I just finished a fresh batch of stew."

"Lady, you took the words right out of my mouth, let's eat," Jimmy said while rubbing his hands. He noticed a girl standing at the door where Mrs. Sanders had entered, and when his eyes met hers she winked at him, curling one of her black tresses on her finger.

Jimmy looked away, not knowing what to make of the girl. She couldn't have been a day over sixteen, and though pretty, was a little under his age preference, plus, he had Cindy now.

Cindy noticed the girl, too, and stepped up closer to Jimmy, sliding her arm into his own. "Who's that?" She asked, curiously.

Mrs. Sanders turned at her question and slapped her hands together with gusto. "Oh, that's my daughter, Missy, she's harmless." Mrs. Sanders pointed at her daughter and gestured for her to shoo. "Go on, girl, get into the kitchen and get that stew ready for these nice people, I'm sure they don't want to be lookin' at your bony behind."

Missy made a face and then slipped into the kitchen, the sounds of rattling pots overriding Beethoven.

"Come on then, follow me, the dining rooms in here," she said, waddling away from the companions.

"Well, if it's all the same to you, I'll be going," Collins said. "My wife's probably waiting on me with supper."

"Wait a minute, don't you have someone in charge, a mayor or head man that we need to talk to?" Henry inquired as the man slid out the door and into the cool night.

"Sorry, mister, we don't have anything like that. The mayor died months ago, before the rains became safe. He got infected and the Chief-of-police died of a heart attack before the winter started. Since then we've all just got along. When we really need to get something done we just call a town meeting. So far it's worked out pretty well, so we decided to keep it that way."

"Sure, son, okay, just checking. Well, if anyone needs to talk to us you know where we'll be," Henry said as Collins waved and disappeared into the darkness of the street.

Turning back to the others after the door was closed; cutting off the cool air outside, Henry clapped his hands together, rubbing them cheerfully. "Well if it's all right with you guys, I'm starving, let's eat."

With Jimmy in the lead they all flowed through the dining room doorway, the smell of Mrs. Sanders stew already making their mouths water.

Mary stopped Henry at the door and spoke low. "What do you make of this place? No one's in charge, and so trusting, it has to be too good to be true."

Henry shrugged. "I know what you mean, Mary but I really think what we see is what we get. These people have a good thing going here, why fix what isn't broken?"

She nodded and took a seat at the wide table. Henry sat next to her while Mrs. Sanders ladled out bowls of stew from a large, copper kettle.

She paused when she reached Henry.

"Here you go, handsome, an extra big scoop for you," she said, making sure to brush her ample bosom against his arm.

Henry blushed, not exactly happy with the attention he was receiving. The woman had to be almost a decade his senior and she was a little heavy for his tastes in women. Still, he smile politely and thanked her, catching Mary's grin as she watched the scene.

Mrs. Sanders exited the room, going to retrieve some bread and Mary's smile widened. Henry picked up his spoon and waved it at her threateningly. "Not one word from you, or so help me..." he said, playfully.

She held up her hands in surrender and then picked up her own spoon, digging into the rich stew.

Henry did likewise and as he bit into the scalding food, Mary whispered out of the side of her mouth. "Pretty good stew, ay *handsome?*" She chuckled.

Henry flashed a mean look her way that quickly turned into a grin. Chuckling himself, he continued to eat, Jimmy and Cindy doing the same, the four of them laughing and talking, enjoying the safety of the inn.

Mrs. Sanders stood at the entrance to the dining room, eyeing the man with the rock hard abs and powerful biceps. The second she had walked into the foyer and saw him standing there, she knew she wanted him. He was different from the men of the town.

He had a hardness to him, though his eyes were soft.

Most of the men in town were all a bunch of pussies that wouldn't know a real woman if she were to rub up against their cocks.

No, what she saw here was a real man, someone who could keep her warm on those cold New England nights.

Wiping her face clean and plastering on her most sincere smile, she straightened her outfit and with bread in one hand, and a pitcher of water in the other, stepped out into the dining room to check on her guests.

Her eyes glanced quickly to Henry and she felt her loins grow moist.

She would have this man, she promised herself, and the other man would go to her daughter. She needed a good man and Missy had already told her she had liked the way the younger man looked.

Mrs. Sanders watched the way Jimmy and Cindy were talking and eating, knowing in her gut the two were lovers.

That was okay, once the blonde and brunette were out of the picture, the two men would stay with her and her daughter...whether they liked it or not.

Chapter 7

With the meal finished, the four companions were led up the ornate oak staircase on their way to their rooms for a good nights rest.

Standing in the hallway on the second floor, Mrs. Sanders showed each of them the door belonging to their rooms, the hanging flesh swinging back and forth on the under side of her arms as she gestured wildly.

"So how many rooms do you need, two I assume," she said, looking at Jimmy and Cindy and then at Henry and Mary.

Henry realized what she meant and raised his hands to deter her. "Whoa, wait a sec, you've got it all wrong," he said. "Mary and me are just friends. She could be my daughter, for Christ's sake. Those two are together, though," he finished, gesturing to Cindy and Jimmy.

Mrs. Sander's eyes went wide in surprise, the gesture almost seeming staged. "Oh, really. Well then, call me Connie, won't you, Henry?" She said, rubbing herself against him, oblivious to the stares of the other companions.

She smelled of old grease and potatoes and Henry tried to keep his face blank, not wanting to offend their host.

"Okay then... Connie. Could you give us our rooms, please? I don't know about them, but I'm exhausted," he said, looking at his three friends.

Jimmy nodded as well. "Yeah, I'm pretty wasted myself. It'll be good to sleep in a bed again. I forgot how good we had it at the mall until we had to sleep on the ground again.

"Mall, what mall?" Connie inquired. "Is it near here, are there a lot of people there. Maybe we could get together with them, you know, pull our resources."

"I'm sorry, Connie, but the mall we're talking about was back in Massachusetts, on the other side of Boston. Even if you wanted to go there you'd have to fight your way through hundreds of deaders just to get through Boston. The entire city is filled with the dead."

"What's a deader? Oh wait, you mean a zombie? Ha, that's clever; I haven't heard that one before. We've had other strangers come through our town and I've heard some of the slang. Let's see, there's rotters and biters, and stenches, and walkers, and oh, there was one more, it's on the tip of my tongue..."

"Ah, listen, Connie, how 'bout we pick this up in the morning; I really want to get some rest. We'll settle up with your payment, too." Henry said as he edged further down the hallway, hoping one of the doors next to him might be his room.

"Oh, sorry, luv', I do go on, not enough people to talk to I guess, I spend all day in that blasted kitchen, need to get out more, I think." She reached into her apron pocket and pulled out a handful of keys. "Here you go, take your pick, the whole floor's empty, there's a few guards on the top floor, but this floors got no one." She moved a little closer to Henry. "My rooms on the third floor. You know, just in case you get lonely."

Henry plucked a key from her chubby hand and quickly scanned the number. Directly across from him was the same numbered door and he slid to his right, opening the door and slipping inside.

"No thanks, Connie, I'm beat," he said, feigning a yawn. "Good night and thanks for dinner, it was fantastic." He looked at his three friends and waved briefly. "'Night guys, see you in the morning, and remember what I said at dinner."

"Okay, Henry, don't worry, now go to bed and let the young folk have some fun," Jimmy said, Cindy giggling in his arms as he squeezed her butt.

Jimmy plucked another key from Connie's hand and after a few seconds to figure out which way to go; both he and Cindy moved down the other end of the hallway, opened their door and were gone with a wave to Mary.

Connie handed Mary a key and pointed to the other end of the hallway.

"Your rooms down that way, dear, all the way to the end," she smiled sweetly.

Mary took one look at Henry's door and then gazed down to Jimmy's, not understanding why they were so far apart from each other, but then she shrugged, taking the key from her hand and moving down the hallway.

"Good night, dear, and there's plenty of water and towels if you want to shower. Since the rain became clean it's been wonderful. All the water we can collect and no boiling like before. I tell you, one less thing to do in a day full of hundreds of chores."

Mary only smiled, not really interested in the woman's day of cooking and cleaning.

"Well, good night, sleep tight," Connie said.

"Thanks, Mrs. Sanders, good night," Mary said, opening her door and slipping inside. She closed the door and leaned against the door, glad to be alone for even a few minutes.

She frowned as she tossed her key on the bed. The entire floor was empty, yet they were spread out all across it. If you had to take care of three guests, wouldn't it make more sense to keep them together, instead of having to walk all over the floor?

Deciding she was just being paranoid, she headed for the bathroom, already disrobing as she went.

Setting her .38 on the sink, she finished undressing, turning the shower on, pleased to see water shoot out of the nozzle. Though it wasn't hot, it wasn't ice cold either, the sun heating the water tank on the roof.

Stepping into the shower, she felt the cool water wash away her concerns, sluicing down her body and she closed her eyes and enjoyed her first shower in more than a week. Her eyes went to the scar of her left arm as she washed herself. The white line was the only defect in an otherwise perfect body. She had almost died from that wound, but thanks to Henry and Jimmy she had pulled through.

She had already decided once out of the shower she would relax, clean her gun and then get to bed early. Knowing Henry, he would want to get an early start out on the road again bright and early the next morning.

With the clear water cascading over her flawless skin, she let out a breath of pure pleasure, wanting the shower to last forever.

*   *   *

Jimmy stripped off his clothes in two seconds flat, then jumped onto the full size bed in the middle of the room. The room was sparsely furnished with a few paintings on the wall and a beautifully carved bureau sat in the far corner unobtrusively. The carpeting was a rich, wine color and the drapes were of a material that denoted wealth. Two nightstands bordered each side of the bed, clear glass lamps on each. The walls were a rich crème color, not so much as a scratch to mar the painted surface.

Lying on his back with his hands under his head, he let out a soft whistle. "This place is alright; bet it cost a pretty penny before the world fell part. I bet I couldn't have even got into the foyer before, but now, look at me!" He said, waving his hands over his head.

His shotgun and .38 were spread on the carpet in a pile, his hunting knife lying askew on top like a drunken dock worker.

"Come here, baby, you know what I want," he breathed huskily.

Cindy made a face. "Are you kidding, do you have any idea how bad you smell?" Shaking her head, she gestured to the shower. "Get in their, Romeo, and wash up, a shower will do you good; then we'll talk." She flashed him a smile that said their talk would be much more than conversation.

After placing his nose near his armpit and wincing at the odor, he decided she was correct.

Jumping from the bed like a ten year old going to the circus, Jimmy jogged into the bathroom, letting out yet another whistle at the beautiful marble tile and carvings around the window.

After getting the water running in the shower he stepped in, letting the water cascade over his body. Taking in some water in his mouth and spitting it out like a fountain, he quickly washed his hair and then peeked out of the curtain to see Cindy using the toilet.

"What do you think you're doing?" He asked her, bluntly.

"I'm using the bathroom, what does it look like?"

"Yeah, but you couldn't wait for me to finish in here? Gees, Cindy I don't want to see you going to the bathroom, I mean, I eat at that restaurant sometimes."

She made a sour face and shot him an angry look. "What the hell are you talking about? You've seen me use the toilet lots of times when we're out on the road."

Water dripped down his face to fall onto the tile floor of the bathroom. "Yeah, but then it's different, I mean, we're roughing it, but now..." He trailed off, leaving his words to hover in the air like the rapidly growing moisture from the shower.

She stood up, and flushed the toilet, secretly enjoying the sound of the toilet as it emptied and refilled. To many times they were without running water and proper facilities, it was nice to use the basics in life once more.

Taking the two steps across the bathroom toward Jimmy, her clothes already in a pile out in the bedroom, she crossed her arms in front of herself and frowned at her boyfriend.

"You know, Jimmy, you keep this shit up and I have a feeling your favorite restaurant is going to be closed for the foreseeable future." She snapped, her eyes icy.

Jimmy made a sad face, not liking where the conversation was going. "I'm sorry, babe, come over here, will you? I want to show you something," he said seriously.

Doing what he requested, she leaned closer to the shower curtain, not understanding what was so important.

In a flash of motion, Jimmy's arm shot out and grabbed her wrist, tugging her into the shower with him. She let out a squeak, falling into his arms, feeling the soothing water fall across her smooth skin. Her nipples grew hard in the cold water and her hair became plastered to her face.

Wiping hair from her eyes, she looked up into the wet face of Jimmy. He was grinning mischievously as he pulled the curtain closed again.

"Jimmy, what do you think you're doing?" She asked coyly.

His grin grew wider, like the Cheshire cat in Alice in Wonderland. "Why, I'm doing my best to get my favorite restaurant to reopen for at least one more night." He said slyly and began nibbling on her neck, his hands caressing her breasts.

She moaned in pleasure and sighed. "Jimmy Cooper, what am I supposed to do with you?"

Jimmy looked up at her, his mouth around one of her pert nipples, his right hand somewhere between her legs. "Oh, I think I have an answer to that question."

With the water sluicing over their bodies, the two started a round of lovemaking that would end hours later in the full-size bed in the middle of the room.

*   *   *

Henry stepped out of the shower feeling ten years younger. Drying himself off, he walked back into the main room and sat on the edge of the bed. With just him on it, the full size bed was more than enough room. His weapons sat on a chair near the bathroom door, his clothes spread out on hangers in the open closet door. Hopefully his clothes would get a good airing out as he slept.

A television set sat at the foot of the bed, against the wall, and he was tempted to go try it, though he knew it was a useless gesture. Even if there was power to operate the television, there were no more stations broadcasting.

Glancing around the room and leaning back on the bed, he let his mind wander.

He'd come so far and had changed so much in the past nine months or so since his walk in the park when he had first witnessed a pool full of children turn into blood thirsty ghouls; attacking and killing their parents.

He thought back to the friends he'd met and had then subsequently lost in his travels to survive and of course his thoughts found their way to his wife, Emily.

He had spent more than half his life with his wife, until he had returned home after the initial outbreak to find her sitting at the kitchen table with pieces of their housecat in her mouth.

She had turned as well, not his wife anymore, but something from the bowels of hell come forth to wreak havoc on the human world. He had put her down himself with a skillet that had been sitting on the stove. Then with Jimmy and Mary at his side, he had left his home and his wife forever.

He felt a chill on his body, so he slipped under the covers of the bed, enjoying the coolness of the sheets. His mind continued racing, images of the past flooding to the front of his mind. He was under the illusion he would never get to sleep, too worked up about past memories, but almost as soon as his head hit the pillow, he felt his eyelids becoming droopy and before he realized it he was fast asleep.

But his mind wouldn't let him rest and past images flooded across his subconscious. Before he had been asleep for more than an hour dreams came to him, some pleasant, others terrifying.

He found himself in a graveyard, the trees waved gently in the light breeze, the sun flashing against some of the polished tomb-stones.

He began walking through the place, not quite knowing where he was going, his eyes glancing at the names of men and women long gone, now only dust in the earth.

He slowed as he came upon a simple tombstone, cut from a piece of marble. On the front were a few simple words etched into the surface. **EMILY WATSON, LOVING WIFE AND FRIEND, 1966-2006.**

He knelt down to stare at the marker, not quite understanding how this could be. He hadn't buried her, in fact her corpse was probably still lying on his kitchen floor at his house, perhaps nothing more than a dried up skeleton.

Tears slid down his cheeks and he let out a silent wail; God how he missed her.

He didn't know how long he stood there, but finally, he gathered the strength to stand up, still looking down at the grave of his wife.

He was about to leave when he saw the dirt below his feet begin to shift. Slowly at first, but then gradually it parted faster until a skeletal hand shot out and clasped around his leg. There was a wedding ring on the ring finger of the rotted hand.

Though he was surprised, he did not move, as if some unseen force was keeping him rooted to the spot he was standing on.

Slowly inch by inch the arm slid from the earth, as if the depths of hell were giving birth. Soon a head appeared, skin like dried leather and eyes long rotted away; the lips ruddy and slick with maggots.

But despite the condition of the zombie crawling out of its hole, Henry knew it was his wife. The hair was her color, and even with the caked in dirt he could tell it was her style, the bangs brushed to the side in the way he had always loved.

With both hands on his legs she pulled herself out of the hole until she was kneeling in front of him. He looked down at her, voiceless, too shocked to speak.

She looked up at him with her hollow eye sockets and then smiled, her brown and rotting teeth peeking through her swollen lips.

Henry didn't know what would happen next, but he didn't expect what his dead wife chose to do. She unzipped his pants, quite smoothly for hands of shredded flesh and fingernails that were far too long, as they had continued growing after she had been put to rest.

Henry tried to break free of his stupor, but he was held tight in whatever invisible bonds had hold of him.

Emily leaned forward, taking his soft member in her mouth and Henry pleaded for her to stop. It was then that he let out a blood-curdling scream that snapped him awake.

He lay perfectly still in his room, the dream still hovering, like fog on a rainy day, in his mind. For a moment he thought he might be sick, but regained control of himself.

The room was dark with the exception of a thin line of light coming in from the partially ajar door that led into the hallway.

Two things happened at the same time for Henry. The first was that he realized he wasn't alone in his room, now seeing clearly his door was open to the hallway. The second was that someone was under the covers with him and if he wasn't sure at that precise moment, when he felt a warm feeling over his genitals, he knew for sure.

Throwing the blanket off himself, he looked down and saw Connie Sanders lying naked on the bed. She had her head on his stomach and she was doing her best to give him fellatio. Henry's member was hard as a rock, the unconscious response to the stimuli beyond his control.

She looked up into his face and grinned happily. "Hey there, lover, I was starting to wonder when you'd wake up. Now we can have some real fun," she breathed passionately.

Despite the living breathing woman lying next to him, visions of his dead wife flew into the forefront of his mind.

Jumping out of bed, for the moment ignoring his nudity, he glared at the woman.

"What the fuck do you think you're doing, Connie?" He yelled at the woman.

Connie rolled to her side, coming up into a sitting position. "I just thought I'd consummate our love, Henry. I saw the way you were looking at me tonight and I feel the same way. I want you to stay here and live with me, your friend Jimmy, too. My daughter Missy has already taken a shine to him. All we have to do is get rid of the two women you're with and then everything will be wonderful."

Henry stared at the woman almost too shocked to believe the woman's delusions.

"Look, lady, I don't know what the fuck you've been smokin', but I am not staying here and neither is Jimmy. You're crazy!"

Connie jumped to her feet and was across the room before Henry had even realized it; the woman's speed a shock for her size. Connie slammed him against the wall, placing a large kitchen knife at his throat.

Henry didn't dare move, the razor sharp blade already pinching his throat, a slim ribbon of blood trickling down his chest. He looked up when Connie's daughter walked into the room. She was wearing nothing but a see-thru Teddy, no panties or bra to be seen. In her right hand was a small .22 pistol, the barrel aimed at Henry.

"Do you need any help here, ma?" She asked sweetly.

"No honey, I've got it all under control, what are you doing in here, I thought you were going to take care of the single woman down the hall?

Missy swirled one of her tresses with her finger, around and around. "Thought maybe we could do this one together, you know like before when them other men come to stay with us."

Connie flashed anger at her daughter. "Not this time, Missy, I want this one for myself, you can have the younger fella, he was a little too scrawny for my tastes. Now this one here, he's a real man, just look at those abs, and look at the size of his dick, I'm looking forward to riding that," she said, licking her lips.

"Now look, ladies, I'm flattered, really, but you can't just come in here and claim me, it's not right," Henry said nicely, tried to make friends with the two women; at least until the knife was away from his throat. "Now, if you want to date or something, that could be arranged, let me get to know you a little better." He turned to look at the daughter. "And Jimmy will be sure to like you if you give him a chance to get to know you, Missy," he lied, trying his best to sound cooperative.

Connie seemed to mull over what he said, her forehead crunching up as she thought about it. "Really, you mean it? But what about the two women?"

"They're not a problem, Jimmy doesn't like Cindy that much and I barely know Mary. We'll send them on their way in the morning and then it'll just be me and Jimmy here, you'll see it'll be great."

"I'd like that, Henry, but first I'd like to finish what we started so get on the bed and we'll get it done. Kind of like a handshake, so I know you're not pullin' my leg."

She gently led Henry towards the bed, the knife never leaving his throat. Not moving a muscle she didn't know about, he climbed back onto the bed, his hard on so far gone he wondered if he'd ever have one again.

Connie climbed on top of him, her thighs resting on either side of him.

"Put your hands on my tits, Henry, and rub them," she ordered him. Swallowing hard, he did as he was told, squeezing the massive mounds of flesh, the chore reminding him of kneading dough.

Connie started moving back and forth on top of him, her body slowly bringing him back to an erection, despite his derogatory feelings. He couldn't stop it, his penis having a mind of its own. He hadn't been with another woman for almost four months, and despite being forced into it, the sexual act was still appealing.

Connie started moaning and Henry noticed Missy with her eyes half shut. She had one of her hands between her legs, watching him and her mother having sex. Then the knife fell from Connie's hand to clatter onto the floor as she writhed with passion, close to an orgasm.

The moment the knife left his throat, Henry went into action. As Connie bent over him, wanting to kiss him, Henry slammed his forehead against her nose, the sound of crunching cartilage filling the room. She sucked in a loud breath, like an asthmatic on his last breath and her eyes squeezed shut with pain.

Connie opened her eyes, not aroused anymore and snarled at him, preparing to wrap her hands around his throat. Henry freed his right hand from under her breasts and punched her in the throat, crushing her trachea. Connie gagged for air and Henry bucked his hip, his penis slamming into her one last time and then tossing her off of him, where she fell to the floor in a heap of flab and limbs.

Missy had her eyes open and was staring in shock at her mother now writhing on the floor, struggling to breathe. For a precious second, she forgot about the pistol in her hand. Henry used that second, pulling the pillow from behind his head and throwing the pillow as hard as he could. The soft object hit Missy in the face, distracting her for another instant. When the pillow had been removed from her face, Henry had already crossed the room and was slapping the weapon from her hand. She hissed at him, trying to claw his eyes out and he punched her hard in the face, knocking her to the floor. Her head caught a corner of an end table near the door and she plummeted into unconsciousness.

Breathing heavily, Henry stood over the girl, too pumped up with the fighting spirit to care that she was half his size. She had trained a gun on him and would have used it if given the chance. In Henry's book that put them on equal footing.

Closing the door to the hallway so as not to be discovered, he walked over to Connie on the other side of the bed. Rolling her onto her back he saw her face had turned blue, no oxygen reaching her lungs.

Henry did nothing, just sat on the bed and waited as the woman slowly suffocated in a room full of oxygen. When her flailing limbs finally went still, Henry dragged her over to the bathroom and with a mighty heave that threatened to throw out his back, placed her in the tub. He checked her pulse one final time, grunting when he found none.

Walking back to the girl, he looked down at her prone form. He debated killing her too, Lord knows the little bitch deserved it, but he just couldn't bring himself to kill her in cold blood.

Call it a remnant from the way things used to be.

Instead, he tied her and gagged her mouth, making sure to shove a sock he'd found in one of the bureau drawers into her mouth before securing the gag around her head.

Then he dragged her into the bathroom as well, closing the door and locking it.

Looking around the room, he tried to decide what to do next. Should he wake the others and fill them in? Or wait until morning.

Sitting on the bed, he wrestled with different ideas, finally deciding to wait until morning. After going back into the bathroom, and with a leg on either side of Missy, he washed up, wanting to clean himself up from his scuffle with the large mother. Then he quickly redressed and stretched out on the bed, his weapons next to him.

Closing his eyes, he tried to slow his heart. With the adrenalin slowly leaving his body, he felt himself becoming drowsy again.

He relaxed and let sleep come if it would. Though he didn't actually sleep, he did manage a blissful sort of meditation. This time he had pleasant dreams of his wife, where she was young and healthy and the two of them were happy.

And there was no such thing as the walking dead.

Chapter 8

Mary opened her room door and stepped out into the hallway. The newly risen sun barely penetrated into the hall, but when she turned to look back into her room one last time, bright rays of sunshine flooded through the room's only window, bathing the room in a heavenly glow.

With a sigh, she closed the door. She was going to miss that room with its running water and clean sheets.

But it was time to return to the real world and the dangers it held.

She walked down the hallway, bypassing Henry's room, figuring she'd grab Jimmy and Cindy and then the three could collect Henry, the group then going downstairs for breakfast.

Mary's stomach growled as the smells from the kitchen swam up the stairs, suffusing the inn with fragrances of baking bread and bacon.

Two knocks on Jimmy's door and Cindy appeared, still tucking in her shirt as she smiled a greeting to Mary.

"Hey, Mar', good timing, Jimmy should be out of the bathroom in a minute and I'm all set to go."

"Good, because I'm starving. I haven't seen Henry yet, figured we'd all go see him together and then go downstairs as a group."

Cindy nodded as she reached over the bed to pick up her rifle. She had secured it from one of the security men when they had been at the shopping mall and had taken a liking to the weapon. While only a .22 caliber, Cindy was an excellent shot, the weapon more than deadly in her hands.

The toilet flushed and Jimmy opened the bathroom door, his hair still wet from his earlier shower.

"Man, I'm going to miss this," he muttered as he retrieved his .38 and shotgun. He pumped it once, sending a round into the chamber, and then let the weapon hang from its strap over his shoulder. "The next time I have to take a dump in a strand of trees I'm going to think back to this place and how civilized people live."

"Yeah, but at least when you pee out in the woods you don't miss the toilet or have to put the seat down," Cindy jibed him, sliding her feet into her hiking boots. Before the companions had left the shopping mall they had made sure to stop by one of the numerous camping stores. All were wearing hardy footwear, as well as hiking vests with pockets full of miscellaneous items they would need on their journey.

"I told you, I was still sleeping when I got up last night, it was an accident," he said, hands out apologetically at his sides.

Mary's eyebrows went up curiously and Cindy turned to her and grinned. "My darling boyfriend took a pee last night and left the seat up, so when I went in there myself I fell into the toilet. Nothing wakes you up better than a wet butt, I have to say."

Mary chuckled, trying to hold back the full blown laughter, the look on Jimmy's embarrassed face hilarious. "I've been there," was all she said, supporting Cindy.

"Look, are we going or what? Or are we just going to stand here and keep busting my balls for the rest of the day," Jimmy snapped with more bark than bite.

Cindy rubbed her chin as if she was pondering the subject, then she moved to the door. "No baby, we can go. Besides, I have the rest of the day and many more to come to bust your balls."

Mary chuckled at her statement and then stepped back out into the hall, Cindy right behind her. "It's nice to know there's someone else around to give him shit, you know it was a full time job for me before I met you," Mary added.

"Happy to help, it's a labor of love," Cindy said happily, winking at Jimmy.

Jimmy frowned at her statement, sometimes wondering if women were really worth all the trouble, but as he watched Cindy's shapely form sashay out the door and remembered the previous night's bout of lovemaking, he decided, yeah, it was worth every second of it, and then some.

Seconds later the three friends were standing outside Henry's door. Mary was first and her guard went up when she noticed the door was ajar. Pulling her .38, she slowly eased the door open, both Jimmy and Cindy alert, as well. They had traveled too long together not to give each other the benefit of the doubt when one didn't feel comfortable about a particular situation.

Mary stepped into the room, finger on the trigger of her weapon and let out a sigh, when she saw Henry spread out on the bed, his Glock in his right hand, but otherwise calm.

"Hey, Mary, what's up, you look tense," he said, staring down the barrel of her gun.

Mary quickly slid the weapon back into its holster and then opened the door for Cindy and Jimmy. In less than ten seconds the three companions were in the room, Henry now sitting up.

"I'm glad you guys are here, I've got something to share with you, something you might not be too happy about," he said.

"Let me guess, you found out the price of gas is going up," Jimmy joked. "Come on, old man; spill it, what's up? We're all starving and want to go downstairs and eat."

Henry made a mournful face and stood up from the bed, walking over to the bathroom door. "Yeah, that's kind of what I need to talk to you about, but it'll be easier if I just show you."

He opened the door, the opening exposing the two bodies within. Mary gasped and Cindy put her hand to her mouth, surprised to see two bodies in Henry's bathroom.

"What happened here, how did they get in here?" Mary asked moving closer. "Are they both dead?"

"No, the girls just unconscious, I didn't have the heart to kill her, despite the fact she deserved it, figured I'd wait for the rest of you and we could decide together."

Jimmy moved into the opening, crouching down over the daughter. "I don't know how to tell you this, Henry, but the girl's dead too, looks like she choked on her own throw-up."

"What? Shit, you've got to be kidding me," he said with anger in his voice as he moved into the bathroom to check on the girl. Sure enough she was dead. Her eyes were wide open, bulging, and a small amount of bile had seeped out of the side of her gag.

Henry stood back up and punched the door. "Dammit, it wasn't supposed to go down like this. We finally find a nice town where we're welcomed and these two bitches have to go and try and pull something!" He spit, almost wanting to kick the dead girl in his rage.

"What actually happened here, Henry, what did they try to do?" Cindy asked, after she had closed the door to the room. It wouldn't be very good to be discovered by the help with the mother and daughter of the inn lying dead in the bathroom.

Henry sighed and went back to the bed, sitting down on the edge. He quickly filled the others in on what had happened and why the two women had been in his bedroom, though he left out the part about the attempted rape, some things he felt could stay between himself.

"And then they said they wanted to kill both you girls and keep me and Jimmy here forever as their mates."

Cindy and Mary shared a look and then both turned to Henry. "Jesus, Henry, I don't know what to say, what do we do now?" Mary asked, glancing back into the bathroom at the two corpses.

"Well, I've had all night to think about that and I think I know what we should do. We need to act natural, just go down and eat breakfast and then pay our tab to one of the helpers that work in the kitchen and then slip out of here before anyone's the wiser. I'll wedge the bathroom door shut and with luck we'll be long gone before anyone finds out they're dead."

Jimmy nodded, agreeing. "Sounds good. I wouldn't want to have to try and explain this shit to the town. They'd probably kill us all without a trial." He chuckled at his statement. "Shit, do people even have trials anymore?"

Henry jumped up from the bed and grabbed his shotgun, making sure he had everything with him. "All right then, if you guys have everything then I say we go downstairs and do exactly what I said. With luck we'll be out of here and on the road in one hour or less."

Everyone gathered their supplies, Mary and Cindy already having everything with them when they left their rooms. Henry hung the *do not disturb* sign on the outside of the door, hoping it would deter anyone for a little while longer.

The group of four walked down the stairs and upon stepping into the dining room walked into one of the helpers Connie had on staff. The girl who looked at the four companions was no more than sixteen with brown hair tied into ponytails and faded jeans.

She smiled at the entrance of the four guests and quickly picked up a pot of coffee sitting near the end of the table.

"Morning, folks, hope you slept well. Breakfast is ready, if something's not right, I'll have to say sorry now. Mrs. Sanders and her daughter didn't show up this morning to fix breakfast and their rooms are empty, so I had to fix breakfast myself."

"Oh, really? Does this happen often?" Mary asked, sitting down at the table and reaching for a piece of toast from a silver tray.

The girl nodded. "Actually it does. Mrs. Sanders likes her men and so does Missy. There's times when the two of them go off and spend the night with one of the men in town. They both share him, taking turns, kind of gross if you ask me," she said and then her eyes went wide with fear. "Oh, I shouldn't have said that, don't say anything to the Missus, please?"

"Don't worry, hun, we won't say a word. In fact, after breakfast we'll be moving on. If it's all right we'll just pay our bill to you," Henry said, munching on a pastry, and washing it down with a cup of coffee. He was in heaven. Connie might have been a sadistic bitch, but she knew how to feed her guests. He would miss the inn, despite the previous uncomfortable night he'd spent there.

"Oh, okay I guess that should be fine. While you folks eat, I'll go get your bill. I know Mrs. Sanders had it on her desk." The girl disappeared into the kitchen and the four companions ate quickly, each of them stuffing themselves to the brim. When food was in front of you, you always ate heartily because the next meal could be a long way off. Jimmy made sure to sneak a few rolls into his backpack for later, when they were out on the road once again.

Cindy saw him and he flashed her a mischievous grin.

"What? They're dead, it's not like they can complain," he said.

Ten minutes later the meal was just about complete and the girl came into the room with a piece of paper in her hand. Handing it to Henry, she frowned.

"I hope it's okay, if it's not you'll just have to wait for Mrs. Sanders to come back. You can discuss it with her."

Henry took the bill and glanced over it. It really didn't matter how much the woman had charged him, he would pay it without question and then all of them would get the hell out of Dodge. Luckily the woman hadn't tried to gouge them and Henry reached into his pocket and pulled out the right amount of rounds; the bullets spreading out on the table.

The girl counted them and when finished, swept them into her apron. Smiling, she backed into the kitchen.

Henry looked at the others. "Well, if we're all done, let's get going and hope our luck holds out."

Everyone gathered their backpacks and weapons and then left the inn, each with a small longing in their eyes. The inn had been the most lavish place they'd spent a night in a very long time and none of them was looking forward to the cold ground come nightfall at the end of the day.

Walking through the edge of town and back to the opening in the barricade, they were able to get a better idea of the town now that it was daylight. The streets were clean and those that they passed were friendly.

"It's a goddamn shame, I tell you. We could have stayed here for a while, maybe even for good," Henry said as he watched a few children playing kickball in the street; the picture a paradigm of domestic bliss.

Mary patted his arm. "It just wasn't meant to be. Besides, if it wasn't us, it would have been some other travelers. You probably saved someone else's life by killing that bitch."

"Oh, I don't know, that Missy was kind of cute, I reckon I could have survived having to be with her night after night, despite her age," Jimmy said, strolling along the street.

Cindy flashed him a stare that would have melted ice in the middle of winter. "You would, you pig. I swear, sometimes I don't know why I put up with you," she snarled and started walking faster, leaving Jimmy and the others behind.

Henry chuckled as Cindy walked by, seeing the fire in her eyes. "You better go after her, old buddy, I think you put your foot in your mouth that time,"

Jimmy shrugged. "Wouldn't be the first time," he said, but picked up his pace to catch up with Cindy.

"And it definitely won't be the last," Mary added when Jimmy walked by her.

Henry and Mary walked together, while the two lovebirds hashed out their differences.

"So she really wanted to kill me and Cindy and keep you and Jimmy here as her studs?" Mary asked, askance of Henry.

"Yup, said she couldn't live without me and that I was the man of her dreams," Henry said with an air of truth.

Mary frowned and stared at Henry as they walked. After almost a minute, Henry's face cracked into a smile; not able to hold back under her withering gaze.

"I knew it," she said pointing her finger at him. 'You are so full of shit. She probably just wanted you because you were the first through the door."

Henry pretended he was hurt by her remark and he made a face. She saw it and grinned. "Oh stop, don't give me that look, you're a hound dog just like the rest of the men in the world."

"Well, I'd like to think I'm a little better than the rest."

"Perhaps, but only a little," Mary said, holding her hand up and placing her thumb and finger only an inch apart.

"I'll take it," he said. "Look, it seems Jimmy has worked his magic once more and calmed her down."

Mary watched Cindy and Jimmy and smiled as Jimmy took her hand in his, the two of them walking together side by side. "He sure is a smooth one, I'll give him that."

Henry nodded. "That he is."

Fifteen minutes later they had reached the barricade.

One of the guards looked down on the companions, but didn't seem that interested.

Henry was the first to speak. "Hey, there, we stayed for the night and are ready to move on," he glanced over to where the motorcycle had been, but didn't see it. "We had a motorcycle with us last night, it was parked over there. Did you see it?"

The guard nodded. "Yeah, afraid I did. Some of the town's kids got to it last night and stripped it. There's nothing left but the frame and the handlebars and if they'd had more time, they probably would've taken those, too. It's over there behind that dumpster if you don't believe me." He said, pointing to a beat up green dumpster that was part of the barricade.

"Jimmy, go check, will you?" Henry told him, not really caring if the bike was there or not. Truth was, they needed to leave before the bodies were found back in his room at the inn and anything that slowed their egress could spell their doom.

"It's here, all right, Henry, though there's nothing left," Jimmy said, jogging back to the others.

"Sorry about that, mister, we never even saw them. Our eyes are always focused outward, not inward," the guard said apologetically.

"That's okay; it was just about out of gas anyway. Besides, one bike and four people really didn't work to well. So can we get going, we need to be somewhere before the sun's too high overhead," Henry said politely.

The guard gestured to one of the men to open the gate. While they waited, the guard tried to keep the conversation going. "So where do you have to be in a few hours? I know everything around this town worth going to, I might know where you're going, maybe can give you a better route."

"No that's okay, we're fine, we know where we're going," Jimmy said nicely, trying to stop the guard's questions.

"No, really, tell me; I'm sure I can help," the guard said not letting up. By now the gate was open for the companions and Henry started forward, the others close behind.

Henry's face grew hard. "I reckon that's my business and no one else's, friend, so we'll be going now. Thanks for your help," he said with a wave.

The guard looked hurt, but Henry ignored him. The man was just trying to be friendly, but at the moment all Henry wanted to do was get out of town.

Just as Jimmy--the last in line--moved through the gate, a yell went up from behind them. All four friends turned as one to see a man running hard across the street directly toward the gate. In his hand was a long barreled rifle, what kind was unknown from the distance, but the man was moving fast and would be at the gate in only a few minutes.

"Come on, people, let's get moving, our business here is over," Henry said picking up his pace as they left the barricade behind.

"Should we run? Get as much distance from here as possible?" Jimmy asked, while looking over his shoulder.

Henry kept walking, his pace as fast as one of those speed walkers of old. "No just keep moving, but nothing that would draw the guard's attention. Up on that palisade they have an advantage over us, don't attract attention."

Three minutes past and the barricade receded behind them, though not fast enough for Henry's taste. Then what he knew would happen, did, though he'd hoped to be wrong. A shot rang out, ricocheting off the asphalt only a few feet from him.

"Shit, our luck's up, they must have found the bodies, come on, let's get the hell out of here!" He yelled, pushing the rest of them to the side of the road where trees and grass would make them a more difficult target.

More shots buzzed around them and Jimmy turned around, .38 in hand, prepared to answer back with a few rounds of his own. Henry placed his hand on his arm, stopping him.

"No, Jimmy, let's just go, the sooner we're gone the better. Those men didn't do anything to us and they don't know the whole story, so just go!" Henry said, pulling on Jimmy to get moving.

With a glance over his shoulder, Jimmy gave in, though it went against his grain to run when someone was shooting at him.

The four of them ran into the brush, a few more rounds following them, but soon they were out of range. Henry didn't slow, but kept up their pace. He had no way of knowing if the town would send out a posse after them. He hoped not, but the possibility was there. Running down the shoulder, he spotted an old farmhouse about a half mile away.

Pointing to it, he started moving towards it, the others behind.

"Let's hold up there for a while and make sure no one from the town's following us and looking for blood. Besides, on foot we're sitting ducks," Henry said, jogging through the waist high grass.

The sound of an engine came to his ears and he turned just as an old truck appeared on the highway from the direction of the town and closing fast.

"Down, into the grass!" Henry ordered the others, all of them falling to their bellies to wait to see if they had been spotted.

The truck slowed when it was only a few hundred yards from them. With his head low in the grass, he couldn't see the truck and didn't want to raise his head and give away their location.

Holding his breath, he counted to twenty and then with a sideways glance at Jimmy, poked his head up. The truck was still there, but was just pulling away, moving further down the highway. If the posse had spotted them, they sure as hell wouldn't be driving off.

They had made it.

Tapping each one of the others on the shoulder, Henry turned and started crawling through the grass. The possibility of the truck returning was always there and he didn't want to risk being seen when they were so close to escaping.

With the dry grass irritating their faces and infiltrating their clothes, the four companions continued crawling to the abandoned farmhouse.

Chapter 9

Within fifteen feet of a dilapidated fence, Henry slowed, straining his ears to hear anything out of the ordinary.

All he could hear was the wind blowing the entangled tree branches and the sound of a screen door that had somehow become unlatched.

"So what do you think, should we go for it?" Jimmy asked by his side. His hair was covered with bits of grass and he resembled a boy half his age as he lay there on the ground.

"Looks okay, but let's not take any chances. I want everyone triple sharp. Be prepared for anything," he ordered the others.

An engine sounded from across the field and Henry poked his head up enough to see the truck returning down the highway. The truck slowed as the men in the bed surveyed the field and surrounding landscape. Evidently someone in the posse was bright enough to know there was no way Henry and the others could have gotten away so quick and had figured out they had gone to ground somewhere along the highway.

After slowing for a few minutes, the truck rolled away. The companions moved forward until they were under the broken gate, but stopped when the truck's engines could be heard again.

Henry chanced a look, and sure enough, the truck was there again. One of the men hopped off the back of the truck and walked to the shoulder of the road, looking out across the field at the old house and barn. But the man didn't move, just stood there, staring; perhaps waiting in hopes of spotting movement. Then the man went back to the truck and it rumbled away again, disappearing after a few seconds.

Dropping back to the ground, Henry cursed under his breath. "There still out there. Either they know we're here or they think we're somewhere in the area. Either way, we're trapped, unless we want to fight our way out."

"That should be our last option. That truck has at least eight people in it. Two to one odds aren't my favorite," Jimmy said, after sneaking a peek himself. When the truck had driven away again, leaving the highway quiet, Henry took the opportunity to rally his people and get them through the fence and to the other side of the barn.

Pointing to Mary, he gestured to the other side of the barn.

"Mary, go see what's over there. Maybe we can circle around and just head west away from the highway. For some reason our pursuers don't want to check this place out and that makes me nervous."

"Okay, I'll be right back," Mary said, jogging away with her .38 in hand.

"Cindy, go check around the back of the house, see what's there. Hell, maybe there's even an old truck or something we can use, but the chances of that is too damn slim to hope for," Henry told her.

She nodded and with rifle ready, her finger over the trigger, she headed off on her errand, winking at Jimmy as she passed by him.

"What about me, what are we going to do?" Jimmy asked, looking over his shoulder. So far the farm was quiet, only a few horse skeletons lying in a corral near the end of the barn to prove there had ever been life present.

"We, my boy, are going to recce the house. Maybe there's something we can use inside. When we're done with the house, we'll all get together and recce the barn."

"Okay, let's do it," Jimmy said, turning to move across the yard, until they both stopped at the screen door that led into the house. Henry placed a hand on the door, which was still flapping in the wind. Without the constant slapping of the metal door, the areas around the farm seemed almost eerily silent.

There was a piece of rope hanging from the handle and Henry used it to tie the door open, assuming the rope was there for this purpose.

Jimmy nodded and reached out to open the wooden door with four sets of small panes of glass above waist height. Though he tried to see inside the house, a curtain across the door prevented it and he had no choice but to go in blind.

Turning the handle, he was surprised when the door opened with a creaking of old hinges, evidently unlocked. Jimmy flashed Henry a smile, proud of himself.

"Well, at least something's going our way today," Jimmy said, using his foot to open the door the rest of the way.

Henry only grunted, his shotgun in his hand, ready to blow anything to hell stupid enough to get in his way.

They stood in the doorframe, their eyes trying to adjust to the gloom of the kitchen, the rays of sunlight cascading into the small room between the bodies of the two men. All the windows were filthy, only the smallest amount of light penetrating the opaque glass panels.

"Well, go ahead tough guy, you first, but I got your back," Henry said, nudging his friend.

Jimmy frowned. "Thanks a lot, I feel so much better now," he said, but he stepped into the kitchen, expecting something to jump out at him, fangs trying to tear open his throat.

But the kitchen was empty and in another moment both men were standing inside the quant old room. An old Formica table and two chairs sat in the corner and the refrigerator looked to be about a hundred years old. Jimmy was about to open it when Henry stopped him.

"Ah, I wouldn't do that if I were you," he said. "There's been no power in here for quite a while. Whatever was in there probably looks like the science experiment from Hell."

Jimmy stepped back from the fridge, as if the appliance might try and swallow him whole. "That's a good point, I'll take that advice."

The sounds of squealing brakes floated into the kitchen and Henry ran to the closest window facing the highway. The posse was back, but still made no move toward the house. Two men walked along the shoulder and then climbed into the bed once again and the truck drove away, backfiring as it went.

"They're gone," was all he said, turning back to inspect the kitchen. Jimmy had one of the cupboards open and was rewarded by more than two dozen spiders. The arachnids poured onto the cabinet and then scurried up to the ceiling, dispersing and disappearing under the molding that lined the walls with the ceiling. Jimmy shook his hands and stepped away. "Oh shit, I hate spiders. Man, they creep me the fuck out!" He shouted, moving to the opposite end of the room.

Henry chuckled at him, and took his place. "Let me get this straight. You fight the animated dead everyday of your life now and its spiders that give you the creeps?" He laughed, while wiping a few stray spider webs away with his hand and reaching inside the cupboard. A few boxes of cereal and crackers were destroyed, the insects having a mighty feast, but a few canned goods were tucked in the back and after a search of the other cabinets more canned goods were found. Henry grinned as he placed them on the table, taking off his backpack to start loading them up.

"Come on, ya big baby, give me a hand. Put some of this in your bag. We'll divide them up with the girls later," he told him.

Jimmy did as asked, slipping out of his pack, his eyes constantly looking up to the ceiling for more spiders.

Henry couldn't resist teasing the man and as Jimmy was shoving cans into his pack, Henry pointed at his shoulder, his eyes going wide.

"Oh my God, Jimmy, there's a big spider on your shoulder!"

Jimmy dropped the can of peas he'd been holding and spun in a circle, arms slapping his shoulders frantically. "What, oh shit, get it off of me; help me Henry, for Christ sake!" He screamed fumbling to get his vest off, shaking it against a wooden chair around the table.

Jimmy kept this up until he saw Henry with a big smile on his face watching him. Jimmy slowed his movements and slowly realized he was being fooled.

Shrugging back into his vest, he pointed a finger at Henry. "You really are an asshole, you know that. Taking advantage of a man's fears, you should be ashamed of yourself," he said, trying to regain some of his lost dignity as he shoved can after can into his backpack.

Henry stood there laughing, his shoulder heaving. "I'm so sorry, Jimmy, I couldn't resist, but you should have seen your face," he said, chuckling some more.

Jimmy held up his right hand to Henry, the middle finger exposed prominently. "Screw you, old man, I'll get you back, you just wait. Payback's a bitch, now what's next; are we checking the rest of this house out or what?"

Henry slowed his laughter, actually having to wipe a few tears from his eyes. Oh how he had needed that. Sometimes a good laugh made all your troubles go away.

"No, Jimmy, we're done. Whatever's in the house can keep. We need to be out of here before that posse decides to check this place out. I still don't get why they haven't come over here yet."

"Fine, then I'll meet you outside," he said, brushing past Henry and stepping back out into the denuded yard.

Henry picked up his backpack, a few more chuckles escaping his lips, then he followed Jimmy back out into the small yard, leaving the kitchen alone with the shadows of the past once more.

By the time Henry and Jimmy had reached the barn the two women had returned. Neither looked happy.

"So what's the verdict?" Henry asked Mary first.

She shook her head, her brown hair shifting over her shoulders. "We're not going that way anytime soon. There's a deep ravine that looks like it became deeper after the winter; maybe some flooding. We'd need climbing gear to get down it. Without the gear, we'd be risking our lives easily.

Henry scowled at the information, but then glanced to Cindy. "Tell me you've got better news," he asked her hopefully.

"I'm afraid not. Nothing in the back yard but a bunch of old lawnmowers and tractor parts."

"The only other option is to try and circle around the posse and head east, but that's going in the wrong way, huh?" Jimmy asked, sucking his lip.

"Yeah, it is. I don't know about you three, but I've had my fill of New England. I wanted to keep us moving south, maybe see what's happening in Florida. I mean, all that sun and humidity can't be good for all the deaders walking around out there. Shit, they should be falling apart even as we speak."

"Well, we're not there yet, so what's our next move?" Mary asked, leaning against the side of the barn. Her shoulder was already covered in paint chips, but she didn't seem to care.

Henry nodded toward the barn's front entrance. "Let's see if there's anything useful inside there and then we'll decided what to do next."

"Hey, maybe there's rope and junk we can use to get down the ravine," Jimmy added, moving alongside Henry.

"Exactly. Until we know what we do and don't have, talking is just blowing wind, so come on," he said.

Pushing away from the barn, Mary brushed her shoulder clean of paint chips, repositioned her .38 and followed the two men, Cindy next to her.

"You know, if things keep going like they are, we might just have to fight our way past that posse," Cindy said thoughtfully.

Mary slowed and looked at her. "Perhaps, but that'll be a risky venture and Henry wouldn't condone it unless there's absolutely no other choice. Besides, there's always a way out, haven't you spent enough time with us to know that yet?" She joked, as much for herself as Cindy.

Cindy smiled back. "I sure hope you're right, because shooting against live people is a hell of a lot different than facing dead ones."

"Amen, sister, amen," Mary answered.

"Are you two hens done jabbering or what?" Jimmy asked from the front of the barn, only his head visible. "Henry wants all of us to stay together in case there's trouble."

"We're coming, Jimmy, keep your panties on," Cindy said, jokingly.

Jimmy made a face, not happy with the comment and then pulled his head back, mumbling something about '*women*'.

The two women shared a glance, unspoken words of friendship easily read in their faces and then picked up their pace to catch up to the others.

Henry already had his hand on the barn door when Mary and Cindy reached him.

"About time you two showed up. We're going in; maybe if we're lucky there'll be a car or something to get us out of here."

"Don't wait on us, Henry, go if you're going," Mary said gesturing to the door.

Henry nodded while swinging the door wide, the rusted hinges creaking in protest.

All four of them tried to peer inside the dank, dark barn, but the shutters were closed, and only a few thin slices of sunshine pierced the gloom. The edges of the barn were wreathed in shadows, seeming to have a darkness so deep one could fall into them forever.

Henry took the first few steps inside and immediately stopped. His nose was overpowered by the smell of death, though whether it was fresh or old was still a mystery.

Jimmy hawked a wad of phlegm and spit it to his side, gagging from the stench.

"I don't think there's anything we need in here, Henry," Cindy said, askance of him, her rifle held at an odd angle as she tried to cover her nose with her arm to keep the smell from overwhelming her.

Henry nodded, breathing through his mouth. "I think we should all turn around and leave here, right now," Henry said, turning to leave, but he stopped in his tracks to see the exit was blocked.

More than twenty animated corpses were in the doorway and to the sides, more coming out of the dark corners with each passing second.

"Shit, it's a goddamn trap!" He snarled, looking every which way at the same time, the others next to him.

From the highway came the sound of an idling engine and a car door being opened and then closed. That told Henry the posse was back. Either the men trailing them knew they were at the farm or were just guessing, but it told Henry that all it would take is one gunshot blast to signal to the posse exactly where they were.

Throwing the shotgun over his shoulder by the strap, he reached down and pulled his panga, the blade reflecting the dim light inside the barn.

"Blades only, people, one gunshot blast and the men out on the road will know we're here. We need to do this quick and quiet."

Mary nodded, bending over and picking up a stray pitchfork lying in a small pile of hay. Cindy did the same, reaching out and grabbing an old, rusted shovel from off a hook on one of the wooden pylons supporting the barn's roof. Jimmy pulled his hunting knife, the blade more than sufficient for close infighting like what was called for at the moment.

From the time Henry had pulled his panga and the others had holstered their own weapons and pulled knives or shovels, only a few seconds had passed.

The ghouls had seemed to hover for a moment, themselves, as if they were surprised to see prey simply walk into their hiding place. But then the first one, a middle aged man in dirty, blue overalls and only half a face, lunged at the group, mouth open, hands outstretched to grasp whatever came within reach.

The four companions moved back to back, forming a square so every corner was covered as the creatures surrounded them. As the overall ghoul jumped at them, Henry was closest and he swung the panga in an overhand chopping motion that severed the corpse's head from its neck, the decapitated head rolling across the floor to stare up at the roof, eyes still moving.

"Watch out, Jimmy, you got one on your left!" Henry yelled, seeing a small ghoul, once a child of seven or eight, trying to take a bite out of Jimmy's calf.

Jimmy saw her and swung his knife downward and then left, the blade sliding into her ear canal. The tip of the blade pierced the dried brain and the small body slumped to the hay-covered floor.

Jimmy pulled his blade free, already looking for the next one. There would have been a time when taking down a child, even if it was a zombie, would have been difficult for him, but now the man was a killing machine, willing to do what it took to stay alive and keep the lives of his friends safe.

"Mary, deader on your right!" Jimmy spat, before he became occupied once again.

Mary saw the one he meant, an old woman with a once white dress with an apron covering the lower half of her body. The woman's mouth was devoid of teeth, her dentures lost somewhere on her travels as one of the undead. Still, her nails were sharp and even a small cut would spell doom for her or the other companions.

Swinging the pitchfork hard as she could, the points caught the woman in the cheek, slicing her face to ribbons. Mary pulled back and then with the garden tool never slowing, rammed the pointed blades into the woman's stomach, only a small trickle of black ichor dripping from her wounds, staining her already filthy dress.

Mary pulled the pitchfork to her, the ghoul following and Mary used her leg to kick the woman off, sending her sprawling into a dozen more, like a bowling ball to pins.

Cindy was doing her best to pull her weight, swinging the shovel hard to impact on a rotting ghoul that had tried to come at her. The sound of metal on bone sent a dull clang reverberating in the barn, Cindy feeling the impact as the vibration traveled up the wooden shaft to her shoulders. But the shovel had done its work, caving in the creature's skull, the corpse crumpling to the dirt floor like a sack of flour.

Henry swung his panga, severing digits from a dried hand that got too close.

"We need to get out of here, there's too many of them!' He yelled swiping at two more that tried to get past his guard. "Start moving back to the opening, and clear a path, hopefully we can get out of here!"

Jimmy started doing what he said, sliding his feet across the blood-red mud that was once the floor of the barn. His knife never slowed, his blade slicing throats and severing spines, jabbing into eye sockets to pierce the brain's within.

Time seemed to stand still, the four people slowly trying to cross the six feet that separated them from freedom. Henry swiped at another zombie; this one looked to be almost brand new, the skin still soft on the body. As Henry's panga slashed across the deader's throat, a spray of blood shot out and Henry had to do some dancing to keep out of the deadly spray. True, none of them knew if simple contact from a ghoul's blood would cause infection, but neither he nor his friends were ready to try that assumption out just yet.

The spray shot by him, striking another corpse in the face. The man seemed to sputter, similar to when a clown shoots a man with seltzer. Clearing its eyes of the viscous fluid, it was greeted by the sight of an approaching shovel, the blade striking it in the fore-head, crushing its head like a melon.

Grey matter and bits of skull splattered to the ground, causing the footing to become treacherous.

Henry continued swinging thc panga, feeling like an explorer working his way through the thick jungle foliage.

Finally, the four were on the verge of crossing the threshold of the barn, Mary and Cindy now facing the brunt of the onslaught. The two women weaved their garden tools like gladiators, striking one zombie after another down in pieces or with new holes in their desiccated bodies.

Henry spotted a heavy rope tied to a pole only a foot inside the barn door. His eyes followed the rope, seeing it end over some kind of lift system. His eyes took it all in, less than half a second pass-ing. This was the pulley system that allowed the owners of the farm to get the bales of hay up to the lofts of the barn. Even now, a wide pallet swung slightly over their heads, waiting forever to be placed with the other bales of hay.

Henry flashed a smile and after kicking two zombies away from him, yelled to the others. "Heads up, I've got an idea!"

The others glanced at him when possible, not able to ask him what he meant, when Henry punched the two closest zombies and swung the panga across the rope, severing it, his blade sticking into the wooden pylon until he was able to yank it free.

The rope hummed as it slid through the elaborate pulley sys-tem, the rope like a living thing. Up near the roof, the pallet full to overflowing with bales of hay, dropped to the ground, gravity claiming dominion now that the rope was no longer supporting it.

With a crash and a thump, the pallet crushed almost all the walking dead, a soft mushy, meaty sound overriding all sound in the barn.

The companions turned their faces away, not wanting to get any blood or spray in their mouths or on their skin.

Blood spattered like rain as the four friends dove through the opening, Henry rolling onto his feet and slamming the doors closed, the sound of blood striking the inside of the door resembling rain.

Sliding the wooden bar across the door, Henry slid to the ground, turning as his butt hit the dirt. The others were all lying in one position or another, breathing hard and checking and rechecking to make sure no contaminants were on their skin.

Cindy could barely move her arms, swinging the shovel over and over feeling like she had been lifting weights. Mary had faired better, the pitchfork a little lighter, but she could still feel a pain in her shoulder from the odd exertions of swinging and lunging over and over until she had lost count.

Jimmy sat up, dropping his bloody knife to the dirt. "Jesus, that was close, nice one with the pallet, Henry, it probably saved our asses."

Henry only nodded, breathing in air, lungful after lungful. "Glad to oblige you," he whispered. Inside his mind he was repeating the same mantra over and over. "I'm too old for this shit. I'm too old for this shit."

The barn door rattled as the seven or so remaining undead that had survived being flattened now tried to escape, wanting the companions badly. It had been quite a while since a live body had wandered into their domain and they were not about to waste the opportunity to feed and add more to their ranks.

Henry rolled away from the door when it shook on its hinges, swinging his panga in front of him. Bloody red drops splattered the barn door and Henry made sure to keep his knife far from his body, at least until he could clean it.

"I think it's time to go," he said, watching the barn door shaking, as if he expected it to explode outward, disgorging the undead inside.

"I agree, wholeheartedly, let's move from here. I've had enough excitement for one day," Mary added, moving away from the door

Jimmy was looking at something on the side of the barn and he stood up and jogged away, the others still wondering where he was going. Less than a half minute had passed when he came back into view, carrying a coil of rope over his shoulder.

"Hey, look what I found. It was hanging on the fence over there. Would this get us down that ravine?"

Cindy nodded. "Hell, yeah, it's long enough and then some. There's lots of trees we could tie the end to, as well, and then climb down."

Backing away from the barn door and picking up his backpack, which he had left lying in the dirt outside the barn, he shrugged into the straps, Jimmy doing the same with the only other one the four of them had left.

"Well then, if it's all the same to you guys, I'd just assume we get going and once we're down the ravine we'll find someplace to hold up and recuperate for a while."

Mary nodded, tossing the pitchfork to the ground and moving next to Henry. "Sounds good, the sooner we're away from here the better."

"All right then, lets go, I can't wait to stretch out and take a nap," Jimmy said, with the rope hanging from his left hand, his right still holding his bloody knife. He'd tried cleaning it in the dirt, but it didn't help much. He'd need at least a few minutes to get the job done right. Henry was doing the same, not wanting to sheath the panga until it was properly cleaned.

With Henry in the lead, the four companions started walking round the barn, Mary taking one quick glance over her shoulder toward the highway.

The truck was still there, the posse just standing around the vehicle, still not moving towards the farm. Mary thought about that. Is it possible the townspeople knew about the barn full of zombies and was that the reason they refused to venture too close?

If it was true then going to the farm had save her and her friends from a firefight with really bad odds on their side. Luckily, Henry had pulled a miracle, saving them again.

If God wasn't looking out for them than it had to be the Devil. Either way, she was glad someone, somewhere, seemed to be watching their backs.

With one last look at the posse, she moved behind the barn, the others only a few feet in front of her.

The ravine was only a few dozen yards away and with luck they would be down it and away from the tainted farm in an hour or so.

She chuckled at that. Luck, she thought. Before the fall of things, she hadn't given much credence to luck. Now it was a part of her everyday life.

That and the will and the skill to survive.

With a smile on her face, she looked up at the sun, glad to still be alive to enjoy it. Then she picked up her pace to catch up with the others.

She wasn't looking forward to the pain of climbing down the ravine, but then again, she was lucky to still feel pain.

If you felt pain, that meant you were still alive.

Chapter 10

Captain Snyder walked back down the dock and boarded his fast-attack submarine, saluting the two sailors on watch just before the boarding ramp. His eyes washed across the deck, admiring the sleek lines of his command.

The vessel was almost at its twenty year mark and would have probably been decommissioned in a few more years, but a lot had changed in the past year. Now he would keep the boat running for as long as he could find the parts to do so, his engineers all capable men.

Climbing down the ladder into the vessel, he walked down a small hallway, no wider then the width of an average man. In fact if two men wanted to pass at the same time, both would have to put their backs to the opposite walls and slide past each other, usually with chests brushing.

Stepping into the Con, he glanced over at the Executive Officer or *XO*, for short.

The man looked up, his glasses pulled down low over his nose. The man only needed them when reading; otherwise they hung from a thin chain over his chest.

"Hey Dan, how'd it go?" Lieutenant Lewis Marshall asked, looking up from the map at the quartermaster's desk.

Snyder tossed his baseball cap with the gold wings on a nearby chair and slumped into the helmsman's chair. With the boat in dock there was no need for the station to be manned.

"About as well as you'd expect with an asshole like Raddack," Snyder said with the distaste for the leader of the base apparent in his voice.

"But you made the deal, right?" Marshall asked, moving closer to his commander and friend.

Snyder sighed. "Yeah, I made the deal, what else could I do? We're dangerously low on food and fresh water, not to mention our supply of oxygen candles are almost depleted, of course I made the deal, I just don't like it, is all."

Marshall leaned against the nearest bulkhead, looking down at Snyder. "Why? It's not like we can use the stuff, and if Raddack wants it, I say give it to him. With the supplies we get from him we can head to the Mediterranean. I hear Italy's nice this time of year and they didn't get hit as bad as the states did."

"True, but do you really think they'll let us near their borders? Last we heard, they'd set up a blockade about one mile from their shores, how do we deal with that?"

Marshall chuckled. "Hello, Captain, we're in a goddamn submarine. We'll just stay submerged longer and only surface when we're inside their blockade, piece of cake."

Snyder looked at his friend and frowned. "Piece of cake? I doubt it, not with their advanced sonar, but I tell you what, I'll think about it. Maybe we could head for the Archipelago of La Maddelina, last I heard our base is still up and running. If we reached there, then we'd be safe, at least until our supplies went dry again." He sighed, looking at the dials and gauges on the wall in front of him, most of them useless with the submarine on the surface of the water. "I just hate taking it one day at a time, is all. Up till now we've done an excellent job of planning what we would do next, but with most of our ships gone, well, it's just not the same anymore. Our chances of surviving are slowly shrinking day by day, Lewis, and I just don't know what to do about it."

"Well, we could find a nice island and stay there," Lewis suggested. "There's nothing that says we have to keep floating around the world, is there?"

Snyder thought about that, but he already knew his answer. "Listen, Lewis, this is my boat and I'll be damned if I leave her anytime soon, if you ever want to leave, well then, go with God, but you know what my answer is today and every other day to come."

Snyder's voice had gone up a pitch, upset at even the thought of abandoning his command.

"Whoa, all right there, simmer down, Dan, even if I wanted to, we're a long way from any deserted islands, so relax, I'm with you as always," he said placing his hand on Snyder's shoulder.

Snyder patted Lewis's hand and then stood up. "I know that Lewis, I know that." Just as he finished talking, a crewman walked into the room, a package in his hand.

"Captain, this just came down the tube, Nelson said one of Raddack's men was told to give it to you," the crewman said, handing it to Snyder.

He took it, holding it in both hands. The thin paper was taped closed and Snyder ripped it open, exposing the bottle of vintage wine beneath the paper.

"Thank you, Peters, that'll be all," he said brusquely, the crewman turning and leaving. No salute was required inside the vessel, only topside.

"What is it, Dan," Lewis asked by his side.

"The son-of-a-bitch sent me a bottle of wine," Snyder snarled, almost throwing the bottle against the nearest bulkhead.

Lewis saw his Captain's anger and took the bottle from him, opening the small card that came with it.

"Here's to a mutual friendship," he read, setting the bottle down on the quartermaster's desk. "What do you want me to do with it?"

"Throw the goddamn bottle overboard for all I care. Christ, the damn thing's probably poisoned." Snyder snarled, his rage boiling inside him. "Look, Lewis, I'll be in my quarters. I need some time to think."

"Okay, Dan, but when does this trade take place with Raddack?" He asked softly, not wanting to agitate the other man anymore then he already was.

As Snyder left the command center, he tossed his words over his shoulder. "Eighteen hundred," he said briskly and then was gone, sliding down the ladder towards the officer's quarters.

Lewis stood there for a few seconds, pondering his conversation with his Captain. Then looking down at the bottle of wine he shrugged and popped the cork. Sniffing the wine, he like what he smelled and took a swig that lasted for almost a full minute.

Breathing heavily, he wiped his mouth on his sleeve and pushed the cork back into the spout.

"Shit, that ain't half bad," he said to himself, and then stopped and made sure he was alone. It wouldn't do for the XO to be found talking to himself with a bottle of wine in his hand.

He relaxed when he saw he was still alone, most of the crew either sleeping or in the mess hall, probably watching some movie more than six months old.

Deciding he had nothing to do at the moment, the maps he had been perusing not a priority at the moment, he left the Con, planning to relax in his cabin with the rest of the bottle of wine as company.

Captain Daniel Snyder stepped into his small quarters and sat down in the single chair in the room. To his right, less than a foot away was his bed, which could be folded into the wall when he wasn't in it. In front of him was a small desk, no more than two feet wide which could also be closed to allow him more room. A small television was set inside the wall, so he could watch his own movies when he was so inclined, though usually he would watch them in the wardroom with the other officers under him. It was good to be with them every so often, so they felt relaxed near him. To remain too aloof was not always a good thing. His men needed to know he was the Captain, yes, but he was also a man like them, and was willing to hear their problems, whether personnel or about his vessel.

A picture leaned against the wall at the rear of the desk and he leaned over and picked it up.

The picture was of him and his wife.

Behind the smiling couple in the picture was a beautiful blue sky, their trip to the Caribbean on their honeymoon.

As he studied the woman in the photo, her hair and how her clothes fit her, he smiled, remembering back to more than fifteen years ago when the picture had been taken.

They had stopped and asked another tourist to snap the photo, the ridiculously tanned man happy to oblige them.

Thinking back to a better time, he wondered if his wife was even still alive. Though he hoped and prayed she was, the truth was she was probably long dead. He tried not to think about her too much, the loss he felt stinging to much. Maybe some day, if he lived that long, the pain would become better, less intense.

Setting the picture back down, he sighed. Sometimes he wondered if it was all worth it. To be trapped inside a tin can, floating under the waves day after day and week after week.

His melancholy threatening to envelop him, he stood up and left his cabin, walking through the small hall until within seconds he was in the crew's mess hall.

The room was ridiculously small.

There were five tables, three on one side and two on the other. Each table sat four crewmen and most of the crew would eat in shifts. The goal was to eat and get the hell out because there were plenty more of your fellow crewmen waiting to get in and eat themselves.

The submarine was running on battery power, the fuel for the backup diesel engines dangerously low. Once upon a time when he pulled into port his vessel would have been connected to the base electrical, but those days were past.

Leaning against the bulkhead, he smiled at a few of his men as they passed him, sliding into a few seats near the television to watch the movie playing.

Snyder didn't recall the movie, but it had something to do with a guy in a red and blue costume shooting ropes out of his wrists and swinging through what looked like New York City. If he was right it was some kind of character from a comic book, Spider...something. He honestly didn't know, not watching television for years and his childhood a distant memory.

He was sure if he thought about it for a moment it would come to him, but decided it wasn't really that important.

The boat's cook had made a cake and Snyder pilfered a piece, nodding to the man as he picked it up.

"Enjoy it, Captain, it'll be one of the last unless we resupply," MS3 Wolfe said to him.

Snyder nodded to the man, the man's black skin covered in sweat as he scrubbed a pan in the deep sink. The galley was the size of a closet, everything the man needed to cook with from grill to deep fat fryer, expertly placed for a maximum amount of room and efficiency. Despite the size of the area the man could make a meal to feed two hundred men easily, though the crew was only half that at the moment.

"Don't worry, Mr. Wolfe, I'll get you what you need, I promise."

"That's great, Captain, thanks, thanks a lot." Then the man got back to scrubbing his pot. Dinner was only a few hours away and he needed the pot he was cleaning for the next meal.

Snyder walked away with his piece of cake still in his hand. Waiting until he reached the wardroom, one of his officers grunted a greeting.

Ensign Robbins was going over a few status reports, checking and double checking the reactor printouts.

"Afternoon, Captain, how's it going?" Robbins asked, placing his pen on the table and looking up at Snyder.

Snyder poured himself a cup of coffee and grabbed a plate from the pantry just off the wardroom, setting his cake on the table.

"Fine, Robbins, fine. Tell me the reactors all right; I could use some good news."

Robbins shifted in his seat to be able to talk to Snyder without having to turn his head.

"Things are fine, Captain. My men are keeping up on maintenance and even if the military was up and running I'd say we were fine. As for the future..." he trailed off, leaving his unspoken words hanging.

Snyder grunted, taking a bite of the cake. It was vanilla and it tasted wonderful. Out of all the military forces it was the Navy that had the best chow, thanks to its supplies and trained specialists. After all, any army, whether they were on land or sea, worked on their stomachs.

"That's good, Robbins, that's great actually."

Robbins picked up his pen and stood up.

"If you'll excuse me, Captain, I really should get back to engineering."

Snyder waved the man away. "Of course, Ensign, go. Do what you have to do to keep my boat running."

"Yes, sir, I will, good day, sir," Robbins said, and left the ward-room, the thin door closing slowly after he'd exited.

Snyder sat quietly, listening to the sound of his crew as they watched their movie only a few feet from him. To his left was another door, opposite the room from the one Robbins had exited with and if Snyder wanted to walk the four feet after using said door he would find himself back in the crew's mess hall again. A fast-attack submarine was truly a small vessel with most of the space dedicated to the torpedo room and the rear of the boat dedicated to the reactor and engineering.

He didn't mind. Though not as grand as a Boomer or a Triton class submarine, it was still his first command and he treasured every moment.

Taking another bite of his cake and washing it down with another sip of coffee, he glanced at the clock on the wall.

Only a few more hours to go until he met with Raddack. Then he could finish his business in Groton and get the hell out of here, perhaps even leave the tainted country all together.

Alone with his thoughts, he ate his cake and tried to keep his mind clear, but his eyes continually were pulled to the clock.

Just a few more hours to go and it would all be over.

But if that was true, then why did he have such an unsettling feeling in his gut that even the cake couldn't fill?

Chapter 11

Henry stopped at the foot of the ravine, frowning when he saw how steep the incline was. Months of flooding had washed away the soil at the bottom of the deep tear in the earth, causing it to become a much deeper impression then originally planned by the farmers that had once lived on the farm behind him.

Jimmy stopped behind Henry and whistled softly. More than fifty feet deep with loose soil mingling with tree roots for walls, the ravine was a formidable opponent, but to go back the way they'd come would mean a firefight with the odds against them, so they prepared to climb down into the rift and try to circle around the posse, and then continue south.

Jimmy dropped the rope into the ravine, holding on to the other end. While the rope didn't fully reach the bottom, it was close enough to the ground so they could each slide the few remaining feet easily once letting go.

Jimmy grunted, satisfied and then walked to the nearest tree, tying the rope tightly in a secure slip-knot. With the rope securely around the tree, he jogged back to the others, a smile on his face.

Mary knew that smile. Sometimes Jimmy would perform the simplest task and want to be complimented like a child, so to keep things moving she moved closer to him, patting his shoulder. "Great job, Jimmy, now we can go," she said, with a wink to Cindy, who hid a slight smile. She too, knew of Jimmy's need for praise and was pleased it wasn't her that had to stroke his ego.

Henry gestured to Mary, and then Cindy. "Ladies first, and then Jimmy can go, followed by me in the rear," he said, dictating the order the group would descend the incline with.

Mary nodded and with a little help from Cindy, swung her legs over the edge of the ravine and with hands firmly gripping the rope, started to lower herself down.

The ravine was covered with small tree roots and bushes grew straight out of the dirt walls, reaching up to the sun like they were natives worshipping their god; most already taking hold of the soft soil from where they had been uprooted the previous fall.

Now, as Mary shimmied down the rope, her eyes were unable to spot the desiccated hand that squeezed the soil behind a few shrubs and fallen logs at the bottom.

Concentrating on lowering herself, she let out a loud sigh when she reached the bottom, dropping lightly, bending her knees to absorb the impact. Her shoes sank an inch in the muddy floor. Only a few days ago, after a heavy rainstorm had blanketed the area, saturating the ravine, it would have been twice as deep, but lack of rain in the vicinity and the warm spring days was helping to dry the earth, transforming it back to hard-packed dirt.

Waving up to the others, she stepped back and waited for Cindy to start her climb downward, unaware that only a few feet away, almost entirely covered in dirt and leaves, a moving corpse crawled toward her.

As Cindy slid over the edge, the rope started dancing and Mary reached up and grabbed it, holding it steady while Cindy started her downward climb.

The young girl was athletic and Mary felt a tinge of jealousy as she watched her friend quickly descend the rope, barely slowing.

When she was only a few feet from the ground she let go; landing cat-like on her feet. Flashing Mary a smile, she stepped away from the dangling rope, allowing Jimmy to start to lower himself down.

With his shotgun on his back, the backpack leaning to his right, Jimmy started to lower himself downward, the extra weight from the backpack causing the rope to stretch. The rope was old and too much weight would cause it to snap, unknown to the others.

A crash from above told Henry the barn door had given in to the weight of the surviving ghouls and he mentally hurried Jimmy down the ravine, but as he watched him and looked over his shoulder as the first of the undead rounded the corner of the barn, he realized if he waited for Jimmy it would be too late for him, so calling down and warning Jimmy, he slid over the edge and started his own climb into the mouth of the ravine.

The rope stretched a little more, sounding like a leather couch when someone sat on one of the cushions and he prayed the rope would only hold on from breaking for a few more seconds.

Henry was almost halfway down when the first zombie reached the edge. The creature stared down at its prey, uncertain how to proceed. Its mind was made up for it when one of its brethren pushed forward, knocking the ghoul off the edge.

With no sound, the animated corpse fell like a fallen rocket, its head striking first, plowing into a small pool of mud. The arms and legs spasmed for an instant, but the neck snapped from the corpse's impact, all neurons shutting down, the body falling to the earth, twitching but not a threat.

Jimmy was almost down when another speeding body came shooting at him. He let go of the rope with his left hand, allowing his body to swing away from the falling corpse. The body only grazed him and he struggled to grab the rope again, now moving faster to get off the rope and out of danger.

Henry continued downward, his backpack at an odd angle, throwing off his balance. One after another, the zombies above him fell off the edge like lemmings, to plummet down like rocks as the few behind pushed forward.

One struck his shoulder and he let out a yell from the pain as his arm was pulled nearly out of its socket. Some of the ghouls were still functioning as they hit the ravine's floor and Mary and Cindy made short work of them, stomping faces into the churning mud and using rocks as bludgeons, while keeping watch above their heads for falling bodies.

Jimmy dropped the six or so feet to the floor, letting out a yell of happiness. Kicking a ghoul in the face, he stepped away, calling Henry to hurry up.

"What the hell do you think I'm trying to do? If you haven't noticed it's raining people," he screamed, as arm after arm lowered him closer to the floor.

Looking over his shoulder, he saw the mud-caked corpse inching towards Mary. The others hadn't seen it, the body camouflaged to the point it was all but invisible in the surrounding terrain, hidden by the shrubs that lined the ravine.

He reached for his panga, but realized he couldn't reach it and his eyes went wide as he watched the ghoul come within inches of Mary's leg, its mouth prepared to clamp down around the flesh of her ankle.

Knowing there was no time to call a warning and having no other alternative, he pushed off from the wall of the ravine, and let go of the rope. He fell more than twelve feet, his arms spinning in the air as he tried to maintain his balance.

The others saw him and all mouths were open in shock as he plummeted to the ground below.

Henry had done his best to line up his falling body with the prone zombie and his aim was true. Feet first, he landed on the back of its head, bending his knees and rolling to the side. The wind left his body and he struggled to suck in his next breath, not knowing if his plan had worked and Mary was all right.

His face landed in some mud and he tasted wet dirt, spitting it out as fast as it seeped into his mouth.

Rolling onto his back, he looked up at the blue sky, only a thin line now; the walls of the ravine cutting the rest from view. His face was covered with wet soil, giving him the look of an ancient warrior preparing to go into battle against his enemies.

Cindy moved to him, helping him to sit up as he cleared his vision.

"Jesus, Henry, what the hell was that?" She asked, opening his backpack and handing him some water. All their water bottles had been topped off before leaving the inn, just incase they had trouble finding more.

"Deader, near Mary, no time to warn her..." He sputtered, trying to wish the pain in his chest away and splashing some of the water on his face. On top of that he had a mighty pain in is right thigh, his landing not as perfect as he would have liked.

After only a few minutes, Henry was feeling better. His fall had been cushioned by the body of the ghoul, and he had tucked and rolled enough to prevent himself from breaking or spraining anything. With Cindy's help he hobbled back to the others, just as

Jimmy used a rock to crush the head of the last body that had fallen over the edge of the ravine.

The floor was littered with bodies, arms and legs seeming to be everywhere. It was almost impossible to walk in the small area without stepping on a body part, the squishy feeling enough to make the companion's stomachs roll.

Mary pointed at the deader Henry had stopped, its back was broken in two, the spine pulverized by the weight of Henry's body when his weight had crushed the ghoul to the floor of the ravine.

Henry nodded, glad that what he had wanted to do had worked so well and Mary was fine.

Jimmy wiped the sweat off his brow with his shirtsleeve and waved the others away from the pile of corpses. "Come on, this place is already ripe and it's only going to get worse with the sun cooking them like a cannibal's barbecue."

"Oh, Jimmy, you're always so poetic," Mary joked, stepping over a decomposing, bloated body which was well on its way to exploding from internal gasses long before it fell into the ravine.

Waving flies from his head, Henry stood up straight, breathing better. He was lucky, he could have easily broken a leg, and if he had, he might not have made it out of the ravine alive, but luckily he had made it through once more. Rubbing his thigh, he felt only a slight twinge of pain that seemed to grow milder as he moved across the floor of the ravine.

Stepping over the bodies, he looked up at the sky and sent a silent thank you to whatever Gods or God watched out for him and his friends.

What Henry didn't realize is that fate had nothing to do with it; he had simply not been high enough for his limbs to not be able to withstand the impact of the fall. If he had been only a few feet higher things may have gone down a lot differently. But to focus on what might have happened was useless, the companions only focusing on the present and in a small way, the future.

Leaving the twitching corpses behind, the four people moved further into the ravine, now thinking of how to escape the same ravine that had been their salvation only minutes before, but could now turn out to be their graves if they couldn't find a way out and back up to level land.

*   *   *

The sun was starting its descent, high in the sky a crow flew overhead, looking down at the four humans, the four people seeming like ants from above as they wove their way through the slowly shrinking ravine.

After more than an hour the ravine had shrunk to half its size, now only wide enough for two people to walk shoulder to shoulder.

And it was continuing to shrink with every step the companions made.

The sun's angle gave the small tear in the earth some shade and Henry called a halt so they could all rest for a few minutes.

He kicked the carcass of an animal away from him, one of many they had found on the floor of the ravine. Evidently a few animals not very skilled at climbing had found their way down the steep incline and had died trying to get back out.

That didn't bode to well for the rest of them, but Henry tried to stay positive. If there was a way out then he or one of the others would find a way.

"Hey, Henry," Jimmy asked as he took a swig of water from his dwindling bottle.

"Yeah," Henry answered.

"What do you think was the deal with that barn? I mean, what the hell were all those deaders doing in there, it was like they were hiding or something."

Henry shook his head. "No, I don't think that's what they were doing. They were just getting out of the sun and over time more and more showed up. Did you see the area around the farm? Nothing but grass. Any roamer in the area would eventually make it there or keep going to the town where they would be put down." Wiping his brow, Henry frowned. "No, Jimmy, all that was, was bad luck on our part. Should have never gone in there in the first place."

"Now, Henry, don't go second guessing yourself, there was no way of knowing what might have been in there, for all we knew there was a brand new car with a hundred miles on it and a full tank of gas," Mary said.

"Yeah, like one of those new Mustangs, those are cool, I wanted one so bad when I worked at Pineridge, but I couldn't afford it." He said, kicking a few pebbles away from his feet.

Cindy put her arm around him and squeezed. "Don't feel so bad, Jimmy. Even if you had one, finding gas would be a bitch, almost as bad as before the shitstorm came down. You remember how much a gallon of gas went for?"

Jimmy kissed her on the cheek, tasting the salt of her sweat. "Thanks, babe, you always know what to say." Then he squeezed her stomach, causing her to giggle.

Henry smiled as he watched them and then stood up and fixed his gear.

"All right, people, breaks over, let's see if we can find a way out of this hole."

With Jimmy in the lead, they headed off once more. As they walked, their eyes constantly roamed the walls of the ravine looking for some form of handhold to allow them to climb out, but the now twenty foot walls yielded nothing but loose soil and fragile tree roots exposed when the ravine became larger.

Twenty-five minutes later Jimmy stopped the others with a fist held in the air. By now the ravine had shrunk to the point where only one person at a time could walk, and even then shoulders would brush the loose soil on the walls, cascading it down onto the rocky floor.

"We've got a problem, Henry," Jimmy said from the front of the line, Henry taking up the rear.

"Well spill it, what's wrong, keep moving," he snapped, hot and tired and short on patience.

Mary turned around to face him, having a clear view over Jimmy's shoulder. "That's just it, we can't. The ravine just stops."

"Stops? That can't be. It should at least continue to get smaller and we could climb out or something by bracing our shoulders and legs."

"Afraid not, old man. There's a big honkin' boulder in front of us, smooth as a baby's ass and the ravine just stops!" Jimmy yelled over the heads of the others.

"That's crazy, let me see," Henry said, forcing by the two women, the going tough as they could barely fit. After pushing through, he reached Jimmy and looked over the other man's shoulder.

Sure enough their was a huge boulder more than twenty feet high, the width unknown as the body of the formation was buried in the walls of the ravine. Looking up, the top of the boulder was more than five feet above the land, showing just how massive it really was.

"Jesus, this rock is huge," he breathed, looking at the small lines on the boulder's face, far too small to try to use as handholds.

"So, oh mighty chief, what the hell do we do now? Go back?"

Henry shook his head hard in the negative. "No way, we are not going back and wasting all the time it took us to get here, we can find a way out; we just have to think on it." Looking around their small prison he shrugged out of his backpack. "We're about as safe as you can get down here, so I say we make camp for the night and think on it. Any idea is worth saying, no matter how farfetched. Then, in the morning, if we still have nothing, I guess we'll have to backtrack back to the farm, distasteful as that sounds."

Henry looked at the faces of his friends, Mary's face partially hidden by Cindy's due to the closeness of the ravine's walls and one at a time the companions nodded.

"Okay, Henry, sounds good, besides my feet are killing me, it'll be good to rest for more than a few minutes," Mary said, sliding to the floor of the ravine and taking off one of her boots, shaking dirt and pebbles out of it.

"Amen to that," Cindy said, doing the same.

With night falling, casting the land around them in perpetual darkness, the companions got comfortable, preparing to spend the long night in the relative safety of the ravine, each one of them racking their brains for a way out.

It was a long walk back to the farm, and if they had to return back to where they had started, then a lot of time and energy would have been wasted for nothing. Plus, there was know way of discerning if the posse still waited for them and if they had to go back and they were still on the hunt, then a firefight would be inevitable, with the odds vastly against them.

With nothing inside the small ravine but a few sparse weeds and some shrubs, a campfire was out of the question, so curling up side by side to conserve body heat in the growing cold, they all relaxed and talked quietly amongst themselves until each became too tired to stay awake. It had been a long, hard day and when each had finally decided to succumb to the drowsiness they each felt, they were asleep in minutes.

Henry was still awake, taking the first watch. Whenever they were out on the land one of them would always be awake, ever watchful for the undead or other humans eager to take the few possessions the companions had.

It was a harsh world now, more ruthless, but the four friends had learned to adapt to it, because if they didn't, they would die or become one of the undead, cursed to roam the land for far to long for any of their tastes.

Henry stood up and moved a little ways from the others, their steady breathing threatening to encompass him as well and pull him into the slumber he so desperately wanted.

Leaning back against the ravine's dirt wall, he watched the others, only darker shapes in the growing darkness.

As he watched them sleeping, his eyes went to the shape of Jimmy, the sleeping man had started twitching slightly, looking for all purposes like he was dreaming.

Henry smiled and took a sip of his water bottle. Whatever the young man was dreaming, Henry hoped it was pleasant.

*   *   *

Jimmy tossed and turned in the tempest that was his nightmare. At first he was walking along a beach, the small form of Cindy far away calling to him on the distant shore. Like so often happened in dreams, space and time transformed so that when he started running to her, the closer he came to her the farther she moved away.

Slowing his running, he stopped and breathed in the cool, sea air. Then she vanished, like wisp of smoke on the gentle breeze.

Now he was alone on the beach, nothing but seaweed and a few stray sand crabs to keep him company.

He looked for Cindy again to find she was gone. Turning round and round he couldn't find her anywhere.

With no other ideas as what to do he started walking, the water lapping at his bare feet.

He had no sense of actual time and eventually he reached the end of the beach. A large park covered with oak trees and a playground filled with different size jungle-gyms and monkey bars was off to his right.

A group of children were playing near the edge of the playground and as he moved closer he saw they were playing jump rope. Two girls were holding the rope, one at each end, while two other girls jumped up and down with a steady rhythm.

The closer he came to the children the better he could hear the song they sang in cadence with the spinning rope. At first he thought he heard one of the many jingles kids would sing as they jumped rope, but when he was close enough to hear the song clearly, he stopped walking and listened, finding the song of choice odd.

The children sang the song in a lilting voice, the first parts of the song high and then the latter, low.

As he listened, he felt a chill go down his spine and he stood perfectly still, as if the haunting jingle had glued him to his spot.

When you die, you go to hell.
With the ringing of the steel church bell.
They put you in a big pine box.
And bury you up with dirt and rocks.
The worms dig in and crawl about.
The worms sing and dance upon your snout.
They eat your eyes, they eat your nose.
They eat the flesh between your toes.
The mean old worms will never stop.
They'll eat and eat till you swell and pop.
In your stomach and out your eyes.
The worms share your corpse with the bugs and flies.
Your stomach swells with pus and gas.
But decompose, you will at last.
So listen well and heed this tale.
For life is naught but a shrouded vale.

Then the girls stopped singing and turned as one to look at Jimmy. For the first time he saw their faces clearly and as the girls moved closer he saw they were dead.

But not just dead, they were some of the most horrendous decomposing bodies Jimmy had ever seen. Their eyes hung from their faces on thin strings of gristle, their faces were shriveled and cracked, maggots crawling through the wounds. Their mouths had swollen tongues incased within, and they could barely speak, the blackened tongues were so huge.

As they moved closer, worms spilled from their ears to wiggle on the ground and one of the girls lips were so misshapen, they resembled night crawlers more than lips.

The torpid, treacle like movements of the dead girls was unsettling as they made their way towards him and it took all of his will to snap out of the trance-like state he seemed to have fallen into.

Jimmy backed away, relieved his legs would move again and as the girls slowly moved closer, a macabre grin on their undead faces, Jimmy reached for his weapon, hoping to blow the little demons to hell where they belonged.

His hand went to his holster to find it wasn't there and he let out a small yelp that he quickly silenced.

Turning, he started to run, deciding retreat was the better part of valor at the moment, despite the fact they were only children. Though Jimmy had faced more than his share of the undead, there was something about the zombie girls that made him fear them.

He ran from them but stopped to discover the beach was gone, nothing but an empty void in front of him. Running back into the park, he skirted the quartet of death and ran to one of the large oak trees. Climbing into the high branches he held his breath and waited for the girls to come to him, hoping he could fend them off.

He didn't believe there was any help for him, he was alone and he would live or die by his own choices. A squirrel chirped at him, angry that he had invaded its home. But when Jimmy looked at the furry creature he saw it too, was a living corpse, its wasteland of skin and bone poking through its matted fur.

Jimmy broke a small branch of the tree and hurled it at the squirrel. The animal hissed one more time and then scurried down the tree and away into the shadows.

The girls reached the tree and tried to scurry up the trunk, their arms too small to reach the branches above them.

Jimmy let out a laugh of victory. They were too short and couldn't reach him!

Then the girls did something he didn't expect and one climbed onto the back of another.

Looking like acrobatics at a circus, another climbed on top of the second, the human ladder balancing as the girl reached out for the branches of the tree to resume their chase of Jimmy.

Jimmy shook his head, denying the intelligence of the girls. No zombie had ever been bright enough to pull a trick like the one the girls were using to catch him.

He climbed up further into the tree, trying to keep out of reach of the small hands as the girls pulled themselves ever higher onto the branches.

Then the small bodies shifted, the undead creatures bending forward, backs arcing and changing shape.

The girls began to scurry like dogs, using their hands and feet to quickly traverse the branches as they moved ever closer to him.

Jimmy had climbed as far as he could, the top of the tree only a few feet above his head. Looking through the branches and leaves, he could see the girls jumping like monkeys from tree limb to tree limb.

Then it happened, one of the girls reached him and a claw like hand snapped out and wrapped itself around his ankle, only the hand had transformed into tendrils that slid into his pants and burrowed their way into his skin.

With a shout that sent birds in the nearby trees fluttering away into the air, Jimmy fought with the creature below him, knowing he was losing with every tick of the invisible clock in his head.

The second creature had reached him and had grabbed a hold on his other leg and the two shook him back and forth like a rag doll. Jimmy screamed, but a moment later, one of the tendrils slipped into his mouth, gagging him. His vision dimmed and he knew he was suffocating while his body was tossed back and forth in a jerking motion.

He let out one more scream, muffled by the tendrils and then his eyes snapped open and he was awake, staring up at the night sky, Henry looking down on him, removing his hand from Jimmy's shoulder where the man had been trying to shake him awake.

"Huh, what? Where am I?" Jimmy stuttered, tendrils of his dream still prickling at the back of his mind.

"Wake the hell up, Jimmy. I want to get some rest. Christ, you're harder to wake up than my wife was," Henry said, with irritation in his voice.

"What? Oh, Jesus, Henry I'm sorry, guess I was having a bad dream," he said, scratching his head and stretching.

"Oh, yeah, what about? The way you were moaning in your sleep it sounded pretty bad."

Jimmy shuddered, a few wisps of the dream still in his mind but quickly dissolving like morning fog on a summer's day. "I don't quite remember and you know what? I think it's for the best. I don't think I was in a good place."

"Suit yourself," Henry said, stepping back from him. "Listen, the others are sleeping and you can wake Mary in a few hours. It's your decision when exactly. As for me, I'm gonna get some sleep, keep sharp, all right?"

Jimmy nodded, standing up to stretch the knots in his back, feeling for his .38 and looking down to see his shotgun where he had left it before he had fallen to sleep.

"It's cool, man, go to sleep, I got this," Jimmy said.

Henry nodded and went into the corner, leaning against the large boulder, his butt on the ravine's floor. Closing his eyes, he was out almost as soon as he breathed in his first breath, the long day hitting him hard.

Jimmy smiled at him and then at Mary and Cindy, the two women curled up together like two sisters who were scared of the dark.

Letting out a sigh, he gazed up at the thin ribbon of night sky he could see between the ravine's walls.

He realized the wall was about as high as three people if they were standing one on top of the other and something from his dream came back to him.

"Oh my God, it's so damn simple," he whispered to himself, and then quickly shut up, not wanting to wake the others.

He had figured a way out of the ravine.

With a proud smile on his lips, he leaned against the dirt wall, pleased with himself.

He was looking forward to morning when he could tell the others how *the great* Jimmy Cooper had figured a way out of their little predicament and saved the day.

Chapter 12

Captain Snyder checked his watch for the fifth time in less than a minute, the hands glowing in the falling dusk. Night came quickly in the early spring of Connecticut and he silently wished he could be back inside his sub, safe from the horrors of the world.

Ten minutes to six it read, and he frowned, his XO standing by his side on the dock noticing his discomfort. Lewis heard the sigh and turned to look at his Captain.

"What's wrong, Dan? Having second thoughts?"

"Hell, yes, I'm having second thoughts. You do realize what we're handing over to that madman, don't you?" Snyder asked his friend.

Lewis shrugged, taking another puff of the cigarette he'd just lit. The things were becoming harder to find and he was running low. Only another two cartons and he'd be out.

"I don't see how it really matters one way or the other. It's not like we can use the stuff, so why not give it to him in trade for the supplies we so desperately need?"

Snyder turned at the sound of footsteps. Five of his crew walked up the dock, two of the men carrying a canister the size of an air tank.

All were armed with side arms and two carried M-16 rifles. When they were no more than a few feet from Snyder, he held up his hand to stop them. "That's far enough, men. Now keep your weapons ready. I don't expect trouble, but better safe than sorry, right?"

The men nodded, some mumbling "yes sirs", others fidgeting as they set down the canister and waited for what they all knew was coming next.

A few lit cigarettes, trying to relax, but Snyder knew they were on edge as much as he was.

Five minutes later headlights appeared, quickly approaching the dock. The shape of the familiar black Hummer appeared out of the darkness, seeming like a creature racing out of the shadows, and Snyder knew it was Raddack's.

Another smaller vehicle pulled up alongside it.

A pickup truck with a .50 caliber machine gun mounted on the rear bed jostled to a stop next to the Hummer, the man standing in the bed making sure to have a clear line of sight on the open dock.

The rear door of the Hummer opened and the large body of Raddack climbed out, his feet dangling for a moment from the high vehicle like a child's, before he slid onto the pavement.

Other men spilled out of the Hummer and pickup truck and Snyder counted almost twice the men with Raddack than Snyder had decided to accompany him and Lewis.

With the water slapping at the dock, Raddack wobbled down the wooden planks, his men behind him.

When he was ten feet from Snyder he stopped and held his left hand up for his men to do the same.

"What the hell's the meaning of all the firepower, I thought we were on good terms now," Snyder spit at the man.

"Nice to see you again, too, Captain, do you have what we agreed on?" Raddack asked, his mouth turning up into a sneer, ignoring Snyder's question.

"You know I do, Raddack, now stop fucking around and let's get this done." Snyder spit, his distaste for the man obvious and the extra men making him even more uncomfortable then he already had been, if that was at all possible.

Raddack's sneer turned into a smile. "I couldn't agree with you more, Captain," he said, moving to the right of the dock, his men following suit.

Snyder watched this and wondered what the hell the man was doing until Raddack pulled his sidearm and aimed it at Snyder.

Lewis saw this as well and his eyes went wide. An instant later the .50 cal. started chattering and rounds chewed up the dock, their target Captain Snyder.

For two heartbeats Snyder stood dumbfounded, too shocked to believe Raddack would pull such a sleazy move and double cross him, then he snapped back to reality, only it was too late to avoid the bullets as they walked up the dock, screaming death.

Lewis threw himself in front of Snyder, his body absorbing the impact of almost all of the rounds. The bullets punched through the man's body, chewing organs to pieces and splintering bone as they passed through the man's dancing body and struck Snyder.

With most of their force gone after passing through Lewis, Snyder received flesh wounds as he fell to the dock and tried to escape the rounds seeming to be everywhere around him. The cacophony of the gun battle filled the night, excluding all other sound.

His men swung their weapons at Raddack and his guards and fired indiscriminately at them. Raddack ducked behind a pile of crates, his men taking the brunt of the barrage of bullets. Some fell to the docks, dead, their eyes still open, while others returned fire, knocking crewmen off their feet, others falling into the water to drown, knocked unconscious from the impact of the rounds and mortal wounds to their person.

Snyder tried to fight back, but Lewis' body was on top of him, the man's cigarette still in his mouth, the small tip still burning brightly in the falling twilight.

Snyder was trapped; all he could do was watch his men be slaughtered by the superior fire power. Small arms fire could be heard now, coming from the direction of the submarine and he turned his head to see what was happening.

More of his crew climbed through the boat's bow hatch, firing as they ran across the wooden plank that separated the boat from the dock.

One at a time the .50 cal. knocked them off the plank, the men falling to their deaths, already punctured dozens of times by the machine gun.

Footsteps could be heard slapping the dock as Raddack's men raced down the dock toward his vessel, boarding it and sliding into the hatch. One of the men dropped a stun grenade into the hatch and a moment late the muffled pop and white light flashed out through the opening; then the guards dropped down into the boat.

Muffled gunshots could be heard, Snyder's ears still ringing from the initial onslaught from the .50 cal.

Raddack walked up to Snyder and kicked Lewis away from him, the XO rolling into the water. His body floated for a moment and then started to sink, the water pouring into all the holes the man had in his body only helping the process, the murky water becoming dyed a reddish, brackish color from all the dead now floating near the dock. A few Bluefish skimmed the surface of the water, curious about all the new food floating in their home.

Snyder looked up into Raddack's grinning face. "Why, you no-good bastard, we had an agreement," he spit, trying to reach for his side arm.

While drawing his weapon, Raddack kicked the .45 from his hand just as he pulled it from its holster, the weapon sliding across the dock a few feet.

"Yes we did have an agreement and I've decided to alter it. I figured why just take the one prize when I can have it all, namely your ship."

Raddack turned to one of his men. "Smith, pick up the Captain and take him to the pickup. I don't want him in my Hummer; I don't want his blood getting on my upholstery. Have him bandaged up and then tossed into our brig. I'll see to him later."

"Yes, sir," Smith said, picking up Snyder and securing his hands with a pair of plastic handcuffs. Just one of many tools he'd found in the MP's shack after the men had abandoned their posts.

Raddack turned to another guard, a burly man with a heavy assault rifle in his hands. "Norton, how many men did we lose?"

"Only three dead, sir, and Williams is wounded. He should be okay if we get him medical attention quickly." Norton said, shifting back and forth on his feet, eager for more action.

"Good, get it done and send the rest of the men down into the ship. Don't kill everyone, we'll need a few of the crew to tell us how to operate the ship's controls and run it. Some will probably join us if the alternative is death. The rest you can lock up. Perhaps they'll change their tune after a few days without food and water."

Norton saluted and ran off to see to his orders and Snyder felt sick after seeing the lackey salute the piece of shit in front of him. He said as much. "You'll never get away with this, you fucker, my men will die before they help you," Snyder spit as he was dragged down the dock toward the pickup truck.

Raddack laughed at that. "Oh you think so? Well, my dear Captain, it appears I already have gotten away with it, and I have the nerve gas to boot," he said walking over to the canister lying on its side on the dock. The words **CVX-NINE** were stenciled in black lettering on the side of the canister, the military nerve gas now in Raddack's possession, as well as the submarine.

"Just what the hell do you think you're going to do with a submarine, Raddack?" Snyder asked, resisting the attempts to drag him to the truck. It was as if as long as he stayed on the dock, the Victory was still his.

"That's the easy part, Captain. I'm going to use it to grab a bigger piece of the pie. Sure this base is nice, but I want more and what better way to get it than with a fast-attack submarine? With that ship I can rule what's left of the United States."

"You're fucking crazy, you fat bastard, you know that?" Snyder spit, losing ground inch by inch as the guards overpowered him and continued dragging him farther from his boat. "You can't use my boat. There are command codes that only my XO and I have access to. It's the only way to get that boat underway and you killed my XO. As for me, I'll die before I give them to you!"

"Perhaps, Captain, perhaps. I assure you, I will be putting your statement to the test. As for your other rather rude comment, well, I'd prefer to be the crazy man with the guns and ship than the sane man locked up in jail. Now, I have better things to do then debate politics with you. In fact, I think I'll inspect my new ship."

Snarling, Snyder kicked free of his captors and started running towards Raddack. He planned to knock the fat Boss over the side of the dock, hopefully drowning the bastard even as his own life was extinguished. But his plan failed before he had taken three steps and a plastic butt of a rifle cracked the back of his skull, knocking him unconscious.

As his vision grew dark and he fell into oblivion, he could still hear the laughter of Raddack as the man headed for his boat, then footsteps pounded the dock and he was picked up and unceremoniously tossed into the back of the pickup truck, then he heard no more as he blissfully fell unconscious.

Chapter 13

Henry opened his tired eyes to see Jimmy's grinning face staring down at him.

"Will you back up a little, please? Looking at your ugly mug first thing in the morning isn't as easy as you might think."

Jimmy did as he was asked, taking a few steps back from the sitting man. Henry sat up, rubbing his eyes as he looked around the ravine. The sun was just peeking out of the clouds, a new day dawning.

Looking past Jimmy, he frowned to see no sign of Cindy or Mary.

Jimmy saw where his eyes were looking and nodded, gesturing to the rear of the ravine.

"The girls went to freshen up, you know, go to the bathroom and stuff. They said they'd be right back."

Nodding, Henry stood up with a small groan. Though he was in the best shape of his life, now, he still had a few aches and pains that wouldn't go away. No matter how hard he fought, he just couldn't fight the will of Old Father Time.

Looking back to his friend, he saw Jimmy had a smile as wide as his face. "What's put you in such a good mood," Henry asked, scratching his chin. The stubble would soon become a beard and he hadn't decided if he would keep it or shave it off.

"I figured out a way out of here," Jimmy said proudly.

"Oh, really," Henry said with derision, rummaging in one of the backpacks for a bottle of water. Finding one, he took a swig, rinsed his mouth out and then spit it out, the water sluicing off the ravine wall to puddle on the dirt floor.

"Really," Jimmy stated, ignoring his doubt. "It came to me in a dream last night, if you'd believe it. Once the girls come back, I'll fill you all in at the same time."

"Okay, fair enough," Henry said sitting back down and stretching. Though he felt tired, his limbs wanted to move, to feel the miles flowing under his feet as he walked.

Jimmy and Henry made small talk until the girls returned and once the four were together once more in the cramped area, Jimmy shared his idea.

"It's really simple, Henry, you're probably going to kick yourself for not thinking of it first, but why don't we just make a human ladder and climb out that way?"

"A human ladder? What the hell are you talking about?" Mary asked, not understanding, her mouth set into a frown.

After an uncomfortable night on the dirt floor of the ravine, she was a little cranky, but she did her best to try to hide it, not wanting her mood to spread; it still poked through her facade of normalcy, though.

"Simple, Mary. Henry is on the bottom and then you two girls climb onto his shoulders, in fact, I could stand next to Henry and each of your feet could go on both him and me. With the two of us as the base it should be easy for you guys."

Cindy looked to be deep in thought and then a hint of a smile played across her lips. "Damn, Jimmy, that's not half bad, it should work, come on, let's give it a try."

"Fine, what do we have to lose but a broken neck? Okay, let's get started, the sooner we're out of here, the better," Henry said, moving against the ravine wall.

Jimmy stood next to him and a moment later Mary climbed onto their shoulders. Mary's right foot was on Jimmy's left shoulder and Mary's left foot was on Henry's right shoulder. The two men balanced her easily, Mary nothing but hard muscle. The days when she had even had an ounce of fat on her lean body long gone.

Next came Cindy, her athletic body scurrying up the others until she was balancing on Mary's shoulder. With her hands touching the ravine wall for balance, she tried to reach the edge, but came up only a few inches shy.

"I can't reach, I'm too short," she gasped, stretching as far as she could with no results.

"All right, come back down and we'll try to figure out what we can do to get an extra few inches," Jimmy said, taking charge of the situation, and well he should, it was his idea after all.

Cindy climbed down, and then Mary hopped off with a little help from Henry. With the companions breathing from the exertion, Jimmy racked his brain for a way to make Cindy taller.

Looking at Henry, the older man shrugged. "Don't look at me, Jimmy, I got nothin'. Good idea though, shame it didn't work. Well I guess we should start back and deal with whatever's there when we get there," Henry said, picking up his backpack.

Jimmy's eyes lit up, and he smiled so wide Henry thought his teeth would fall out.

"No wait, I got it, I know what to do," he said, pointing to the backpacks.

Filling in the others on his new idea, they all nodded, liking the sound of it and in no time they were once again following Jimmy's instructions until all was ready.

"Okay, let's try this again, Jimmy said, balancing on one of the backpacks. But instead of it being filled with their supplies, it was now filled with loose rocks and soil, creating a stepping stone for both him and Henry. Henry was standing on the other one, wobbling back and forth; unfortunately there had been no usable sized rocks in the ravine, all of them being baseball size or smaller.

"Come on, Mary, get up there before I lose my balance," Henry said brusquely, his hands firmly against the walls of the ravine.

Mary climbed up once again, followed by Cindy, and with the added lift, Cindy was able to scrabble over the edge.

But instead of Cindy spinning around to reach her hand down for Mary, she had disappeared from view.

The sound of a scuffle carried down to Mary and she waited quietly, not knowing if she should call out. Mary could definitely hear Cindy grunting.

She was fighting something, but whether her opponent was dead or alive was unknown.

Mary looked up, watching the edge of the ravine, feeling helpless and exposed, expecting something grotesque to show itself. If something came to the edge and swiped down at her, she'd have nowhere to go but down.

Her hand had already wrapped around the grip of her .38 in preparation of the danger to come and she was just getting nervous enough to call out, when Cindy's head reappeared.

"Coast is clear, figured I'd do a recce before I tried to pull you up," she smiled. "Good thing, too, there was one deader hanging around up here, but I took care of it. Nothing but skin and bones, a few kicks took it out."

"That was good thinking, Cindy, but next time how about filling me in before you do it, okay? I was starting to get worried down here, I can't see a thing."

"Sorry, Mary, I didn't think, just acted."

"Is everything all right up there?" Henry called from below.

"Things are fine, Henry, Cindy's going to pull me up now!" Mary answered.

"Okay, give me your hand and I'll pull you up." Cindy said, lying on her stomach and reaching for Mary.

Mary did as she was told, stretching as far as her arms would allow and a few seconds later she was on flat ground, lying on green grass in an open field. The highway where the posse had been was far away to the east, the meandering ravine taking them further inland.

The sun was playing hide and seek in the clouds, looking like it was going to be a beautiful day, if a little cloudy.

Cindy lay next to her and for a moment, forgot where she was, the landscape so beautiful. Then Henry's voice came from below. "Hello, ladies, how about a little help here. We'd like to get out of here, too!"

The women looked at each other and laughed. "I guess we should get them out of there, huh?" Mary asked.

Cindy shrugged. "Yeah, I guess so, but the next time Jimmy pisses me off I'm going to remind him of the time I could have left him in the ravine."

The two girls rolled to their feet and Mary shrugged out of the light jacket she was wearing over her vest, Cindy doing the same. Tying the clothing together, the women formed a crude rope, dropping it over the edge for the men to use.

Jimmy came first, his head popping up at the edge like a mole. "Hey, guys, miss me?" He joked, pulling himself over and turning to help with the extraction of Henry.

But Henry wasn't ready yet, as he was taking a few extra seconds, repacking their supplies back into the backpacks after emptying the debris from them.

Jimmy looked across the landscape and his eyes caught something a few yards away. Walking towards the zombie Cindy had taken down, he picked up a piece of it to carry back with him. He had a use for it, which he was looking forward to using in a few seconds.

With his hand behind his back, he walked back to the two women to help pull Henry out of the ravine.

After throwing the backpacks up, the women catching them, Henry started up the clothing-rope, his feet digging into the wall for purchase.

It took only seconds, his shotgun repeatedly whacking his head as he pulled himself to the edge.

Just when he was about to crawl over onto the flat ground he felt something touch his shoulder. Looking to his right, his eyes went wide when the sight of a desiccated, skeletal hand appeared grasping his vest.

Working fast, he pulled himself over the edge and rolled away, coming up in a crouch, with his Glock in his hand, prepared to blow away the dead menace he expected to see.

Instead he saw Jimmy, with a severed arm in his hand, a large smile on his face. "Need a hand, Henry?" Jimmy asked, waggling the severed arm in front of him.

"Jimmy, you bastard, you almost gave me a heart attack, what was that for?" He scowled, holstering his weapon and breathing out a sigh of relief.

Chuckling to himself, Jimmy tossed the hand away from him and pointed at Henry. "That, my friend, is for the spider joke in the kitchen yesterday. I told you I'd get even."

Henry held out his hands. "All right, all right, then we're even, truce?" He asked, moving closer to Jimmy, his hand out for the man to shake.

Jimmy stared at the out-stretched hand and then took it, pumping quickly. "Deal, but remember, no more spider jokes."

Chuckling softly, Henry slapped Jimmy on the shoulder. "Deal, buddy, deal. Now come on, let's get moving. I want to see where we're at and how far it is to the nearest settlement."

Jimmy nodded and the two friends walked away from the ravine, hoping to never see it again.

*   *   *

Henry slowed the companions, his eyes catching something in the tall grass. The ravine was more than a few miles behind them, the lush grassy field seeming to go on forever. Looking at all the open, austere land, Henry wondered if the world had kept on moving forward if all this land would have ended up being developed into a housing development or a strip mall.

A few rooftops of homes had started appearing the closer they came to the edge of the giant field.

Then he caught movement out of the corner of his eye and he stopped walking.

Pointing to the disturbance, Henry nodded to the others.

"Saw something over there, near the tree line; get sharp people until we know what it is," Henry ordered them while pulling his shotgun from over his shoulder and cocking the weapon.

The others all pulled their weapons; the soft click of safety's being flicked off carrying on the gentle breeze. With Henry in the lead, the companions crossed the plain, the waist high grass swaying like a living thing.

Slowing only a few feet from where Henry spotted the disturbance, he held up his hand and moved away from the others, Jimmy sliding to the left to catch whatever Henry found in a crossfire.

A soft mewling sound came to Henry's ears and he parted the grass, looking down at a three foot wide section of crushed grass.

Lying on the ground was a reanimated corpse.

Henry studied the creature, wondering how it had managed to make it as far into the clearing as it had.

The reason for his curiosity was the condition of the undead thing lying before him.

The pitiful creature was missing both arms and legs; nothing more than a torso and a head.

The deader looked up into Henry's face and its teeth gnashed violently, clacking together like cordwood slapping a rock. The deader tried to roll towards Henry and it was obvious how the creature had made it as far as it did.

It had rolled.

"What's going on, Henry? Is everything all right?" Mary asked from ten feet away.

Henry held out his hand to Mary and waved. "Yeah, everything's cool, I'll be there in a second." He turned to Jimmy. "Check out that tree line, will you?"

Jimmy hesitated for a moment, watching Henry. "Go ahead, Jimmy, I'll be fine," he said. Jimmy nodded and headed off towards the tree line, less than two-hundred feet away.

Henry swung his shotgun over his shoulder and pulled his panga from its sheath. There was no reason to waste a bullet on the macabre thing lying before him.

Mary and Cindy watched Henry's arm rise into the air, the blade of the panga flashing in the sunlight. Then the arm came down, a soft crunch of metal on meat carrying to the two women.

This happened two more times, and then Henry leaned forward, popping back into view moments later, the women unaware Henry had wiped his blade clean on the ragged shirt of the small corpse.

Walking back to Mary and Cindy, he grinned. "Nothing to worry about, just a lone deader. Took care of him with this." He said, patting the sheath of the panga.

"Okay, Henry, whatever. You know, I understand we're just women folk, but it would be nice to be let in on what the hell's happening," she snapped, a small bit of her foul mood seeping out. Then she turned and walked away from Henry, going in the same direction as Jimmy. Henry turned to look at Cindy, his face blank with surprise at her outburst.

Cindy looked back at him and shrugged, not understanding why her friend had flew off the handle, then she followed Mary across the plain.

Jimmy came up next him, returning from his recce. He had seen Mary's outburst and smiled at Henry.

"What's her problem? That time of the month?"

"Don't let her hear you say that, Jimmy, or she's liable to gut you like a fish," Henry said, watching Cindy and Mary talking together in the grass a few yards away from him.

Turning to Jimmy, he gestured towards the tree line. "So what'd you find? Anything out there?"

"Hell, yeah, there's a fenced in community there," he said and gestured with his right index finger. "There's a chain-link fence just past the trees. Those rooftops over there are inside the fence."

"See anybody moving about?" Henry asked.

"No, but I was only there for a few seconds. Didn't want to be spotted," Jimmy said.

Henry nodded. "Good move. Well, let's get to the fence and follow it. We're bound to find a gate sooner or later."

Jimmy nodded, and the two men went over to collect the women. Henry flashed Mary a smile, but she was having none of it, and turned away from him, moving off in the direction Jimmy pointed.

Jimmy chuckled at that and patted Henry's shoulder with understanding. "Don't feel so bad, pal, it happens to all of us, just be glad you're not sleeping with her, then it's ten times worse."

Henry sighed, *women*, what can you do but just go with it and pray for the best? He thought, then started walking behind the others.

With Mary on point, the companions stepped through the tree line, and with the chain-link fence in view, started walking parallel with it. Either they would see someone inside the camp or they would find a gate. Sooner or later one or the other would happen.

Twenty minutes later they were still walking, the steel mesh fence on their right never ending. Henry had moved up next to Mary and for a while she pretended he wasn't there.

Finally Henry spoke up. "Look, Mary, I don't know what's troubling you, and I can't try to fix it if you don't tell me, so for the hundredth time, what's wrong?"

Mary looked askance at Henry and when she saw the genuine concern on his face, her own countenance melted.

"Fine, I'll tell you," she sighed. "It's just, sometimes you act like I can't protect myself, you know? I mean, haven't I proved my worth to both you and Jimmy enough times already? I'm not the helpless waif you and Jimmy found on the road last year."

"Of course you're not. So where's all of this coming from?"

"Coming from? What just happened a little while ago? You saw something in the grass and you told me to stay away, like I was some small child that needed to be protected. I'm not Henry, I can shoot just as good as you men and I think I've learned a lot about hand to hand combat in the months we've spent together."

"You have, I'd have you at my back anytime, you know that," Henry said, emphatically.

Mary stopped, Henry and the others stopping as well. Jimmy and Cindy hung back, wanting to give the two of them some privacy.

"Oh yeah? So then why didn't you have me come into the grass with you?"

"You want the real answer? The truth?"

"Yes, I do," she said, her eyes wide with frustration.

"Jesus, Mary, you already know the answer. It's because I love you like a daughter and I don't know what I'd do if anything ever happened to you. I guess sometimes I get a little over protective and I'm sorry, but I can't help it." Henry said, emotion filling his eyes.

Mary stepped closer to him and reached out her hands for him to take. He did, and the two stood staring into each others eyes.

Whatever anger Mary had bottled up inside her seemed to disappear. "I'm sorry Henry; I don't know what got into me. I should be glad you care so much about me, not angry."

Henry squeezed her hands, and then let go. "That's okay. So, are we good now?"

She nodded and a slight smile crossed her lips. "Yeah, we're good...Dad."

"What? Don't do that. That's not funny. That daughter thing was just a reference. I'm nobody's father."

Jimmy ran up to Henry and almost jumped on his back. "Oh, don't be like that, old man; you're certainly old enough to be a father to all of us."

Henry slid out of Jimmy's grasp and pointed a finger at him. "Now cut that out. I feel old enough as it is without you guys reminding me every five minutes. Now enough of this shit, we need to get moving. It'll be dark in a few hours and I want to be either inside this fence or somewhere else. And seems we don't know where that might be, I think you should all move your young asses."

"Fine, fine, I hear ya. Come on, Cindy, us youngin's need to keep moving," Jimmy told Cindy.

Cindy flashed Henry a grin and then the two of them took point, leaving Mary and Henry alone for a few seconds.

Henry held out the crook of his arm for Mary, like he wanted to escort her to the Prom. "Shall we, my dear?"

Giggling slightly, she slid her arm through his, her other hand on her weapon.

"Why, thank you kind sir, I would be delighted."

With the birds singing in the treetops, the four companions continued onward, following the chain-link fence to its ending.

* * *

The gate to the fence appeared almost unexpectedly as the four companions walked out of a group of trees and into the open road that once led into the community.

Henry saw the brown sign almost as soon as he turned around. The sign had the words: **GREENWOOD ESTATES**, in neat script across its surface.

A guard shack stood on the left, the roof modified to have a man stand on it. On the roof the man would have a perfect firing line to the road.

Where there was once an open road with a single pole going across it to stop vehicular traffic, now there were car tires filled with sand piled six feet high.

Behind the tires two men stood with automatic rifles. Weapons were cocked the moment Henry and the others stepped out of the woods, but thankfully the guards were professionals and didn't shoot first and ask questions later.

Henry noticed the asphalt of the road was stained a dark maroon in several places, a telltale sign of a battle or an attack against the settlement, the manifestations of violence hard to erase.

Henry cursed his carelessness and said a silent thanks that he wouldn't have to pay for his mistake with the lives of his friends and himself.

With hands to his sides, as far away from his weapons as he could, he moved toward the barricade.

"Halt, stranger. One more step and I'll fill you full of holes. State you name and business here," one of the men said, racking a round into the rifle.

"Whoa there, easy fellas. My name's Henry and these are my friends, Mary, Cindy and Jimmy. We're travelers. We came upon your town by accident and wondered if we could stay for a night or two. We have a few things we could trade for room and board."

The guard seemed to ponder Henry's words, and Henry was starting to become concerned when the second guard raise his rifle and aimed it directly at Henry's head, squeezing the trigger and sending a round directly at him.

There was no time to move, let alone try to get off a shot of his own. All Henry could do was wait for the impact of the round and then the sweet oblivion of death.

Chapter 14

The bullet flew past Henry's head, taking a few stray strands of hair with it. Henry opened his eyes and fell into a crouch, his right hand reaching for his Glock.

He was about to shoot the guard who had shot at him, when he saw Jimmy take aim and send a barrage of bullets at something behind him.

Swiveling on his heels, he saw more than a score of shambling dregs of dead humanity coming up the road and the tree line bordering the shoulder of the asphalt, the piles of branches and leaves slowing them down somewhat.

Henry looked back to the guards to see them quickly opening a small gate to the right of the guard shack, the guard motioning for Henry and the others to get inside.

Turning back to the horde of undead charging at him and his friends, he sent a few rounds into the main group of ghouls. Only one round was a head shot, the others striking arms and shoulders.

Henry frowned at the wasted ammunition. He was rushing his shots, unable to get a handle on the situation.

He saw Mary take aim and fire, emptying her revolver and then reloading with rounds she had in her vest pocket. Every shot she took was a headshot, the corpses falling to the road to entangle the ones behind it.

Cindy was also putting her rifle to good use, every shot striking a zombie in the eye or forehead, the now very dead corpses falling to the pavement to join the others slaughtered before it.

But it didn't slow the rest of the undead army; they knew no fear or doubt or trepidation; only hunger. And Henry and his friends were on the menu if they didn't get away quickly.

"Fall back, into the compound, now!" He screamed, starting to move towards the barricade. The guards used their automatic weapons sparingly. The weapons on single shot only, despite the fact they had a clear line of fire to the undead.

Making sure his friends were with him, he sent two more rounds into the heads of the closest ghouls, dropping them to the ground like sacks of dirt.

One got under his guard and tried to take a bite out of his neck.

His gun was at stomach height and he fired three quick shots into the creature's abdomen, shredding dried muscle and splintering ribs, the rounds continuing out of its rotted body to strike another behind it. He kicked it away with his foot and turned to run, but the creature lunged once more, unfazed by the body shots.

But behind it was others, preparing to jump on him. With a quick look over his shoulder, he saw Jimmy and the women running into the compound, and he realized he was alone.

With his left hand keeping the snapping teeth at bay, he spun the zombie around so its back was to him and he jammed his gun and arm through the hole he had made in the creature's torso, the barrel of his weapon sticking out its stomach.

Pointing the weapon at an upward angle, he shot round after round at the attacking ghouls until the clip went dry.

But it had worked, his bullets striking their targets, knocking some to the road, the others only hesitating for a moment and then coming toward him again.

"Henry, get its head up!" Cindy screamed from behind the barricade. She had her rifle resting on the topmost tires, her eye against the gun sight. Henry did as he was told; ducking low, knowing to hesitate was to die.

Forcing the deader's head as high as it would go; he shifted his body to give Cindy a clear view of its head.

The rifle cracked and a neat little hole appeared in the back of the zombie's skull, black ichor dripping out to roll down its back. The body went slack and Henry slid his Glock out of its torso, shaking the gore from his arm. His weapon would need the best cleaning of its life when he had a chance, he thought, shaking the blood from the barrel.

Turning on his feet, he charged toward the barricade, jumping through the opening as it was slammed shut behind him; a ghoul bouncing off it a split second later, the animated corpse was so close to Henry's escaping body.

Cindy swiveled her rifle and shot the ghoul in the ear, brain matter flying out the other ear with the rest of the bullet.

With the guards help, the few remaining undead were put down in no time, the barricade keeping them at bay, allowing the companions to pick their shots and make them count.

Jimmy used his shotgun, the street sweeper blowing off arms and legs, the road becoming a bloody mess of gore.

When the last zombie was put down, everyone breathed a sigh of relief. Henry walked over to the guard who had shot at him and reached out his hand, the guard taking it. "I thought you were trying to kill me. I'm glad I was wrong," he said with a grin.

The guard took the hand offered to him and pumped it three times, smiling widely. "The name's Richards and I agree with you one hundred percent, plus, if I had wanted to kill you, well then, you never would have gotten a word off."

Henry stopped shaking with the man and his grin turned into a slight frown. "I suppose so. Still, thanks for taking that deader out."

"Deader? What the fuck's that?" The second guard asked, moving next to Henry. Henry was pleased to see the man's rifle was hanging by its strap, the man not feeling threatened by Henry or the others.

"It means a zombie," Mary said, walking up to the men. "We got tired of calling them zombies. Too 1980's horror movie, you know?"

Richards nodded, understanding. "Oh, sure, we always just called them *retreads*. One of our guys used it once and it kind of stuck, but I guess your name works too." He said, smiling at Mary. She smiled back and Henry noticed for the first time that Richards was about the same age as her.

Richards turned to the other guard and pointed to the guard shack. "Hey, Owens, get on the radio and tell them we need a cleanup crew out here, stat. It's gonna get pretty ripe, pretty quick, if we don't burn those retreads."

Owens nodded and ran into the shack, Jimmy following curiously, Cindy by his side.

"So why do you call them retreads? What's the significance of the name?" Mary asked Richards.

Richards kept one eye on the gate at all times, not shirking his duty. "Well, one of the guys worked in a tire place, you know, putting retreaded tires on trucks and stuff. That's how he got the name. Retreads are tires that were no good and then were given a new life. Kind of like those poor bastards out there, don't you think?"

Mary nodded. "Sure, I get it. It's pretty clever, actually."

Owens stuck his head out of the doorway. "Hey, Richards, they said they'll get us a few people in about an hour and wanted to know if you needed any help, otherwise."

"Nah, tell 'em we're fine, thanks to these nice people," he said, flashing Mary another smile. "And tell them we have strangers visiting for a day or so and that they should treat them well. They helped destroy the retreads that just came at us."

"Wilco, no prob'," Owens said and disappeared back into the shack.

"Does that happen often? Do you still have that many zombies around here?" Henry asked, Richards pulling his eyes away from Mary.

The guard shrugged. "It's not as bad as it used to be, but they're still out there. They usually gather together and come at us in twos and threes, but not usually like that. I'm just glad you guys were here." He held up his rifle. "These babies will fire a shitload of rounds a minute but without the ammo, they're nothing but clubs."

Henry nodded. "I saw, both you and Owens were firing on single shot. I thought that was odd."

"Yup, we've been low on ammo for a while now. We're trying to figure out how to make the ammunition, but it isn't as easy as you might think. But we've got books and encyclopedias. We'll figure it out eventually."

"If you don't, then there's always bows and arrows. An arrow to the brain is as good as a bullet." Henry said.

Richards laughed at that. "So it is, Henry, so it is. Come on, I'll get you heading in the right direction. There'll be someone to meet you when you get to the center of town. I can't leave until my shift is over."

"Oh, and when is that?" Mary asked, coyly.

Richards looked at his wristwatch and smiled at Mary. "I get off in about an hour or so. Maybe once you're settled I can show you around?" He asked.

"That would be nice," Mary said, batting her eyes sweetly.

Richards walked them to the end of the small road, and pointed down a fork that bent to the left. "Just follow that road for a half mile and you'll be in the town center. A man named Conrad will be there to get you set up for the night."

"Okay, thanks, Richards, see you later," Henry said.

Richards nodded and waved, jogging back to the barricade where Owens, Jimmy and Cindy were waiting. Once Richards had reached them, both Cindy and Jimmy moved away with a wave and a goodbye. Henry and Mary waited for them and in less than a minute the four companions were together again.

"All right then, let's go, I'm interested in what the town looks like," Mary said, starting off.

Henry chuckled at her back and glanced at Jimmy and Cindy. "The only thing she's anxious to see is that guy Richards again. Did you see the way those two were looking at each other?"

"So, and what's wrong with that?" Cindy asked a little defensively. "Doesn't she deserve to be with a man? Or do you think she's going to be celibate for the rest of her life? I swear, you men think sex is a one way street. You can have it anytime you want but when a woman wants it she's a slut." She turned her head away from Henry and Jimmy and moved down the road, trying to catch up with Mary.

Jimmy glared at Henry, his eyes angry. "Now look what you did. Do you think I'm gonna get any if she's in that kind of mood. Damn, Henry, we need to get you a girlfriend, and fast." Then he, too, moved off down the road, making sure not to get too close to Cindy when she was in one of her moods.

With a heavy sigh, Henry started off as well, walking all alone behind his temperamental friends.

And at the moment, that suited him just fine.

The two bodies hanging from the wooden gallows at the beginning of the town square could have been there for a few weeks or a few months, the condition of the corpses making it hard to tell.

The eyes were missing in both bodies, the birds eagerly plucking out the soft morsels from inside the eye sockets. The skin on the corpses was similar to parchment, the skeletal fingers clicking in the wind, while the bodies swayed gently back and forth.

Wooden signs were hung around each of the bodies, a rope tied around the shriveled and cracked necks.

TOOK WHAT WASN'T THERE'S TO HAVE, the signs read in loose script, the words carved into the wood with a chisel.

Henry slowed as the companions walked by the gallows, his eyes taking in the executed men. From the rope around each body it was clear they had been hanged.

Rough justice for a rough land.

"Well, at least if there are still executions going on, then there's some semblance of civilization left," Henry said, moving past the gallows.

"You think those dead bodies means there's civilization here?" Mary asked. She was over her mood swing and back to her normal, cheerful self.

"Yup, sure do. If those men were put to death for stealing, then that means it's not total anarchy here. There are still laws to follow and rules to obey. Best we watch ourselves. Don't want to step on some toes and wind up next to those poor bastards."

"I hear that," Jimmy said with a glance over his shoulder.

The streets were eerily quiet; no other people could be seen moving about. Henry had to admit it made him more than a little uncomfortable.

"Hey guys, look, a bar. Maybe we can get something to drink there," Cindy said moving onto the sidewalk and through the door.

"Cindy, wait a minute for the rest of us, you don't know what's in there!" Henry called after her, but it was no use, she was gone, having entered the building.

"I'm on it Henry, I got her," Jimmy said running towards the door. Mary looked to Henry for directions and he nodded for her to go as well.

Meanwhile he slowed his pace, his hand on his sidearm as he opened the door to the bar.

His concerns were unfounded. The place was empty except for one lone man behind the counter. The bartender was already in deep conversation with Cindy and when the others walked in he stood straighter, a smile on his lips.

"Welcome strangers, to Mickey's pub, sit down and I'll get you a drink," he said in a jovial tone.

"We don't have money, but we have ammo, if that's okay to trade with," Henry said. Despite the air of normalcy, he never took his hand off his Glock. If you let your guard down for only a second it could be your last.

The bartender nodded. "Sure, that'll be fine. Can always use more ammunition, but you don't need to pay here. You're the strangers that just helped defend the town right?"

Henry nodded, curious on how the man could have heard the news so fast.

The bartender pointed to the two-way radio on the shelf behind him. The man had heard the news just as soon as it had happened.

"So what'll it be?"

Jimmy swallowed hard and took a chance. "How about a couple of beers," he said hesitantly.

The bartender nodded. "Okay, four beers coming up," and proceeded to fill glass mugs from a keg sitting on the counter behind him.

"Holy shit, you have beer here?" Jimmy asked, unable to hide his amazement.

"Sure do," the barkeep said, placing a mug in front of Jimmy. "We have a fella in town who knows how to make it. So far his supplies are holding up, but in time I suppose he'll run out. Still, once he does he already said he'll start making moonshine, so we'll always have something to wash those troubles away."

Jimmy grinned, picking up his beer and taking a sip. Henry and the women waited to see what his opinion was and when Jimmy's face lit up and he took another sip, they each started to drink from their own mugs.

Wiping his mouth on his sleeve, Henry let out a loud belch. "Not bad, a bit bitter for my tastes, but damn good." He turned to look at the bartender. "So, is it Mickey?" Henry asked the man.

Shaking his head while he wiped the countertop, the bartender sighed. "No, I'm not Mickey. Mickey was the owner of this place. He died back when the rains came. Poor bastard ended up like one of them things outside the fence. He ended up with a bullet in his brain, but I don't know who gave it to him. I was his friend and so the town gave me the bar to run in his absence. Name's Giles, Giles Mason."

Henry introduced himself and the others and once all the introductions were finished, Jimmy spoke up.

"Speaking of the town, where the hell is everybody? It's like a ghost town out there," Jimmy said, taking another sip from his mug. Though the beer wasn't cold, it still tasted wonderful.

"The townspeople have all gathered together at the day care center, though it's not used for that anymore. No, now it's where we decide the fate of lawbreakers. That's where everyone is now. We found Thomas Mallory behind a dumpster with old man Simmons' grandson. The sick bastard was trying to molest the boy. He's only seven for Christ's sake. That's where everyone is, there sentencing him today. In fact, I was just about to close up and go over there myself, if you'd be interested in joining me."

Henry shrugged, looking to the others for their opinions on the subject.

"Why not, Henry, it'll give us a chance to see civilization still in action," Jimmy quipped, Henry flashing him a frown.

"Fine, we'll go, but remember, whatever happens, it's none of our business. That goes especially for you Mary," he said, glaring at her.

She knew what he meant. Mary had a soft spot for others and sometimes it would get in the way of their survival. Henry had no problem with helping another human being in distress, but only if it didn't put his life, or the life of his friends, at risk.

She only nodded, understanding what he was telling her. "I'll be good Henry, I promise, after all, we're only guests here; their politics are none of our concern."

Finishing off the rest of his beer, Henry nodded. "Good girl, I'm glad you agree with me. Well then, Mr. Mason, we'd be glad to join you."

"Please, call me Giles, everyone does," Mason said.

"Fine, Giles, let's go." Henry added.

As Mason stepped out from behind the counter, Henry's eyes went wide at the sight of a double barrel shotgun, a 30-odd-6, if Henry was right. The weapon could blow a man clear in half, if he was shot the right way. Mason saw Henry's face and chuckled, lowering the weapon.

"Oh, sorry about that. Had it ready when you folks came in, just in case; you can never be too careful."

"Glad we passed the test," Jimmy said, admiring the large weapon. Looking at his own shotgun he felt like a man comparing the size of his penis, and feeling grossly outmatched.

Cindy patted his shoulder, sensing his mood. "Don't worry, lover. It's what you do with it that matters, not the size," she said, holding up her small caliber .22 rifle.

Jimmy grunted and then slid off his stool, following the others out the door.

Jimmy noticed Mason didn't lock the bar as they walked across the street. Then he decided the man probably didn't have to in a town where men were hanged for stealing.

Mason talked the entire way to the day care center, Henry and the others listening patiently. All the companions knew if you had someone willing to talk, let him. You never knew what small bit of information you might pick up that could be useful somewhere down the road.

Mason led them in and out of the warren of streets until Henry believed he was definitely lost. Sometimes he would catch site of the perimeter fence, the chain-link surrounding the entire town.

"Now, we didn't have enough fencing to surround the entire town, mind you. So we moved everyone into a few square blocks and just sealed it in. So far it's kept the retreads from getting in here. Well, that and a few good head shots."

Henry nodded, not saying anything. There was really nothing to say. It had been the same all across America and most of the world.

When the undead attacked, towns everywhere barricaded themselves in and hoped they would be safe for another day.

Only when the rains fell and turned unsuspecting people into undead zombies, then the same fences became deathtraps as the people became trapped inside their own man-made prisons with the undead nipping at their heels. Luckily, though, many towns had overcome the rains and had continued to survive, scraping by with hard work and a will to overcome whatever came their way.

If there was one species that would fight 'till its last breath, then it was man.

"Looks like you guys did a bang up job of it, too, this place looks pretty safe compared to some of the places we've been," Jimmy said, looking around the street and the nearest buildings. A few first floor buildings had broken windows, a clear sign that not all had been peaceful in the quiet little town.

The five of them continued on and as they moved through the streets, Henry started hearing the sound of a large crowd of people. With every step they took, the sounds of yelling and cheering grew louder until they couldn't have been more than a block away.

Rounding a corner at an intersection, the stoplights all dark with lack of power, Henry and the others slowed as their eyes took in the tableaux in front of them.

Inside a waist high chain-link fence, which was once used to keep toddlers inside the playground while their parents worked their day jobs, were more than fifty people, all yelling and screaming at the man on a small podium.

Next to the man were three others, two men and a woman. Each of these people wore black robes, similar to what a judge would wear while presiding over court, but also resembling a clergyman's cassock.

The man the crowd appeared to hate was tied with his hands behind his back, his legs shackled with a metal chain. Henry glanced over the crowd, his eyes immediately spotting at least five men with automatic rifles. If he had to guess, he would have said they were security for the little shindig he now found himself in.

Mason smiled at the companions and then ran off. "You guys can do what you want, but I'm going to get a front row seat." Then he was off, disappearing into the crowd almost immediately.

"Let's hang back here!" Henry shouted over the crowd. "We can see fine and if things turn bad we can run for it!"

The others nodded, understanding him. The faces of the crowd were wide with anger, all of their emotions being taken out on the man on the podium. Henry frowned. If the man charged with the crime of molesting a child was true, then he was glad he was being punished, but he couldn't help wonder what the punishment would be. If a man was hanged for stealing, then what would be the penalty for molesting a boy?

The woman wearing the black robe stepped up to a small dais on the podium, raising her hands for silence. At first the crowd continued yelling, but after only a few short seconds they began to quiet down, obviously respecting the woman on the podium or the weapons of the guards who shifted them uneasily in their hands.

The woman waited patiently until all were silent, only a few muffled voices still being heard and eventually, they too, were quickly quieted.

The woman held a clip board in her hands and she rifled through the papers on it, pushing them over the top of the clip-board to see the next page.

When she spoke, her voice was loud and strong, filled with confidence and authority; this was a woman used to being obeyed.

"Thomas Mallory, you have been accused of the crime of pedo-philia and have been found guilty by myself and my two peers. For this most abhorrent act, we sentence you to death."

The crowd cheered at the verdict, some tossing empty cans and rolled up paper at the bound man. Henry could see the man's face and saw the tears streaming down his cheeks; the man's counte-nance one of abject fear.

He sensed Mary's uneasiness next to him and he moved closer to her. "You okay?"

She nodded. "Yeah, I'll be fine, it's just a little unsettling; that's all."

"Don't see why, Mary," Jimmy said, "the friggin pervert's gonna get what he deserves. Way I see it, they should have done this to all of those freaks before the world fell apart, anyway. Maybe the world collapsing has knocked some sense into a few people, like the rulers of this town.

Henry didn't answer. "Whatever his feelings about the subject, they really didn't matter here. This was all out of his control. This time he was just an innocent bystander.

The woman was speaking again, her voice carrying on the wind loud and clear.

"Though we would normally hang you for a crime against this town, we feel your crime is so vile, so disgusting, that you should be killed in one of the most painful ways we can conceive, so as your crime is so barbaric and sick, so will your death be the same. Thomas Mallory, I sentence you to be stoned to death, carried out immediately, here, in this yard." She turned her attention to the crowd and gestured to the pile of stones and bricks off to the side of the podium.

"People of Greenwood, gather one projectile a piece and then line up. But pay attention, we don't want an ambitious soul to end up striking a fellow member of the town. Take your time and aim your shots, accordingly.

The crowd shuffled to the pile, someone handing out the stones to make the process move faster. In no time at all, the entire crowd of people were each holding a piece of stone, brick, or mortar.

Someone with two bricks tried to hand Henry a piece and he politely said no thank you, the man moving away eager to give his extra piece of brick away to someone who wanted it.

"Oh my God, it's so barbaric. If they want to kill the man, then put a bullet in his head or just cut his throat. This isn't civilized, it's just plain inhuman," Mary said, disgusted at what was taking place. "How can people do this to another human being?"

"Now, Mary, you promised," Henry said. "Besides, by killing this man it keeps the rest of the populace in line. No one wants to wind up in that poor bastard's place."

"No shit, If I was him, I think I'd be trying to bite my own tongue off and drown in the blood before I'd let myself be stoned to death," Jimmy said, shaking his head.

Cindy was silent, merely watching everything with an almost quiet detachment.

"Guards," the woman on the podium said, "place Mallory on the grass in the middle of the crowd and secure him to the flag-pole."

Mallory whimpered as two guards pushed him down the podium and into the center of the large yard. Off to the man's right were a jungle-gym and a see-saw, strangely out of place in the execution area.

"Ready! Aim, and throw your stones!" The woman yelled, a fierce light in her eyes, as if the woman was getting off on the carnage to come.

The crowd let fly their projectiles, a barrage of heavy items striking the man almost at the same time.

All Henry could do was watch and hope one of the bricks knocked the man unconscious, sending him to oblivion with the least amount of pain.

But luck wasn't with Thomas Mallory this day. The first blow he felt was across his cheek, a sharp stone slicing it open. Another stone struck his front teeth, knocking them out, the man spitting teeth like watermelon seeds.

A large chunk of mortar struck his left eye, puncturing the orb and blinding him.

He tried to look away and protect his right eye but there were people all around him, tossing and hurling bricks and stones.

A large concrete block struck his ribs, breaking three of them, and he tried to suck in air as one of his lungs became punctured.

Both his shoulders became dislocated and he tried to slide to the ground, only the ropes securing him holding him upright. Another sharp brick glanced his forehead, leaving a red gash that seeped bright blood over his face.

The man was screaming in pain, begging to be killed and end his suffering, but the crowd only became more agitated.

Another rock struck his nose, crushing it, blood running freely to soak into his shirt.

Through babbling gibberish, the man pleaded to die; praying one of the rocks would just crush in his skull and end his suffering.

Henry watched, sick to his stomach, the scene of wanton violence hard to take for even the hardened warrior. In practice what the citizens of the town were doing made sense, but to witness it or to take part in it was another thing, altogether. The more he watched the grotesque execution, the more he started to agree with Mary.

At least the men who had been hanged on the gallows had been killed quickly when their necks had snapped.

Another thin rock struck the bloody man in his right eye, piercing the socket like a small spear. The man let out an ear splitting squeal, now fully blind. Still, he remained conscious; none of the wounds so far inflicted enough to kill him.

For a moment there was a lull as the townspeople exhausted their supply of projectiles, but then a few men and women started gathering the rocks from the grass, the few who were close enough to Mallory taking the time to spit on him in disgust.

When their arms were full, they started to hand out the bricks and stones again, most stained a dull red now, and prepared to continue the onslaught.

Henry watched quietly. The way the organized men and women picked up the rocks and then handed them out while the others waited patiently told him this town had done this before. The question was, how many times and for what crimes?

When the crowd was once again armed, the woman on the podium raised her hand.

"Ready, Aim, throw your rocks!" The woman screeched out to the crowd, her hair having come undone in a few places, the woman looking like she was having sex, she was so excited and covered with a fine sheen of perspiration despite the coolness of the day.

More rocks and bricks struck the wounded man, this time his anguished cries becoming dimmer as he lost pint after pint of blood.

Henry looked away, deciding he'd had enough. He was about to ask the others if they would leave with him when he turned to see Mary crossing the street, her .38 in her hand.

"Mary, stop, where are you going?" Henry asked.

She ignored him, her face set in stone, her jaw set.

"Dammit, I knew this would happen!" Henry yelled, slapping Jimmy hard on the shoulder and pointing to Mary.

"Holy shit, not again," Jimmy yelled.

Mary strode through the edge of the crowd and stopped. She'd had enough of this excuse of an execution and her soul could stand it no longer. Pushing a few people away from her, which quickly turned at the intrusion, but when they saw the woman with her gun drawn, they quickly moved out of her way.

Without preamble, Mary lined up the bloody head in her sights and pulled the trigger, sending a round into the man's skull.

His head snapped back and the man remained still, brains and blood dribbling out of the hole in his skull to fall onto the grass.

Mary lowered her weapon and seemed to come out of a trance. She had been so upset she hadn't realized what she had done until it was over, her subconscious seeming to take control of her body. With the sound of the weapon firing, the crowd stopped hurling rocks and all eyes turned to look at Mary.

The woman on the podium swung her face to the dead prisoner and then like radar, her eyes found Mary.

"Seize her! She has disrespected our ways! She must be punished!"

Mary stood there, her mouth falling open, too shocked to say anything, when Henry grabbed her arm and pulled her off her feet.

"Come on, Mary, it's time to go. I think we overstayed our welcome!" He yelled, pushing back through the edge of the crowd, thrusting people out of his way in his urgency to escape.

The guards chased after them, not firing in fear of striking the townspeople.

Henry used that to his advantage, weaving his way through the mob. Jimmy was right there as they exited the last line of people and he fired his shotgun over their heads, causing instant panic.

Like tossing a firecracker into a flock of pigeons in a park, the crowd erupted in mass hysteria. No one knowing where the danger was, but all wanting to escape from it.

Cindy was waiting for them across the street and was soon joined by Henry, Mary and Jimmy. The four of them took off down a small alley, hoping to become lost in the winding streets.

Just before he rounded the corner of the alley, the wall exploded, a missed shot coming from behind him. Henry spun on his heels to see two guards at the entrance to the alley.

Henry sent two shotgun blasts of his own down the alley, the small confines of the walls an easy killing zone.

The two guards were thrown from their feet, landing heavily on the sidewalk. Whether they were dead or not, Henry didn't know as he was around the other end of the alley and was running down the street, hot on the heels of Mary.

The companions ran for almost fifteen minutes, the heavy backpacks on both Jimmy and Henry slowing them down.

Mary spotted a building with boarded up windows and she pulled a few planks out with her hands, the sheer adrenalin giving her added strength.

With a quick look over their shoulders to make sure no one had spotted them entering the building, they all climbed in, Henry doing his best to re-secure the planks over the windows. It would do for a cursory inspection, but if anyone looked too hard, it would be easy to see the planks weren't sitting properly in their frames.

Deciding one worry at a time, the companions moved deeper into the shadows of the dusty building while figures floated by the boarded up windows, the townspeople on the hunt for them.

In the wan light of the room, only a few slivers of sunshine piercing the gloom through the wooden slats, Henry looked at Mary, his face stern.

Mary smiled slightly, not really having an answer for her lack in judgment.

"Look at the bright side, Henry. We probably weren't going to stay long here anyway," she joked, her voice cracking at the end of the sentence.

Henry repositioned his shotgun, keeping it ready to fire on a seconds notice. Glancing over to Jimmy, who was hovering near one of the windows, watching the street warily, Henry sat down on a wooden crate sitting in the middle of the room and let out a deep breath he'd been holding in.

"That's okay, Mary," he sighed, "to tell you the truth, I was almost ready to shoot the poor bastard myself."

Chapter 15

"What the hell were you thinking?" Henry gasped at Mary, while Jimmy watched the window for signs of movement.

"I'm sorry, Henry, I didn't think, I just couldn't stand to see that man suffering like that. It was barbaric, like we've returned to the middle-ages." Mary apologized.

"Middle-ages? Mary, the man was as good as dead. At most you saved him a few minutes or an hour of suffering. Now we need to get out of here before they find us. God knows what they'll do to you when they find you...and us for being with you."

"All right, Henry, you said your peace, now lay off. She was only doing what she thought was right and you said it yourself, you wanted to do the same thing," Cindy said as she moved next to Mary for moral support.

Henry nodded slightly. "Sure I said I wanted to, not that I would," he retorted brusquely.

Moving from the window, Jimmy gathered next to the others. "Well, whatever would or could have happened is irrelevant now. We need to get out of here. There's still people on the street, so I guess we're stuck here for a while, at least until it gets dark," Jimmy said, sitting down on an old office chair. The chair had more than an inch worth of dust on it, but the man barely noticed.

Henry moved to the window, taking Jimmy's watch. A shadow stopped in front of the window, seeming to hover there, the streaks of sunlight surrounding the dark form.

The companions held their breath, weapons ready in case they'd been found, but then the shadow moved on, everyone letting out the breath they had been holding unconsciously.

"So what's the plan?" Jimmy asked, laying his shotgun across his lap.

Henry rubbed the stubble on his chin, his face feeling like course sandpaper. If they ever got a second to stop and breath he wanted to shave.

"The plan is simple. We stay here until nightfall and then we get the hell out of town. Maybe we can accommodate some supplies as we leave, but it's not a priority."

"Okay, then, who's up for a game of cards?" Jimmy asked pulling a cracked and ripped deck of playing cards from his backpack. He had found the cards in a souvenir shop at the shopping mall and had traded it for a shotgun shell. Since then, he used them every chance he got. Henry believed it was a small way for the young man to stay attached to the life they had all left behind.

"I'll play you, Jimmy." He glanced at Mary. "Hey, Mary, how 'bout taking over here?" Henry requested, leaving the window.

Mary nodded and Henry and Jimmy sat around an old barrel, another office chair in the corner perfect for Henry to use. After clearing the layer of dust from the barrel's top, the two men got down to playing blackjack, Cindy watching silently.

From Mary's vantage point she couldn't see the cards the men played with, so she turned her attention back to the window, her eyes peeking through the wooden slats to monitor the street outside.

Inside her mind, her thoughts floated around like a piece of paper in a hurricane, the tempest tossing the object around without care.

Though she wasn't ashamed of what she'd done, putting that man out of his misery, she did regret putting her friends in danger. Sometimes she forgot she wasn't alone in the world anymore. She had moved out of her family home when she had turned eighteen and had never looked back.

Settling in the Midwest, her parents had been far away and she had been alone, one young woman against the world.

Sure they were only a phone call away, but it wasn't the same as having them close enough to touch and see.

But she had persevered; becoming a successful secretary and saving to one day buy a home of her own. But then the world had fallen apart, the dead unbelievably returning to life.

She smiled back to the first day she had seen a real zombie, he had been a telephone repair man and had attacked her. She might have died that day if Jimmy hadn't arrived with a heroic rescue, pulling her into the car he had been driving and the two of them making a run for it.

Glancing across the dimly lit room, she stared at Jimmy. There had been a time when the two of them might have become an item, but the moment had passed and now the two were closer than most brothers and sisters. Running and fighting for your life everyday, side by side, will do that to people.

Her eyes drifted to Henry, his stern face crinkling in disproval as he lost to Jimmy once more, apparently. Though he could be gruff at times, she knew the man had a heart of gold and she loved him deeply.

She had never really been close to her father and Henry had filled that role easily, the two forming a bond that was as strong as iron.

Cindy laughed when Jimmy pulled a card from the deck that made Henry curse and Mary glanced to her. Cindy's flowing blonde tresses still looked beautiful, despite the sweat and dirt in her hair and streaks covering her face.

The moment Jimmy had seen her, he had been smitten and the two had become an item, to the point the blonde girl had elected to travel with them. Mary was glad for that. It was nice to have at least one more female in the boys club that had become her life. Cindy understood things the two men would never understand as long as they had a penis between their legs.

Another shadow crossed the window and muffled voices could be heard coming from the other side.

At the exact same time all four of them raised their weapons, but once again luck was with them and the shadow moved on.

After a few tense heartbeats, nerves relaxed and the card game continued.

Leaning her head against the window, Mary tried to get more comfortable. It was hours until night would come and until then they were trapped in the small building with nothing but the dust bunnies in the corners of the room to keep them company.

*   *   *

"All right, I guess it's dark enough to move out," Henry said, stepping back from the window.

The past few hours had passed agonizingly slow, all of the companions wanting nothing more than to escape the town and get as far away as soon as possible.

Shrugging into his backpack, Jimmy grinned mischievously in the dark room. "So what's the plan? How do we get out of this crazy town?"

Henry moved closer to him, not wanting to talk too loud and risk being overheard by someone out on the street. In the last hour or so the search for them had dwindled to nothing and in the last ten minutes Henry had seen no sign of movement on the dark and lonely street outside the boarded up window.

"I figure we should keep to the shadows until we reach the perimeter fence. Once there, we can either climb it or cut our way to the outside," Henry said.

"Sounds too easy," Mary said, checking her .38. She had reloaded the spent rounds hours ago, but it still felt better to double check the weapon every once in a while. It just put her at ease.

"Too easy," Cindy said from next to Jimmy. "I just hope there are no surprises on our way there."

"I guess we'll be finding out in a minute, so if everyone's ready, let's get this show on the road." Henry said, picking up his shotgun.

With the soft clicking of weapons being cocked, Henry took the lead and approached the door. He had checked the place earlier to find there were no windows to the rear of the building and the one back door, an emergency door, was locked with a heavy chain and padlock. Without access to tools it would have taken a point blank round from the .38 or the shotgun to shatter the chain, and if they did, it was an almost definite possibility that someone on the outside would hear and sound the alarm, so it was back out the way they had entered, through the front door.

Henry cracked the door an inch, his eyes peeking out into the street. Nothing stirred.

Turning back to look at the others, he nodded curtly and opened the door wide enough to slip through, the others right behind him.

They had made it no more than a few feet from the building when a startled cry sounded from across the street.

"They're here! They're over here!" A voice yelled.

"Shit, I don't believe it!" Henry said, cursing under his breath.

A gunshot popped from across the street and a moment later a street sign clanged from the stray round.

All four of the companions stood perfectly still, their eyes scanning the darkness for the origination of the gunshot.

Then another weapon cracked, coming from the opposite end of the street. Henry saw the muzzle flash and sent a round toward the point he guessed the gunner would be.

No sound of pain came to his ears but multiple imprecations floated on the air, so he figured he'd missed his target, but gained some respect. Flashlights were appearing, the townspeople running toward the sounds of gunfire. Henry counted more than twenty and stopped counting.

"Shit, Henry, what the fuck do we do?" Jimmy asked, his shotgun waving in front of him. He fired into a group of approaching lights and was rewarded with a few cries of pain, some of the lights winking out.

Henry's mind was in a daze as he calculated the odds of standing their ground or trying to run for it, the later not a very good option. Once the crowd had found them, it would be easy for them to be hunted down and captured.

"Back in to the building. At least we have some cover there," he ordered the others, though he was loathed to do so.

Firing shots at the twinkling lights and muzzle flashes, they quickly retreated back into the building.

Firing one more round from his shotgun, Henry dove through the door, kicking it shut with his foot, the wood splintering as rounds chipped out divots in the heavy wooden door.

One round sneaked past the closing door to shatter a light fixture across the room, shards of glass raining down on Mary. She rolled away from the raining glass and shook her head free of any stray shards, glad it was only glass and not something more deadly.

Jumping to his feet, Henry pointed to Jimmy. "Get on the second floor. Anyone comes near us, take them out!"

Jimmy nodded and took off toward the stone stairwell, taking the steps two at a time.

"Cindy, go with him," Henry told her, the woman jumping to her feet and following Jimmy.

Henry moved to the boarded window and knocked one of the lower planks away with the butt of his shotgun. Sending a few shots into the night, he was immediately forced to fall to the floor as round after round flew threw the window, the planks like paper to the heavy caliber barrage.

"Jesus, they must be using those automatic weapons the guards were carrying," Mary said, crawling across the floor to come up next to Henry who was quickly reloading his shotgun with shells from his pockets.

"Ya think?" He replied.

"What are we going to do?" She asked, a little uncertainty evident in her voice.

"Simple, we get out of here and live another day," he prevaricated. Though he was trying to stay positive the truth was they were in a bad situation, but he wouldn't give up until he was dead, and nowadays even that didn't stop some folks.

"Get to that back door and blow off the lock, the time for stealth is over. If the alley's clear, then get back here and let me know. Then we'll get the others and get out that way!"

She nodded and crawled toward the backroom, bullets flying over her head.

Reaching the backdoor, she heard Henry firing his shotgun again, answering fire peppering the building.

Putting the muzzle of the .38 against the chain, she squeezed the trigger, the chain jumping as one of the links shattered under the round.

Pulling the chain free, she cracked the door and with no sound or cries of alarm, she opened it a little more.

In the darkness she made out the shapes of a dumpster and an old car with flat tires. Opening the door wide enough to stick her head out, she almost fell back when a round ricocheted off the door only inches from her head.

Jumping back, she slammed the door closed, sliding the large bolt into place, securing the door once more.

"Shit," she muttered under her breath. Mary wasn't one for cursing, but in really dire circumstances she had always felt warranted. And at the present moment, this was one of those moments.

Running back to the entrance to Henry's room, she dropped to all fours and shimmied over to him.

"So how's it look back there?" Henry asked, sitting with his back to the window. Jimmy's shotgun roared from above and the sound of Cindy's rifle cracked repeatedly.

"No good," she said, shaking her head, "the alleys got people in it. I nearly got my head shot off before I closed the door."

"Dammit," he spit, chancing a look through the window. The planks covering the window were riddled with holes, resembling a mock Swiss cheese. He was still amazed they were still on the frame at all. "I've got to tell you, Mary, I have no goddamn idea how we're going to get out of here."

"Oh, God, Henry, I'm so sorry I shot that man. If I could take it all back I would," she said apologetically. "Now my foolish action is going to get us all killed...or worse."

"It doesn't matter. Forget about that now. It's water under the bridge. What you need to do is focus on the here and now. We've been in worse scrapes, hell; you remember when you and Cindy were trapped in that house in Pittsfield with the streets full of zombies? Betcha didn't think you were gonna get out of that one, or what about the time we had to hide out at Pineridge Labs and had to crawl into the ductwork. The odds were against us then, too, but we made it."

"Yes, we did, but we didn't all make it," Mary said with sadness in her voice.

Henry poked his head up to the window and fired the shotgun and dropped back down, continuing the conversation as if he had never moved.

"Yeah, I know. You're talking about Blackie, aren't you?"

She nodded. "Yeah, he was a good dog. I still miss him, but even if he'd survived, he wouldn't have made it this far, not with the things we've seen and done. Still..."

More rounds shot through the window, one of the planks finally falling to the sidewalk. Cindy's rifle cracked twice more and then the barrage stopped.

Henry heard Jimmy's footsteps as he ran down the steps and came running into the room, his body silhouetted in the wan light.

"Get down, you damn fool, before you get shot," Henry told him.

"It's not a problem, Henry, they've stopped. There's a woman outside in the street, I think it's the same one from the stoning. She's just standing there, waiting for something. I think she wants to talk to us."

Henry turned around on his knees and peeked out the window. "What? That's crazy, only a damn idiot would walk out there in the middle of a gunfight," he said.

But sure enough, Jimmy was right.

Standing in the middle of the street, still wearing her black cloak stood the woman from the podium.

Henry had an itch in his trigger finger, almost wanting to gun the woman down where she stood, but he stopped himself. Maybe this could be their way out of this mess.

Then the woman started talking.

"Strangers, hear me! You have desecrated our town by killing one of our own and interfering in our ways. If you come out now, with your weapons lowered, I promise you will receive fair treatment. You are charged with disrupting an execution and the manslaughter of ten men who were trying to capture you!"

"Not bad, we've killed ten of them so far," Jimmy said next to Henry.

"Shut up, Jimmy, I want to hear her," Henry snapped as the woman continued.

"If you are found guilty of the crimes you have been charged with, you will be hanged. The most compassionate form of execution we have." She turned to look behind her, the street filling with men and women, most of them guards. All carried torches with them.

"If you do not comply, we will be forced to set fire to the building you are presently occupying and force you out. If that occurs, you will not be treated with such leniency."

"Leniency? Is she for real? We're supposed to just go out there and give ourselves up like cows to the slaughter? I don't think so." Jimmy spat, shock filling his voice.

"I agree." Henry said standing up, only his head showing in the window.

"No deal, lady. If you want us, then you're gonna have to come get us and I promise you, you're gonna lose a lot more than ten men if you try! Just let us leave and we'll never return!"

The woman pursed her lips, as if she was unaccustomed to being told the word no.

"Very well, you bring this on yourselves. Guards, do your duty!" And then she quickly stepped back, almost running away from the building. Henry smiled at that. He wondered if the people she ruled over knew she was a coward like most people when the chips came down.

The townspeople with the torches started forward and Henry opened up with a shotgun blast that knocked a man onto his back, the shells hitting the man in the neck, his head hanging from his shoulder by a few strands of tenuous flesh.

Despite the fact he was shooting live targets, Henry had become accustomed to head shots after killing hundreds upon hundreds of the undead.

Mary and Jimmy opened up with their own weapons, one on either side of him, while Cindy, hearing the gunfire, opened up with her rifle.

More than half the guards were taken down, some of them, Henry saw, were wearing body armor and crawled away after being shot.

He grunted at the sight.

Maybe head shots were the best shots even now.

While the guards continued to advance, a few went to the sides and came up to the building out of the companion's field of fire. Three torches flew into the windows, the guards retreating before they were shot. Cindy managed to hit one in the leg, the man hobbling away.

A crashing against the backdoor sounded and Mary jumped up and ran to the secured door, avoiding the spreading flames. Touching it, she pulled her hand away quickly, the door hot to the touch. As she watched, smoke began to creep under the door, curling upward in the darkness.

Cursing under her breath, she ran back to the others. "The backdoor is on fire, it's blocked!"

"Shit," Henry said while he tried to put out the flames of the spreading fire with an old moth-eaten blanket.

But the fire was spreading quickly and it was hopeless. Jimmy pulled a fire extinguisher off the wall and tried to put out the blaze. The canister sputtered for a few seconds and then was silent. Checking the gauge that read *empty,* Jimmy tossed the extinguisher away, disgusted.

It was getting hard to breath, the conflagration sucking all the oxygen from the room. Henry was already coughing, trying to breathe through his nose; the fumes making his nose run like a spigot.

Mary was coughing uncontrollably and Henry grabbed her. He retrieved his backpack and with Jimmy doing the same, the two men carried the almost unconscious woman up the stairs to the second floor.

Cindy turned as they entered and she rushed over to them, helping set Mary on a pile of crushed cardboard boxes.

"Oh, Henry, I'm sorry I couldn't stop the men with the torches, but they came at me tight against the building. If I leaned out I would have been shot." Cindy said, worry on her face.

"It's okay, Cindy, it's not your fault. Just stay positive. We've gotten out of worse scrapes than this.

Coughing hard, Jimmy came to his feet and moved to the window. No one was shooting, instead the townspeople were cheering as the building slowly burned.

"Sick fucks, they're gonna roast us alive and they're cheering like it's a friggin' barbecue," Jimmy spat, ducking back inside. He sent a shotgun blast into the crowd, some of the people scattering, most seeming to ignore it in the party-like atmosphere, their furor apparent.

It was like they were all lost in a trance-like state. Remembering how the townspeople acted at the stoning, he wondered if that wasn't a real possibility.

At least with the fire downstairs they were safe from an attacking enemy, but the fire was an even worse problem.

"We're safe up here for a little while. This building is mostly steel and concrete, but the flames will continue spreading until it'll be too much. In fact, it'll probably be smoke inhalation that kills us, not the fire. We'll just fall unconscious and that'll be that," Henry said solemnly.

"Well thanks for the fire lesson, Fire Marshall Bill, but I'm not quite ready to die just yet," Jimmy quipped, his eyes inspecting the room.

There had to be a way out of the building, the trick was to find it.

With the blaze consuming the first floor and already starting to work its way into the ceiling, and the smoke crawling up the stairs, the companions waited.

The question was; were they waiting to escape, or were they simply waiting to die?

Chapter 16

With the fire raging uncontrollably around them, Henry knew they had only minutes before the smoke overwhelmed them. Spotting a small door no more than two feet wide across the room, he quickly ran over to it, coughing and gagging from the toxic fumes.

The door was locked, so he leveled his shotgun near the doorknob and lock and sent a round into the door, the wood splintering like it was nothing more than paper.

Pulling the door inward, he looked up a steep flight of metal stairs. He didn't know where the steps led, but at the moment it really didn't matter.

Turning to the others, he started up the stairs.

"Up here, quick! It might be a way out!" He called, gesturing for them to hurry.

"A way out? It goes up? That's not much help," Jimmy said but still went and helped Mary to her feet. The woman was falling in and out of consciousness, the fumes overwhelming her.

"Doesn't matter. Even if it's another floor it still buys us some time. Now, move it!" He ordered.

Jimmy listened and half-dragged, half-carried Mary to the door, Cindy hanging on his other arm.

Henry came to help and he picked Mary up in his arms, carrying her up the stairs.

The stairs were steep and he was barely able to walk up them with Mary slumped in his arms, but he managed to finally reach another door.

Putting all of his weight behind his foot, he kicked the door open, the lightweight material almost falling off its hinges.

Stumbling onto the roof of the building, Henry fell to his knees, trying to clear his lungs of the smoke he'd inhaled. Jimmy followed him out the door a second later, falling to the rooftop, Cindy collapsing with him. The two were hacking and coughing, trying to gain their breath.

Despite the smoke blowing around them, every now and then a patch of clear air would appear and they sucked it in greedily.

Once they had regained a small measure of their composure, everyone retreated to the rear of the building. Henry looked over the side to the alley below, frowning. The fire escape was wreathed in flames, the entire back of the building glowing a bright orange with tinges of red.

"Jesus Christ, these sick bastards are willing to burn down the whole building just to get to us," Henry said, watching the flames crackle and snap.

"You've got to give them an 'A' for determination though, don't ya think?" Jimmy said askance of him. The man's eyes were red from smoke irritation and his nose was still running, but for now they were alive and breathing.

Henry grunted at his remark and then walked away, traversing the edge of the roof.

With the smoke billowing out the windows of the burning structure, he could barely see the street below.

That was good. If he couldn't see the townspeople below, then they couldn't see him on the roof.

When he had reached the west side of the building he looked down at the adjacent rooftop. It was a one-story brick building, its occupation unknown, but what he did notice was the roof was only twenty feet from them.

Jumping was out of the question, the distance from rooftop to rooftop far too high, plus he was two floors higher than the neighboring one.

His eyes inspected everything until he saw what he needed.

It had been hard to see in the darkness and with the smoke it had been nigh impossible, but once his eyes had spotted it, he'd wondered how he had ever overlooked it in the first place.

A telephone or cable wire ran from the roof he was occupying down to the neighboring brick building.

"Jimmy, get over here. I think I found our way out!" He called, careful not to speak loud enough to be heard from the ground.

Mary was coming around and Cindy was seeing to her, giving her a bottle of water to wash her face and clear her throat.

Jimmy jogged across the roof, his backpack left with the women. Henry noticed this and did the same, sliding out of the heavy burden and dropping it to the roof with a dull thud, the canned goods from the farmhouse adding weight to the pack.

"What's up? What you got?" Jimmy asked, looking around, but seeing nothing.

Henry pointed to the almost invisible black wire and smiled.

"Do you think that will hold us if we slide down it one at a time?"

Jimmy squinted, looking for the wire and his eyes opened wide when he finally separated it from the surrounding blackness.

"Son-of-a-bitch, yeah it might work, but if we're wrong, you know what'll happen to the first person over."

He nodded, his face set in stone. "Yeah, I know; whoever goes first will fall to their death...or worse, receive a broken limb and be caught and slaughtered by those bastards."

An explosion came from somewhere inside the building, the rooftop rocking slightly. Huge black clouds of obsidian smoke poured out of the building's sides, threatening to engulf the entire building in mere moments.

Henry turned and ran across the roof, stumbling over an object in the darkness. When his hands landed on the gravel roof, he had to immediately pull them back, rolling back to his feet.

"Jesus, the roof is hot and it's not residual heat from the sun. The fire's burning through the ceiling below us." Henry said, wiping the hot rocks from his hands, black tar sticking to his palms.

"Then let's go, either the cable holds us or it doesn't. No use putting it off," Jimmy stated at his side.

Henry nodded and they joined the two women, quickly filling them in on the new plan...the only plan.

Mary was conscious now, the light in her eyes burning bright as it reflected the light from the growing fire and said: "Well, then gentlemen, what are we waiting for?"

Less than five minutes later the companions were ready to make their escape from the rooftop. Jimmy had cut another electrical wire into multiple pieces using his hunting knife. The pieces of wire would be used as a make-shift sling, each of the companions wrapping it around the cable and then, *hopefully,* sliding to the safety of the neighboring rooftop.

Henry prepared to go first, not wanting the others to risk it when Cindy shoved herself between the cable and himself.

"No way, Henry, I'm first," she said, glaring up at him. "I'm the lightest. If the cable won't hold me, then what chance do the rest of you have? Plus, once I'm over on the other side I can help hold the wire steady for the rest of you."

Henry shook his head from side to side. "No way, out of the question. I'm the leader here and I say who goes first and that's me. I won't have one of you doing something I wouldn't do."

Mary pushed in front of him and said: "Fine, you said you would go, but this time Cindy is the better man for the job. Look, Henry we don't have time to argue, so this one time just give in and let her go," she finished, pleading with her eyes. She knew how stubborn Henry could get and this was one of those times that he needed to just let go and let someone else take the risk.

"She's right, Henry, Cindy is the lightest and the most athletic," Jimmy said, chiming in his two-cents.

Sighing, Henry turned his head away, realizing they were right. Turning back to face Cindy, he held out his hand to her.

"All right then, go, but you better make it or I swear to God I'll follow you to hell and tan your hide," he said to Cindy.

She leaned up and kissed him on the cheek and then turned and did the same to Jimmy. Jimmy flashed Henry a sly grin. "So now my girls kissing you? When I said you need a girlfriend, I didn't mean mine."

Henry scowled at Jimmy, insulted by the remark, but when he saw the younger man's face, he realized he was only joking.

"Very funny, smartass, how about paying attention to your girlfriend now," he quipped in return.

Cindy crawled out onto the edge of the roof, her rifle hanging from its strap and with a flash of her blue eyes and a smile, she pushed off.

Henry watched, his breath in his chest. She reminded him of a young girl out on the lake, sliding down the rope to fall into the water, only if Cindy fell, only hard concrete would break her fall.

But the cable held and Cindy zipped down the line, looking like a Ninja on a silent recon. The young girl dropped to the lower building's rooftop, rolling across it to come up against a metal box a few feet high, a ventilation unit or an air conditioning unit for the building's air system.

She wiped herself off and waved to the others that she was okay.

"She made it," Henry said, relieved. Turning to Mary, he helped her onto the edge. "Okay, honey, you're next. Just hold on tight to the electrical wire and let gravity do its thing."

Swallowing hard, she nodded. "I can do this, Henry, piece of cake," she joked, trying to psych herself up.

When she was ready, Henry gave her a push and she slid down into the darkness.

Cindy was waiting on the other side, pulling the wire taught to make it a smoother ride for Mary. It worked and Mary made it across with no problem.

Just before she reached the other roof, she had thought she had felt a slight jarring on the wire, but figured it was just her imagination and nerves combined. Then she was preoccupied with rolling across the rooftop and trying not to break anything.

Standing up, a little dizzy after her tumble, she waved to Jimmy and Henry.

Back on the roof, Henry cleared his throat, spitting a wad of phlegm onto the rooftop. The smoke had cleared his sinus' well, and he wondered if he would ever have mucus in his nose again.

"Okay, Jimmy, you're next. Once you're over, I'll send you the backpacks," Henry said while the man stepped up onto the edge and got into position.

Looking down into the side alley, nothing was moving. If there were townspeople down there, they were lost in the blackness of the night and smoke from the building.

With a tremble a piece of the roof fell in, the flames thrusting through like demon hands looking for victims.

"It's now or never, Jimmy, best get going. I'll be right behind you," Henry said.

"See you on the other side, old man," Jimmy said and then sailed off into the night.

With his added weight compared to the girls, Jimmy flew across the cable in no time, the cable dipping a little more from when Mary had crossed. Falling to the rooftop, he rolled until he came up hard against the metal structure on the roof.

The metal gave with a wrenching sound and Jimmy found himself becoming buried under sheet metal. An instant later both Mary and Cindy were there, pulling him free of his small prison.

Wincing as he stood up, Jimmy flexed the wrist on his right hand. He had fallen badly and had pulled something, but the more he opened and closed his hand, the more he was confident nothing was adversely damaged.

Waving to Henry, he waited as the backpacks were sent one at a time across the void. The second backpack had Henry's shotgun strapped to it and after a few seconds to untie the wire wrapped around the handles, Jimmy removed them from the cable.

Waving back to Henry, he gestured for him to make the crossing.

Henry stepped up to the ledge, prepared to swing out into the void, glancing behind himself one last time.

The rooftop resembled a lava field, fire shooting up from multiple holes as the tar melted, falling back into the openings.

Another explosion rocked the building; something inside igniting from the heat of the conflagration. Henry sucked in his breath like he was diving into a pool of water and stepped out into nothing.

Gravity took hold of him and he started sliding, but what he wasn't aware of was the flames had been slowly burning the cable and when he was no more than halfway across, the fire finally completed its mission and the cable snapped, the end falling to the alley below.

Henry felt himself falling, his stomach lurching inside his body.

On instinct alone, he reached out and grabbed the snapped cable, releasing his hold on the cut wires he had been using to transport himself across.

One moment he was falling, the next he was slamming against the wall of the shorter building, the air forced from his chest by the impact.

He was more than six-feet below the ledge of the roof, hanging like a piñata at a birthday party. If one of the townspeople checked the alley and looked up, they would easily spot him, his body illuminated by the fire across the void.

He wanted to pull himself up, but his strength was gone, only enough left to keep himself from falling the twenty-feet to the alley below.

He managed to wrap his hand around the cable and pull himself up the smallest bit, wrapping the cable around his wrist to prevent himself from slipping.

His feet dangled, only smooth brick next to him so using his feet to brace his body weight wasn't an option and the cable was cutting into his wrist.

He knew he was going to fall, his last reserves almost depleted.

Then what he prayed wouldn't happen, did.

One of the town's guards wandered into the alley. Henry stayed motionless watching the man. He watched as the guard lit a joint and started to smoke it. The man looked neither right nor left, too preoccupied with his joint to care about anything else.

Henry swallowed hard, hoping the man would leave, but as the seconds passed and the man didn't leave, Henry knew he was in trouble. His hands had started to slip and he had less than a minute to move and try to readjust his position. Perhaps calling attention to himself in the process.

The man leaned against the wall of the building Henry was hanging from, looking over his shoulder to make sure he wasn't being watched by one of his fellow guardsmen.

Then Henry felt the cable move and he looked up to see Jimmy's face smiling at him. Seeing the guard, Jimmy signed to Henry that they were going to pull him up. Henry could only nod, not knowing if Jimmy could see him in the flickering light of darkness and shadows.

Cindy and Mary, along with Jimmy, started pulling him up an inch at a time.

Henry only had eyes for the guard, who so far didn't seem interested in anything but his smoke break.

Little by little Henry was pulled to the top until he was almost close enough to reach over the ledge and climb up.

Cindy had left the pull line and was even now looking over the ledge, seeing the guard lazily taking a break. Henry watched her frown and a moment later her head was gone. He gave it no more thought and concentrated on being pulled up.

Only a few more feet would do it.

Cindy appeared again, further down the roof. Henry realized she was directly over the guard, high over his head.

In the flickering light, Henry saw her pick something up and set it on the ledge, but the shadowy shape was a mystery.

Just before Henry was able to reach up and pull himself to freedom, the guard's peripheral vision caught movement above him and he looked up. Henry's and the guard's eyes locked for a fraction of a second and Henry could see the man was about to sound the alarm.

Just as the man's mouth opened, the joint falling from his hand, a large concrete block fell from the roof and crushed his head to nothing but a bloody pulp, Cindy looking down at her handiwork.

The body swayed for a moment in the darkness and then fell back against the wall, slumping to the ground like he had decided to take a nap; the cement block still lodged on the man's shoulders, like a replacement head.

Henry had reached the ledge and he hauled himself over it, Jimmy there to help him. Falling to the rooftop in a heap, he sucked in a breath of fresh air, the air on the new roof less tainted by smoke.

Closing his eyes and trying to slow his hammering heart, he couldn't believe he was still alive.

Jimmy knelt down next to him and Henry opened his eyes. Behind him Cindy and Mary were talking, the latter complimenting the younger woman on disposing of the guard.

Jimmy patted Henry's chest. "See, what did I tell you? Piece of cake."

Henry could only chuckle at Jimmy's carefree response as he sat up, his head spinning from the ordeal.

True, they were free of the burning building, but they were still in enemy territory and the perimeter fence was a long ways away.

Chapter 17

Captain Daniel Snyder was in a well of inky blankness. He had no way of even perceiving exactly how long he'd been there, as time was irrelevant. He felt like he had spent an eternity there until he felt a slap on his face and he opened his eyes.

Quickly closing them, blinded by the bright light shining into his face, he turned his head to the left.

Then, slowly, he opened his eyes once more. In time his eyes became accustomed to the glare and he looked up into the face of Raddack.

Snarling a curse, he tried to charge at the man, but realized he couldn't move.

Looking down at his arms and legs he saw he was restrained.

Taking an inspection of the room, he found he was in the base dentist's office.

Pictures of happy people with Hollywood smiles gleamed back at him from the walls.

Behind Raddack, on a countertop sat a pair of teeth, a mold made for some sailor that was probably long dead.

Raddack took a step closer, the man's body order assaulting his senses. The heavy set man's forehead shone with perspiration and his armpits were darker than the rest of his cotton white shirt.

The ex-criminal still dressed like he was in the Mafia, despite the fact he had never been affiliated with the group or that the organization was dust along with a thousand others of its kind.

Leaning over Snyder's face--a few drops of sweat rolling off his forehead to fall onto Snyder's shirt—the man smiled.

"Welcome back to the world of the living, Captain. And I use my analogy loosely. You were correct in what you informed me about. Although a few of your men decided to cooperate with me, instead of being shot, and even with their help, I just can't seem to get that marvelous vessel to run. It seems I will need those codes you mentioned."

"Go to Hell, you fat bastard, I won't tell you a thing!" Snyder spit, struggling futilely with his bonds.

Raddack chuckled at him. "That's very heroic of you Captain. Did you know that almost all of the men who have sat in that chair have said the very same thing to me at the beginning of their session? But at the end of the session, they usually can't be made to shut up. I guess we'll see if you are the former or the latter, yes?" He motioned to a small, Chinese man in a white lab coat. The man had been standing behind Snyder, his hands folded in front of him. With Raddack calling him, the man wheeled a small, stainless steel cart in front of him, stopping when he was next to Snyder.

The man sat down in a chair with wheels, an odd front rest connected to it. The dentist would have used it to lean on as he worked on a patient.

While the man moved about the tools on the table, Raddack continued to talk. "You see, Captain, though we use this room for what it was built for, namely dentistry, I've found it has another wonderful use as well. The same tools used to save your teeth and gums can be used as wonderful tools for torture. Some people would agree there isn't much of a difference, but I'll let you be the judge of that." He chuckled at his own joke. Snyder merely stared at the man, the veins in his arms taut as he struggled ineffectually with his restraints.

Realizing he was most definitely not breaking free, he relaxed, his chest moving up and down heavily from his exertions.

"Now, I'll make this simple. Give me the codes to use your ship and you can save yourself a lot of pain."

"And if I refuse?"

"Well then, you'll get to experience Mr. Wong's expertise. So what is your answer?"

"Listen to me, Raddack, and listen close. As far as I'm concerned, my boat will never leave that dock, so you might as well pretend it's a giant dildo and shove it up your ass, because that's all the use you'll have for it!" Snyder screamed at the man.

Raddack's face grew hard, but an instant later the expression was gone, and his jovial countenance was back. "Quite a descriptive insult. Well then, I'll be leaving now. I'm not ashamed to say I don't have the stomach for what is going to happen to you next. Mr. Wong is a master at his arts. You'll talk, Captain Snyder, or you'll die. The Chinaman has never failed me yet."

Raddack turned and left the room, the two guards standing at the door following him out.

Mr. Wong's face was impassive, like Snyder was nothing more than a lab experiment to be dissected and categorized.

The door to the room was closing slowly, the pneumatic hinges preventing it from slamming. As Raddack's footsteps echoed down the hall, he paused before leaving the building. Just before the dentist's room door closed completely, he heard the first screams coming from the room, Captain Snyder receiving the attentions of Mr. Wong.

Then the door clicked shut, the hall becoming quiet once more.

Raddack smiled; then turned and continued on. There was a canister of nerve gas that needed his attention and a small town no more than a few miles away that had quite a lot of supplies and food that Raddack wanted and needed desperately if he was to keep his base healthy and happy.

*   *   *

Snyder's head bounced against the cell wall as two guards tossed him into the room. Despite the impact, Snyder barely felt it.

Sliding to the cold, concrete floor, he lay exactly where he had fallen. He was in far too much pain to move.

All he wanted to do was pass out, to let unconsciousness take the pain away, but he knew that wouldn't be happening anytime soon. His nerve endings were on fire from the torture he had just received. He had passed out many times from the intolerable pain but each time he had been revived with smelling salts. Then Mr. Wong would set to work again.

Snyder had told the man nothing. True to his word, he had kept the security codes for his vessel to himself. He would rather die with them then to give that sadistic bastard the boat he had worked his entire life to command.

Mr. Wong had been relentless, the torturer extremely good at his craft. Snyder had tried to leave his mind a few times, like they say you should do when something is too unbearable to deal with, but each time he tried, the pain he suffered would pull him back to reality.

No, there would be no escape in his mind. After the second hour he felt the only way he would escape would be in death, but even that was denied him. An IV had been connected to his arm to make sure he was being hydrated. Almost as quickly as his torturer had sliced into his flesh, a bandage had been applied, or a tourniquet when necessary.

A shadow loomed over him and Snyder tried to open his remaining eye. His left eye was swollen shut, a black eye large enough to impress any pro boxer. His right eye was now blind, the eyeball nothing but a memory.

Snyder could still feel the blade slicing into his retina and the man's slimy gloved fingers scooping his eye from its socket. The man had cut the nerves and blood vessels connecting the eye, and like a television set being turned off, his vision had disappeared on one side.

The evil, little bastard had held the removed eye up to his face so he could get a good look with his one remaining eye.

Snyder had spit in the man's face, one of his last defiant acts that day other than remaining silent.

After that it was all a blur, mingled with pain and suffering. The Chinaman had tried everything to get him to talk. Needles under his fingertips, peeling his skin from his back like peeling an orange. Even simple water torture by covering his face with a towel and then pouring water over it, trying to drown him.

He had resisted it all. His superiors would have been proud of him, if they still existed, of course.

Now he lay on the cold cell floor, battered and bruised, but still alive.

Closing his eye, he laid there, trying not to move or risk sending agony screaming through his limbs, a thousand nerves telling him their sorrow. That was when he made a silent vow that one way or another Raddack would die. He didn't know how or even if it would be possible, but if it was the last thing he did in this life, the man would die painfully.

Chapter 18

Rolling to his feet on the rooftop, Henry swayed slightly, trying to regain his balance. Jimmy reached out to steady him and a moment later he was feeling a little more like his old self.

Mary walked up to him and handed him his shotgun and then she gave him a quick hug.

"Thought we were going to lose you there for a moment," she smiled, stepping back from him. Henry reached up with his hand to her face and wiped a smudge of ash from her cheek with his thumb. "Now come on, Mary, you know it'll take a lot more than a little fire and a twenty-foot fall to get rid of me," he joked.

With a large smile on her face, she reached up and cupped his hand in hers. "Don't I know it."

Jimmy poked his head between the two of them. "Uh, excuse me, but if you two are done with the Oprah moment, maybe we could get the hell out of here?"

"Sure, Jimmy, let's go." Henry looked around the roof until he spotted what he had been looking for. Walking across the rooftop, he picked up his backpack, the familiar weight seeming almost comforting. Double checking his holster, he was pleased to see his Glock was fine, as was his panga, still tied securely to his hip.

Walking back to the others, he caught the last of the conversation.

"And we should just have to get down the fire escape and disappear into the shadows. From there we can get to the fence and over it we go. Just like that," Jimmy said, snapping his fingers for emphasis.

"Sounds good if it works. It seems ever since we got into this crazy town it's one thing after another," Henry said, turning to glare at the fiery building.

Parts were collapsing, only the brick outer shell keeping most of the flames contained.

He felt a chill go up his spine as he thought about what would have happened to them if they hadn't been able to escape. But they had, so dwelling on what ifs was nothing but trouble. Better to keep your eye in the present and in a small degree, the future.

"Well, let's get going, where's the fire escape?" Henry asked the three faces, looking for an answer.

Cindy answered for the rest. "Over there, on the other side of that a/c unit. I saw it earlier when I grabbed the cement block." She pointed to the unit and the pile of blocks lying scattered on the roof, placed there for some project that will never reach fruition.

Everyone ran across the roof, feet crunching on gravel. Seconds later they were all looking down the metal ladder that would lead them to the back alley of the building. Off to the left was a pile of cement bags, now all solid rock after spending months out in the elements, useless; their original purpose unknown.

After checking to make sure the alley was devoid of life, Henry climbed over the ladder and started down to street level.

"Jimmy, watch my back in case there's a lookout down there," he said, hands and feet working in tandem to slowly lower him downward.

"Will do," Jimmy said, pulling his hunting knife and watching the shadows. If he spotted trouble he would at least try to throw the knife. If that failed, then he would just have to use his gun and risk detection.

Cindy picked up another cinder block and hovered near the roof's edge. What worked once would work twice if needed.

Henry reached the bottom rung and stepped into the alley. The burning building was on the opposite side of the wall behind him, the orange glow like a spotlight. The darkness wasn't as pervading as he would have liked, the fire illuminating everything for more than a hundred feet in every direction.

He gave the hand signal to Mary that the coast was clear and to come down. The woman quickly climbed down and a minute later was standing next to Henry, her .38 in her hand.

Next came Jimmy and a minute later Cindy jumped from the third rung to lightly land on the ground like a cat. Swinging her rifle around, she watched the shadows, but so far all was quiet.

"All right, move out, but stay triple sharp. If we make it to the perimeter fence without some opposition, it'll be a friggin' miracle."

The others nodded and Henry took point, followed by Mary and Cindy. Jimmy brought up the rear, his shotgun sweeping back and forth as he turned at the waist to scan the darkness.

Slowing at the entrance to the street, Henry snuck a peek around the corner of the building. The townspeople were still there, some of them now sitting down, getting a little bored. Others were still whooping it up, cheering at the burning building like they were at a bonfire.

Henry pulled his head back and glanced at the others. In the blackness of the alleyway their faces were only outlines.

"They're still there, but if we go one at a time we should be okay. Once we get past this opening we should be home free."

"Then let's go, man, all this sneaking around is driving me crazy," Jimmy whispered from the darkness.

Henry nodded and then looked out into the street once again. He waited for the right moment and seconds later had it when a piece of the burning building collapsed, the crowd cheering in unison.

Henry took the distraction as a blessing and bolted across the alleyway.

Reaching the other end, he poked his head back to see if he had been spotted.

Nothing. No one had seen him. He wondered if it was possible that in the shadows of the alley he was doing this all for nothing and in truth they couldn't be seen from the street.

Deciding it was irrelevant, he waved the next person on. The more caution they took, the better. Careless people got dead real fast and Henry was planning on sucking air for a long time after this day was finally over, as well as his friends, with him.

Mary sprinted across the alleyway, her feet slapping the concrete. Once she was with him, Henry checked yet again.

All was the same.

"Jimmy, you and Cindy run side by side. Decreases your chances of being seen. Ready, one, two...three, go!"

Jimmy and Cindy sprinted across the alley and moments later were safe on the other side. Henry looked one last time and noticed a guardsmen looking down the alleyway. He had spotted something, but didn't seem to realize there was any danger.

Henry watched the man moving closer and debated whether they should just run or deal with the man, hoping to leave him behind.

His decision was quickly taken from him when two more guards could be heard talking as they walked down the back alley the exact way Henry wanted to go, so they could escape the town.

Cursing his luck, he knew to shoot the men down would draw the unwanted attention of the rest of the township.

These men would have to be handled quietly.

An idea struck him, risky, but all he could think of on short notice.

Gathering the others together around him, Henry whispered his thoughts to them, Jimmy at first arguing, but soon giving in, because he had nothing better and time was short.

Separating, the companions moved away on their assorted tasks, Henry hoping his plan would work.

Failure wasn't an option. If his plan failed, they would all be hanging from the gallows by morning.

*   *   *

The two guardsmen walked side by side, their weapons casually slung across their shoulders. Neither believed they were in any danger, the strangers long dead from the flames of the burning building.

Both were talking quietly about what they would do when they were allowed to leave when Guard #1 spotted something moving in the alley a few yards in front of them.

Before either could pull their weapon, a half naked woman stumbled out into their path.

She was beautiful, with light blonde hair and firm breasts. Her porcelain skin seemed to almost glow in the night air. Her face was one of panic as she wobbled over to the two guards.

"Oh, thank God," she said, her voice frantic. "I was attacked by someone, he tried to rape me," she said, pushing her chest outward to expose her breasts even more.

Both men's eyes saw nothing but Cindy's chest as the woman fell into Guard #1's arms.

"Don't worry, miss, we'll get you help, you'll be fine," the man said, looking down at her beautiful face. Despite the woman below him needing his help, he still couldn't help but become slightly aroused at her exposed flesh.

Her eyes seemed to flutter and for a moment the guard thought she might faint.

"Miss, are you all right?" He asked.

Cindy's eyes snapped open and she smiled cruelly, baring her teeth. "I'm fine, Doll, but I can't say the same thing for you," and then she pulled the six-inch hunting knife she had strapped to her back, inside her pants waistband, and thrust the blade into the guard's throat.

The man's eyes went wide and he dropped Cindy to the ground, the knife sliding free as she fell. A geyser of blood shot out from the man's sliced jugular, in the dark alley the fluid resembling a black ichor.

The second guard remained motionless, the shock of seeing this helpless, beautiful woman slaughter his friend like a pig to much of a surprise for him to do anything other then stare.

If the guard had another three seconds, he would have come to his senses and swung his rifle around, shooting Cindy where she lay on the ground, bloody knife still in her hand.

But the guard didn't get those precious seconds. While Cindy was falling to the ground, Jimmy had appeared at the guard's side, his own hunting knife in his hand.

Just before the hapless man could swing his weapon around, Jimmy brought his arm over the guard's shoulder and dragged the blade across his throat, adding to the waterfall of blood now covering the alley.

Cindy rolled away from the spewing fluid, her chest now covered in blood. She looked more like a demon-hellcat than his girlfriend and Jimmy blinked twice just to make sure it was her.

The guard in his arms had raised both hands to his throat, still not fully comprehending what had happened to him. He called out, but only gargling sounds came from his frothing mouth.

Cindy took a step into the man and stabbed him through the heart, thereby ending the man's suffering.

The first guard Cindy had skewered was falling to his knees, the blood flow slowing as he pumped out what was left in his body.

Falling over, he landed on his friend, already lying dead in the alley.

Jimmy stepped away from them and stared at his girlfriend.

"Cindy, my darling, you are one hardcore bitch."

She smiled in the darkness. "And don't you forget it, come on, let's go see how the others are making out," she said. Bending over and ripping a piece of cloth off one of the dead guard's shirts to use as a rag, she attempted to wipe off some of the already thickening blood.

She would need a shower soon or she was going to smell like a charnel house, but one thing at a time.

The couple turned away from the prone corpses and jogged back down the alleyway to find Mary and Henry.

The plan Henry had fabricated for Cindy and Jimmy was much different for the one he planned with Mary.

Risky at best, he didn't know if his plan would even work, so he chose to mix it up a little.

The curious guard walked down the alley in front of him, still looking for what had caught his attention.

Reaching the end of the long alleyway, the man paused at the sight of a man and woman seeming to be having sex on the alley floor, surrounded by a pile of boxes and crates.

At first he thought everything was fine, that he had walked upon a couple having a little outdoor sex, probably aroused by the burning building, but when the woman let out a muffled cry of: "No, stop, please," he knew something was off.

"You picked the wrong time to take advantage of a woman, buddy. You'll hang for this," the guard said, comfortable in his authority. No one in the town ever tried to fight one of the guards, there were simply too many. And even if said person managed to escape, then where exactly would they escape too?

The guard walked up to the couple, the woman still struggling under her assailant. He reached down and grabbed the man's shirt collar, smiling as he did it.

He was about to put the fear of God into the rapist and perhaps the woman under him would be so relieved he had saved her that they might get together once she had recovered.

Thinking back to other times he had saved a damsel in distress, he knew it was a possibility.

Hauling the man off the woman, he saw she had brown hair and a nice body.

Expecting to see surprise, shock, or perhaps fear of being caught, the guard didn't expect the icy cold gaze the man shot back at him.

The guard immediately knew something wasn't right about the situation and as he looked toward the woman and saw the cold determination on her face, as well, he knew he was correct.

Then a large blade, more than twelve inches long was coming at him, the man swinging it like he was trying for a homerun. The blade struck the guard in the side of the neck, slicing down to stop halfway in his chest.

Muscle and tendons were severed and the man felt agonizing pain like he had never experienced before.

Henry tried to pull his panga free, but the knife was stuck in the man's ribs.

Mary was on her feet now and she swung a four foot two-by-four in an overhand blow that crushed the guard's head like a watermelon.

The guard wavered on his feet, only Henry's panga and his grip holding him up. Henry raised his right leg and planted it against the man's stomach, then pushed off. The panga slid free in a bloody spray that painted the wall of the alley.

The guard fell to the alley floor and remained still.

Knowing time was of the essence, Henry wiped his panga clean on one of the man's pant legs, the only one not covered in blood, and sheathed the blade.

Then he picked the dead man up by his boots and dragged him into the crates and boxes. Mary helped, tossing papers and boxes over the corpse.

Picking up the man's rifle, Henry checked the clip and frowned to see he only had five rounds. Barely worth the trouble of carrying.

Deciding five rounds were better than nothing, both he and Mary turned at the sound of pounding footsteps.

Everyone breathed a sigh of relief when Jimmy and Cindy came around the corner.

Jimmy saw a boot sticking out of the boxes and grunted, nodding to Henry and Mary. "Everything all right?"

Mary wiped some blood from her cheek. "Couldn't be better, it worked perfectly. These damn guards are so full of themselves they can't even entertain the idea that someone would defend themselves against them."

"I hear that," Cindy said, buttoning the last button on her shirt. "The only thing those two idiots could see were my breasts, the rest of me was invisible," Cindy finished, gesturing to the prone bodies behind her.

"Well, they are pretty fabulous," Jimmy said, looking at Cindy with a childish grin.

"Men," both Cindy and Mary said simultaneously.

"All right, then, if everybody's done, let's go before someone else shows up," Henry said, wiping his forehead from some stray gore from when he had pulled his panga free.

Everyone agreed and started off. Jimmy had the other guard's rifles with him and Henry pulled the clips. After adding all the rounds in the combined clips, there was less than fifteen rounds.

The guards might have fancy weapons, but they had no ammunition for them. That could be useful if they got cornered again. That would also explain why they set the building on fire instead of continuing to shoot at them.

They didn't have the ammunition to waste, better to just burn them out.

Quickly gathering their shotguns and backpacks, Henry handed the extra rifle to Mary--with the spare clips to combine later--and the companions moved away from the alley and deeper into the town.

The streets were deserted, everyone either still at the burning or finally going to bed for the night.

Checking his watch, Henry saw they had only a few more hours before sunrise. It had been a long night and he hoped when the sun finally rose, spreading its brilliance down on this town in the morning, he and his friends would be far away.

*   *   *

The town wasn't that big, and it didn't take them long to reach the perimeter fence. Jimmy inspected it, trying to gauge the best way through it, either over or under. With barbed wire covering the top of the fence, over wasn't very popular.

On the other side of the fence was nothing but trees and foliage. Anything could be lurking in the wooded growth, but at the moment that danger was only secondary. The first problem was to get out of the town, anything after that would be dealt with as the problems came.

Jimmy stood up from where he'd been kneeling on the ground. He had a handful of dirt in his hand and he sifted through it, the soil falling through his fingers.

"The dirt's pretty soft here, Henry. We should be able to dig a hole under the fence," Jimmy said, wiping his hand clean on his pants.

"Okay then, get started, after a while, if needed, one of us will relieve you," Henry told him.

For the briefest moment Henry thought Jimmy was going to protest, but the moment passed and the young man knelt down and started digging.

Henry smiled at the man's back. Jimmy was growing more mature everyday. There would have been a time when he would have complained, about being the one to dig, but now he just did what had to be done, no complaints, no protests.

Cindy knelt down next to him and helped pull the dirt away while Jimmy dug deeper.

Mary and Henry guarded their backs; prepared to shoot anything that appeared.

The spot they had picked was behind a small row of one-story buildings. Henry hadn't seen what they were used for but if they were inside the fence then they were probably used for something.

With most of the town still awake and thinking they were successful in killing the companions, the odds of being discovered was still great. Not to mention once the dead guards were found someone would figure out something was wrong and sound the alarm.

Jimmy looked like a puppy trying to escape his yard as he swiped dirt from the ever growing hole.

Ten minutes passed and Henry was growing anxious when Jimmy leaned back with sweat in his eyes and breathed out a sigh.

"Finished at last," he gasped. "The dirt got harder as I dug down more and with nothing but my hands it was a bitch. Remind me to get a small shovel for my backpack the first chance we get."

"Deal," Henry said, stepping back when Jimmy stood up.

"Okay, toss the backpacks over the fence and then we'll go one at a time. The women go first, then Jimmy and then me," Henry told them, the others doing as he said.

Once the backpacks were over the fence, Cindy slid under first, the smallest and therefore the quickest. Once she was through, Jimmy slid her rifle under the fence and Cindy brought it up, her eyes scanning the dark greenery for signs of movement.

Mary followed next, and waited as Henry slid her newly acquired rifle under the fence for her. Jimmy nodded to Henry and then with a little bit of effort, slid under the fence as well. His shirt ripped on one of the links and he cursed out loud. "Shit, I just got this shirt, too. I really liked it."

"Oh, quit whining, we'll get you another one," Mary said.

"Nuh-uh. This came from the mall, I doubt very much we'll find another one like it," he protested.

"Knock it off, Jimmy; it's just a friggin' shirt. Focus dammit, we're not in the clear yet," Henry snapped.

Jimmy closed his mouth, but the look on his face said the discussion was far from over.

Henry sat down on his butt and pushed his shotgun under the fence. He was about to slide under when he heard the distinctive sound of a rifle being cocked.

The companions turned as one and Henry saw he was looking down the barrel of a semi-automatic rifle, the man carrying it seeming to appear out of the darkness like magic. He had no way of knowing how many rounds the rifle carried, but even one would be enough to end his days.

He looked up at the face behind the rifle and saw it was Richards, the guard they had first met when they entered the town.

"Don't move a muscle. I don't want to shoot you," Richards said, his voice never wavering.

Henry leaned back on his hands, trying to look calm. "Oh, really? Well, then you'd be the only person in this entire place who didn't."

Jimmy and Mary both had weapons trained toward the man but with the chain-link fence blocking the bullet's path it would be unknown if the rounds would strike the guard before the man could shoot Henry.

Jimmy flashed Henry a look that said: What do you want me to do?

Henry just shook his head, no, ever slightly. If the guard had wanted to shoot, then he would have done so already. Henry hoped he could talk his way out of the situation.

"So what are you going to do now? Turn us in?" Henry asked casually, sounding like he was having a beer with an old friend instead of being held prisoner by gunpoint.

Richards ignored the question. "You know, a lot of people think you're dead. That you burned up in the fire. You killed a lot of my friends tonight, do you know that? Why shouldn't I give them justice and just kill you now?"

Henry leaned forward a little, sliding away from the fence. Even if he was shot down at least he knew his friends would escape.

Not a lot of comfort, but better than nothing.

"Justice, for whom? We were the ones attacked. We didn't start this; your people did when they butchered that man with stones and bricks. What the hell is wrong with you people? If the man was guilty, then fine; banish him or kill him, but don't torture the man. That's just sick and I think you know it. That's why you haven't pulled that trigger or sounded the alarm that you found us." Henry turned toward the man and stood up, wiping his hands clean on his pants. "You want justice? Then don't let your friends die in vain. Change this town for the better, because in case you haven't noticed it's all you got. If this place falls, there's not exactly a lot of places that would just take you in. Look at what happened to us, yesterday. Shit, we didn't even last half a day here, what do you think would happen when others arrive like ourselves? Look, Richards, I don't know you that well, but I'd like to think I can measure up a man pretty quick and I think you're a good man with honor, so let us go. Everyone already thinks we're dead. What will killing me or my friends really do but add more blood to the flames?"

Richards chewed his lip, mulling it over. He glanced sideways at Mary and then back to Henry.

Henry waited patiently. His right hand itched to reach for his Glock, but there was no way he could pull it out in time before Richards could get off a shot. And he really didn't want to kill the man if it could be avoided. All he wanted to do was escape the cursed town.

He was at the man's mercy. Not a pleasant place to be in the current state of the world where mercy was at a premium and hatred was plentiful.

Richard's seemed too tense and Henry braced himself for the impact of the round into his body, but then the man relaxed and slowly lowered his weapon.

"Some of what you say makes sense, mister, and you're right, there has been too much bloodshed already." Gesturing with his head, Richards said: "Go on, get out of here, and never come back. Next time I see you I may not be so forgiving."

"Fair enough, take care of yourself, Richards, and remember what I said," Henry said and slid under the fence.

Once on the other side of the fence, Jimmy handed him his shotgun. Richards stood still, watching the companions for a few seconds and then he nodded and turned and walked away to be lost in the darkness.

Mary hugged Henry and Jimmy patted his back. "Jesus Christ, Henry, I really thought he was going to shoot you," Jimmy said.

"Yeah, he was really on the fence about it, but I guess he decided on mercy. Not something we see too much anymore," Henry said.

The companions moved off, away from the fence, the tall grass waving as they moved through it. The goal was to just get a little ways from the town and then hold up till it became light. Moving around the landscape in the dark was tantamount to a death wish.

The undead never slept and were always hungry.

"I'm so sorry I got us into that mess, Henry, I can't tell you how much. Next time I'll try to control myself," Mary said apologetically.

Henry wrapped his arm around her, and squeezed. "Look, Mary, sure I'm mad at how things went down, but not at you, not really. You shot that man because he was suffering and you couldn't take it anymore. You showed him mercy even when the bastard probably didn't deserve it. It's your compassion that makes you so special. Don't let this damn world take that from you."

She smiled up at him and he kissed her forehead, then they broke apart and continued walking. There would be time for contemplation later, but for now they needed to stay focused on their environment.

With a few night birds chirping in the nearby trees, the companions moved away from the town, still together and still strong.

Chapter 19

Captain Daniel Snyder blinked away the bright light spilling into his cell as the only door into the room was opened. At first nothing but white filled his vision, but as the seconds ticked by he was soon able to see again.

He didn't like what he saw.

Raddack stood in the doorway, two armed guards at his side. The man looked like a fool, with a yachting cap on and a jacket that any yuppie would have killed for.

"Do you like it? I thought I'd wear this when I take my new submarine out for its first trip under my command. There's only one thing stopping me and that is the goddamn codes. Give them to me or so help me I'll..."

"You'll what? Kill me?" Snyder asked, his voice hoarse from lack of water. "Go ahead, kill me and you'll never get them."

Raddack sighed. "Yes, I thought you might say that, well Captain, you leave me no choice." Turning to the guard on his right, he nodded and the man disappeared. Snyder lay on the floor, not understanding what was happening.

Raddack was just standing there, a slight grin on his face, like the cat that had just caught the mouse.

Minutes ticked by and still nothing happened, until the sound of voices in the hallway disrupted the silence.

A man was pushed into the room, losing his balance and falling to the floor. One of the guards stepped in and picked the man up, keeping the man on his knees, both hands secured behind his back. The man had a black eye and a bloody nose, but otherwise seemed to be unharmed.

Snyder recognized the man immediately.

"Petty Officer Wolfe, what are you doing here?" Snyder croaked.

Wolfe shook his head. "I have no idea, sir. I wouldn't help them so they locked me up in a cell with a bunch of the crew. I hear some of the men are following him, but most of us are still loyal to you, sir."

Snyder nodded, the motion causing him great pain. "That's good to know Wolfe, thank you. When you see the other men, tell them the same."

"Yes, sir, I will," Wolfe said.

"How very noble, but I didn't bring this man here so you two could catch up with each other. Now Captain, I will ask you one last time, what are the codes that will allow me to use your ship?"

Snyder laughed, the laughter sounding more like an animal in pain. Two of his front teeth had been torn from their roots, just one of many souvenirs from the Chinaman. "Go to hell, Raddack, I told you I'll never give you those codes. I'll die first."

"That's what I thought you would say." Raddack gestured with a slight nod to the guard holding Wolfe by his collar.

The guard grunted an acknowledgement and in one fluid motion, with no hesitation, pulled his sidearm from its holster, placed the muzzle against the back of Wolfe's skull and squeezed the trigger.

Inside the small cell the bullet shot sounded like a cannon had just gone off. The smell of burned hair and gun smoke filled the room, assailing Snyder's nostrils. Wolfe's head was tossed forward as the bullet blew out the front of his forehead, peppering Snyder with bone fragments and blood spray.

The guard let Wolfe go and the dead man fell over to land not more than a foot from Snyder. Blood leaked out of the wound to pool on the painted floor.

"I'm done playing with you, Snyder. Either you tell me those codes or I will kill one of your men every hour. And keep in mind that if I have to kill too many and there's no one to operate the ship, then I really won't need you at all, will I?"

"Fuck you, you fat piece of shit!" Snyder yelled as he stared at the destroyed head of one of his men. "You're nothing but a filthy murderer."

"Just for that you can keep him for company. As you watch him rot, you can reconsider your position." Raddack placed a small, battery powered digital clock on the floor inside the door. "You can use this to keep track of how long it will be until you kill your next crewman. Yes, Captain, you, not me. You can stop this whenever you want. Don't let another man die."

With that said, Raddack left the cell, the two guards following. This time the lights stayed on, Snyder figuring Raddack wanted him to see the face of the slaughtered crewman.

With tears in his eyes, Snyder squeezed his hands into fists. How the hell did it come to this? How did he go from being a Captain of a nuclear submarine to a tortured prisoner in only a few short days?

Realizing it didn't really matter; Snyder closed his eyelids and cried.

Not for himself, but for his men.

*   *   *

Raddack walked down the hallway and out into the dark night. Walking away from the brig, he looked down at his base. The brig sat on a hill overlooking the lower half of the base, his sleeping quarters as well as those for his men off to the right and up the sloping road. To the left just over the trees was the roof of the galley, the smoke floating out of the chimneys as the cooks prepared breakfast.

He couldn't see his new acquisition from where he stood; the lower base of the station out of sight. But he knew the submarine was safe for the moment. He had stationed six armed guards on the pier and two guards inside the ship. No one would be taking from him what he had in turn worked hard in taking from someone else.

Walking to his Hummer, he was greeted to the sight of Smith waiting for him. Smith was as close as a man could come to being the second in command, but Raddack new better than to let that happen. He only gave the man enough power and information to perform his given tasks, and thereby ensuring the man's loyalty.

"Report, Smith, how goes the preparations for attacking the next town. Is the nerve gas ready?"

Smith made a face that Raddack didn't like, a frown. "I'm afraid not, sir. We still haven't figured out how to release the gas without killing ourselves in the process."

"What are you talking about? Simply put the canister in the middle of the town and open it, how hard can that be?"

Smith nodded agreeing with him. "Yes, that's true, Boss, but we still haven't found a man who will do such a suicide mission and even if we did, we can't have our men close by. If the wind shifts towards us then we'll all be killed as well."

"So, why can't we wear gas masks? That'll solve the problem, won't it?" Raddack asked.

Smith nodded again. "Yes, sir, but we don't have enough for all of our attacking force. We only have about twenty, the rest are either damaged or missing pieces. We managed to cobble together a few more from combining pieces of broken ones, but that's it."

Raddack had decided he had heard enough and climbed into his Hummer, his driver starting the motor.

Raddack leaned out the open door at Smith, his chubby face hard, sweat building up on his forehead.

"Listen, Smith, find someone to bring that gas to that town or I'll send you instead, got me?"

Smith swallowed a large lump in his throat, "Yes, Boss, I'll find someone."

"Good, you do that. Check in with me later and fill me in on the status, until then, I'll be at my quarters. It's been a long day and I'm tired." The Hummer started to move and then the squeal of the tires told Smith his meeting was over.

The vehicle hadn't gone ten feet when the tires locked up, sliding on some loose sand in the dirt. Smith turned to look at the Hummer, waiting.

Watching the window roll down, Smith jogged over to the Hummer, knowing his commander wasn't through with him just yet.

"Sir?" He asked politely.

"Yeah, I almost forgot. If Snyder doesn't talk, then have one of his crew killed in his cell every hour. And leave the bodies there with him. That ought to change his mind."

Smith hesitated for a second, but then regained his composure. "Okay, Boss, I'll see to it personally," he said.

"Good, Smith, good. Keep this up and I'll make sure you receive a promotion, how does that sound.

"That sounds wonderful, Boss, thank you."

Raddack grunted and the Hummer pulled away. Smith watched it roll down the small road and disappear out of sight.

Checking his watch he realized he had fifty minutes to go before he had to execute another prisoner, distasteful as that sounded to him.

Shaking his head with conflicting thoughts running through his head, he went back inside the building that was once used by the MP's and was now the jail for the base and Raddack's enemies.

Sometimes he wondered if what he was doing was justified and if he would be going to hell when he died.

But what was the alternative? To be running around out there in the world always looking over your shoulder, waiting for the walking dead to bite you in the ass?

No, though he may have to do some distasteful things once in a while, he still had it better than the rest of the civilians who made up the population of the base. All the guards received better food and preferential treatment as part of the risk they took protecting the base.

Yes, sir, George Newton Smith was a survivor and that was what he was doing, surviving, and to hell with everybody else.

Besides, if he didn't follow Raddack's orders implicitly, he'd end up occupying the cell next to Snyder.

With a reality like that it was easier to rationalize doing bad things because the alternative was just too difficult to face.

*   *   *

Raddack pulled into the front driveway of the barracks now exclusively used for himself and his guards. The base had an entire section dedicated to housing. Raddack had taken one of the closest buildings to the docks and had then transformed the top floor of the six-level structure to one giant apartment. His men had taken weeks to knock out the walls, and even now a few steel girders could be seen throughout the grand room.

On the floors below him were housed his men. He preferred to keep them close, that way he could keep an eye on them.

Walking into the lobby, a guard stood up from behind the desk placed in the middle of the area. Before the world had collapsed this desk would have had a man sitting behind it whose sole job would have been to keep track of visitors coming and going from the barracks.

A sign still hung on the wall that read: **Curfew 23:00. All visitors must be off premises by designated time.**

Raddack strode up to the desk, the guard sitting at attention. Raddack held his hand up to the man, gesturing for him to sit back down. Sometimes it was good to be casual with the men, made them feel they could identify with you, he thought.

"Relax, Johansson, you're fine. Any news on that bar the last team found?" He asked politely. He was referring to one of the many teams of men he sent out daily to scavenge for supplies. Toilet paper, alcohol, gasoline, these things weren't easily fabricated and so teams would constantly be searching the ruins of the nearby towns. On the last outing the team had found a bar that had been virtually untouched, the stockroom still full to the ceiling with alcohol, popcorn and pretzels. The only negative was that the area was swarming with the undead, the walkers had been everywhere, the commander of the team had told him.

Raddack didn't care. He wanted what was in that building and what he wanted, he got, end of story.

"Yeah, Boss, Nelson's team is heading out in the morning. He said he's bringing enough firepower to level a city. It should be enough to take down a few walkers," Johansson said.

Raddack nodded, listening to the guard, then he slapped his hand on the countertop.

"Tell Nelson I'll be joining him in the morning. It's been a while since I've been off base. I could use a distraction while I try to get those damn codes from our uncooperative Captain."

The guard seemed surprised. "You're going, Boss? Are you sure?"

Raddack's face grew red with anger. "Are you questioning me, Johansson? Yes, I'm fucking sure, now get me up an hour before Nelson leaves and tell him he better wait for me!" Then he turned and headed for the stairs. The only negative to being on the top floor was the damn climb, but he hoped one day to have power restored on the base, at least, then he could ride the elevator in style.

Pulling his bulk up the stairs, Raddack huffed and puffed, looking forward to finally going to bed. It hadn't been a bad day overall. He had a brand new submarine to play with as well as a canister of deadly, military nerve gas. Soon he would get those codes from Snyder and then he would be king of the seas, not just an ex-crime boss hiding out on a military base.

Looking forward to shooting a few walkers the next day, he huffed and puffed up the stairs, idly thinking maybe he should move his quarters a little closer to the first floor.

Chapter 20

RING, RING, chimed the bell on the handlebars of the girl's bicycle Jimmy was riding while the companions walked down the middle of the lonely highway.

They had spent a long night in an old trailer home waiting for the sun to come up, every noise making them jump, wondering if Richards had changed his mind and told the town about them escaping, and the town had then sent out a posse to find them.

But the night had been uneventful and when the sun had sent its first rays out to banish the darkness for another night, the companions had started on their journey once again.

Jimmy had found the bicycle strapped to the back of an old camper sitting derelict on the side of the road and had immediately taking a liking to it. Though the bike was three sizes too small and the tires were flat, he rode circles around the companions as they slogged onward.

"Jimmy, for Christ's sake, will you knock it off? You're driving me crazy," Henry snapped while Jimmy drove so close to him, he almost ran over his foot.

Mary chuckled next to him. "That's why he's doing it, Henry. You know he loves to aggravate you."

Henry grunted, trying to ignore Jimmy as he went round and round. He was about to pull his shotgun out and blow away the front tire, he was so pissed, that he almost didn't see the group of roamers coming out of the tree line a few hundred feet in the distance.

"Heads up, boys and girls, we've got company," he said, gesturing with his chin towards the shambling figures.

Cindy hadn't heard a thing he'd said. She had been fortunate enough to find an ipod in one of the abandoned cars littering the highway and the device still had power. With the earphones in her ears, she sang quietly to the music. Henry had allowed it, figuring that while they were out on the open highway, they would see danger coming long before it became a threat.

So far he'd been right.

The shambling ghouls crossed the shoulder of the road and started walking towards them, moving faster now that they were on solid ground. There were ten in all, all in different classes of decay and rotting anatomy.

Some looked to be no more than a few weeks old, while two at the back of the line looked to be one of the first ones to fall and return as soldiers for the dead. These were nothing but dried skin and bones with rags for clothing. Henry watched them slowly move closer, the fresher ones pulling away from the others.

He smiled at that. One of the only things still going in humanity's favor was the fact that the average ghoul was an idiot. Only there large numbers would ever cause a person to actually be threatened. If you just stayed calm and kept your head, it was usually easy enough to dispatch them quickly and efficiently.

Jimmy stopped riding and stood up, the bike falling over on to the pavement. Swinging his shotgun around, he aimed the barrel at the approaching zombies, ready to send them back to the hell that was waiting for them.

Henry held up his hand for him to wait.

"Why? Let's just take them out and move on," Jimmy said, his finger pressing on the shotgun's trigger.

"Slow down there, Tex. Lets see what happens. Besides, we've got at least five minutes before they're close enough to be a problem."

Cindy had seen the roamers, as well, and had pulled the earphones from her ears, moving closer to Jimmy.

Mary watched the stumbling walkers move ever closer and she nudged Henry with her new rifle. "What are we waiting for? Either we try to get around them or we take them out. Which is it?" She asked, curiously.

"Neither; just wait a little longer and you'll see. If what I'm thinking works, we'll take them out with one bullet."

"One bullet? I'd like to see that," Jimmy said sarcastically.

Henry turned to look at his friend. "Oh, really, want to make a wager on it then?"

One to never back down from a challenge, Jimmy nodded. "Fine, but what do we bet on?"

Henry gave it a few seconds thought and then he smiled. "I've got it. Winner has to carry the other guy's backpack for a day and clean and strip the winner's weapons for a week."

Jimmy thought it over, but as he was sure there was no way Henry was going to win, he nodded and held out his hand to Henry. "Deal, shake on it."

"Okay, sucker, remember you started this," Henry quipped pumping his hand twice.

Jimmy paused for a moment, wondering if he had just made a mistake in taking the wager,

"Umm, guys, the roamers are almost here," Mary said nervously. She would always prefer shooting them from a distance then getting up and personal. The last time she had to battle close and personal, she had been accidentally shot in the arm, striking a vital artery, and had nearly died.

Henry stood perfectly still, his Glock in his right hand, while the abominations of half-life moved ever closer. The others were starting to get uncomfortable, hands caressing triggers in preparation for the coming fight.

The large group were less than fifty feet away when Henry looked at the others and calmly said: "I think you all should get behind that car over there," and he gestured to an old station wagon sitting in the middle of the two lane blacktop with the barrel of his Glock.

Jimmy was about to ask why, when Henry fired the Glock, sending one round at an old, metallic blue, Buick Skylark with jacked up chrome, rear wheels, tinted windows and a sunroof; the car sitting sideways on the yellow line in the middle of the highway with four flat tires.

The gas tank exploded in a blazing fireball of orange and reds, the added lift from the shocks pushing the rear of the car up high enough so Henry had an easy shot at the car's gas tank. With all the doors open wide, and a pair of fuzzy dice hanging from the rearview mirror, the car disappeared into the inferno, swallowed whole; someone's once loved car now nothing but scrap metal.

He had timed it perfectly.

Just as the first of the roamers passed the front of the car, the bullet impacted with the gas tank, igniting the quarter tank of gas still sitting in the bottom of the tank and sending an erupting fireball outward that consumed both the car and the approaching zombies surrounding it.

Mary and Cindy had done as Henry suggested and moved behind the station wagon, ducking down when the Buick exploded.

Jimmy had stayed next to Henry and was now ducking for cover as debris and body parts flew across the area. Dropping down, as well, Henry raised his arm to shield his face, and felt his ears pop from the explosion.

A brisk breeze blew the smoke away from the burning wreckage and in only a matter of minutes the companions were able to move closer to inspect Henry's handiwork.

Jimmy looked down at the severed body parts and wreckage, shaking his head in disbelief. "Son-of-a-bitch, I can't believe you did that," he spit, mad that he'd lost the bet."

"Told you you'd regret it," Henry smiled. "Never bet against an old horse, he still might surprise you."

A high pitched wail sounded from behind Jimmy and he turned to see a zombie walk out of the flames, its entire body on fire. Jimmy raised his shotgun to fire on it, but Henry stopped him.

"Wait a second, Jimmy. It can't see you; just get out of its way!" Henry yelled, taking his own advice.

Jimmy hurried to the side of the wreckage and sure enough, the flaming ghoul stumbled past him to fall over onto the shoulder of the highway, the corpse still smoking. It flailed for a few more minutes and then remained still.

"See, no bullets used but mine," Henry said. "Let's check the rest out, make sure they're down and don't shoot just because and try to welch out on our bet." Henry said to Jimmy.

"Hey, I wouldn't do that, you know me," Jimmy said hurtfully.

Henry nodded. "Uh-huh, exactly."

Mary and Cindy left the shelter of the station wagon and moved to the burning car as well, checking to make sure all the zombies were finally and truly dead.

Three minutes later they were finished and gathered at the other side of the fire, prepared to move on.

With a wide grin across his lips, Henry handed Jimmy his backpack. "Here ya go pal, carry it with pride."

Jimmy took it and hung it on his shoulder, muttering about it all being fixed or rigged.

The companions started off again, leaving the burning Buick behind. After a few minutes Mary moved closer to Henry and asked: "So, Henry, how did you know there was gas in that tank? It could have just as easily been empty."

Henry shrugged and wiped his forehead. With the sun up, the day was becoming warm and he was glad to have the backpack off his shoulders.

"Would you believe I guessed? That I just took a chance and got lucky?"

Mary cocked her head to the side and grinned. "Yes, I would; in fact, it seems our entire lives since we've met have been one gamble after another."

Wrapping his arm around her, he chuckled. "Amen, to that, honey."

Walking down the highway Cindy listened to her ipod again, this time keeping one ear open to listen for trouble, while Jimmy mumbled next to her, clearly unhappy about carrying two backpacks.

*   *   *

Three hours later Henry called a halt. They were somewhere inside of Connecticut, the highway in their back trail, but their exact whereabouts was unknown. Every time they saw a street sign or marker it was knocked down or just missing, only the pole it had been attached to still standing.

Only one sign still stood. It was made of plywood and in painted, messy red script were the words: **DEADTOWN, POPULATION 0**

"Well, that's a little dramatic, don't you think?" Jimmy said, softly.

"Boy, whoever lives around here doesn't want any visitors to know where they are," Mary said as she looked around the beginnings of the deserted street.

After leaving the highway they had walked another half hour, and had now stopped at the beginnings of what looked to be another town. Only this town had no barricades or fences.

They had seen countless places like the one in front of them. Towns where all the people had either been killed or had abandoned the buildings for safer climes.

Sometimes they would get lucky and scavenge food and supplies from the picked over shelves, but more than likely the entire town was swarming with the undead, the ravenous creatures just waiting to be woken from their hiding places by some sound or noise.

"I don't like this, guys," Cindy said, looking around at the abandoned houses. "I think we should just keep going."

Doors hung open and roof gutters were filled with weeds and walkway shrubs were three times their normal size. Windows were broken and more than one home had the looks of being on fire in the distant past, the siding and woodwork charred a deep black.

"I think your girlfriend makes a good point, Jimmy," Henry said. He took another few steps down the street, stopping and listening to the air.

Nothing but silence mixed in with a few screen doors flapping in the wind. He caught the chirping of a few birds in the trees, but otherwise the town was dead silent.

Stray newspaper rolled across the street, the wind blowing it here and there. A piece blew up against Jimmy's leg and he reached down and read it. Though the date was almost a year old he let out a laugh.

"Hey, guys, guess what? The President says the unemployment level will be down another five percent by years end. And guess what? They're finally going to raise minimum wage, how 'bout that. Oh, and there's a sale at the Gap. Buy one pair of jeans and get one free!" Then he let the paper go, it blew out of his hands to join the rest of the debris spreading across the sidewalk.

No one answered him. Each of the companions dealt with the loss of the world in different ways. Jimmy enjoyed making jokes. It was just his way of coping.

Henry turned and walked back to the others, his hand never far from his sidearm.

"Cindy's right, I think we should keep moving, see what's further down the road. This place gives me the creeps," Henry said, his face looking more than a little unsettled.

Everyone was about to head out when the distinctive sound of multiple engines floated to them on the air. At first they all looked at each other, surprised by the sound. There were almost never any motor vehicles about anymore.

Henry snapped out of his stupor first. "Everyone, hide, get out of the road," he told them, the others jumping to action.

As one group, they ran off the road, diving into the overgrown hedges of the nearest house just as two Hummers and a beat up pickup truck came into view from around the corner of the nearest intersection. Jimmy tumbled more than dived into the shrubs, the two backpacks pulling him off balance. Mary was near him and helped him get righted and undercover.

Seconds later the motors of the Hummers grew louder and the three vehicles rolled by.

Henry watched them and inspected the men in the rear of each vehicle as they passed. A large machine gun, a .50 caliber or larger, was mounted behind the rear seat, each man looking mean and serious as they scanned the area around them.

The road vibrated with the Hummers passing and once they were gone, Henry and the others stepped out of the bushes, watching the road.

"What the hell was that about?" Jimmy asked, shouldering the extra pack. Henry saw this and immediately took the backpack, nodding to the man. Jimmy returned the nod with one of his own, knowing what Henry was doing. This was no time for childish bets. Right now each one of them needed to be ready to move quickly; not weighed down by too much gear so they couldn't move.

"I don't know, but I tell you I'm damn curious," Henry said, watching the road where the Hummers disappeared.

"Well then, let's go see what's so interesting around here, who knows, maybe they know a good hotel in the area," Jimmy said, starting forward.

Mary held back and Henry turned to look at her. "What's wrong, Mary?" Henry asked.

She hugged herself, her rifle hanging from its sling. "I don't know for sure, but I have a gut feeling you were right the first time and we should just leave."

"Maybe, but I want to know what two military Hummers are doing here. If they're part of some kind of government agency around here then don't you think we should try to hook up with them?" Should be a lot better than being out here on our own."

Mary stood motionless, thinking over what Henry had said, when Jimmy turned and called to them. "Are you guys coming or what? If we don't get moving, they'll be gone and we'll never catch them!"

That helped make up her mind and Mary started walking. "All right, but I want to go on record as saying this is a bad idea."

Henry laughed a little, trying to hold it in, not wanting to upset her anymore than she already was. "Duly noted, we'll have our record keeper log it in as soon as we can."

She made a face at him that said: *I don't think you're very funny* and then walked past him. Henry stood in the middle of the street and took one last look around him, then he, too, moved out, following behind Mary. Jimmy and Cindy, now in the lead, were setting a good pace, Jimmy anxious to catch up with the convoy.

With Henry moving further down the street, leaving the darkened houses behind, he had no way of seeing the dozens upon dozens of walking dead that were starting to appear from inside those same houses and from behind overgrown foliage and backyards.

The noise of the Hummers had woken them and they stirred, climbing forward, eager to see what had shaken them from their fugue.

Jimmy's laughter floated on the wind and all heads turned as one, knowing what that sound proclaimed.

Humans, live ones! They all thought in their limited way.

Stumbling and crawling into the street, they started down the road, following the same path that Henry and the others had taken only minutes before.

Hunger consuming them with each step they took.

Chapter 21

The Hummers pulled up to the front of the bar in the middle of deserted town and five men jumped out, running towards the front door of the building.

Raddack stepped out into the bright light of the morning sun and blinked a few times, waiting for his eyes to readjust.

"So, where are all the dead people I heard about that supposedly inhabited this town?" He asked the guard next to him. Raddack thought the man's name was Carter, but he wasn't too sure. Frankly as long as they did what he told them, their names could be whatever the hell they wanted them to be.

Carter looked around the desolate street and shifted nervously on his feet.

"Don't you worry, Boss, they'll be here. They seem to go into hiding when there's no food around, and guess what? When we pulled in, our engines were like the dinner bell."

Raddack grunted. "Hmmm, we'll see about that."

As he walked into the dark building, the fragrances of old beer and rotten food assailed his olfactory senses.

Breathing through his mouth, he moved deeper into the building.

His men were already in the back, picking up boxes and hurriedly carrying them into the front again, setting them down on the wooden tables and floor.

Raddack wandered over to the countertop of the bar and looked at himself in the full-size wall mirror. Bottles lined the shelves, most of them full and Raddack ordered one of his men to make sure he grabbed all of them, as well, but stopped the man and retrieved a bottle of Vodka from his arms.

Opening the bottle, he took a sip, wincing at the warm taste. Vodka needed to be chilled or better yet, placed in a freezer, but the odds of that happening were slim.

Setting the bottle back on the counter, he turned to watch his men work.

Boxes upon boxes were being piled up, two other men already bringing the items outside to load into the pickup truck.

He smiled. Things were going excellent.

At least until he heard the sound of the.50 cal on one of the Hummers start firing, the staccato of short bursts filling the bar. The sound of rifles firing, the guards picking targets of their own, filtered in also, and Raddack new they had company.

Running back to the door, Raddack's face went blank at what he saw.

Hundreds of desiccated human beings were spilling out of the closest buildings, others appearing on the side streets.

Every dead face was turned toward the bar and the men therein.

The .50 caliber continued rattling its staccato of death, riddling bodies left and right. Body parts flew everywhere, littering the ground and striking other creatures behind it.

"Shoot the head, you stupid bastard, the head!" Raddack yelled from the doorway. But the gunner didn't hear him and continued to fire into the torsos of the undead crowd.

Finally the weapon cycled dry and the gunner turned to the other men around him. "I'm out!" He screamed.

Raddack was so pissed at the ignorant man he climbed up onto the Hummer, pulled his magnum and pressed it to the man's head. Before the hapless gunner could even ask what was wrong, Raddack squeezed the trigger, sending the gunner to hell with a fist size hole in his cranium.

The gunner fell over the side of the bed and lay still, blood pooling under the rear tire of the vehicle.

"Now reload this weapon and get somebody up here who knows what the hell they're doing!" He yelled at the men below him. "And get those boxes loaded. I didn't come all the way out here for the hell of it and I'm not going to lose a man's weight in ammunition for nothing!"

"Yes, Boss, right away," Carter said, disappearing back into the bar to retrieve another crate.

With the guards reloading the machine gun and the other Hummer's gunner now firing his own .50 cal, as well, the guards did their best to keep the undead army away from them.

But slowly and surely the horde of dead grew closer.

*　*　*

Henry called a halt at the sound of gunfire. "You guys hear that?" He asked.

"Yeah, sounds like a major battle is going on. What do you want to do?" Mary asked, askance of him.

"I want to see what's happening. If there's a military outpost still active around here, I wouldn't mind checking it out. Maybe we could help them or they could help us."

"Yeah, I know, it would be nice to be behind a solid wall again, preferably cement. Jesus, I miss that mall. Three squares a day and a roof over our head, plus a warm place to sleep."

"Oh, Jimmy, I think that place spoiled you," Cindy said, nudging him with her elbow. "You were a lot tougher when I first met you. You remember how you handled that asshole in the bar I worked at and how you made my Uncle let me go with you?

"Hell, yes, it spoiled me. We haven't had it that good since we were back at Pineridge. And I'm just as tough as when you met me, so stop saying I'm not," he said; his ego slightly bruised.

"If you two are done with your stroll down memory lane, I'd like to keep moving," Henry said.

Mary tapped him on the shoulder and moved closer to him. "Oh boy, ah Henry, I think we may have a problem," she said, pointing behind them.

All heads turned to see what she was pointing at and when they did, muffled imprecations came from their lips, hands reaching for weapons.

A massive crowd of walking corpses were coming down the street, a few more spilling out of the nearest homes lining the sidewalk.

"Shit, they're everywhere!" Henry said, as he took a step backward.

"What do we do? There's too many to shoot, they'll overwhelm us?' Mary said, her rifle in her hands ready to fire.

"Now, stay calm. Remember, we're faster than them. Come on, let's get to those trucks. It's our only way out of here!" Henry told them.

Running down the street, Jimmy raised a suggestion." What about going to one of the deserted buildings and barricading ourselves in?"

Henry kept jogging and shook his head.

"No way, Jimmy, that's a bad idea. There's so many, we'll be trapped with no way to fight our way out. Sooner or later we'll starve. No, the best chance we have is to get to those Hummers and catch a ride with those men, now shut up and run!"

The companions ran, dodging in and out of ghouls that were pouring out of the houses they passed.

They used their weapons sparingly, only firing when absolutely necessary. Most of the time one of them would simply push or kick an attacking creature as it lunged at them, then continued running.

There were far too many to even hope to stop enough to escape death at their hands.

Fifteen minutes later, with everyone panting with exhaustion, they reached the town square. They had heard gunshots for more than half of that time, knowing they were going in the right direction.

The undead were in front of them, but they were facing the other way, trying to get at something Henry and the others couldn't see. If he was right, then they were trying to reach the men in the Hummers.

Coming from behind, the companions ran past the undead army before they had even realized humans were in their midst.

Henry's panga was covered in gore, as he swiped swing after swing at the closest bodies.

"There's the Hummers, make for them, hurry," Henry yelled, but it was quickly obvious that Jimmy and him were becoming separated from the women.

The more he tried to reach them, the more both he and Jimmy were forced back.

Bodies were everywhere and Henry waited for the moment he felt rotten teeth sink into his arm. But he continued moving, weaving a whirlwind of death as he chopped at arms and fingers.

Mary and Cindy did as they were told and continued running towards the Hummers. One of the guards saw them and pointed to the other men and the guards started shooting the closest bodies around them as they ran through the undead horde.

Cindy was grabbed by a large zombie that must have weighed more than three hundred pounds when it was still alive and she rammed her rifle under its chin and blew the top part of its skull out, the brittle bone no match for even the small caliber .22 slug.

Jumping away from the toppling body, she ignored the chill that slid down her spine. If that undead behemoth had fallen on her, she would have been crushed to death before the first set of teeth would have bit into her.

Reaching the Hummers, the guard's faces were wide with surprise. "Holy cow, ladies, where did you come from?" One of the guards asked, a country boy from Maine, his accent heavy.

"Doesn't matter. We have friends in there, they need help. There are more of them coming; they'll be here in a few seconds. We have to go, now!" Mary screamed at the man.

Then she turned and saw a large man with almost no hair waddle over to her. His eyes scanned both her and Cindy and he licked his lips malevolently.

"Well, well, and who are these lovely ladies?" He asked, his voice heavy with sexual excitement.

Mary looked at Cindy, her eyes rolling in her head. Was this the first time this guy had seen a woman?

Turning back to the man, she stepped close to him, his body odor almost as bad as one of the corpses.

"Look, buddy, they'll be time for introductions later, but right now we have two friends out there, you need to help them."

Raddack's eyes went up in surprise. "Oh, really? Are they women, too?" He asked hopefully, his forehead covered in sweat.

"No, they're men and one of them is my boyfriend, now help them, please!" Cindy yelled and pleaded at the same time.

Raddack stared at the two women and then pulled one of his men off loading duty of the boxes from the bar. "You, get these lovely ladies relieved of their weapons and then get them into my Hummer," he ordered the man.

"But what about our friends?" Mary asked while she and Cindy were disarmed under the watchful eye of another guard and the .50 cal over their heads continuing to spit lead at the approaching zombies.

"Don't worry, ladies, I'll take care of your friends," Raddack said with a smile.

Mary and Cindy were shuffled into the first Hummer and locked in, their faces plastered against the windows as they pounded to be let out.

"What about their friends, sir, should we try to save them?" Carter asked, preparing to tell the gunner firing the .50 cal to adjust his aim.

Raddack laughed. "Save them? What for, so I can have two more men that are not under my authority running around my base? No, Carter, I don't think so. I think I'll keep those two lovely ladies for myself. I'm tired of having to screw the same sluts over and over at the base. It'll be nice to have some new blood around." He looked Carter straight in the eyes. "Tell the gunner to kill those two men. I don't care if it's by us or zombies, but I don't want them to reach us. What the ladies don't know, won't hurt them." He walked back to his Hummer and slid into the passenger seat, both Mary and Cindy bombarding him with questions

"Please, ladies, give me a second; we're still in mortal danger here." He emphasized this by drawing one of his magnums and shooting a ghoul that had managed to get by his guards. The head almost disintegrated by the powerful weapon, the body falling to the sidewalk at his feet.

"Are we ready to leave yet, Carter? I think it's getting a little to close around here." Raddack called to the man.

Carter checked inside the bar and nodded. "We can go, if you want, Boss; there's only a few more boxes left."

"Yes, Carter, get the men and let's get the hell out of here. I'm sure we have enough to last us for a while, anyway." Then he closed the passenger door of the Hummer and had to contend with the two women.

Carter climbed up onto the back of the closest Hummer and sounded the retreat, yelling over the cacophony of gunshots.

The guards immediately started to fall back and climbed into vehicles.

The guard from Maine was bitten in the arm just as he tried to climb into the pickup truck, his screams rising over the moans of the dead and the gunshots of the other soldiers.

Another guard witnessed this and before the man from Maine could even scream *no*, the other man put a bullet in his head, ending his suffering.

Once bitten it was over. The infection would spread and finally kill the host only bringing the body back to life moments later as an undead warrior.

Carter pointed to the two armed men struggling towards the Hummers in the midst of the undead horde and told the gunner to kill them. Nodding, the gunner swung his weapon around and acquired the new targets.

Without hesitation--trained to follow orders--the gunner opened fire on the two men, white hot tracers streaking through the air to find their intended targets.

Just as the Hummer with Raddack, Cindy, and Mary pulled away from the bar, knocking zombies to the street and crushing them under the wide tires, the man turned and looked sorrowfully at Mary and Cindy.

Mary saw the look he was giving them and knew something was wrong.

"What's wrong? Why are you looking at us like that?" She asked, worriedly.

Raddack sighed. "I'm afraid I have bad news for you two. It appears your friends were overwhelmed by the undead crowd around us and killed; ripped apart and eaten. There's nothing left. I'm so sorry."

Mary looked at Cindy, both of them in shock. Then Cindy started crying and Mary couldn't hold it in any longer. Together, the two of them hugged each other, consoling one another. Rad-dack turned around in his seat, facing forward again and with his back to the crying women, smiled widely.

Chapter 22

Henry cut the head off another body, the brittle muscle slicing like dried parchment. Before the head struck the ground, he was swiveling around, his Glock firing at the next ghoul.

They were everywhere, both he and Jimmy fighting back to back.

Jimmy was using his shotgun like a baseball bat, the ammo long gone and with no time to reload, he had thought quickly, twisting the butt around and bashing in the face of the closest ghoul.

Henry saw the girls reach the small convoy out of the corner of his eye, relieved to see they were safe. Now all he had to do was worry about himself and Jimmy.

Suddenly the bodies around him exploded as .50 caliber rounds impacted with the ghouls.

Henry dropped to the ground, seeing Jimmy at his side. "Holy shit, are they trying to help us or kill us?" Jimmy screamed while bullets whined over their heads.

"Don't know, but keep sharp. Maybe things went bad for the girls and there's trouble."

Jimmy nodded and the two sprang up, Henry punching the closest ghoul under the chin. Bone cracked and the neck snapped back, the head lolling on its shoulders at an unnatural angle. Henry turned and looked off to the bar and the Hummer. The second the gunner spotted him and Jimmy, the man opened up with the machine gun again.

Henry fell to the ground, pulling Jimmy with him. The surrounding zombies, thinking their prey had collapsed, prepared to pounce, only to be blown apart into a hundred gory pieces a moment later.

Gobbets of flesh and bone rained around Jimmy and Henry, the two men covering their faces to protect themselves. But this time the bullets kept coming, walking along the asphalt as they slowly moved closer to where Henry and Jimmy were laying.

"Jimmy, grab a couple of these dead bodies and get underneath 'em or your going to have a few new holes you might not want!" Henry yelled to him, doing the same himself, after holstering his Glock. He had been through too much with the sidearm to lose it now.

Burrowing under the stinking corpses, the stench was overwhelming.

Jimmy thought back to a scene in the *Empire Strikes Back* when Han Solo cuts a wampa open and says how bad they smelled on the inside. Well, Jimmy just wished ol' Han could smell what a few hundred decaying, dead bodies smelled like, then come back and talk to him.

Trying to breath through his mouth, Henry pulled his shirt over the lower half of his face and pulled the bodies over him, burying himself under the mounds of rotting flesh. He could feel the impacts as the bullets tore up the bodies on top of him, all the flesh and muscle keeping him from being shot.

More corpses fell over, covering him even more as rounds destroyed dozens at a time.

The gunner continued for a few more seconds and then stopped, the barrel glowing hot. Then the man jumped off the back and climbed into the passenger seat, the driver ready to go. With a surge of the engine, the Hummer prepared to leave, following the other Hummer and the pickup truck as it rolled over bodies.

Though Henry would have preferred to wait for the Hummer to leave and then come up for air, that wasn't an option. The only way out of the town would be by vehicle and the Hummer was it.

With dozens of the undead surrounding him and Jimmy, he had only seconds before they were on him. Sliding out of the meat pile, covered in gore, he crawled over to Jimmy. Jimmy had more bodies on him than Henry did and Henry had to tug hard to get the man free of his flesh prison, stopping every few seconds to thrust yet another walking corpse away from him.

"Oh my God, that was awful," Jimmy gasped, wiping his hands free of blood and gore. "That is the number one thing I never want to do again," he gasped, kicking a zombie in the chest, and knocking it over. "Do you think we're screwed with all this blood on us?"

Henry shrugged. "Don't know, Jimmy, guess we'll have to wait and see; one problem at a time. If none got in our mouth or eyes, we should be all right," Henry answered.

Henry punched one in the side of the face, throwing it off balance, then he hauled Jimmy along with him, toward the Hummer.

The first Hummer and the pickup truck were long gone, the other vehicle hanging out longer to see to Henry and Jimmy.

While Henry didn't know what was happening, he did know when someone apparently wanted him dead, and he wasn't happy about it. If Mary and Cindy had been accepted willingly into the group of men, then they would have never allowed the gunner to fire at them so callously.

No, the girls were in trouble.

Weaving through the few zombies still standing, his empty shotgun bouncing off his back while he ran, he pulled his Glock from its holster and flicked off the safety. Just as the Hummer swung around to leave, Henry jumped onto the driver's side roll bar that was welded to the frame as a step into the vehicle.

The window was cracked open just a little to let in fresh air and Henry shoved the barrel of his Glock into the opening and fired three rounds at the driver and passenger. He would have fired more, but found that was the last of his clip.

The bodies danced in their seats and the Hummer rolled to a stop, hitting a parking meter and denting the bumper of the Hummer, the meter leaning a little to the right. Henry's eyes caught the orange pop up tab in the meter, the black words: **EXPIRED** showing clearly.

At the moment it kind of summed up the world.

Jimmy ran up next to him and jumped onto the back of the Hummer, dropping his empty shotgun in the rear bed and swinging the machine gun around, opening up with what was left of the ammo.

Zombies danced and heads exploded in a visceral scene of death.

Henry opened the driver's door and pulled the driver out, letting the body fall where it may.

"Come on, Jimmy, it's time to go!" Henry yelled to him over the machine gun.

"Go, I'll stay up here, just watch the bumps!" He called, blowing away three ghouls at the same time. He grinned, having fun. He could get used to this kind of firepower. Beat the hell out of his little broomstick of a shotgun, he thought, swiveling the gun around to take down a few that thought they could sneak up on him.

"Die, you dead bastards, die!" Jimmy screamed, his eyes gleaming with the adrenalin.

Henry climbed into the Hummer and closed the door, ignoring the bloody passenger for now.

Gripping the wet steering wheel, the blood already sticky, he slammed the Hummer in drive and drove over the parking meter, pulling onto the street and taking off in the same direction as the first two vehicles.

Jimmy fired the last of his ammunition and then held on for dear life as Henry swerved through some of the corpses and just ran over others.

He struck one head on, the decaying corpse snapping in two like a twig. The upper part seemed to stick to the grille for a few minutes and then it slid down and fell to the road. The Hummer bucked as it rode over the wet, bloody speed bump, churning the body into dog food as it spun in the tire well. Then it was spit out the rear where it lay glistening in the hot sun.

Henry drove for five more minutes until the town was more than a mile behind them.

Pulling over to the side of the road out of habit, he placed the Hummer in park and climbed out.

Jimmy came around the passenger side and opened the door. The other guard fell out and lay face down in the dirt.

"Hey, this guy is dead," Jimmy said to Henry.

"Really? I wondered why he was a lousy conversationalist. I just thought he was the quiet type." Henry said sarcastically.

Jimmy stared at his friend, for just a moment thinking he was serious. Then he saw Henry's face and knew he was just being a wiseass.

"Well, nice to see you still have your sense of humor, now do you mind telling me how we're going to find the girls?" He said, while dragging the dead guard away from the Hummer and letting the corpse roll down a small incline into the grass lining the road.

"I haven't thought of that yet, God, Jimmy, will you give me a chance to catch my breath?" He looked at the gore covered Jimmy and pointed. "Have you seen yourself? The first thing we need to do is get cleaned up. It can't be good to have this much contaminated blood on us."

Jimmy frowned. "Sorry, Henry, but we lost our packs and spare clothes. What do you have in mind?

Henry looked over at the dead guard lying in the grass and Jimmy frowned. "Oh sweet Jesus, you don't mean..."

Henry nodded. "Yup, a dead man's clothes are a lot better than going naked. Come on, let's get started."

Mumbling under his breath, Jimmy knew Henry was right and together the two men stripped the dead guard and used the clothes for themselves. Jimmy found another shirt, discarded under one of the back seats and together they changed. Henry chose to keep the pants he was wearing, but washed them as well as he could with water he found in a canteen inside the Hummer.

Jimmy finished dressing and frowned. "Isn't it bad luck to wear a dead man's clothes," he asked, buttoning the last button on his shirt. With the exception of a blood stain on the front of the shirt, the material was relatively clean. There was a urine stain on the pants from the man's bladder when he had expired, but compared to the smell of Jimmy's old clothes, the urine was almost like scented flowers.

"Look, I told you, the guards clothes were to small for me. I'm just glad you found that shirt, thanks again."

Jimmy made a sour face. "Don't mention it. Then he pulled a map from the dash board and handed it to Henry. "I found this too, I think you'll want to see it; take a look at what's circled."

Henry took the map and opened it on the driver's seat. He would have preferred to lay the map out on the hood of the vehicle, but the hood was too high for it to be used comfortably, plus, the bits of blood and gore would contaminate the map.

It was a map of Groton and New London Connecticut. The Groton Naval Base was circled and a line followed the highway out of town. Henry traced it all the way to where he thought they might have been when they were attacked in the Dead Town.

Pushing his finger over the naval base, he smiled at Jimmy. "There you go, that's got to be where the girls are. Good job, Jimmy, if you hadn't found this map, I don't know what we might have done."

"I know what we would have done. We would have driven over this entire state until we found them, that's what."

Henry nodded. "Oh yes, you better believe it, but still, this is a hell of a lot better."

"So, are we going?" Jimmy asked, eager to get Cindy back, and of course Mary too. Though they might fight a lot, he loved her like a sister.

Henry held up his hands, "Whoa, slow down there. First we need to take stock of what we have and don't have. Then we'll see about the base. Don't worry, if there's one thing we both know, it's that those two girls can take care of themselves. In fact, by the time we find them they'll probably be running the place."

"I sure hope you're right," Jimmy grunted in reply and then returned to checking their weapons and supplies.

* * *

Mary and Cindy were done crying for the moment when the Hummer and pickup truck pulled up to the front gate of the Groton naval base. Dead bodies littered the gate area, some torn limbs stuck in the links of the fence. Both women saw the pile of charred flesh off to the side, the bodies still smoldering.

At least these people were smart enough to burn the dead bodies once the ghouls were taken down. Many towns she had visited had been too scared to leave their barricades to clean them up and when the corpses started to rot, infections and disease would follow. Not just the zombie virus could kill. There were plenty of other viruses still waiting to claim humanity if given a chance.

Both women stared at the tall fences with razor wire and the efficient men guarding the gate.

A gate on rollers was pulled open, the once electric gate now having to be opened manually.

The Hummer and pickup truck pulled through the gate and followed the main road that led into the base, while the pickup truck turned at the first intersection, disappearing from sight.

Raddack turned around and smiled at the women. "Well, ladies, what do you think?"

Mary looked at him with red eyes, her cheeks still moist from crying. "About what? You've seen one town you've seen another, don't' make a difference if it was once a military base. What are you going do to with us? Why did you take our weapons?"

Raddack pursed his lips, considering his answer. "Now you two just relax. Let's just say you won't have to worry about the outside world anymore. I'll be protecting you from now on."

"Protecting us? From what?" Cindy asked, "We've been handling ourselves just fine up till now, we don't need your help. Thanks for getting us out of that death trap, but if it's all the same to you, once we've cleaned up and paid you for your hospitality, we'll be on our way."

Raddack laughed then, a full out loud, I don't care who hears me, laugh. "Oh, I don't think so, ladies. You see, I'm not one to look a gift horse in the mouth and you two," he let his eyes roam across their bodies, stopping at their chests. "Well, you two are the gift I won't be letting get away anytime soon."

Mary was about to protest when Raddack pulled his magnum and pointed it at the two women. "Now you two just sit tight, we'll be at my quarters in another minute or so."

Mary and Cindy looked at each other, knowing either woman would back the play of the other, but both realized for the time being they were stuck. All they had was each other now, better to stay quiet and see where the next hours led.

*   *   *

Snyder rolled over onto his back, staring up at the fluorescent light humming inside the ceiling. A mesh metal grating covered it so a prisoner couldn't get at the long tubes or the wiring within the ceiling. Turning his head, he looked to the door of his cell. The door was only partially visible, the lower half hidden by the bodies of his crewmen.

True to his word, Raddack had one of his henchmen bring one of his men into the cell and had the man kneel down on the floor every hour. Each time he would be asked to give up the command codes for the submarine and each time Snyder would refuse. He had to stare into the eyes of each of his men as the guard had pulled the trigger, blowing the man's head off.

Then the guard would leave the body where it fell. The last three crewmen had been blindfolded so that as they were ushered to their deaths, they would have no idea of the fate that awaited them, not until they felt the bullet blow through their skulls.

Snyder wept openly, remembering the eyes of the first few men. Each man had stared at him, their eyes pleading for him to give up the codes and save them. Each one had carried a shred of hope that he would live to see another day. At least until Snyder refused and the man would die.

The cell reeked of death and excrement, the bowels of the men letting go upon their death. As the hours passed, Snyder had almost become accustomed to the smell, but the odor of his failure permeated everything. Even if he held his ground and stayed silent, his men would all be dead.

He wondered if he was truly doing the right thing. Was it worth trying to live up to ideals of a world that no longer existed? Or should he just capitulate to the crime boss' demands and give him the submarine, and let the man commit chaos on a grander scale.

Snyder pushed the palms of his hands into his eye sockets, pressing hard until he felt pain. At least this was pain he had chosen to inflict upon himself, not like the hundreds of other spots on his body that ached with a throbbing that would never stop.

But as he thought about it, he realized the pain and suffering would stop; just as soon as he died.

That made him feel slightly better and he smiled slightly until the pain in his teeth caused him to stop.

He stared at the bloody corpses of his men. Sooner or later everything ends, whether you like it or not.

Chapter 23

"There it is, exit 84," Jimmy said, pointing out the window at the large green sign on Route 95 South. The sign was a standard highway sign with a green backing and white reflective lettering. The sign, read: **EXIT 84, GROTON NAVAL BASE**.

Henry swerved off the highway, taking the exit at speed. Just as he took the off ramp and barreled around the tight curve that led to the main street, two roamers stumbled out into the road.

Henry grinned and swerved toward them, aiming the front grille so they would hit the two bodies' dead center.

The Hummer bucked for a second as it absorbed the impact, the two corpses flying twenty feet into the air to land in the slight ravine running along side the road to help with drainage.

When the Hummer sped past, Jimmy caught a quick glimpse of the bodies. The limbs were still moving, twitching really, but the two roamers weren't going anywhere for a while, if ever.

Henry glanced in his rearview mirror and then pressed the gas pedal, the vehicle surging forward.

"Two more down, three million to go," he muttered to himself.

Jimmy heard the end of the statement but let it go. He wasn't in much of a mood for talking, his concern for Cindy and Mary filling him with dread despite Henry's pep talk.

Pulling onto the main road, Henry floored the pedal, the vehicle surging forward yet again as it almost seemed to fly across the road. The large tires crushed dead and rotting bodies lying in the road as the Hummer shot up the two lane blacktop, avoiding dozens of derelict vehicles.

A school bus was lying on its side in a nearby parking lot for a shopping center. Henry slowed the Hummer as they drove by it, seeing a few small skeletons lying near the bus. Neither man said anything, the tableaux saying everything that didn't need to be said. Henry stepped on the gas and the Hummer surged forward, leaving the dead school bus in their back trail.

Jimmy couldn't help but look out the window at all the stores, nightclubs and bars. At one time this large street would have been a booming commercial area. All the personnel from the naval base using the different businesses. He imagined what it must have looked like on a Friday night, all the sailors off for the weekend, looking to spend some of their paycheck before pulling out on their ships the following Monday.

Now, all that lined the highway was shattered wrecks and charred buildings, a remnant to a different time that despite being less than a year ago; seemed like a lifetime.

Henry spotted another sign with an arrow pointing down a side street. The sign said that the base was only a mile away and Henry swerved around the turn, knocking the sign down to land in the dirt.

Powering down, he slowed the vehicle and turned to Jimmy. "All right, if the areas clear of deaders, then I want to park this thing and do a recce on foot, see what we're up against. Once we do that, we can formulate a way to get in there and find the girls."

"What about if we just pull up to the gate and ask to come inside? Say we found this Hummer on the road and the map in the glove box?" Jimmy suggested.

Henry shook his head side-to-side. "No, that would be a bad move. The second we stop at the gate we're vulnerable to an attack. We have no idea if they're friendly or not and considering their men tried to gun us down in cold blood, I'm going to lean to them not being very welcoming."

Jimmy nodded. "Fair enough, lead on, chief."

Henry drove further down the road, slowing when he believed he was as close as he could get without being spotted by anyone patrolling the base's perimeter. Parking the Hummer behind an old building that looked like it had once been a gas station; the pumps long gone, he and Jimmy slid out of the vehicle and gathered by the front bumper.

Henry noticed the steaming gobbets of flesh and gristle cooking on the grille, but ignored them. He'd seen more of people's insides in the last year to last a lifetime.

"All right, stay behind cover and keep your eyes out for deaders. I don't want to be so focused on the base that we get cornered by some damn *retread*," he said, using the slang name from Greenwood.

Jimmy nodded, pulling his shotgun from the back seat. It was now clean of blood and gore, Henry's as well. Per their previous bet, Jimmy had stripped all their weapons, using all the gun oil they had left. Luckily, Henry had been carrying a small bottle in his pants or they would have been unable to clean and strip the weapons properly, though Henry would have considered taking some oil from the Hummer's oil pan to at least grease the outer mechanisms of the weapons and keep them moisture free.

Not the best of ideas, but better than nothing in a crucial moment.

Two .45 pistols and a box of bullets for them was found in the rear of the Hummer. Now both carried the new side arms. Though small caliber weapons didn't have much stopping power, they would do well if the marksman was skilled enough, and both Jimmy and Henry had become superb shots since they had first met.

Moving away from the Hummer at a slight jog, the two men hugged the buildings and trees for cover. The base was just around the bend in the road and Henry was wary for either men patrolling the perimeter or other vehicles leaving the base.

Leapfrogging for ten minutes, the two warriors stopped behind the husk of a burned out automobile.

The main gate could be seen clearly from where they hid, and Henry frowned as he watched the guards patrolling the perimeter fence.

"Look at their weapons, Jimmy," he said gesturing to the closest guards. They were too far away to see the men's faces, but the weapons they held reflected the sunlight like polished mirrors.

Jimmy nodded. "Looks well maintained. Think they've got the ammo for them or are they just for show like back in Greenwood."

"No, If I had to stake my life on it I'd say they've got more than enough rounds. Remember how that gunner shot that machine gun like he would never run out?" Henry counted the guards, trying to keep all the bodies straight. "I count at least ten men, maybe one or two more. I can't get a good count, the bastards won't stay still," Henry said frustrated.

"Yeah, me neither. If we're going in there, I think we need to find another way in." Jimmy turned sideways and looked into Henry's eyes. "How the hell are we gonna find the girls once we're in there? If we're seen, there's no way we can fight off a whole settlement. We need a distraction."

Henry looked down at the dirt around his shoes, thinking. "I know, I've been thinking about that, too. Listen, you know I'd kill a thousand people to save Mary and Cindy but I just can't start killing innocent people indiscriminately. Once you go down that road there's no going back. At first I thought we could cut a hole in the fence and let a shitload of roamers inside the base. With the guards dealing with that we could look for Cindy and Mary."

"So, that sounds good, what's the problem?" Jimmy asked, not understanding.

Henry looked around them, making sure they were alone, neither live nor dead enemies near them. "The problem is there are innocent people in there, people just trying to stay alive. I won't be the cause of their death, not intentionally and neither will you. What do you think the girls would say if you told them that's what you did to save them? Do you think Cindy would be okay with that?"

Jimmy sighed, kicking a stone away from his feet. "No, she wouldn't. In fact I don't even want to think of what she would do. Okay, Henry, that's not an option, but then what is? We've only got the two of us and a few guns and we're both low on ammo. Not exactly the cavalry."

Henry didn't answer, his eyes looking through the husk of the car, staring at something Jimmy couldn't see. Jimmy was about to ask him what was wrong, when Henry stopped his gaze and turned to look back at Jimmy, a big grin on his face.

"What? What the hell are you smiling about? What were you looking at?" Jimmy demanded.

"I just figured out our way in and it requires no cutting or climbing at all."

Jimmy started to smile as well. "Great, sign me up, let's go get them," he said enthusiastically, not even knowing what the plan was.

"We will, Jimmy my boy, we will. But first we need to get back to the Hummer and gather everything we're taking with us. Then I want to camouflage it better so that we can get to it once we get the girls. I don't want to be running for my life and find out at the last second some other asshole had stolen our ride."

Agreeing with Henry, Jimmy started backing away from the car, Henry right beside him.

As the two men ran back to the Hummer, Jimmy asked: "So how long is this going to take?"

"If everything goes smoothly, we should be inside the fence within the hour."

With a wide smile on his face, Jimmy looked to Henry. "Sweet," he said and then concentrated on running, eyes always scanning the dark corners of the nearby buildings and tree line for any undead activity.

*　　*　　*

Mary and Cindy were escorted by gunpoint into a large building with a large oval driveway that let the Hummer drive right up to the lobby doors. Raddack had already exited the vehicle and waited for them to reach him inside the lobby.

Mary made sure to take notice of the guard he had been talking to. Whatever they had been discussing the guard didn't look to happy and Raddack seemed displeased as well.

When the women reached him, he smiled, the gesture making Mary want to kick him in the face, but she kept her temper in check for a better time when she might be able to escape; though she couldn't resist flashing him a contemptuous glare.

If he noticed, he didn't let on.

Both women stopped simultaneously, waiting for what would happen next.

"Oh, don't be like that, ladies. I promise you, you'll like it here. I have all the comforts of home. Even running water, and the toilets work. We're lucky here. We have engineers and electricians and even a few farmers. We are almost entirely self sufficient and when I finish with a few loose ends, I'll be able to branch out and take even more. You'll see, one day you'll be thanking me for taking you in."

Cindy crossed her arms and stared at Raddack, her eyes flashing fire. "Don't bet on it, chubby. I'm warning you now, let us go or you'll be sorry."

Raddack's eyes went wide with first shock and then anger. He stepped closer to Cindy, the smaller woman having to take two steps backward or risk being knocked over. She had to stop when the muzzle of one of the guard's rifles jammed into the small of her back. "Now, you listen to me, you little bitch. This is my house and no one talks to me like that in my house. I'll let you off with a warning this one time, but if you speak to me like that again, I warn you that you will regret it. Do you understand me?"

Cindy swallowed hard, realizing she was in way over her head. This was not the time for foolish rebellion, better to wait until they knew more about their situation. She nodded slowly and her eyes looked away from him. Raddack reminded her of her Uncle, a man who had done despicable things to her and though Cindy was a strong woman, even she had her weaknesses and her Uncle was one of them.

Raddack could see he made his point and so stepped back, wiping sweat from his brow. "Good, if that's settled, then these men will escort you to my quarters. They'll send up a change of clothes for you, until then, feel free to have something to eat and drink while you wait for my return."

Raddack turned around then and walked away, dismissing the two women.

Raddack said to the guard, "Make sure there are two guards outside my door. I have a feeling these two ladies are a tricky pair."

"Yes, Boss, I'll make sure it happens," Smith said.

Raddack nodded and then left the lobby, climbing back into his Hummer and disappearing down the drive.

Smith turned to Mary and Cindy and smiled half-heartedly. "Come on, ladies. You heard the man," he said.

Mary looked to Cindy and she shrugged, they had no choice but to do as they were told, so both allowed themselves to be led to the stairwell. They could worry about Raddack later. At least when they reached his quarters they could eat and clean up, then figure out a way out of their new prison.

Which wasn't so bad actually.

If you had to be kept like a pet, this was the way to do it.

After the guards had pushed Mary and Cindy through the doorway and closed the door behind them, securing the lock--Mary had tried it anyway, not surprised to find it locked--she had kicked the door and frowned, looking around the room unhappily

The walls of what were once the rest of the floor had been knocked out so that the apartment was huge, consisting of nearly half of the entire floor of the building. Paintings raided from art galleries lined the walls and teakwood and oak furniture was scattered across the wide open space. Plush carpeting covered portions of the room, mostly near where the bed was. A grandfather clock, looking to be worth thousands of dollars, ticked quietly in the far corner.

Despite the opulence the items were all thrown about half-heartedly, looking for all purposes like a designer's worst nightmare.

Taking it all in with a casual look, Cindy walked over to one of the large glass windows and peered out. She could see numerous building tops and off to the side was a huge structure she believed to be the commissary. None of the windows opened, the building originally being cooled by air conditioning alone.

Off to her right she could see the ocean. Raddack had mentioned the lower base of the station and she assumed that must be where it was. Looking past the water into the canal, she could see the burnt out husks of other buildings and structures that had once bordered the coast, now nothing more than dark skeletons still standing defiantly despite the damage they had suffered.

An old submarine dry dock floated in the middle of the channel, one side of it listing so much it was a miracle it hadn't tipped over yet. The side closest to the water had a large crane connected to it, the mast now bent and hidden in the dark water. There was a set of binoculars sitting on the window ledge and she picked them up, looking at the dry dock closer. She was just able to read the name on the front of the bow. **WATERFORD**, it said in faded white paint.

Mary walked over to her and glanced out the window as well. She looked down below her. All she could see was a parking lot full of cars that had been left when their owners had gone to sea only to never return for them. Some of the vehicles were missing parts and tires, scavenged by the people of the base.

Mary glanced to her left and noticed some small campfires and saw two other barracks. In these she saw ordinary people, children, old men and women doing what people did every day of their lives. Some could be seen cooking, washing and there appeared to be someone trying to fix an old van.

On the roof of the building, laundry could be seen blowing in the wind and when Mary squinted, she could just make out a figure still up there, hanging clothes to dry in the sun.

Backing away from the window, Mary walked passed a few openings where walls once stood and stopped by a large dinner table. On the table were set canned fruits and homemade bread. A cooked chicken, some feathers still attached, but having been burned off when it had been roasted on an open fire, sat in a silver serving dish. Mary pulled a piece off and making sure not to see any residue from the feathers, tried a piece. The bird was still warm and her taste buds went wild with the taste. It had been hours since they had eaten anything and before she could stop herself, she was pulling off yet another piece. She ripped a leg from the carcass and walked over to Cindy, who seemed to be hypno-tized as she gazed out the window, binoculars hanging by her side, her vacant stare making her seem like some form of statue created from the mind of a sculptor.

"Here, try this, it's incredible," she said over a mouthful of meat. Cindy shifted her head and looked down at the leg. "I'm not hungry," she said quietly. Mary finished what was in her mouth and then moved closer to her friend.

"You're thinking about the guys, huh?" She asked quietly.

Cindy nodded, her shoulders drooping. "I just can't believe they're dead. I really don't know what I'm going to do without Jimmy," she said so quietly Mary almost didn't hear her.

Mary did though and she grabbed her shoulders and spun her around. "Now you listen to me, missy, I know exactly what you're going to do, you're going to keep fighting and live. That's what Henry and Jimmy would have wanted us to do. Do you really think the guys would just want us moping around, crying for them? Of course not. In fact, if Jimmy knew I cried for him I'd never hear the end of it. So as of right now you need to suck it up and get focused. Eat something, drink something, then we'll get cleaned up, and then we'll see if we can get out of here. Okay?"

Cindy listened to what she had to say and her eyes seemed to cloud up. Then she blinked them clear and nodded. Her face cleared of sorrow and her countenance took on one of resolve. "You're right, Mary, I know you are. Okay, let's eat and then let's get the hell out of here. If that fat prick thinks he's going to lay a hand on me, he's got another thing coming,"

Mary smiled; glad she was back onboard again, the melancholy mood gone. They would mourn the guys later, when they were free, but for now they needed to prepare for what was to come. Henry had taught her a lot and if she was going down she would go down fighting, and take a lot of bad guys with her.

Chapter 24

Raddack opened the door to Snyder's cell, wrinkling his nose at the smell. More than ten bodies were piled in the corner of the room like cordwood. Blood dripping from them like a weak waterfall.

Holding his hand to his nose, Raddack stepped inside the cell, but only a foot or so. That was as far as he wanted to go into the charnel house of death.

Snyder looked up from the floor where he had been laying. More bruises and cuts covered his arms and face, leftovers from his latest visit with the Chinaman.

"My, Captain, you look terrible, though not as bad as your men over there. I think you should know that more of your men have defected to me. When some of them heard what you're letting happen to the crew in here, they quickly changed sides. Smart lads, I don't blame them." He knelt down so he was closer to eye level with the Captain. "So, what do you say? How 'bout giving me those codes. I give you my word, I'll release you. Even though you've been difficult, I have to respect you for keeping your silence," He leaned in a little closer to Snyder, whispering his next words as if the Captain was a confidant. "You know, I don't believe if I was in your shoes that I would have lasted as long as you have. I don't think I'd have had the resolve, the loyalty. But what you seem to forget is your loyalty is wasted on something that doesn't even exist anymore. Some of your crew has told me you haven't received word from NORAD or any other higher chain of command for what, months? Why don't you just except that the old world is gone and embrace the new one. Your world is dead, literally and figuratively. Though the old world had its perks, I have to say the new one isn't that bad. That is, if you're at the top of the food chain, which I am. So how about those codes? Would it help if I said please?"

Snyder had remained perfectly still the entire speech, not wanting to give away that he was in fact able to move if he desired to, though the action would cause him a great deal of pain. As Raddack slowly grew closer, Snyder prepared himself for a last ditch effort to get his revenge on the man.

Snyder waited patiently, listening to the man's speech about his world being gone and when Raddack had finished, the word *please* leaving his mouth, Snyder lunged at the man, wrapping his fingers around his throat.

Raddack screamed and tried to jump away, but Snyder's grip was like iron, every ounce of his strength being put into the attack.

Raddack started to turn blue and Snyder smiled just a little, not wanting to break his concentration.

"Tell you what, Raddack, why don't you just die, yourself," he hissed. But then it all went wrong as one of the guards jumped into the room and slammed the butt of his rifle onto the back of Snyder's neck.

The Captain saw stars and when the rifle butt came down for the second time, he was knocked unconscious, his grip loosening as he slumped to the bloody floor.

Raddack pulled himself away from the unconscious man, breathing in great gasps of air. The color returned to his face and with another guard's help, managed to regain his footing.

Raddack was so relieved to still be breathing, he didn't think to chastise the guards for their lax behavior, but instead walked over to Snyder and raised his foot over the unconscious man's skull, prepared to crush it under his heavy boot heel.

The foot hovered there for more than a minute until Raddack seem to realize what he was doing and lowered his foot, stepping back. Pushing one of the guards out of his way, he stormed out of the cell, realizing if he stayed he would surely kill the man for what he had done and lose all hope of recovering the lost command codes.

Rubbing his sore neck, Raddack stomped down the hallway. "You two, clean those bodies out of there and get the Captain cleaned up. Let me know when he regains consciousness," he snapped before he turned the corner of the hallway to walk out into the main room of the building.

"Yes, Boss, we'll get right on that," one of the men said, but Raddack didn't hear him, he didn't need to. All of his men knew what would happen to them if they disobeyed one of his orders. If they did and he found out, they would feed the zombies in the corral by the galley.

Rubbing his neck and trying to soothe his raw skin, he grinned malevolently. He had to give Snyder credit. The man was tougher than he thought and might have killed him if it wasn't for his guards.

Ah, well, with Snyder under wraps for a while he figured he'd go back to his quarters and play with his two new toys, namely the blonde and brunette.

As he climbed into the rear seat of his Hummer, the driver driving off after he had closed his door, Raddack wondered which one he'd take first.

Then realizing that he had come so very close to death and that life is truly shorter than it should be, he decided what the hell, maybe he'd just have the two women at the same time.

*   *   *

Henry and Jimmy dashed across the small side street to the rear of the base, keeping a watchful eye out for any undead loiterers and the guards patrolling the perimeter fence of the naval station.

Slamming against the side of an old ice cream truck, now parked, half-on and half-off the curb, the two men surveyed their surroundings.

They could only see a tiny portion of the rear gate, the rest hiding from view because of distance and obstructions.

After hiding the Hummer better, the two men had loaded up with every piece of weaponry they had and had set off for the opposite side of the base.

In his left hand Henry held a tire iron he'd taken from the tire kit that was in the back of the Hummer. Without the metal bar his entire plan would be useless.

The sun was high in the sky, the time, somewhere in the late afternoon. Jimmy looked around himself, frowning at the moving shadows in the buildings and trees around them. There were deaders everywhere and it was only a matter of time before they realized they had fresh meat in their midst and decided to come out and try to get a taste.

Both men had taken down three roamers a piece as they had made their way to the rear of the base. The slow moving targets had been easily dispatched, Henry using his panga and Jimmy a piece of two-by-four with a few nails sticking out of the end like spines on a porcupine. After Jimmy had cleaned and polished his shotgun, he wasn't too keen on getting the butt of the weapon covered in blood and gore again.

With their target now in sight, Jimmy set the piece of wood down, hopefully finished with it.

The need for stealth was just about over and in a few minutes it would be time to use more effective means of stopping an enemy, namely a bullet to the head.

"Okay, just like we rehearsed it. I'll pull the cover to the side and you drop in, then I'll follow you," Henry said while sneaking a peek around the ice cream truck.

Jimmy nodded and then checked their backs once again, and muffled a soft curse at what he saw.

"Henry, we've got visitors," he said, with his hand on the trigger of his shotgun. He was just about to blow the party crashers back to hell where they belonged when Henry placed his hand on the shotgun, stopping him.

"No, don't shoot them, you'll just alert the base we're here, forget about them, just go!" He ordered Jimmy, taking off from around the truck and running out into the open street.

Jimmy hesitated for a half second, his instincts wanting to shoot the attacking ghouls, but he did what Henry told him to, knowing the older man was right.

Turning on his heels, he ran out into the street, where Henry was already at work removing the manhole cover. At their position in the street, the guards at the base couldn't see them, though Jimmy had no doubt they might hear all the noise. Hopefully the approaching deaders would cause a diversion.

Grunting with the effort, Henry managed to slide the heavy metal cover from its seal, the cover making a loud clang as it fell the two inches from his fingers.

He turned to check on Jimmy just as the younger man ran up to the opening in the street and dropped in with a yell of "Geronimo!"

Henry laughed at his friend's recklessness and then, he too, turned around and slid his legs down into the darkness. He was about to try and pull the heavy cover back in place when the first ghoul reached him.

Teeth and hands reached out, trying to grab any piece of Henry that was available. Henry was at a serious disadvantage with half his body dangling on the ladder below the street, his upper body sticking out of the hole like a puppet.

Henry pushed the foul creature away, and grabbed its leg with his right hand, pulling as hard as he could. The deader's leg flew out from under it, and for a heartbeat the creature was horizontal in the air. Then gravity took over, sending the ghoul falling hard onto the street, the jarring impact enough to rattle its teeth.

But with no breath to worry about, the creature rolled onto its side and continued the attack.

Cursing loud and long, Henry realized there was no way to fend off the advances of the dead attackers and still manage to pull the manhole cover back, so he gave up and dropped off the ladder, falling into the shadows of the sewer. Another ghoul had snuck up behind him, the tattered business suit it had worn in life still buttoned, and was about to take a bite out of Henry's shoulder when the warrior dropped into the sewer, his shoulder falling away from the blackened teeth. He could have sworn he heard its upper and lower teeth clack together as he fell away.

Henry landed on his rump in four inches of a dark substance that might have contained water at one point in its existence and he looked up at the circle of light above him. The light was quickly extinguished as multiple decaying, pale heads looked down into the sewer. If they were angry that their prey had slipped their grasp, none of them let on.

"Ha! Better luck next time, ya dead bastards!" Jimmy called up, while helping Henry to his feet.

Standing up, Henry looked down at the lower half of his body, managing a disgusted face when he saw his wet clothes. A brown and black substance coated his lower half and he looked to Jimmy for some comfort.

"What the hell is on me?" He asked quietly, ignoring the shuffling bodies above him. For the moment they were safe, the undead not understanding how to get down into the sewer.

"If I knew, I'd tell you, but I really don't think you'd want to know," Jimmy said with a slight smile. He was doing his best to stop it from becoming wider.

"Forget it, you're probably right, come on, lets get moving," he told him.

Jimmy nodded and the two companions headed off into the darkness of the sewer; one sloshing step at a time.

Five minutes later, the footsteps of the two sojourners had faded into the darkness. The pack of ghouls had continued to grow, a few wandering over to the rear gate where they were promptly put down by the guards, but more than a hundred were still active. They had been waiting for some way into the base, never wandering too far from the fence, knowing there was food inside.

Others still hovered over the opening in the sewer, wanting the food that had dropped down into the darkness.

Completely by accident, one of the corpses stumbled into another one, causing the walking corpse to overstep the hole.

The ghoul dropped away into the darkness to be lost from sight. Seconds passed and another fell in. Soon every zombie was stepping over the hole, each one falling into the sewer below.

After falling they would crawl forward, as others fell behind them. Some weren't so lucky, though. A few had shattered limbs and one broke its neck, ending its mobile existence.

But the undead didn't feel pain and merely pulled themselves to their feet and shuffled into the blackness. Some small amount of intelligence, what could be compared to the minutest spark of energy deep inside a massive supernova, told the lead ghoul to head into the darkness, that was where the meat had fled.

Single file they went, more falling behind the others, the sewer becoming packed with undead, moaning bodies.

They were hungry and now they knew where to go.

*   *   *

"Did you hear that?" Jimmy asked as they made their way through the obsidian darkness.

"Hear what, the moans and groans of the animated dead coming from the shadows to eat you?" Henry remarked sarcastically as they continued deeper into the dank and fragrant sewer.

"That's not funny, they could be in here and we wouldn't know it until it was too late," Jimmy said.

Henry was counting his footsteps, hoping his estimate was correct as to when they would be under the base. "It's probably all the deaders at the sewer opening. Noise carries down here, echoes and stuff, you know? Shit, I still wish I could have gotten that cover back on. Now if there are any patrols around they'll see it and know something's up. With only the two of us, surprise is our best weapon. Hopefully, we can get in the base, grab the girls and then get out with no one the wiser, then we'll get the hell out of here, maybe find a secluded house and hole up for a while."

Jimmy nodded, but realized Henry couldn't see him. "Sure, sounds good, I just hope the girls are all right. They must know we're coming for them, right?" He asked; the worry and concern in his voice clearly audible in the darkness.

Henry reached out and found his shoulder and squeezed it. "Don't worry, they'll be fine, they have to be, right?"

"Yeah, sure, of course, I mean, what could happen in half a day? Hell, they're probably just hanging around, waiting for us."

"That's the spirit, Jimmy, think positive. Now come on, there's a little light up ahead. It's probably another opening to the street. Let's get to it and get the hell out of this disgusting pit."

"Okay," Jimmy said and picked up his pace, their feet churning the black water around their feet as they walked.

"I'm just glad we can't see the shit we're walking in," Henry said, his hand sliding across the moss covered, sewer wall while he moved constantly forward.

Jimmy thought about Henry's statement and then asked softly: "Do you think there're spiders down here?"

Henry chuckled. "I'm sure there are. Some of them big enough to eat a man whole. But don't worry, I'll protect you."

"Gee, thanks, I feel a lot better now, thanks a lot," he said, glad Henry couldn't see the worry on his face. He didn't know why he had such a fear of spiders; after all, when you got right down to it what could the small arachnids ever do to hurt him?

But he just couldn't control his fear, irrational or not, every time he thought of those eight legs moving up and down, those beady little eyes staring at him, he shivered.

Give him a reanimated corpse any day; just keep the spiders away from him.

Trying to hone his senses to any spiders that might be in the darkness, he bit his lip and continued on, Henry by his side.

Chapter 25

"Stop here, this should be under the base," Henry said, looking up at the small pinholes of light that made up the manhole cover above his head.

"You mean like the last three we've tried. I'm not afraid to say this, but this might have been a big mistake, Henry. Maybe we should just backtrack back to the way we got in here and try something else," Jimmy said.

With a sliver of light shining down on his face, Henry could see how dirty he was. Henry held his hands out in front of him, the diffuse light barely illuminating his hands. But he was still able to see the filth covering his hands and arms. When and if they ever got out of the sewer, they would each need a bath for a month to get the stench off their bodies.

"Nonsense, this one will open, you'll see," Henry said with more confidence than he felt.

Since walking enough distance to be under the base, Henry had tried every manhole they had come across. Each one had been blocked by something. One time Henry had heard the distinctive sound of a baby crying and had smelled food cooking, a stew or soup or something that resembled that particular fragrance.

With the sewers completely ignored by the residents of the base, the manhole covers had been built over, what exactly was on top of them unknown.

Now as Henry climbed up the small ladder to the cover, he glanced down at the dull outline of Jimmy's face. "You'll see, this one will work, I promise."

Jimmy just grunted and watched their sides. In the past few minutes he had been hearing sounds. Scraping sounds as well as the sound of water being displaced like something was walking in the sewer. Each time he had looked, nothing had appeared and he realized he was just nervous. It was probably what Henry had said and just echoes from the deaders back at the opening. But should the noise carry all the way to them from such a far distance?

Jimmy was about to bring this up to Henry when a crack sounded above his head and the manhole cover popped up an inch. Sunlight spilled into the sewer and Jimmy finally got a chance to see what he had been walking in for the past half hour.

"Yuck, this is so gross," he said, wishing he hadn't seen the viscous fluid covering his boots. Bits of toilet paper, rat carcasses, some still twitching, and floating turds floated in the black depths of the water.

Climbing on the bottom rung of the ladder, he looked up at the opening, and waited while Henry peeked through to see if it was clear.

"I'm really ready to get out of here now, Henry, is it okay up there?"

"Yeah, seems fine. There's some kind of wall a few feet away, but otherwise there's nothing. Looks like it's some kind of corral. Guess they've got animals here." He pushed the cover off, the lid clanging as it fell.

"Jesus, Henry, make some more noise, why don'tcha, maybe everyone doesn't know we're here yet," Jimmy quipped, starting up the ladder.

Henry was about to give him a snappy answer when hands shot at him and he was pulled from the hole, disappearing from view.

Jimmy looked up from inspecting his boots, not happy with the black sludge covering them and frowned, not seeing Henry. So he climbed up a few more rungs, his head just shy of the opening

"Henry, where'd ya go?" Jimmy asked, wondering what Henry was doing.

But instead of hearing Henry's voice answering him, he heard the unmistakable sound of undead voices moaning.

Jimmy tried to back down the ladder, but before he could let go and drop back to the sewer floor, he too, was pulled out of the hole, skeletal hands with rotting flesh pulling him up and out onto the street.

Jimmy was flat on his back and staring up at five rotting, undead faces.

"Oh, shit," he muttered, and then the faces descended.

* * *

Mary looked up when the door to the apartment opened and Raddack stepped in. The man didn't look as good as when he'd left them alone earlier. For one thing, he had a red mark around his neck like someone had tried to hang him.

Mary leaned back against the window frame and smiled. "Rough day?" She asked, wryly.

"You don't know the half of it, but I'm sure you ladies can make me forget my troubles."

Cindy's eyebrows went up a little at his statement. "Oh, really, and how do you suppose we might do that?"

Raddack walked further into the room, slipping off his leather jacket and tossing it onto a nearby couch. He walked over to the table full of food and poured himself a glass of water.

"Surprise me," he said with a sleazy grin. "And in case you get any ideas, my men are right outside that door. They can hear us, so if I was to say, call out in pain, they have orders to come in here shooting and sort out the mess later. Understand?"

Mary pushed off from the window and strolled over to Raddack. She walked circles around him, her left hand touching his shoulder playfully as she moved seductively.

"So what did you have in mind?" She whispered sweetly into his ear.

Raddack tried to follow her as she moved around him, his head swiveling around, making him resemble an owl. "Oh, I don't know; let's just say that if you want to stay here with me, you'll need to keep me happy. The women that are on this base now are all old and tired. The hardships of just staying alive everyday have crushed their looks. But you two, well what can I say? I haven't seen a pair as lovely as you since before the world went to shit."

Cindy moved closer as well, pursing her lips and looking up into his eyes. "So you want a couple of love slaves, is that it? We service you and keep you happy, and in exchange you'll let us stay here with you?"

Raddack nodded, licking his lips as he looked down at Cindy's breasts, full and soft under her shirt.

"That's right; my, you ladies catch on quick," he breathed.

"And what if we don't agree with this arrangement? What happens then?" Mary asked, calmly, like it was a joke of a question, not something she would actually entertain as a real thought.

Raddack's face went blank, and he grabbed Mary's wrists, holding her tight. Not expecting it, Mary could only stare at the man. He gazed into her eyes and his mouth opened wide.

"Well, if you don't agree, then I really have no use for you. I guess I'll give you to my guards and let them have some fun for a while. Once you're used up, then I'll have you disposed of. You see, we can only have so many people on the base or we'll run out of resources. You understand, don't you, my dear?"

Mary smiled sweetly at him, her eyes closing to slits. "Oh yes, I understand better than you might think."

Before Raddack could do a thing to stop her, she rammed her leg up into his testicles, and pushed the crime boss to the floor.

"Cindy, get his mouth so he doesn't scream," Mary told her while she looked around the room for something to tie him up with.

Cindy dropped down to the floor, grabbing a napkin off the table and shoving it into Raddack's mouth. The fat man was in no condition to argue as he tried to suck in another breath of air. His face was a slight shade of blue and he wheezed from the pain of his crushed groin

"Why don't we just kill him?" She asked, glaring down at the suffering man.

Mary had found a sheet on a shelf by the bed and she used her teeth to start a rip. Then she started tearing it into strips, trying to make a binding for Raddack.

"Believe me, I want to, but if we do kill him and we can't find a way out of here, they'll just kill us. We need him as a hostage. It's the only way to keep the guard's in line. Here, roll him over so I can tie his hands."

Cindy did so, straining with the effort. Raddack was huffing and puffing through his nose, trying to work through the pain he felt. Mary pulled his hands together and then tied his wrists with the long strips of cloth, making sure to wrap one loop around the man's neck. Then she pulled the torn sheet to his legs and tied his ankles. By doing this, Raddack couldn't move and if he struggled to hard he would end up strangling himself.

Reaching down, she pulled the pair of Magnums from their holsters. Studying the weapons with an admiring eye.

"Nice," she said, tossing one to Cindy. The woman caught it easily and then opened the cylinder, satisfied to see it had a full load. Slapping it shut, she made sure the safety was on and then tucked it into the front of her pants.

"What's the plan?" Cindy asked, standing back up. Raddack tried to yell through his gag and Cindy kicked him in the back, shutting him up.

Mary was still holding her own Magnum and after checking it, she gestured to the door. "We call the guards in here and when they come inside the room, we get their weapons and get the hell out of here."

Cindy nodded. "It'll do in a pinch. What about him, do we leave him?"

"No, once we get the guards weapons and tie them up, I want to personally put a bullet in the bastards head."

"What about if I want to do it," Cindy asked, hurt.

"Look, he came on to me first so I should be the one to do it," Mary replied.

Raddack lay on the ground staring up at the two women who had somehow managed to subdue him and tie him up in the blink of an eye. Now they were arguing who was going to kill him. It was madness!

The two went back and forth, each giving a reason why she should be the one to kill him until Mary finally held up her hands. "Whoa, all right, hold up. Look, we both deserve to kill him so what do you say about me shooting him in the head and you can shoot him in the heart?"

"I want to shoot him in the head," Cindy protested.

Mary sighed. "Fine, then I'll shoot him in the heart, okay?"

"Okay," Cindy said, satisfied.

"All right, now that it's settled, lets get out of here," Mary said and moved to the door. Knocking on it twice, she heard a voice on the other side.

"Yes, what is it?"

"Uh, yeah, hi. Look, your boss is in the bathroom and he told me he needs you guys. Something's wrong with his zipper and his... you know. He doesn't want me or my friend to help; he said he needs a man."

She heard a chuckle from the other side of the door and then the door opened; the two guards making jokes about how much pain Raddack must be in.

The first guard stepped through the door, a large smile on his face, his rifle slung over his shoulder. He had no reason to even suspect something was wrong.

After all, the boss was with a couple of women and they had heard no sounds but some huffing and puffing, i.e. they were having sex.

No sooner had the guard entered the room, then he realized things were not as he had expected.

Mary grabbed his arm and threw him to the floor, pressing the Magnum to his cheek. At the same time Cindy kicked the other guard in the stomach, the man doubling over from the pain. She followed her first kick with another to the man's face, knocking him to the floor where he lay perfectly still with a crushed nose.

Cindy walked out into the hall, knelt down over the prone body and checked for a pulse.

"Shit, I killed him," she said unhappily from the hallway. She had kicked him in the nose so hard, she had sent splinters of cartilage into his brain, killing the man in one blow.

Mary didn't seem interested. "Goes with the territory. He wanted to be a guard. Sometimes you win, sometimes you lose. Guess he lost," she said while tying and gagging the other guard.

Mary had just finished and was about to tell Cindy to get the guard's body inside the room and close the apartment's door, when two more guards came walking up the hallway.

Mary and Cindy had no way of knowing it was time for the guards to change shifts. They had picked the worst possible time to attack. If they had only waited five more minutes, the new guards would have been in place and they would have had four hours before being discovered.

The two men saw Cindy leaning over the body of one of their own and immediately drew their weapons. Cindy turned to see them and as she moved back into the apartment, the face of the dead guard was in view to the two new men. Seeing the blood covered face was all the two new arrivals needed to know.

Firing off a shot each, Cindy ducked back inside the apartment, slamming the door closed and jamming a chair under the knob.

A moment later the door started shaking, so she turned, pulled the Magnum, and fired a shot through the door. The round went through the door like it was cardboard and a cry of pain from the other side told her she had struck someone. Whether it had been a kill shot was unknown.

"Stay away from us or we'll kill your boss!" Cindy screamed as she moved away from the door, Muffled cries and men talking filtered inside the room through the door, but other than that, nothing happened.

Cindy looked across the room at Mary who had just finished tying the guard and now had his rifle, as well. Cindy had been unable to retrieve the other guard's weapon, the rifle having fallen into the hallway when he'd gone down.

"What the hell do we do now?" She asked.

Mary shook her head, not having the faintest idea. Their chances of leaving with the guards permission went to hell the moment Cindy killed one of their own. Now, even if Raddack was kept alive the men would be out for blood.

Mary went to the window and looked out across the base. They were six stories up, so there would be no escape from the windows.

They were trapped.

Turning and slouching against the window frame, she sighed, all the steam going out of her.

"Cindy, I hate to say it, but I really think we're in real trouble here. I have no goddamn idea how the hell we're going get to out of here in one piece."

Cindy stared back at her and then at the door, where the sounds of more voices were filling the hallway. Whatever the guards were planning it was going to be happening soon.

Raddack lay on the floor, listening to the two women discuss their fate. While he lay there, still in pain from his throbbing groin, he couldn't resist a bout of laughter, though it was muffled by the gag.

Mary heard him laughing, but ignored him.

With the two women realizing the hopelessness of their situation, Raddack continued laughing, the sound hoarse and sickening to their ears because they knew the man was right, they were screwed.

Chapter 26

At first when Henry was pulled from the sewer opening he didn't panic, though he wasn't happy about being captured.

Knowing he was safe from the undead inside the perimeter fence of the naval station, he just assumed he had been caught by a roving security patrol.

It was only when the stench of death and decay assailed his nose that he realized he was terribly wrong.

Pulled from the opening and forced to the pavement, he never expected to be looking up into the faces of four undead ghouls.

Most men would have gone into a terrified panic attack, figuring their life was over as they knew it.

Not Henry.

The second he realized his captors were of the undead variety, he immediately went into action, knowing to hesitate for even an instant would spell instant death.

His left hand shot out beside him and wrapped around an old leg bone from a past victim. He took the bone and jammed it into the nearest decomposing face, the blackened teeth clamping down on the gristle covered bone.

Rolling to his side, he reached around and managed to pull his shotgun free, only half aware that Jimmy had just appeared nearby, likewise pulled from the sewer the same way Henry had been.

Henry whirled around on his back his legs swinging out and striking undead faces to the side, knocking them off guard. Getting to his knees, he elbowed another that was about to chomp on his neck and then jammed the shotgun sideways into a deader that lunged at his face.

With the ghoul's chompers firmly around the shotgun, Henry used his right hand and slipped it over the trigger. A ghoul to his left was lined up with the barrel and Henry slid his finger against the trigger, the rounds blowing the creature's head clean off.

The shotgun bucked from the force of the expelled shells and flew from the ghoul's mouth, taking a dozen rotted teeth with it. Henry ignored the shotgun, instead reaching down and pulling the panga from its scabbard.

Three ghouls gathered around him, one dragging its legs behind it, preparing to attack. Henry's teeth gleamed in the sun and his eyes held a feral look that was more animal than man.

He grinned wider and waved the panga over his head. "So you boys want to play? Fine, let's play." Then he waded into their midst, panga weaving a wave of death.

*   *   *

Just as the pallid, deformed faces descended on Jimmy, a shotgun roared off to his side. One of the heads about to attack Jimmy disappeared in a spray of bone and brain matter.

Knowing to stay where he was would be suicide, Jimmy swung out with his legs, wrapping them around the closest ghoul's ankles. Twisting his body, he knocked the creature off its feet, the body falling into two more. Like a game of dominoes, the ghouls fell over and landed in a heap on the ground.

Jimmy rolled away and came up in a crouch, swinging his shotgun around and preparing to send the others back to hell.

A few feet to his right he saw Henry cutting up bodies as fast as he could swing his panga. Arms and legs flew from bodies as the man's powerful swings decapitated heads and severed limbs.

Jimmy shot from the waist, blowing the middle ghoul's waist clean off, just as it was regaining its footing. The top half of the decayed body fell over to slap the ground, the sound resembling what a side of beef would make in a butcher shop. The legs continued stumbling around for a moment before falling over, as well. Jimmy watched this macabre dance and shook his head. "Man, that ain't right," he muttered to himself, and then kicked another rising zombie in the face, knocking the jaw free of its head and sending it skittering across the pavement.

Its tongue hung down like a macabre necktie and Jimmy shot it through the eyes, the face disappearing in a red mist.

The top half of the severed torso tried to crawl toward him and he kicked it in the face, knocking it back to the pavement where he then stepped on its head, crushing the skull into a red mash of brains and blood.

His foot made a squishing sound that made even his hardened stomach turn just a little.

Turning to check on Henry, to see if he could assist his friend, he wasn't surprised to see the man just finishing up with his foes. Body parts were everywhere. Twitching and snapping like the ends of a worm that had been cut in half.

Henry turned to look at Jimmy and he smiled, wiping blood from his forehead. "You okay?" He asked, breathing heavily from the exertion of the battle.

Jimmy shrugged. "Sure, no prob', just another day in the neighborhood."

Henry surveyed the carnage around them, satisfied with his results.

"What in the hell were these things doing inside the base?" Jimmy asked. Stepping over a twitching arm and another leg, neither belonging to the same corpse, Henry pointed to the remains of the corpse in the corner, now missing one of its leg bones.

"If I had to guess, I'd say people got tossed in here, maybe for punishment or something."

"Well, if this is the kind of place that does shit like that, then we need to get the girls and fast," Jimmy said, repositioning his weapons and making sure he had everything.

"You're right. Come on, we better get moving. Those gun blasts will alert every resident here that something's wrong. We need to get away from here and under cover."

"Okay fine, which way do we go? Mary and Cindy could be anywhere."

Henry walked over to the gate of the corral and broke the chain with one strong downward blow with the butt of his shotgun. The thin chain snapped and fell to the ground and Henry kicked the gate open wide, prepared for anything, living or dead.

Nothing greeted him and he waved Jimmy onward.

The two men leapfrogged across the open parking lot and disappeared into a copse of trees lining the road.

The base sprawled in front of them, a large majority of it lying in sight on a slight slope so that if you were at the top where the barracks were it would be possible to see the roofs of the buildings below; the two death warriors having no idea of the layout of the naval base.

"We could search for a week and not find them; this is hopeless," Jimmy said exasperated, as he looked across at the rooftops of all the buildings scattered across the base.

Henry rubbed his chin, the stubble scratching his coarse palms. "No it's not, we just need a guide," he said slyly.

Jimmy frowned. "Oh sure, we'll just go up to the first person we meet and ask nicely if they'll help us find our friends. I'm sure they'll be happy to oblige."

Henry shot Jimmy a look that said he wasn't amused and then he patted his friend on the shoulder. "You misunderstand me, Jimmy, who said we're gonna ask?"

Jimmy's eyes grew wide with understanding and he smiled. Then the two men moved off deeper into the base, looking for their first candidate.

Almost ten minutes after Henry and Jimmy had disappeared deeper into the naval base the first pale white, vacant, staring face popped out of the sewer opening in the corral.

With arms and legs that barely functioned, the zombie crawled out onto the bloody pavement, heedless of the blood and gore under its hands.

Pulling itself free, another head appeared only seconds later, followed by dozens more.

One at a time more than a hundred ghouls poured out of the sewer, each one following the one before it. Fanning out, they moved across the naval base, looking for prey.

An old woman came walking by the galley parking lot, on her way to a friend's quarters when the first of the zombie horde saw her. Not knowing what to do, she tried to run, but tripped over her own two feet in her despair.

Walking dead covered her body and tore into her like senior citizens at a Las Vegas buffet. In less than a minute the woman was nothing but a pile of meat and exposed organs.

Only when she opened her one remaining eye and sat up did the undead leave her alone. The old woman somehow managed to pull herself erect and with internal organs falling out at her feet and trailing a long red, string of intestines behind her; she started off after the rest of the undead horde.

She was hungry as well, despite the fact that she had no stomach anymore. But that was fine with her, she didn't really mind.

With the ghouls spreading out across the base, finding, killing, eating and then reanimating the residents, the screams of pain and horror grew until no other sound could be heard.

*   *   *

The pounding on the door made Mary turn and stare at it yet one more time. So far the noise was only a distraction. After putting another Magnum round through it, the guards had learned to keep their distance.

Cindy had gone through the rest of the apartment trying to find a way out. Because the large room had originally been multiple dorm rooms, she had immediately tried to pry open one of the other doors lining the wall, but none would open, all nailed and screwed shut securely. Plus, even if they managed to get one open they would still be in the same hallway as the guards.

Raddack tried to scream from the floor and Mary kicked the man in the stomach, satisfied when his face turned red with pain. "Now you be quiet down there, it's quiet time for bad little boys," she smiled at him sweetly like a mother to her son.

"What the hell are we gonna do? We can't stay here forever," Cindy said looking like a caged animal.

Mary leaned on a table, sipping some water. "I know, sooner or later they're gonna get through that door, and with only a pair of

Magnums between us, we don't stand a chance. I was thinking about how to get out of here. I have an idea, but it's risky."

Cindy moved closer. "Oh, yeah, and when has any of the ideas we think up not?" Cindy asked.

"Good point, all right, here's what we should do," and Mary went into a long explanation of what they would try.

At the end, Cindy nodded, smiling. "Not bad, Mary, Henry would be proud. I'll get started." Then she was off to gather the supplies they would need to hopefully escape their predicament.

Mary felt a pang of loss as she thought of Henry... and Jimmy, too. Things had been so hectic neither she nor Cindy had even gotten a spare moment to come to grips with the loss of their friends and in Cindy's case, lover.

She had always thought they would go on forever. The three of them, and now four with Cindy, added to the group. They had overcome so much and it seemed almost a cheat that they should die so senselessly.

Deep down Mary had always thought when Henry died it would be in some kind of magnificent explosion that might take out half a city.

She chuckled at that, realizing she may have even had a schoolgirl crush on the man, similar to a little girl's crush on her father.

Shaking her head, she rubbed her eyes. It was hard to believe the day was only a little more than half over. It felt she hadn't slept for weeks.

She knelt down next to Raddack, the gagged man's eyes staring up at her with intense hatred. "You know, if I was a smart woman, I'd put a bullet in your head right now and end this crap. That way even if I go to hell today, I know you went ahead of me." She held the gun over his face, caressing his cheek, Raddack's eyes never looking away from the weapon.

She cocked the weapon and placed it on his forehead.

Then she stood up and backed away disgusted. Looking down at Raddack's groin, she saw the material dark and the unmistakable smell of urine filled the room.

"You have got to be kidding me," she said, looking down at the prone man. "You're supposed to be the big strong leader of this place and you piss your pants? Forget it, I think I will let you live, at least for now. God, you're pathetic. You're so pathetic I want your men to find you with a pant leg full of piss. I wonder what they'll think of you then?"

Then time for ruminating was over, Cindy coming back with a handful of items, everything from bed sheets to a heavy stone statue Raddack had taken from an antique store in the city of New London on one of the foraging trips for supplies.

Mary scanned the pile of items and nodded. "Okay, then, let's get started."

Chapter 27

Smith walked down the small two-way road from the barracks, on his way to the brig. He wanted to check in on Captain Snyder, see how the man was doing. Raddack had told him that under no circumstances was the man to die. He was simply too valuable until he gave up the codes. There had been no available vehicles and being such a nice day out, he had decided to walk, the brig only ten minutes away.

He looked up at the sound of far away screams. Truth be told, he wondered if it was just some of the naval station's children playing in the nearby streets.

He never saw the two men come out from behind a parked car and jump him. Before he could draw his weapon, he was thrown to the road with a knee in his back.

His arms were trussed behind him and he was pulled to his feet. He was about to yell in protest when what looked and tasted like a dirty sock was jammed into his mouth.

Then the two men dragged him down the road and behind an old shed used by the landscapers to keep the station beautiful.

The two men could have been father and son. The older man looked to be around forty, his face set like granite, his eyes hard, streaks of white in his hair. The younger man couldn't have been a day over twenty, but this man, too, looked rugged and confident.

Whoever they were, they weren't residents of the Navy base.

"All right, now. I'm going to take the gag from your mouth and you're going to tell me what I want to know. Do you understand me?" The older man said.

Smith nodded, understanding perfectly. In fact, after seeing the armaments the two men carried and Smith's eyes looking directly at the wicked looking sword on the older man's thigh, he truly believed he would do anything they wanted.

Smith had never really been a man of courage and the zombie apocalypse had only accentuated his flaws. He had been lucky to hook up with Raddack and his men, where he was usually safe behind the high, chain-link fence of the station.

"Go ahead, Jimmy, take the gag out," the older man said.

With the gag gone, Smith tried to spit, to work the taste of the sock out of his mouth. Jimmy took the sock and then removed his boot, sliding the sock back on.

"Sorry about the sock, pal. Believe me; you don't want to know where it's been."

"Jimmy, please, for once will you stop with the wisecracks," the older man said.

"Sorry, Henry, go ahead, ask the guy where the girls are."

Smith's ears perked up at the raised questions of two girls, but he feigned ignorance.

Henry turned his face from Jimmy and then looked Smith square in the eyes. He held the man's gaze. Neither looking away nor wavering in its intensity. Finally Smith had to look away, the gaze to uncomfortable.

Henry grunted and then leaned so close, Smith could smell his breath. "Now I'm only going to ask you one time, friend, so if you want to live to see the sun come up tomorrow, I recommend you tell me the truth. You understand me?"

Smith nodded and then realizing he could speak did so. "Y..yy..es, I understand," he stammered, more than a little intimidated by the two men standing in front of him.

"Good. We're looking for two women that were taken from a small town about twenty miles from here. One's a blonde, pretty, and the other is a brunette, also pretty. They were with us until they were taken by some of your men and then said men tried to kill us. What do you know about that?"

"If I t..t..tell you will you p..p..promise not to k..k..kill me?" Smith stuttered nervously.

Henry nodded brusquely. "If the information is true."

"How do I know you're telling the truth and that you wont' kill me as soon as I tell you what you want to know?" Smith asked.

Henry's eyes grew to slits and he moved so close to him, Smith thought he was about to be kissed by the man. "You don't, now talk," Henry growled.

"Fair enough. They're with the Boss of this station. His name is Raddack. He used to be a small time crook out of Hartford. He managed to take this place over when most of the soldiers and sailors abandoned it to go to their families. Others joined him, the rest he killed. Raddack's in his quarters with your two friends. It's the large brick building with the blue stripe across the front at the top of this road. Every barracks has different color stripes on the building so the soldiers would know which one was theirs." Smith gulped and looked down at the ground, not wanting to tell them the rest, but hoping it was his best shot at survival. "He plans on keeping them as his women. In fact, he should be up there right now with them...doing stuff."

The eyes of both men went wide with surprise and then shrank down to slits as anger took over.

"He wants to make my girl his woman?" Jimmy said, fiercely. "I'll cut the bastards balls off and feed them to him!"

Henry stepped away from Smith and took Jimmy by the shoulders, shaking him. "Jimmy, stop it, get a hold of yourself! If we're going to get them free, then we need to stay focused. Bottle those emotions away for another time. Right now I need to know you're all there and not prepared to run off like a jealous boyfriend."

Jimmy stopped trying to break free from Henry's grip and after a moment his face seemed to calm, his breathing slowing down.

"Sorry, Henry, but it's just...well you know...what would you do?"

"I know and we'll get them back." He turned to Smith who had stayed absolutely still, not wanting to be the brunt of the bad news he was giving these two men. "All right, guy, so where are Raddack's quarters and how many guards does he have there?" Henry asked.

Smith nodded and then ticked off everything Henry and Jimmy needed to know, the two men listening closely. When Smith was done, Henry pulled open the door to the shed and then tossed him inside.

Standing in the sunlight of the doorway, Henry called to Smith. "Now listen to me closely. If your information is true, then we'll get our friends and let you out on our way back. But if you've been lying to us..."

"No, I swear, it's all the truth. Everything I've told you is true!" Smith pleaded.

Henry ignored his protest and continued. "If you've been lying to us I'm coming back here to slit your throat." Then the door was slammed closed and Smith was in almost total darkness, only a few slivers of sunlight piercing the cracks in the shed's walls and around the door.

Smith sat down on a box of fertilizer and sighed.

Now all he could do was wait and hope the two men found their friends and then took the time to set him free.

Fifteen or so minutes later, Smith looked up at the few thin lines of sunlight. Shadows were walking across the shed, breaking the streaks of light. He thought it must be the two men coming back to free him or kill him but no one tried to enter the shed.

He was about to call for help, knowing whoever was out there would unlock the shed and free him, when something made him pause.

Was it a sound he heard that had made him hold off from calling out?

Standing up, he shuffled to the wall of the shed and put his ear against the cool metal. He could hear a little better now and he pulled his head off the wall like it would burn him when he heard a very distinctive sound.

It was a moaning, combined with a weasing sound.

He'd heard that sound before from the ghouls in the corral by the galley.

Had they gotten out? If so, it shouldn't take too long to clean the mess up.

But as he watched the shadows crossing the light in the cracks, he started counting. After stopping at twelve, way more than the corral held, he realized if the undead had somehow penetrated inside the fence, then the base was in for a world of hurt.

Backing up and sitting back on the fertilizer box, he remained absolutely still. Maybe it wasn't so bad to be in this shed, after all, he thought. In fact, maybe those two men had just saved his life.

* * *

The undead poured out of the sewer and into the base, hungry for fresh meat. Once leaving the galley parking lot, they quickly spread out across the landscape. Soon they were infiltrating every home, building and work place.

Screams of terror and pain filled the base as the residents of the Groton Naval Station were slowly slaughtered.

No one was spared; children were pulled from playgrounds and devoured while screeching parents tried to protect them. The old were easily run down and cornered, ripped apart and killed until they revived and joined the ranks of their murderers.

With nearly all the security for the base at Raddack's quarters trying to capture the two rogue prisoners and recover their Boss, there was no one to sound the alarm.

The few guards on watch at the gates were overrun before they could so much as pick up their two-way radios, not expecting to be attacked from inside the base. Bloody hands and teeth tore into them, the soldiers getting off a few shots before they were ripped to pieces.

Some of the defenders were devoured to the point that reanimation was impossible, the undead ravenous to the point that entire bodies were ripped to pieces

Soon nearly the entire base would be converted, a bright light of humanity extinguished as so many others had been before it.

But the dead didn't care. They felt no emotions, no sorrow or loss for what they once were and had become.

Slowly they swarmed through the base, seeking out every ounce of life they could find.

* * *

The door rattled on its frame yet again as the guards outside strove to break it in. Mary had pushed a small bureau in front of the door, but it was beyond inadequate to stop the door from giving way eventually.

Cindy turned to the door and sent another two rounds into the middle of it. She was rewarded with the sound of screaming, but an instant later the door began to vibrate again.

"I think it's time to go, Mary," Cindy said, turning to look at her friend.

Mary couldn't agree more and picked up the long make-shift rope made from torn sheets and curtains and tied it around her, Cindy doing the same. "I agree, let's get the hell out of Dodge, you ready?"

"Is the Pope Catholic?" She answered.

"All right, watch your eyes; I don't know how the glass will fall. This shit is probably tempered or something."

Cindy nodded and looked away from the window, the corner of her eyes still watching Mary.

She picked up a heavy statue and tossed it at the closest window. The statue bounced off the glass and fell to the carpeted floor with a muffled thump, shattering into a dozen pieces; Mary jumping to the side to avoid being struck by the heavy objects.

Raddack chuckled behind his gag and Cindy kicked him, shutting him up again.

Turning to Cindy, she frowned. "Okay, time for plan B."

Mary shifted, once again, so she faced one of the many windows that made up the large apartment, pulled the Magnum free of her waistband and fired three rounds into the tinted glass; one on top and two on the bottom, spaced three feet across. If she had wanted to trace the holes with a marker she would have had a perfect triangle.

With the window spider webbing minutely, she picked up a heavy oak chair Raddack had behind a grand desk in another part of the room and she threw it at the window with all her might.

The chair was heavy and she had to spin like a discus thrower until letting it go. The chair arched through the air, barely staying above the window frame, but the heavy, solid object did what Mary had planned. With the bullets weakening the glass, the chair punched through the window, shards of glass falling to the ground below like hail.

The chair smashed into a hundred pieces as it struck the parking lot in the front of the building and before the last pieces of glass had landed, both Mary and Cindy were climbing out the window, each on their own rope.

Just before Cindy jumped out the window, she saw the door crack and then it fell in, crashing over the bureau so that the bottom of the door was in the air.

Guards poured into the room, rifles ready to shoot anything that moved. Cindy sent three more rounds at the approaching guards and then the Magnum cycled dry.

Cursing her luck, she threw the weapon at the closest guard, hitting the man on the forehead and with bullets flying around her; she jumped, dropping from sight.

Mary was now hanging five stories up and she wasn't feeling too confident about her plan anymore. She looked up and saw Cindy literally jump out the window, the sounds of gunshots following her.

As Cindy flew out into the air, her body arcing wide, Mary shot the closest window to where Cindy should end up at the end of her fall. Spacing the shots carefully, she used up the rest of her ammunition, dropping the useless weapon when it cycled dry. The Magnum followed the empty shell casings to the ground below and Mary watched as Cindy plummeted downward.

Then her rope went taught and she started to swing toward the building. Mary's guess was true and Cindy crashed into the window with the bullet holes, her body shattering the glass as she disappeared amongst the curtains.

Mary looked up in time to see one of the guards lean out the window. She could hear Raddack screaming for someone to untie him and she would have smiled if she wasn't looking up at the barrel of a rifle aimed at her hanging body.

The guard fired, the round zipping by her head, missing her by only inches.

Cursing, the guard fired again, but then Mary felt herself yanked forward, her head snapping back and she looked up to see Cindy pulling her into the shattered window.

"Thanks, Cindy, another second and I would have ended up a Piñata."

Helping Mary to the glass covered floor, she smiled. "Happy to oblige."

Mary could see Cindy had picked up multiple cuts from crashing through the window, but they all seemed superficial. A small cut in her forehead trickled down her cheek, like a stream of red tears. Cindy wiped the streak away and then moved to the door.

Opening it, she looked out into the hallway. All was quiet.

"No one's there, that's a good sign, right?" She asked.

Mary chuckled. "How about we take it as one." She had finished getting out of her harness and ran to the door.

They were just about to go into the hall and try to make their way to the ground floor when footsteps could be heard coming from the stairwell at the end of the hall. Mary closed the door, keeping it open just enough to peek out and watch the hall.

Seconds later the fire door was thrown open and men with rifles charged out, looking every which way at once.

"There somewhere on this floor, find them. Raddack says he wants them dead." One of the guards said as he directed the other men to take opposite ends of the hall. "Check every goddamn room until you find them, and check everything, closets, bathtubs, shit, under the beds for Christ sakes, now get moving!"

Men ran off, obeying the order and Mary closed the door quietly.

After locking it, she turned back to Cindy and stared at her.

Cindy's eyes were wide and trusting. "That's okay, right Mary? I mean, you've got a way for us to get by them right?"

Mary said nothing, only smiling reassuringly. The truth was she had nothing. They had five, maybe ten minutes, before they reached the room Cindy and she were in, and for the life of her, she was all out of ideas.

Chapter 28

Henry and Jimmy came around the sharp corner in the road, breathing heavily from the uphill run, there eyes trying to look everywhere at once. The bright light of the day was fading and rain clouds were beginning to roll over the base. If it started to rain that would only add to the confusion on the base and help the companions escape.

Gunshots floated on the wind and Henry looked over the nearby treetops to see one of the windows on the top floor of Raddack's building explode outward, raining shards of glass onto the ground below; a large chair shattering in the parking lot out of their eyesight.

He watched as Mary jumped out the window, followed a moment later by Cindy.

They were too far away to do anything but watch as Cindy swung in an outward arc and then crashed into a fifth story window. Henry saw the guard stick his body out the window and train his weapon on Mary. Then he heard the gunshot and his heart leaped into his throat.

"Come on, Jimmy, we've got to get up there, they're in trouble," he said putting on a burst of speed. Jimmy looked up and saw Mary as well, missing Cindy's swinging body.

Henry continued watching the building while running and saw Mary being pulled inside the window, probably by Cindy, he assumed. Then the moment was over and he concentrated on running some more, his arms pumping, his legs eating up the distance.

Two minutes later both men slowed as they ran over the glass littering the walkway in the front of the building.

Henry pointed to Jimmy to take the left side and Henry took the right. The large glass doors looked unimposing as the two men prepared to enter the building.

Henry weighed his options and decided he was through screwing around. It had seemed like for the past three days all he had been doing is running and hiding, trying to survive other people's rules in what they thought should be the order of a new society.

This was it, he'd had enough running. From now on he was taking the fight to the enemy and be damned the consequences.

Cocking the shotgun, he ran at the glass doors, firing two shots as he went.

The glass shattered into a thousand pieces and Henry ran through the opening, Jimmy covering his side.

There were two guards at the desk. One was sitting behind the desk, the other talking to him from the front. His back had been to the doors and when they shattered, he swung around, surprised, not understanding what had happened.

He would never get the chance.

Jimmy shot the man in the chest, throwing him back to fall over the desk, almost landing in the sitting guard's lap. This man was better prepared and he ducked below the desk, a moment later popping up to spray the lobby with automatic fire.

Henry dived behind a couch off to the side, once used for visitors to hang out in the lobby while waiting for a pass to go into the building to a dorm room or to wait for someone to come down.

White stuffing flew into the air like fake snow, covering everything, including Henry's head.

Jimmy dived behind a small stone column that looked like it was holding up the ceiling, but when the guard fired at Jimmy, the plastic column cracked and shattered, pieces of plaster falling to the floor, the bullets going right through it.

"Jesus Christ!" Jimmy yelled and ducked down lower to try to make the smallest target he could. "A little help here, Henry, this guys killing me!"

Henry crawled to the end of the couch and poked his head out to check on the guard. He would have given his left arm for a grenade at the present moment, but despite the lobby looking like Christmas, with all the stuffing lining the floor like snow, he knew

Santa Claus wouldn't be around to grant him his wish anytime soon, so he reached over the couch and grabbed one of the partially destroyed sofa cushions.

Counting to three, he threw the cushion high into the air and in the opposite direction from Jimmy. The guard, seeing movement out of the corner of his eyes, instinctively turned and sprayed the pillow with fire, blowing fist size chunks into the plush cushion.

Henry rolled out from behind the couch, his shotgun aimed at the man's legs. The guard was facing the wrong way and as he swiveled to try to recorrect his aim, Henry sent a barrage of death toward the man.

Screaming, the guard fell to the floor; his legs a mangled mess of flesh and bone. Jimmy saw his chance and ran across the lobby and jumped over the desk, his butt sliding across the polished, wooden counter.

The guard, his face a mask of pain, looked up just as the butt of Jimmy's shotgun slammed into his forehead, knocking him unconscious. Jimmy surveyed the lobby, looking for more targets, then waved the all clear to Henry.

Standing up, Henry ran across the floor, kicking stuffing as he went.

Jimmy smiled when he saw Henry. "Nice look, going for the dapper, older look?"

Henry wiped the stuffing from his hair, shaking his head back and forth until it was clean.

"Come on, they're upstairs," he said simply, all business.

Jimmy nodded and the two men ran to the stairwell, Henry opening it with his foot, while Jimmy prepared to blast anything inside the stairwell.

Empty.

Henry went first and the two men ran up the stairs, taking the steps two at a time.

By the third floor they heard talking and both men slowed and hugged the wall. Taking it slowly now, both men hung their shotguns on their straps and pulled their side arms. With his Glock leading the way, Henry crawled up the stairs, the voices growing closer.

The stairwell was made of stone steps that circled upward in a spiral design. Because of this design, both Henry and Jimmy were able to make it directly below the talking guards, only the circling stairwell separating hunter from prey.

Henry gestured to Jimmy to take the right side, Henry would take the left.

Henry held his hand up, three fingers showing. Mouthing the words, he started counting, "One, two...three." On three, both men ran up the few steps and took the corner, the three men standing guard startled.

Henry shot the man on the left two times; double tapping his weapon to make sure the man would stay down. Jimmy turned to his right, the .38 sounding like a cannon had gone off in the stone walls of the stairwell.

The guard flew off his feet, the round catching him in the shoulder, just above his heart. The guard in the middle had that extra second to raise his rifle while his comrades were being killed, but he still wasn't fast enough. When Henry and Jimmy had finished with their initial targets, both men turned minutely and shot the middle guard at the same time. Henry's round caught the man in the throat, slicing through to exit out the back of his neck. Jimmy's .38 man stopper struck the man in the lower chest, knocking him to the stairwell landing where he sputtered as his life leaked from two mortal wounds.

Running up the stairs, Henry and Jimmy checked to make sure their targets were down. Jimmy's first shot had knocked his man over, but the man was still alive, now trying to reach for his weapon. Kicking it away from his grasping hand, Henry pulled his panga and leaned over the guard.

"No, please, don't," the guard pleaded, his eyes begging for mercy.

Henry glared at the man, his jaw set tight, his voice soulless. "You made your choice, pal, now play the cards you've been dealt." Then he leaned over and sliced the panga across the man's neck, severing his jugular.

While the man's lifeblood shot out and covered the nearest wall, Henry stepped over the guard and continued up the stairs.

On the next level Jimmy grabbed Henry's arm and stopped him. "Wait a second, Henry, what the hell was that about. You killed that man when he was down. We could have knocked him out. I thought we don't kill live people if we don't have too."

Henry turned to glare at Jimmy, the same look on his face he had given the guard. "And we don't, nothings changed, but that guard chose to be what he was and enforce the status quo for this Raddack asshole. He made his choice and he lost, end of story, now come on, while we're talking semantics your girlfriend could be getting shot by one of those same live people you want to save so badly!"

"No, it's cool, you made your point," Jimmy said. "He didn't mind when he was a powerful guard and got to push others around, now he met someone stronger and lost. It's cool, I get it. Let's go," he finished and ran past Henry, moving further up the stairs.

They had just passed the fourth floor fire door, the fifth only a few steps away.

Henry paused for only a heartbeat, thinking about what Jimmy had said. Then decided now was not the time. Later, if he was still breathing and they didn't have to bury one of their own, they could discuss the right way and wrong way of killing people that seemed to want you dead.

Then he started up the stairs again. So far it had been easy, despite the opposition they'd confronted. He knew the real challenge would be on the fifth floor where most of the guards would be congregating as they tried to capture Mary and Cindy.

*   *   *

Raddack was on his feet again and staring out the broken window of his quarters. He was still in awe. The two crazy bitches had actually jumped out his window. He was six-stories up for Christ sake!

Deciding he'd had enough of women for the time being, he called Carter over to him. The guard was directing his men to go down to the next floor and search it from top to bottom.

Carter noticed the urine stain on Raddack's pants, but the man quickly looked away, pretending he didn't notice it.

Wise man, Raddack thought.

"Carter, I'm going to change and then I'm going to leave the capture of those two she-devils in your capable hands. I need to be somewhere more urgent."

"Can I ask you where you'll be, Boss, just in case you're needed?"

"Yes, I suppose so. I'll be in the brig. I want to check on Snyder. Smith left a while ago but hasn't reported back yet, so I'll go myself. Have my Hummer pulled up front and tell the driver to be wary of glass; I don't want a flat tire. It's not as easy to get it repaired as in the old days, eh? Tell him I'll meet him at the rightside fire door?"

"I'll make it happen, Boss, no problem." Then the guard moved away, directing men here and there in the search to find the two women. Raddack hesitated then, deciding he didn't need the two women talking to one of his guards and filling him in on what they had done to him. With the rumor mill the base had, every resident would know in a few hours, maybe less.

"Oh, Carter, wait a moment, will you?"

"Sir?" Carter asked from across the room.

"I've changed my mind. Those women have caused me enough trouble. I want them shot on sight. Do you understand me? Shoot to kill."

Carter seemed to pause for a second, as if he was processing the order. But then his face regained its normal professional mask and he nodded, yes. "I'll see that it happens, Boss, you can count on me."

"I know I can, Carter, I know I can." Then Raddack went to the opposite end of the room and with clothes from a bureau drawer, he quickly changed into a new set of clothes, pausing in the bathroom to wash his face. Looking at the toilet, he frowned, knowing he didn't need to piss thanks to the two women.

That made him furious and he swiped at the toiletries covering the sink with his right hand, most of them landing in the shower stall.

Then he left the bathroom and took the rear stairs down to the ground floor. By going this route he bypassed the lobby, thus saving himself some valuable time. His Hummer should be waiting by now and he was eager to see how Snyder was doing. By the time he returned, the trivial matter of the two women should be wrapped up and then a work crew could get started cleaning up the mess they'd made.

He figured in a week, ten days at the most, all signs of the trouble would be gone. And he would be glad when it was.

*   *   *

Reaching the fire door for the fifth floor, Henry and Jimmy both paused to do a weapons check. Both men only had a few more rounds for their shotguns, but their side arms were fully loaded, plus the two .45s were still securely resting in the hollow of their backs.

Henry flashed Jimmy a sly grin. "You ready to get our women folk back?" He joked, trying to diffuse the tense situation.

Jimmy chuckled. "Sure am, Paw, let's go get them women folk."

"Good one, okay, you take high and I'll go low. Ready?"

Jimmy nodded. "Just open the damn door for Christ's sake, we're wasting time."

Nodding, Henry prepared to open the door. The two of them had already discussed their tactic for attacking the fifth floor and each man had agreed the best way would be to go in hard and fast. The average man would be taken by surprise at the sight of two attackers charging in, heedless of their safety, as the guards themselves would never do such a foolhardy thing.

It was a delicate gamble that could backfire, but both men were confident of the result and weighed it against the alternative of losing the girls.

Henry sucked in a breath of air, like he was about to dive deep into the ocean and pulled the door open, the greased hinges making no sound. As the heavy metal door swung wide, the two men were greeted by a hallway full of guards, all surprised to see two armed men with guns coming through the door.

Henry dropped down to his knees, spraying the hallway with lead while Jimmy plastered himself against the right-side wall, emptying the .38 in seconds and then pulling the .45 to continue firing.

To anyone standing in that hall at the precise moment the warriors stepped through the fire door, it would have appeared that the world had exploded and all the violence was occurring in that one hallway in the middle of Connecticut, the sound of gunshots and smoke filling the narrow corridor.

At a quick count Henry counted eight guards in the hallway, some standing at open doors that led to other dorm rooms.

With the first barrage of gunfire, four men went down in sprays of blood and screams of pain. Some of the men kept their heads and dived for cover into the dorm rooms. Henry cursed when this happened. If the guards had cover they could hold him and Jimmy off forever, or at least until reinforcements arrived.

"Jimmy, take cover!" Henry roared over the gun blasts, rolling to his left into a side hallway. The building was square, with the hallway circling all four corners like a picture frame. Jimmy followed his order and the two men jumped to the side, the tile where they had stood only a heartbeat before exploding into shards of ceramic and grout.

Henry heard shouting, the guards trying to get organized. He couldn't let that happen, so he dropped to the floor and crawled back out into the hallway, keeping his head only inches from the floor. The guards, expecting their target to be head height, had to realign their weapons. That fraction of a second was all Henry needed to spray the ceiling with bullets, shattering the nonworking fluorescent lights there and raining glass powder on the men. He ducked back just as a round ricocheted off the floor, missing his face by centimeters.

"Jimmy, watch the hall, I'm gonna go to the other end. Either they'll try to come at us from the other side or I'll do it to them, catching them in a crossfire! Either way, it'll end this shit for good!"

Jimmy waved him to go. "Good luck, and watch your ass," was all he said, and then he sent a few rounds into the hall to keep the guards at bay.

"Good advice and that goes for you, too," Henry replied and then ran off to reach the far end of the hall.

Just as he rounded the corner, he could hear footsteps pounding his way. He had been right and the guards were even now coming for him and Jimmy, hoping to trap the two men in a vise of death.

To Henry's left was a fire extinguisher, still in its bracket as if the world had never been overrun by the dead and everything was as fine as a summer's day.

Henry pulled the canister off the wall and threw it down the hall, the red extinguisher bouncing end over end until it slid toward the opposite wall.

Just as the fire extinguisher reached its mark, the guards came charging around the corner, rifles ready to blow Henry to hell.

Henry sent two rounds into the canister, the contents under pressure exploding in a cloud of white mist. The first two guards were thrown backward against the frosted window behind them, the window shattering under the weight of two grown men. Shrieks of fear followed them out the window and then were silent. Henry rolled to a crouch and sent three more rounds into the other two guards who were just regaining their senses, their bodies covered in white. Both men tumbled to the floor, a red spray of blood from their exit wounds painting the wall behind them a scarlet color, mixing with the white powder.

Grunting with the results, Henry turned and ran back to Jimmy. It would be a few minutes before any of the remaining guards would gather the courage to try that again.

Now all they had to do was take out the entrenched guards in the dorm rooms and then find the girls; all before reinforcements arrived.

Chapter 29

"You hear that? There's a gun fight going on in the hallway," Mary told Cindy, her ear pressed tight against the door. The sounds of screaming, yelling and more shots filled the hall and she pulled her ear away from the painted wood.

"What do you thinks happening?" Cindy asked from the bathroom. She had been trying to find some cleaning solutions; maybe she could mix something to throw on the guard's faces if it came down to it.

"I don't know, but whatever's happening is the distraction we need to get out of here. The guards will be too busy with the other fight to worry about us," she said. "I hope," she added after a second.

The door rattled as something or someone fell against it. Mary looked at the door, an idea coming to mind. But if it was going to work, she had to act fast. Without telling Cindy her plan, she ran to the door and opened it. A security guard had been leaning against it, firing into the hallway and when Mary opened the door he fell into the room with shock and surprise.

Before the man could do anything but open his mouth in surprise, Mary punched him under the chin, knocking him unconscious the way Henry had taught her.

"Oww, Jesus, that hurts," she said, waving her hurt hand in the air. She hadn't had time to position her fist in the proper stance and had crushed one of her fingers when striking the guard's jaw.

Still, the desired effect had been accomplished. Slamming the door closed with her foot, she bent over and picked up the guards rifle, popping out the magazine to inspect how many rounds were left.

Cindy appeared from the bathroom, hearing the noise and was shocked to see a man lying on the floor and Mary with a rifle in her hand.

"What the hell happened, I was only gone for a few seconds," Cindy asked, stepping into the room.

She immediately started checking the guard for extra ammo clips and took his side arm from his waist.

"Sorry, but I got a brainstorm and there was no time to discuss it. It worked, right?"

"Yeah, it did, great job!" She stood up; tossing Mary a spare magazine, which the woman promptly slapped into the weapon, then racked the bolt to send the first round into the chamber. The other magazine had only been half full, that she slid into her back pocket for later. Better to go into battle with a full clip, and with luck she wouldn't need the other.

Cindy had finished checking the .45 she now carried and with the one extra clip she found on the guard's belt, she was ready for action.

"So, we're armed, but we're still trapped five floors up. What's the plan?"

Mary's face grew serious and she flashed Cindy a wild look. "Simple, whatever's going on out there, it's distracting the guards. When the moment's right, we jump out there and hit them from behind, hopefully taking them all out or at least enough to allow us to escape. Then we hightail it to the nearest stairwell and hopefully we can finally get away from this crazy place. From there we'll just take it as we go."

Cindy grinned, her wild streak showing through. "Hey, that's good enough for me, when do we go?"

Mary moved to the door and cocked her ear against it, trying to discern what was happening outside. "I'm not sure, but I'll know when it's time, till then, just rest, because I have a feeling we'll need all our energy once we open that door."

Plopping down into the nearest chair and placing her feet on the guard's chest like a footrest, she nodded. "Good enough for me; just say the word."

Mary looked back to the door, listening to the sound of blaster fire. She didn't know what was going on out there, but whatever it was, she prayed it would be their ticket out of here.

Chapter 30

Raddack was sitting in the back seat of his Hummer relaxing, while it drove down the winding road. In only a few minutes he would be at the brig, where he would finally get what he needed out of Snyder.

After the humiliation he'd received from those two hellcats, he was looking forward to dishing out some of his own onto Snyder.

He looked down to where his missing Magnum should be. One of his handguns had been retrieved from his quarters, but the other had been damaged beyond repair when it had fallen out the broken window to strike the hard concrete below.

Mumbling obscenities to himself and hoping his guards killed the two women slowly, he glanced out the window to see the road ahead.

"Watch out!" He yelled to the driver as one of the residents of the base stumbled onto the road. The driver didn't see her in time and the front grille struck her dead center, the body flying twelve feet to land in a tumble of arms and legs.

Climbing out of the Hummer, Raddack walked over to the body. If she was still alive, perhaps she could be saved, but from the way she had been catapulted into the air, he highly doubted it.

While Raddack knelt down over the woman, the driver hovered over him. "Oh my God, Boss, I didn't even see her, she came out of nowhere, I swear!" The driver said nervously.

Raddack felt for a pulse, but there was none. The neck looked to be snapped, the woman very dead. Before Raddack stood up, he noticed a gash on her throat, similar to teeth marks, but then dismissed the wound as something the woman must have picked up from the accident. Perhaps her neck had struck a protrudence on the grille or had landed on a sharp rock as it rolled on the ground.

"Will you relax, Carson? It's not like the old days, there are no police that are going to come and inspect the scene for whose fault it is. I make the rules around here and I say the dumb bitch walked right in front of you." He looked down at the bloody body. "Serves her right, should've paid more attention."

Pointing to Carson, he then gestured to the corpse. "Drag her off the road and we'll deal with it later, have a cleanup crew come and get her later. It's not like she's going anywhere," he chuckled to himself. "Now come on, let's get going, I'm anxious to see Snyder."

Carson seemed to relax a little; relieved he wasn't in any trouble and ran to the corpse, dragging it off the road to let it lie in the grass. Then he quickly jogged back to the Hummer and held the door open for Raddack.

The Boss grunted at the show of hospitality, expecting it, and then climbed into the vehicle, the driver doing the same and a moment later the Hummer was gone, spraying the body with gravel as it shot down the road; the corpse already attracting flies as it sat steaming in the late day sun.

Three minutes after the Hummer was gone, the dust from its passage just starting to settle, the road had some more visitors. Dozens of the undead, most of them freshly revived, poured out of the tree line along the road.

Shuffling and shambling, they followed the Hummer, attracted to movement of any kind. They ignored the battered and broken body, stepping over it when necessary. One not so dexterous tripped over the prone corpse and tumbled away down the hill, flailing limbs snapping from the impact of coming up against a large boulder.

The others ignored it, slowly moving further into the base in their search for more prey.

*   *   *

Captain Snyder rolled over on the floor and stared up at the ceiling, wishing he were dead for the thousandth time.

Every nerve in his body screamed with pain, thanks to the Chinaman. His fingernails were gone and his testicles were charred from where the sick bastard had connected a car battery to them, deciding to use Snyder for a few diathermy experiments.

As he lay there suffering, he wondered if he'd ever be able to manage a hard-on again.

His missing eye wept fluid that pooled onto the floor below him. He could barely talk, his throat was so sore from screaming. His tongue slid across his teeth, those he had left, and poked the gaping holes. Many of the extracted teeth had left the exposed nerves behind and his head felt like it was being squeezed by a vice every three seconds. He had heard about how painful an exposed nerve was to the open air, but he had never truly understood what it meant, the agony of it, until now.

The bodies of the dead crewmen had been removed a little more than an hour ago. Snyder didn't know why they had done it, but he wasn't complaining.

The blood stain was still on the floor where the bodies had once lain. The soap and water used to mop it up not enough to erase what he had let happen to his own men.

A frightened yell sounded from outside his prison door and he looked up idly. It wasn't the first time he'd heard other screams of pain. Raddack was a busy man and obviously had other prisoners he was torturing nearby.

But this time the scream was followed by gunshots, which wasn't altogether unusual either, but when he heard the distinctive sound of automatic rifle-fire, he knew something was wrong.

More screams sounded in the corridor and he managed to pull himself to a sitting position, his back leaning against the wall.

His vision was blurry, but he thought he could see shadows moving from the crack under the door.

More gunfire sounded and the sound of a falling body came to his ears.

Curious what was happening, he felt his heart skip a beat as a false sense of hope filled him.

Could it be that some of his men were staging a revolt and were taking out the guards? If so, then any second now he would see the door open and one of his men would rush in to save him.

Crawling to the door, every inch utter agony, he weakly banged on it, hoping someone out there would hear him.

More gunfire sounded and then, against all hope, the door did open, the sound of the lock being undone clearly coming to his battered ears.

But instead of seeing one of his men, it was one of Raddack's guards.

The man's face was a mask of terror and it seemed he was trying to gain access into the room as if he was running from something.

Just before the man would have stepped into the room, he was yanked from sight, his screams filling the hall and the cell, alike.

Snyder craned his neck upward, trying to see what was happening. He wanted to stand, but his legs were so weak he knew it would be next to impossible.

Raddack had done quite a job on him, but he still hadn't talked.

The hallway was wreathed in darkness, the automatic fire having taken out the overhead lights.

Snyder reached out with a bloody hand and opened the door a little more. Whatever was out in the hall was irrelevant. After what he had suffered, death wasn't something to fear, in fact, it would be welcomed with open arms, like a terminal cancer patient that simply couldn't stand the pain of living any longer.

With the last ounce of his strength, he dragged himself into the hallway, not seeing the desiccated hands reaching down from the darkness behind him.

Chapter 31

Henry hunkered down against the wall next to Jimmy. The wall was a peppered mess of fractured tile and bullet holes.

The guards had slowly been solidifying their position. While one would give covering fire, others would move into a better position to attack.

But that wasn't the worst of it. Security guards were now trying to sneak through the demolished hallway where the fire extinguisher had exploded and others were in the stairwell, blocking off any chance of a retreat. Henry had managed to jam the door latch with a piece of molding lining the hallway floor, but he didn't have much confidence that it would hold for long.

While Jimmy kept the men on their right at bay, Henry did the same for their left.

But with only a finite amount of ammunition, they were doomed to failure unless something happened quickly to turn the tide in their favor.

"Shit, they've got us pinned down," Jimmy cursed, ducking back, bullets rebounding off the corner of the wall where his head had just been. "What the hell are we gonna do?"

Henry bit his lip, trying to think of just that. If only he was able to get word to Mary and Cindy, but it was a large floor and there was no way of even imagining where they might be. For all he knew, they were only a few feet away at the nearest door, or all the way on the other side of the building.

"I hate to say this, Jimmy, but I'm all out of ideas. I think this might be one of those times where the good guys don't win."

"Aww, shit man, don't tell me that. There's got to be a way of getting the girls and getting out of here," Jimmy protested.

Henry shrugged. "Sorry, buddy, not this time," then he turned and sent two rounds down the hall, the guards ducking back again.

"Well, fuck it, if we're going down, then let's see how many of these bastards we can take with us."

Henry slapped his back and smiled. "Wouldn't have it any other way, buddy."

The sound of pounding feet filled the hall and the guards started firing continually, making their rush toward the warriors.

"Shit, here they come!" Jimmy yelled.

"Wait for them to get real close!" Henry yelled over the noise of the discharging weapons. "Maybe we can get in between them and stop them from just mowing us down!"

Jimmy nodded and braced himself for the attack, his hand turning almost white as he squeezed the handgrip on his .38 in anticipation of what was to come.

* * *

"Hear that? Footsteps, a lot of them. And the gunfire, they're using suppressing fire. Whatever's happening out there, it's going down, now. Let's go!" Mary said, preparing to open the door and charge into the hallway

Cindy nodded and looked down at the supine guard on the floor. The man was tied and gagged, neither woman having the heart to kill him in cold blood.

"Now, you take care of yourself, hon," Cindy said with a smile, then she was next to Mary and ready to move.

Mary held the .45 and Cindy held the rifle, she being a better shot with it.

Mary waited for a few more seconds until she believed the last set of footsteps was past, then she threw open the door and the two women jumped out into the hall. Cindy went to her knees and Mary hugged the left wall, both women firing as soon as they had exited the door.

Six guards danced a jig of death as they were struck down from behind. None of them expected a rear attack and were totally caught off guard.

The hallway grew silent for only a moment, then the girls heard the sound of more gunfire coming from around the corner.

Both women moved closer, using the bodies of the dead guards as cover. If there were more men that needed killing, then the two women wanted them dead. They were tired of running and wanted to end this once and for all.

Henry dropped his empty Glock to the tile floor and swung his shotgun into position. Just as the guards came down the destroyed hallway, he jumped across the floor, sliding across it. He only went a few feet, but it was enough to throw the three attackers off guard. All three shot over Henry's head, bullets coming so close he felt their passage, and as they realigned their weapons lower for the killing shot, Henry fired the shotgun again and again, using the rest of the shells to take down the men.

In the small confines of the stone hallway, the shotgun shells were devastating.

The bodies were thrown back, landing in a pile. One man had received a shot through the neck, his head hanging on by a few stray strands of skin and gristle.

Seeing Jimmy had the other side covered, Henry quickly ran to the other end and picked up one of the rifles from a dead guard, running back to Jimmy.

Jimmy turned and looked at Henry, his face showing a quizzical look. "I don't know what just happened out there, but the entire compliment just got gunned down from behind."

"From behind? Could it be the girls?"

"I don't know. I don't want to stick my head out there and get it blown off."

"Shit, all right, stay quiet and wait. If we call out and it's not them, we'll tip our hand, better wait."

Jimmy nodded, and moved closer to the corner, sweat dripping off his forehead.

Henry tapped him on the shoulder. "I'm gonna go around the building and come at them from behind, so make sure you don't hit me. Here, take this, I'll get another one." Henry said, handing Jimmy the acquired rifle.

Jimmy nodded thanks and then turned back to the corner, waiting for the next shoe to drop.

Henry climbed to his feet and ran off down the hall, scooping up another rifle and a spare magazine from one of the guards belts.

Running hard and fast, he only stopped as he reached each corner, checking to make sure there would be no surprises on the other side. He poured on the speed to get to the opposite side of Jimmy and catch the new attackers in a crossfire.

He was just about there when he heard the sound of more gunfire, praying he wasn't too late, he put on a burst of speed, his rifle ready to shoot the second he turned the corner.

Jimmy could hear the soft shuffling of footsteps and the click of a rifle. Knowing it was do or die, he climbed to his feet and prepared to blow the attackers to hell.

Holding his breath, his finger already applying pressure to the trigger, he jumped out into the hall, his finger pressing the trigger, his mouth letting out a loud war cry.

At the exact same time, Cindy saw movement and prepared to take out the next target.

Suddenly a man jumped out from behind the corner and started yelling, his rifle aimed directly at her. She squeezed the trigger.

Within less than a microsecond to decide, both Jimmy and Cindy realized who was on the other end of their rifles and at the same time both pulled up on their weapons, the bullets plowing into the ceiling, making it rain ceiling tiles.

Just then Henry came from around the corner, also prepared to kill anything that moved. Mary heard him coming and swung around, her .45 aiming directly at his torso.

Both warriors stopped in mid-stride, surprise and happiness filling their faces.

"Oh my God, Henry? You're alive!" Mary screamed and ran into his arms.

Henry was knocked to the floor, Mary on top of him, smothering his face with kisses. "I don't believe it, it's a miracle!"

At the same time Cindy had run into Jimmy's arms, tears of happiness and relief flooding down her cheeks.

"Oh my God, how can you still be alive?" She said through sniffles and tears. "Raddack said you were dead."

Jimmy squeezed her tight and then put her down, the woman not wanting to let go. "And you believed that asshole? Come on, Cindy, you should have known better than that. No bodies means not dead yet. Simple."

"But you were surrounded by all those deaders, how the hell did you escape?" Mary asked, climbing to her feet and helping Henry as well. His back was killing him from the tackle Mary had given him, but he ignored it, glad to see the woman was safe.

Henry shrugged. "When that gunner tried to take us out, he took out most of the deaders instead, that and some other stuff got us free. Look, there's time for catching up later. Right now I want to put this place as far behind us as I can."

"You won't get any argument from us. I just wish one of us could have killed Raddack on our way out," Mary said.

"No kidding, that's one bastard who needs to be put in the ground," Cindy added.

"Forget him, once we're gone from here we'll never see him again, now come on. Get as much ammo from the guards as you can, we're not out of the woods yet, we still need to get through the base and past the gate guards."

Everyone did as Henry said; quickly gathering spare magazines and making sure everyone had a rifle with a full clip.

Five minutes later they were ready to go and single file, they moved down the stairwell. The guards that had been in the stairwell were gone, making Henry very concerned. Why would they abandon an attack right in the middle?

Deciding not to look a gift horse in the mouth, he continued on, the others following.

Reaching the lobby, Henry peeked out, not seeing anything.

"Looks clear, but keep watch; those guards from the stairs had to go somewhere."

The companions entered the lobby and moved across the large room till they reached the broken glass doors.

All their faces were wide with shock. The mystery of the stairwell guards was answered. They were all in front of the building, stumbling around in a daze. It was only when one of them turned to look in the direction of the companions that Henry realized what was happening.

The guard's neck was torn out and there was a large hole in the man's stomach. But it was the vacuous stare the man gave him that sealed the deal. He wasn't alive anymore and he wasn't quite dead.

Mary put her hand to her mouth and uttered a soft cry. "Oh, good Lord, they're in the base? When did this happen?"

"Doesn't matter, all that matters is we get back to the sewer and get out of here," Jimmy, you lead the way, the girls next and I've got the rear. Here's the deal, if it moves, shoot it."

"Gotcha," Jimmy answered, and then with a quick squeeze of Cindy's hand, he started out, quickly taking down the guard and his two buddies with bloody headshots.

He had to use a few extra rounds while he got used to the new rifle. That was why he liked his shotgun. Point in the right direction and shoot, no skill required.

Moving down the road, taking out any ghouls that got too close, the companions made their break for freedom, while the naval station crumbled around them.

Chapter 32

Making their way through the base, Henry realized they wouldn't reach the sewer opening without becoming lunch for one of the hundreds of animated corpses around them.

The ghouls were everywhere, some looking to be months old, others looking to be only hours or minutes old.

Coming around a sharp corner, and only a few hundred yards from where they had first entered the base, Henry called a halt.

Jimmy shot the closest ghouls while the girls covered their backsides.

Making it as far as they had, they had already used up more than half their ammunition. The ghouls were everywhere, stumbling about aimlessly until spotting the four companions. Once spotted, they would do a beeline directly at them, with only a well placed head shot stopping them.

Everyone was breathing heavily, tired from all the running and dodging.

A ghoul wearing a Patriots jersey charged at them and Jimmy stitched the creature from toe to head, until finally putting it down.

Henry flashed him an angry look and Jimmy just shrugged. "What, it's cool."

"It's a waste of bullets. Bullets we might need to save our lives, so cut the shit," Henry snapped.

Jimmy made a face like a child being disciplined by his father, but he did as he was ordered; now shooting in single shot.

Mary and Cindy continued shooting; only waiting until the ghouls were so close there was no chance to miss.

They moved onward, leaving a trail of bodies behind them like breadcrumbs. As far as they knew, there was no one around to follow them, all the guards either dead or running scared.

That was fine with them.

By the time they reached the general parking for the galley, they were almost totally surrounded.

Firing almost constantly, Henry quickly realized it was hopeless. The second he put one down, three more would take its place.

With weapons spitting death, he turned left and right, trying to find a place to retreat to.

He found it when he saw the front doors to the galley hanging open.

"There, go over there!" He yelled. The others looking to where he was pointing.

"The doors are open, there could be more inside," Mary yelled as she shot yet another in the head, the body falling to the street to be lost amidst the legs of the others.

"Doesn't matter, it's got to be better than out here, now go! Jimmy, clear us a path!" He yelled, firing continuously, now. The magazine cycled dry and he quickly pulled another one from his pants pocket and slapped it in, then continued firing again.

The footing became treacherous, spent shell casings rolling beneath their feet, but slowly, staying back to back, they moved toward the galley.

What seemed like an eternity but was in fact only minutes later, they entered the entrance to the galley.

Jimmy tried to close the doors and keep the rest of the undead out, but arms and heads clogged the opening as soon as he tried to close the doors.

Henry saw this and slapped him on the back. "Forget it, those doors are too packed. Fall back, there's got to be a back door out of here, maybe we can circle around the building."

Nodding, Jimmy backed away from the door, shooting a few for his trouble.

The companions moved into the galley and continued until they were behind the serving counters and in the massive kitchen. The kitchen was as large as four garages put together, the floor split up into different sections. There were machines for separating the shells from eggs, looking like some form of space robot. Off in the corner was another strange contraption used to alleviate potatoes from their skin. And many rows of stainless steel tables where the cooks would roll out dough and set pans in preparation for each meal.

Mary turned her head so sharp she almost pulled something when she heard the sound of a pan rattling at the rear of the kitchen. She watched the shadows and let out a yell when more than a dozen zombies stumbled in.

"Shit, they're coming in from the back!" She called to the others.

Moving to the middle of the kitchen the companions stood their ground, prepared to make their last stand as they were slowly surrounded. Walking corpses climbed over the serving counters, eager to feed on the companions. Scores of them filling into the galley; like hungry sailors looking for their evening meal.

Jimmy pulled Cindy to him and kissed her hard on the lips. "I love you, you know that, right?" He said quickly.

"Of course I do, stupid, it's about time you said it," Cindy replied.

Jimmy gave her a shit-eating grin that went so well with his personality. "I've been waiting for the right time. So, how'd I do?"

She answered him by kissing him again, holding his face between her hands as she kissed him long and hard. "You did great, baby, you did great."

Mary shot a few of the closest ghouls, the rest still more than twenty feet away but closing fast. She glanced at Henry, watching him fire his own weapon again and again.

She moved next to him and stopped firing, reaching out to touch his arm. He looked down and saw this and he, too, stopped firing, reaching out with his own hand and squeezing hers.

"Is this really it, we're not getting out of here?" She asked. "I don't want to be one of them, you won't let that happen will you?"

Henry's face seemed to soften as he split his attention between her and shooting anything getting too close.

"No way, Mary. Whatever happens, I'll save four bullets for us. You know that."

A ghoul sprinted at him and he clubbed it in the face, then shooting it in the head. Ammunition was low and in minutes, if not less, they would all be dry. Then all they would have is their knives and rifles for clubs.

It wouldn't take too long after that before they were overwhelmed.

"Whatever happens, you know I love you, and I wouldn't change a thing since I met you...well, except the whole end of the world thing. I could have done without that." Mary said.

Henry swung his rifle around and shot a ghoul coming up on Mary from behind.

"Focus, Mary, we're not dead yet!" He screamed. "And I wouldn't change anything either, except what you said, the end of the world thing, yeah, that kind of sucked."

The four continued firing, taking down body after body. There was a waist high wall of bodies surrounding them and with nowhere else to go, they could only keep firing until their ammo was gone.

"My rifle's out," Jimmy yelled, dropping the rifle and pulling the .38 in one hand and the .45 in the other.

"Me, too," Cindy answered a second later. She, too, drew two .45s taken from dead guards at the barracks and started firing them into the crowd of undead faces.

Henry looked around the kitchen, racking his brain for a way out. There had to be a way, there just had to.

Then he saw it. The dozens of bodies seemed to separate a little, like Moses parting the red sea, and Henry spotted the stack of ten pound propane tanks lined up against the wall near the back of the kitchen, near the loading dock.

With the gas company not in service thanks to the apocalypse, the kitchen galley had been adapted to run on propane. The white and tan canisters had probably been salvaged from a hundred barbecue grills across the state; the foraging teams going into backyards in search of them.

But how could that help? Even if he destroyed the tanks, the ensuing fireball would kill all of them in the inferno.

Firing the last rounds in his rifle, he threw it as hard as he could at an approaching zombie. The front barrel slammed into its eye, not enough to kill it, but making it unstable. It wobbled for a moment and then fell into two others, slowing their charge.

Henry looked around him one last time, now looking at things in a different light.

Then he saw the massive walk-in refrigerators and freezers, still kept operational by a generator in the back of the galley.

His eyes lit up when he saw them. When he had first looked at them he had dismissed them as a deathtrap. Even if they went in there, there would be no escaping. Eventually they would die from something, either from exposure or madness. How long could you live in a refrigerator with an army of the undead directly outside the door? It would be a prison sentence that would end in death.

But now he looked at the massive walk-ins differently. Firing his Glock, careful to keep count on how many bullets he had left, he made the others move back to the walk-in.

"But we can't go in there, it's suicide," Jimmy said, down to his last clip.

"Just shut up and do what I say, will you? I don't have time to explain!" Henry yelled at him. "Now everyone, get the fuck into that walk-in!"

Not understanding why, and figuring he was ordering them to their death, the others obeyed, having nothing to lose.

Jimmy backed up enough to open the door, the undead horde crawling over the wall of dead already put down.

Mary and Cindy shot off the last of their ammunition and ducked into the walk-in, Jimmy right behind them.

"Get against the walls and make sure there's nothing above you on a shelf that could fall on you and crush you!" Henry yelled, standing at the opening.

Shrugging and thinking he was crazy, they did what he told them, knocking pickle jars and coleslaw containers to the floor where they smashed open around their shoes.

Henry fired three more shots at the closet zombies and knew it was now or never. In the hubbub to get everyone into the walk-in, he had lost count of his remaining bullets.

Jumping up onto a nearby table, he called out to Jimmy. "Hey, Jimmy, get ready to close that door as soon as I get in!"

"Okay, whatever," Jimmy said, not knowing what was happening.

Standing on the table, Henry kicked the closest zombie in the face and then kneed another as it tried to climb up. Turning to his right, he lined up the shot and then sent a nine millimeter round at the closest propane tank.

Whatever he expected as he turned and jumped off the table and ran for the walk-in door was nothing compared to what happened.

Just as he plowed through the door, Jimmy started to pull it shut and the propane tank erupted into a giant fireball. One after another the other tanks were set ablaze, exploding like a thousand grenades.

Jimmy caught sight of a roaring fireball coming straight at him and then the door was closed, the latch clicking into place.

"Henry, what the hell did you...?" That was all Jimmy could get out before the floor under his feet shifted like a massive earthquake and he was tossed to the floor amid the falling cans of food on the shelves.

The walk-in shook like Armageddon was going on outside the door, and the companions were covered in a pile of food as the shelves shook, dislodging their contents.

For an eternity, the sounds of secondary explosions filled their world and the door buckled from the force of the blast, threatening to cave in and kill them, despite Henry's machinations.

Then just as suddenly as it started, it stopped, and there was no sound in the walk-in but the muffled breathing of the companions.

The cooling fan, operating before, was now eerily silent; the mist still hovering over everything and when they talked, their breath appeared like fog.

Henry was the first to speak. "Is it over?" was all he could manage.

"Is what over? Henry, what did you do out there?" Mary asked, while wiping Ranch dressing from her arms. All four of them were covered in food, the containers breaking open when they struck them.

Pushing himself free of the plastic jars and boxes, Henry leaned against a five gallon tub of pickles. "There was a pile of propane tanks near the back of the building. I ignited them with a well placed bullet."

"You did what? Are you crazy?" Jimmy said while he helped Cindy to a sitting position. Jimmy looked almost comical with a pile of coleslaw on his head. Wiping the white concoction off, he shook his hand and then wiped it on his pants.

"Yeah, I guess I am. Look, it's all I could come up with, we're alive aren't we?"

"Sure, Henry, but what about all the dead guys, there's still a room full of them out there, we can never escape from here, we're trapped," Mary added from his side.

"Maybe, maybe not." He stood up, steadying himself for a moment. When he was sure he was okay, he moved to the door. There was a massive dent in the middle of the stainless steel door and for moment, Henry wondered if he had, in fact, doomed them all to a life inside a walk-in refrigerator.

Pulling the latch, he tried to open the door, but it wouldn't budge. He tried pushing on it but it still didn't move.

"Jimmy, give me a hand here, will ya?" He asked his friend.

Mumbling unmentionables, Jimmy stood up and walked the three feet to Henry.

"Help me get this open. It's stuck, jammed from the blast probably," Henry said.

Jimmy moved to the left side and leaned on it with all his weight. Henry backed up and then charged at the door, putting all his weight against the thrust. The door moved, but not by much.

"That's okay, I felt it give. A few more times should do it," he breathed, rubbing his shoulder where it had struck the door.

True to his word, the door gave after the sixth try, though it would only open about a foot.

Stepping out into the kitchen, Henry could see the large hinges had been warped by the explosion, the door charred and black.

Jimmy and the girls stepped out, as well, Henry guarding them with the only loaded weapon and if he had to guess, he only had a few rounds left in the Glock.

The kitchen was nothing more than a charnel house, bodies everywhere, all burnt to a crisp. A few still twitched, but they wouldn't be a threat, so they were ignored.

Stepping a few feet out into the kitchen and looking around, the companions truly saw the devastation Henry had wrought by exploding the tanks.

The loading dock was completely gone, vaporized in the first seconds of the massive explosion. As for the undead, none could be seen that weren't charcoal.

Henry turned to the others and smiled. "What'd I tell you, I told you we'd get out of this."

Mary walked over to him and hugged him, placing her head on his chest. "Now, no one tell him what a great job he did, it'll only make his head bigger than it already is."

Everyone chuckled at that and Henry moved back to the walk-in. Sticking his head inside, he could see the power was out.

"Let's grab some of this food, whatever'll last for a little while. At least we'll have some grub until the next town, wherever that'll be."

Jimmy was the first to start sorting through the piles of food, but he turned and looked back at Henry. "Well I hope you bring us to a better town than the ones we've been going to, because I gotta tell you, as a tour guide, you've really sucked lately."

Laughing at the joke, Henry nodded. "I wish I could deny it, but you're right. Between crazy women that want to mate with me and towns that kill you for spitting on the sidewalk, I think I've had my fill of civilization for a while."

Mary walked up next to him and patted his shoulder.

"Let's find a nice house somewhere out of the way and just rest for a while, maybe a week or so. Call it a vacation."

"Fair enough. Sounds good to me. All right then, let's pack up some of this food and clear out of here. Keep an eye out for any guards, either dead or walking dead, doesn't matter. We should be able to scavenge some ammo from them."

Everyone got to work, and using some onion bags they found in the corner of the trashed walk-in, they loaded up a reasonable amount of food.

Once finished, they moved out of the destroyed building.

Even outside the destruction could be seen. Body parts were everywhere and there were almost no walking dead in the vicinity.

Moving across the parking lot, Henry spotted the podium and the corral fence where they had come in and they all moved toward it. On the way there, three dead guards, now reanimated, wandered into their sights. Henry put them down one at a time and then the bodies were quickly stripped of usable ammunition.

Mary had carried her rifle into the walk-in and now she had three magazines for it. She handed it to Jimmy, who nodded thanks. Mary now had a full clip for her .45 and to say everyone felt better having guns that work was an understatement.

Henry picked up a burning piece of wreckage and carried it to the sewer opening. Dropping it down into the hole, he saw it looked empty, but as he climbed down into the darkness, he felt something pawing at his boot. Turning to look, he saw a deader on the sewer floor trying to bite him.

Its legs hung behind it as it tried to climb up the rungs. Henry stepped off the ladder and let his full weight drop onto the pathetic creature. His boots landed on its back and the head went under the viscous water. Not needing to breathe, the body continued to flail around. Sighing, not wanting to dirty his panga, Henry pulled it from its scabbard and then separated the ghoul from its head.

When he was through, he picked the head up by its hair, the teeth still chomping, eyes rolling in their sockets, and tossed it the opposite way from the direction the companions would take.

After the splash from the decapitated head, the sewer was quiet. Never taking his eyes from the darkness, Henry called back up. "All clear for now. Jimmy, get some more torches. I think there might be more down here and I don't want to take any chances. Try to get something like a curtain rod or a spear, you know, something long."

Jimmy saluted and then disappeared while the women handed down the supplies. Henry held onto them, not wanting to place them in the black gunk covering the sewer floor.

By the time they were finished, Jimmy was back with a few torches made from some of the wreckage.

He quickly climbed down, in a hurry, and Henry saw the look of concern on his face.

"What's wrong, why so fast?" He asked.

"The natives are getting restless. More dead guys are showing up. It's definitely time to go."

"Well, then, what are we waiting for?" Henry asked. Taking a torch and leading the way.

* * *

The sewer was mostly empty, but Henry had to put down five more ghouls on the way back to the street opening of the sewer.

It had been easy. All the bodies had shattered limbs in some way or another. It was only when they reached the opening at the back of the base that Henry realized what had happened.

Three bodies floated in the muck, all with heads at odd angles. Though they tried to move, it appeared that without a spine, the brain couldn't control the bodies. Henry grabbed each one by its feet and dragged it out of the way of the ladder, leaving them to spend an eternity paralyzed and in total darkness.

Climbing up, he poked his head out to see what it was like. With the exception of a few prone bodies lying near the gate, the street was deserted, every zombie in almost a mile radius finding the sewer opening and following one after another into the naval base.

"Shit, they must have followed us into the base by the sewer. Hey, Henry, remember those sounds I said I heard? It wasn't echoes, it was those bastards following us," Jimmy said once they were all back on the street. The sun could barely be seen, the clouds heavy and slate-gray. They were in for a bit of rain and Henry wanted to be safely inside the hidden Hummer when it came.

Though the rain was safe now, the bacteria dying off after the cold from the winter, he was still wary of it. After months of knowing to get caught in the rain was death, it was hard to want to run around in bare feet singing like Gene Kelly.

"Well, it couldn't be helped. If that prick Raddack hadn't taken the girls and tried to kill us, then none of this shit would have happened." He looked at the back of the base, seeing the numerous smoke clouds from fires as the base crumbled and he turned to the others. "I hope that bastard gets what he deserves."

Mary shrugged, "What happens, happens," she said, the four companions starting to walk down the road.

She put her hand in Henry's and together they walked side by side, while Jimmy had his arm around Cindy.

"So you came all the way here to rescue me, huh? I guess I should be impressed," Mary said softly

Henry tried to act nonchalant. "It was Jimmy's idea," he said casually.

"What? It was both our ideas, Mary; he wanted to find you guys as bad as I did."

"Is that true, Henry, did you?" She asked coyly.

"Will you please stop it? You know I did and I already said as much, now quit it. You know I hate all that lovey, dovey stuff."

Mary chuckled and leaned over and kissed him on the cheek. "Oh, Henry, if I was a few years older and you were a few years younger..."

He looked at her, surprise on his face. "Mary, why I never... I mean, you're half my age...you could be my daughter for God's sake," he stammered.

Everyone started laughing at that and Mary waved his nervousness away. "Oh, will you relax, you know I don't think of you that way, you're like my father, or uncle."

Henry calmed down, walking in silence for a few minutes. "That's good, uncle, I like that."

Mary smiled and walked a little faster, leaving Henry alone with his thoughts.

Twenty minutes later they had made it to the Hummer.

Cindy helped Jimmy take off the trash and branches from the roof and hood and then everyone piled inside. The trip to the Hummer had been mostly uneventful, only a few stray ghouls wandering the area. Henry had taken each one down with a solid blow to the neck with his panga, decapitating each one in turn before kicking the head away to roll in the gutter.

The eyes of each head would follow them down the street, the mouths opening and closing in silence.

Jimmy jumped into the driver's seat and with a surge of power, the engine roared to life.

Everyone climbed in and Henry patted Jimmy on the back from the back seat.

"Find us somewhere with trees, a lake and flowing plains of grass, Jimmy my boy." Henry said.

Jimmy mock saluted and pulled out into the street, taking out a stray ghoul that was coming to investigate the Hummer.

The four companions sat back and talked, laughing and joking about their escapades as they found out what each had been doing when they had been separated; enjoying the comradery of knowing the people you were with had your back and would give their lives for you, and that no matter what the world might throw at you, they would always be there.

With the first cracks of thunder filling the sky, the Hummer made it back onto Route 95 and disappeared into the distance, the clouds in the sky finally opening up and unloading their payload, the rain washing the world clean one more time.

Epilogue

The Hummer pulled up to the front door of the brig and Raddack stepped out onto the pavement. Turning around, he looked around himself, noticing there appeared to be more people around than usual.

If he had chosen to watch them more closely, he might have noticed how they shambled about, their faces slack and drawn, looking nowhere; some with blood stains and life threatening wounds.

But he didn't. Raddack was a self-absorbed man and he barely paid the residents of the base any attention at all. The only time they even saw him was when he was executing some poor slob that had either broken a law or Raddack had chosen to say he did.

Many residents who had attempted to stir up trouble had found themselves hanging over the corral with his pet zombies inside.

Moving to the door of the building, he frowned to see it was hanging open. Someone would pay for that, he thought. Security needs to remain intact.

Carson was behind him, serving as bodyguard, as well as driver.

Before stepping into the hallway, he looked up to the sky at the sound of thunder. Seconds later the clouds opened up, large raindrops splattering the building and the roof of the Hummer.

He nodded. They needed the rain. Even now there would be people putting out rain collection containers to try and collect as much of the fresh water as they could. Lightning crackled across the sky and he jumped when the thunder boomed overhead, sounding like a bomb had gone off. Earlier he had heard what had sounded like an explosion coming from the other side of the base, but after seeing the overcast sky had dismissed it as thunder. Now, as the thunder rattled the building, he was sure that was what it had been.

Stepping into the dim hallway he stopped and drew his only remaining Magnum.

"What the hell happened here?" He said to Carson.

The front of the building had a small desk where a guard would have sat, but now the desk was overturned and blood covered the wall behind it, looking like an amateur artist had tried to make his own Picasso.

The door that led into the back rooms where the cells were, as well as where the Chinaman did his work, was open.

More blood covered the doorknob of the door and as Raddack moved closer, he saw blood on the floor, droplets spread out like raindrops.

Not comprehending what could be happening, Raddack moved deeper into the building. Snyder's cell was the third on the right. Moving closer, he cursed at the sight of the cell door opened wide.

The overhead lights were shattered, the hallway covered in shadows, the exposed wires sparking continually. With power in the wires, Raddack knew the generator was still functioning at the back of the building, but why were the walls and ceiling pock-marked with bullet holes?

Making sure Carson was behind him, he crept to Snyder's cell. Opening the door with his foot, it was plain to see the cell was empty, the faded blood stain still on the floor from all the executed men.

Had Snyder escaped? Perhaps a jailbreak, some of his men perhaps had shifted allegiances once again?

At the end of the hallway, the corridor split into two, like a "T". Raddack moved closer to the junction, telling himself he was a fool for risking himself and he should get some of his guards to hunt for the Captain. But there had been at least five men already stationed at the brig. Where were they and if they'd been killed, where were the bodies.

Stepping into the middle of the intersection, he looked left, see-ing nothing and then turned right. At the end of the corridor about twenty feet away stood a man. At first Raddack didn't know who it was, but then he saw the silver dolphins on the man's chest and the tan color of the shirt, despite the blood covering most of the material.

It was Snyder

"There you are, Snyder, thought you could escape, eh? Well you thought wrong. Now I want those codes, now, or so help me, I'll kill you where you stand and I'll figure out a way to go around your damn command codes."

Snyder didn't move, but remained perfectly still, if swaying a little to his left.

Raddack scowled. "Listen, you bastard, I don't know what went on around here, but I want to know where my men are. What have you done with them?"

Still Snyder didn't move.

Cursing a foul streak, Raddack shot at Snyder, the bullet going wide above his head. He didn't want to kill the submarine Captain, only scare him.

Raddack was shocked to see Snyder remain motionless, not even so much as an instinctive twitch when the round struck the wall less than a foot from his head.

"Speak, dammit, what the hell is wrong with you!" Raddack screamed.

That was when Snyder started walking forward, but he wasn't alone. As he passed each open cell on his left and right other bodies stepped out into the hallway and began following him. A dull moan, some groaning, filled the corridor and Raddack took a step backward, unnerved by the sight.

The faces of Snyder and the men behind him were still hidden by the shadows of the corridor. Raddack would have given almost anything for a flashlight at this precise moment in time.

Carson made a frightened sound, mumbling something and Raddack turned to look at him. "What the hells the matter with you, what are you saying?"

Carson did two things at the same time. The first was to point at the second figure behind Snyder, the second was to drop his rifle and run out of the building.

"Wait, Carson, get your ass back here, they're not even armed!" Raddack yelled to him.

Carson would pay when he got his hands on him, that was for sure, he thought hearing the Hummer start and the tires squealing on the wet asphalt as Carson drove away.

Turning back to Snyder and the men behind him, he snarled. "Fine, I don't need him, I can handle you easily, now get back into those cells before I shoot you all and be done with it!"

Snyder continued moving forward, never slowing; his footsteps slow and methodical.

"Fuck it, I said I'd kill you and I meant it!" Raddack hissed, firing into Snyder's chest from less than ten feet away. Smoke filled the corridor and the smell of burnt meat drifted to Raddack's nose, making him want to gag.

When he looked up from covering his nose he was in awe. Snyder was still coming, except now he had a hole in his chest that Raddack could put his fist through.

"What the fuck?" Raddack said. "That's it, I don't know what's going on, but it ends now. Goodbye Captain."

Raddack opened up with the remaining five rounds in his Magnum, blowing Snyder's torso to shreds. A few of the men behind the Captain jerked from the impacts of the rounds, but still kept coming.

Raddack's mouth hung open, too shocked for words. How could they still be walking with that many holes in them? How could Snyder still be alive?

Unless...

That's when Raddack finally reasoned it out. He had been so safe inside his base, ruling with an iron fist, he never thought to see a zombie he wasn't in full control of.

Snyder crossed the remaining few feet that separated him from Raddack and as he did, a small bit of light from a sparking wire lit up the Captain's face.

Raddack inhaled sharply, realizing his assumption was true. Snyder's face hung slack, the eyes vacant. A large piece of his neck was missing near his shoulder, the blood still glistening in the wan light.

"Oh my Lord, no," Raddack whispered, making the sign of the cross with his left hand. "But how did this happen? You were safe in your cell."

Snyder didn't answer, but instead lunged at Raddack. The fat man tried to run, but tripped over his own two feet.

Just before Snyder's teeth dove in and ripped out Raddack's throat, the fat man could have sworn Snyder was smiling. But that was impossible. Zombies didn't smile.

Then he screamed in pain, feeling his life blood squirting into the air to drop back down and rain on him, like the rain pattering the roof above his head.

Raddack screamed louder, the other ghouls diving in and starting to devour him, tearing off large chunks of meat and fat.

It was when his stomach was ripped open by sharp nails and he felt his intestines pulled out like a magician doing the handkerchief trick, that he truly shrieked in agony.

The pain seemed to go on for an eternity, but finally his heart stopped and he died. But he would not be returning, with one last ounce of vengeance still seething in his non-beating heart, Snyder ripped Raddack's head from his body, tossing the head to the other zombies who eagerly ripped it open for the brains inside.

Then, stepping over the bloody mess that was Jordan Raddack, Snyder stepped out into the rain and wandered away satisfied, his revenge fulfilled.

*   *   *

Smith leaned closer to the shed door, listening intently. It had been nearly an hour since the explosion had rocked the walls of his metal prison. He had managed to free his hands and was now waiting quietly, wondering if it would be safe to leave.

The rain continually tapped the metal roof in a singsong pattern only nature could create. After another twenty minutes had passed and still nothing, he decided it was time to leave.

Picking up an old metal rake, he forced the shed door open, the rain splattering his face.

Looking left and right and seeing nothing, he ran onto the street and down the steep road.

He didn't stop until he had reached the gate for the lower base of the station, where the submarines were once housed.

The gate was wide open, as it always was and he ran along the water until he reached the dock with the submarine moored to it.

Running down it, he paused when he saw the deck of the boat. Wandering around aimlessly were zombies. As he watched, one lost its footing and tumbled overboard to be lost from sight in the water.

Smith idly wondered if zombies knew how to swim and then quickly dismissed the thought as irrelevant.

Watching the bow hatch of the sub intently, he saw a ghoul crawl out and fall to the deck, then another one did the same. At the rear hatch another figure was crawling into the hatch. The crewmen that had remained aboard the sub and had sworn their loyalty to Raddack were all dead, now nothing more than ghosts haunting the submarine.

Some lost thought was telling them they belonged on the boat and they would stay and fulfill their duty even past death.

Smith knew the nerve gas was onboard the sub, hidden in the torpedo room. Smith turned and ran back up the dock, realizing the nerve gas would be protected by the dead forever.

He ran two docks over and ran down it, spotting what he wanted. The rain flattened his hair to his scalp and he tasted a bit of iron in the rainwater, but the rain wasn't killing him like before the winter, so he had nothing to complain about.

Moored to the dock was a small motor boat, Raddack's personal boat.

The keys were in it, as no man would have chanced stealing the boat; for to be caught would have been death, or worse, fed to the zombies in the corral.

Climbing down the ladder and jumping into the boat, Smith paused when he heard the sound of an engine.

His hearty leaped into his throat when he saw the black Hummer pull up and drive down the dock so it was only a matter of feet from the ladder Smith had just climbed down.

He knew he was dead, Raddack finding him now was the worst possible luck.

The driver's door opened and a man stepped out, but even in the rain and shadows, Smith could see it wasn't Raddack. The figure was only half the man's girth.

Carson ran to the ladder and looked down at Smith. "Hey, looks like we had the same idea. Room for one more?"

Smith smiled up at Carson. He liked Carson; the two of them played poker sometimes in the rec room when they had downtime at the same time.

"Sure, hop aboard," Smith invited him.

Carson held his finger up for a second and then disappeared for a moment. Smith was just starting to get nervous; not knowing where the man had went, when Carson reappeared with two packs wrapped in a blanket.

"Here, catch," he said, dropping them one at a time to Smith. After that he left for only a second, coming back with a fuel can that sloshed as he handed it down to Smith.

Then the man climbed down, another rifle banging on his back as he went, found in the rear of the Hummer. Raddack always made sure his vehicle was well armed.

Smith nodded to the man and then started the engine, the motorboat starting easily. Carson untied the mooring rope and pushed the boat from the dock. Smith maneuvered it to face forward and then gave the throttle a little gas, so they slowly cruised out into the channel.

For the next ten minutes neither man spoke, each man lost in private thoughts, then Smith broke the silence.

"That stuff you put in the back of the boat, that's Raddack's supplies from the Hummer, right?"

Carson nodded. "Yup, food—MRE's only, water, extra ammo, a couple of .45's, even a first aid kit, why do you ask?"

"Well, doesn't Raddack need that stuff, I mean, won't he come after you for leaving him, not to mention you're stealing his stuff?"

Carson shook his head, the water sluicing off his face. "Believe me; Raddack won't need that stuff or anything ever again." And to prove his point, he pulled out the keys to the Hummer, which he'd placed in his pocket without thinking, and tossed them into the water, the keys sinking immediately.

Smith laughed at that, feeling free for the first time in almost a year.

Carson started laughing, too, the two friends cruising along the channel to parts unknown.

DEAD RECKONING: DAWNING OF THE DEAD
By Anthony Giangregorio

THE DEAD HAVE RISEN!

In the dead city of Pittsburgh, two small enclaves struggle to survive, eking out an existence of hand to mouth.
But instead of working together, both groups battle for the last remaining fuel and supplies of a city filled with the living dead.
Six months after the initial outbreak, a lone helicopter arrives bearing two more survivors and a newborn baby. One enclave welcomes them, while the other schemes to steal their helicopter and escape the decaying city.
With no police, fire, or social services existing, the two will battle for dominance in the steel city of the walking dead.
But when the dust settles, the question is: will the remaining humans be the winners, or the losers?
When the dead walk, the line between Heaven and Hell is so twisted and bent there is no line at all.

RISE OF THE DEAD
By Anthony Giangregorio

DEATH IS ONLY THE BEGINNING

In less than forty-eight hours, more than half the globe was infected. In another forty-eight, the rest would be enveloped.
The reason?
A science experiment gone horribly wrong which enabled the dead to walk, their flesh rotting on their bones even as they seek human prey.

Jeremy was an ordinary nineteen year old slacker. He partied too much and had done poorly in high school. After a night of drinking and drugs, he awoke to find the world a very different place from the one he'd left the night before.
The dead were walking and feeding on the living, and as Jeremy stepped out into a world gone mad, the dead spotting him alone and unarmed in the middle of the street, he had to wonder if he would live long enough to see his twentieth birthday.

ANOTHER EXCITING CHAPTER IN THE DEADWATER SERIES!
BOOK 6
DEAD UNION
By Anthony Giangregorio

BRAVE NEW WORLD

More than a year has passed since the world died not with a bang, but with a moan.

Where sprawling cities once stood, now only the dead inhabit the hollow walls of a shattered civilization; a mockery of lives once led.

But there are still survivors in this barren world, all slowly struggling to take back what was stripped from their birthright; the promise of a world free of the undead.

Fortified towns have shunned the outside world, becoming massive fortresses in their own right. These refugees of a world torn asunder are once again trying to carve out a new piece of the earth, or hold onto what little they already possess.

HOSTAGES

Henry Watson and his warrior survivalists are conscripted by a mad colonel, one of the last military leaders still functioning in the decimated United States. The colonel has settled in Fort Knox, and from there plans to rule the world with his slave army of lost souls and the last remaining soldiers of a defunct army.

But first he must take back America and mold it in his own image; and he will crush all who oppose him, including the new recruits of Henry and crew.

The battle lines are drawn with the fate of America at stake, and this time, the outcome may be unsure.

In a world where the dead walk, even the grave isn't safe.

THE DARK
By Anthony Giangregorio

DARKNESS FALLS

The darkness came without warning.

First New York, then the rest of United States, and then the world became enveloped in a perpetual night without end.

With no sunlight, eventually the planet will wither and die, bringing on a new Ice Age. But that isn't problem for the human race, for humanity will be dead long before that happens.

There is something in the dark, creatures only seen in nightmares, and they are on the prowl.

Evolution has changed and man is no longer the dominant species.

When we are children, we are told not to fear the dark, that what we believe to exist in the shadows is false.

Unfortunately, that is no longer true.

DARK PLACES
By Anthony Giangregorio

A cave-in inside the Boston subway unleashes something that should have stayed buried forever.

Three boys sneak out to a haunted junkyard after dark and find more than they gambled on.

In a world where everyone over twelve has died from a mysterious illness, one young boy tries to carry on.

A mysterious man in black tries his hand at a game of chance at a local carnival, to interesting results.

God, Allah, and Buddha play a friendly game of poker with the fate of the Earth resting in the balance.

Ever have one of those days where everything that can go wrong, does? Well, so did Byron, and no one should have a day like this!

Thad had an imaginary friend named Charlie when he was a child. Charlie would make him do bad things. Now Thad is all grown up and guess who's coming for a visit?

These and other short stories, all filled with frozen moments of dread and wonder, will keep you captivated long into the night. Just be sure to watch out when you turn off the light!

ROAD KILL: A ZOMBIE TALE
By Anthony Giangregorio

ORDER UP!

In the summer of 2008, a rogue comet entered earth's orbit for 72 hours. During this time, a strange amber glow suffused the sky. But something else happened; something in the comet's tail had an adverse affect on dead tissue and the result was the reanimation of every dead animal carcass on the planet.

A handful of survivors hole up in a diner in the backwoods of New Hampshire while the undead creatures of the night hunt for human prey.

There's a new blue plate special at DJ's Diner and Truck Stop, and it's you!

THE MONSTER UNDER THE BED
By Anthony Giangregorio

Rupert was just one of many monsters that inhabit the human world, scaring children before bed. Only Rupert wanted to play with the children he was forced to scare.

When Rupert meets Timmy, an instant friendship is born. Running away from his abusive step-father, Timmy leaves home, embarking on a journey that leads him to New York City.

On his way, Timmy will realize that the true monsters are other adults who are just waiting to take advantage of a small boy, all alone in the big city.

Can Rupert save him?

Or will Timmy just become another statistic.

SOULEATER
By Anthony Giangregorio

Twenty years ago, Jason Lawson witnessed the brutal death of his father by something only seen in nightmares, something so horrible he'd blocked it from his mind.

Now twenty years later the creature is back, this time for his son.

Jason won't let that happen.

He'll travel to the demon's world, struggling every second to rescue his son from its clutches.

But what he doesn't know is that the portal will only be open for a finite time and if he doesn't return with his son before it closes, then he'll be trapped in the demon's dimension forever.

DEAD TALES: SHORT STORIES TO DIE FOR
By Anthony Giangregorio

In a world much like our own, terrorists unleash a deadly dis-ease that turns people into flesh-eating ghouls.

A camping trip goes horribly wrong when forces of evil seek to dominate mankind.

After losing his life, a man returns reincarnated again and again; his soul inhabiting the bodies of animals.

In the Colorado Mountains, a woman runs for her life, stalked by a sadistic killer.

In a world where the Patriot Act has come to fruition, a man struggles to survive, despite eroding liberties.

Not able to accept his wife's death, a widower will cross into the dream realm to find her again, despite the dark forces that hold her in thrall.

These and other short stories will captivate and thrill you.

These are short stories to die for.

DEADFREEZE
By Anthony Giangregorio

THIS IS WHAT HELL WOULD BE LIKE IF IT FROZE OVER.

When an experimental serum for hypothermia goes horribly wrong, a small research station in the middle of Antarctica becomes overrun with an army of the frozen dead.

Now a small group of survivors must battle the arctic weather and a horde of frozen zombies as they make their way across the frozen plains of Antarctica to a neighboring research station.

What they don't realize is that they are being hunted by an entity whose sole reason for existing is vengeance; and it will find them wherever they run.

DEADFALL
By Anthony Giangregorio

It's Halloween in the small suburban town of Wakefield, Mass.

While parents take their children trick or treating and others throw costume parties, a swarm of meteorites enter the earth's atmosphere and crash to earth.

Inside are small parasitic worms, no larger than maggots.

The worms quickly infect the corpses at a local cemetery and so begins the rise of the undead.

The walking dead soon get the upper hand, with no one believing the truth.

That the dead now walk.

Will a small group of survivors live through the zombie apocalypse?

Or will they, too, succumb to the Deadfall.

ANOTHER EXCITING CHAPTER IN THE DEADWATER SERIES!

BOOK 5

DEAD HARVEST
By Anthony Giangregorio

Lost at sea and fearing for their lives, a miracle arrives on the horizon, in the shape of a cruise ship, saving Henry Watson and his friends from a watery grave.

Enjoying the safety of the commandeered ship, Henry and his companions take a much needed rest and settle down for a life at sea, but after a devastating storm sends the companions adrift once again, they find themselves separated, exhausted, and washed ashore on the coast of California.

With each person believing the others in the group are dead; they fall into the middle of a feud between two neighboring towns, the companions now unknowingly battling against one another.

Needing to escape their newfound prisons, each one struggles to adapt to their new life, while the tableau of life continues around them.

But one sadistic ruler will seek to unleash the awesome power of the living dead on his unsuspecting adversaries, wiping the populace from the face of the earth, and in doing so, take Henry and his friends with them.

Though death looms around every corner, man's journey is far from over.

SEE HOW IT ALL BEGAN IN THE NEW DOUBLE-SIZED EDITION!

DEADWATER: EXPANDED EDITION
By Anthony Giangregorio

Through a series of tragic mishaps, a small town's water supply is contaminated with a deadly bacterium that transforms the town's population into flesh eating ghouls.

Without warning, Henry Watson finds himself thrown into a living hell where the living dead walk and want nothing more than to feed on the living.

Now Henry's trying to escape the undead town before he becomes the next victim.

With the military on one side, shooting civilians on sight, and a horde of bloodthirsty zombies on the other, Henry must try to battle his way to freedom.

With a small group of survivors, including a beautiful secretary and a wise-cracking janitor to aid him, the ragtag group will do their best to stay alive and escape the city codenamed: **Deadwater**.

LIVING DEAD PRESS

Where the Dead Walk

www.livingdeadpress.com

Book One of the *Undead World Trilogy*

BLOOD
OF THE
DEAD

A Shoot 'Em Up Zombie Novel by A.P. Fuchs

"*Blood of the Dead* . . . is the stuff
of nightmares . . . with some
unnerving and frightening action
scenes that will have you on the
edge of your seat."

- Rick Hautala
author of *The Wildman*

Joe Bailey prowls the Haven's streets, taking them back from
the undead, each kill one step closer to reclaiming a life once
stolen from him.

As the dead push into the Haven, he and a couple others are
forced into the one place where folks fear to tread: the heart
of the city, a place overrun with flesh-eating zombies.

Welcome to the end of all things.

Ask for it at your local bookstore.
Also available from your favorite on-line retailer.

ISBN-10 1-897217-80-3 / ISBN-13 978-1-897217-80-1

www.undeadworldtrilogy.com

Printed in the United Kingdom by
Lightning Source UK Ltd., Milton Keynes
140984UK00001B/202/P